"You're right, there is a lot you don't know. I explained that I'm not at liberty to give you all the details at this time. I have my—"

"I don't care about your orders." She grabbed him by the shirtfront and tried shaking him, maybe to make him see she wasn't taking no for an answer.

All she succeeded in doing was sending him teetering closer to the edge. "Tell me the truth, Lyle."

There was no time to develop an intelligent strategy to outmaneuver this precarious situation. No evasive explanation that would satisfy her. His only alternative was distraction.

His fingers dove into her hair. He pulled her mouth up to his and kissed her, hard at first out of sheer desperation, and then softer…because the taste of her melted him from the inside out. To his surprise, she didn't resist.

First published in Great Britain 2012
by Mills & Boon, an imprint of Harlequin (UK) Limited,
Eton House, 18-24 Paradise Road, Richmond, Surrey TW9 1SR

© Debra Webb 2012

ISBN: 978 0 263 89565 0
ebook ISBN: 978 1 408 97250 2

46-1012

Harlequin (UK) policy is to _____ ble and
rec_____ forests. The
log_____ ronmental
reg___

Pri___
by I___

COLBY LAW

BY
DEBRA WEBB

Debra Webb wrote her first story at age nine and her first romance at thirteen. It wasn't until she spent three years working for the military behind the Iron Curtain and within the confining political walls of Berlin, Germany, that she realized her true calling. A five-year stint with NASA on the space shuttle program reinforced her love of the endless possibilities within her grasp as a storyteller. A collision course between suspense and romance was set. Debra has been writing romance suspense and action-packed romance thrillers since. Visit her at www.debrawebb.com or write to her at PO Box 4889, Huntsville, AL 35815, USA.

I want to thank the readers for their love and support of the Colby Agency through all these years!

It's hard to believe that the third book in this trilogy heralds the 50th installment of the Colby Agency!

Enjoy!

Chapter One

Victoria Colby-Camp waited in the cold, sterile room for the man who had requested her presence. Considerable persuasion from the right source had been required to sway the warden of Polunsky Prison to allow this meeting. Lucas, Victoria's husband, though fully retired from his lifelong career with the CIA, still wielded a great deal of influence. One call to the esteemed governor of Texas and Victoria had almost immediate approval to meet with the prison's most infamous death-row inmate.

Raymond Rafe Barker had spent twenty-two years in prison, seventeen on death row, quite an extended period for Texas, where the punishment of heinous criminals was generally carried out in a swift and efficient manner. Many had hoped that the delays would provide the necessary time for him to grow a conscience and give up the locations of the bodies of his victims that were never recovered. But that hadn't happened, and now his time on this earth was coming to a close. In thirty days he would be executed by lethal injection.

Victoria was torn by what she had read in the file provided by the warden and what she might be about to learn. No one wanted to be used as a conduit for an evil man's purposes. Yet, after due consideration of the letter Barker had written, she could not refuse the request.

The door of the interview room opened. Victoria jerked from her troubling thoughts and mentally fortified for the impact of meeting the man whose stunning invitation had brought her here. Two prison guards escorted Barker into the room. The leg irons around his ankles and belly chain coiled about his waist rattled as he was ushered to the chair directly across the table from her. The nylon glides whispered across the tile floor as the chair was drawn back.

"Sit," one of the guards ordered.

Barker glanced at the man on his left, then followed the instruction given. He settled into the molded plastic chair and faced Victoria. His gaze, however, remained lowered, as if his reflection in the steel tabletop had garnered his undivided attention. The second guard secured the leg irons to a hook on the floor and the ones binding Barker's hands to his waist to the underside of the sturdy table that spanned some three feet between the prisoner and his visitor.

"We'll be right outside, ma'am," the first guard said to Victoria, "if you need anything."

"Thank you. We'll be fine."

When the door had closed behind the guards, Barker finally looked up. The move was slow, cautious, as if he too were braced on some level for what was to come. The twenty-three hours per day confined to his cell showed in the pale skin stretched across his gaunt face; a face that narrowed down to slumped shoulders and rail-thin arms covered by colorless prison garb. But the most glaring aspect of his appearance was the faded brown eyes, dull and listless. There was nothing about this man's presence that exhibited the compassion and desperation of the letter he had written to Victoria. Had she made a mistake in coming?

"I didn't think you'd come."

The rustiness of his voice had her resisting the urge to flinch. His voice croaked with disuse and age far beyond his true years. According to the warden, this was the first time he had broken his silence in more than two decades. Reporters, men of God, bestselling authors, all had urged him to tell his story. He had refused. The measure of restraint required to maintain that vigil in spite of so very many reasons not to was nothing short of astonishing.

"Guess you're wishing you hadn't," he offered before Victoria completed her visual inventory of the man labeled as a heinous monster.

"Your letter was quite compelling." Only two pages, but every word had been carefully chosen to convey the worry and outright fear he professed haunted him. Victoria had no choice but to look into the matter. His assertions, though somewhat vague, carried far too much potential for even greater devastation for all concerned in the Princess Killer case. The idea that the man watching her so intently had been arrested and charged with the murders of more than a dozen young girls held her breath hostage as she waited for his next move.

His throat worked as if the words he intended to utter were difficult to summon. "It's true. All of it."

Victoria kept her hands folded in her lap to ensure there was no perception of superiority. She wanted Barker relaxed and open. Even more, she wanted his full attention on her face, not on her unshackled hands. The eyes were the windows to the soul. If she left this room with nothing else gained, she needed to gauge if there was any possibility whatsoever that he was telling the truth about those horrific murders.

The prospect carried monumental ramifications even beyond the added pain to the families of the victims. Her chest tightened at the conceivability of what his long-awaited words might mean. "Why haven't you come forward with this before now?" Having told the truth at or before trial, for instance. Instead, he had refused to talk from the moment he and his wife were arrested.

Clare Barker, on the other hand, had steadfastly stood by her story that she was innocent. As the investigation of the case had progressed, the bodies of eight young girls, ranging in age from twelve to seventeen, had been recovered, but several others remained missing. Clare insisted that she knew nothing about any of the murders. Her husband, a pillar of the small Texas community rocked by the news, had executed all the heinous murders, at least twelve, without her knowledge, and that gruesome number didn't include those of their three young daughters the morning of the arrest. This would not be the first time a community and even a spouse were totally blindsided. Since the evidence had incriminated both Clare and Rafe, there was the remote chance his sudden claims were, in part, the truth.

But why now? There were only two possibilities. First, and most probable, after numerous appeals, his wife had just been released, exonerated legally if not in the eyes of the citizens of Texas, and he wanted revenge. The less likely scenario was that he actually was innocent. Though he had provided no proof in his letter, there was something in his words that Victoria could not ignore. She had explored the depths of evil many times in her nearly three decades of private investigations. Long ago she had learned to trust her instincts. "There was ample opportunity for you to come forward."

"I had my reasons for not speaking out before." He looked away as he said the words, each of which was imbued with distrust and what sounded more like misery than defensiveness.

A deep calming breath was necessary for Victoria to repress any outward reaction. This man, one painted as a monster by the deeds he had refused to deny more than twenty years ago, despite his frail appearance and imminent death now, held the key to closure for so many. Parents who merely wanted to find peace, to provide a proper resting place for their daughters. The warden, Don Prentice, had urged Victoria to tread carefully here. Barker might very well be looking for a last-minute reprieve. No amount of strength possessed by any human fully abated the natural inclination to keep breathing. That cold, hard reality aside, the families of the victims should not have to go through more agony, particularly unnecessary agony. Prentice was right. Too much misery and loss had been wielded by this man and his wife already. Yet, if there was even the most remote chance he was telling the truth... Victoria had to know and to glean whatever good could come of it.

"Mr. Barker, you asked me to come here. You suggested in your letter that it was a life-and-death matter. If you want my help, I need the truth. All of it. Otherwise, I won't waste my time or *yours*."

Barker stared at her for so long that Victoria wasn't sure whether he would respond or simply cut his losses and call out for a guard to take him away. There was no mistaking the fear that had trickled into his weary eyes. Her pulse accelerated as the realization sank deep into her bones that the terror she saw was undeniably real. But was it for his own life or was it because he believed, perhaps even harbored some sort of proof, that the real killer of all those children had just gone free?

He took a breath that jerked his upper body as if it was the first deep gasp of oxygen he'd been physically able to inhale since sitting down with her. "I didn't hurt anyone, much less a child. I couldn't." Again he looked away.

"Unless you have irrefutable evidence," Victoria began prudently, "the chances of staying your execution are minimal." If that was his intent, as the warden suggested, Victoria refused to be a pawn in Barker's game. She would not allow the media to use her or the Colby Agency to that end.

"I'm ready to go." He squared his thin shoulders. "Don't waste any time on me. This is not about my guilt or innocence. It's about my children." His lips trembled. "And the others." The craggy features of his face tightened as he visibly fought for composure. "I can't do anything to bring those girls back, and I don't know that the truth would ease nobody's pain. Dead is dead." He moved his head side to side with the defeat that showed in the deep lines forged around his mouth. "But I can't let *her* hurt anyone else, especially my girls."

Despite the anticipation whirling like a biting snowstorm inside her, Victoria kept her expression schooled. "In your letter you claimed your wife was responsible for the murders. All of them." The bodies of their three small daughters had never been found, but neither had those of at least four other victims. As much as Victoria wanted to ask specific questions, she could not risk putting words in his mouth. Over and over in his letter he had insisted his daughters were in danger. Yet not a single shred of evidence supported the theory that the children had survived that final downward spiral the morning of the arrest. In all this time no one had come forward and suggested otherwise. The little girls had vanished, and concrete evidence that a violent act had preceded their disappearance had been documented at trial. What he alluded to in his letter and now, face-to-face, had to be supported by something tangible. He needed to say the words without a visible or audible prompt by Victoria.

"That's the truth," Barker repeated, the defeat she'd seen and heard moments ago now gone. "I can't prove it, don't even want to. But it's so just the same." He blinked, clearing the definable emotion from his eyes. "I didn't beg you to come here to save me. I died in here—" he glanced around the room "—a long time ago. I need you to help my girls."

Now they were getting somewhere. His leading the way was essential. "What exactly is it you're asking me to do?" Did he want her to recover their bodies and ensure a proper burial? If they weren't dead, why would he not want to prove his innocence of those particular charges? Why had he allowed all involved in the case to believe they were deceased? Was he simply trying to muddy the waters? Whatever his end game, Victoria needed him to spell it out. The warden was monitoring this interview, as well he should.

"As far as the world is concerned," Barker explained in that unpracticed voice, "I can stay the devil they believe I am. That doesn't matter to me." His gaze leveled on Victoria with a kind of desperation that sent a chill all the way to her core. "Once I found out *she* was going to get away with what she'd done, it took some time to find just the right person I could trust with what I knew had to be done. Careful research by certain folks in here who knew I needed help."

That this man had developed a loyal following of some sort during his tenure was no surprise, since the warden had not known the contents of Barker's letter until Victoria had shown it to him. The letter had gotten through the prison mail system without the usual inspections.

"But over and over the results they found were the same," Barker continued. "There was only one place that consistently fought for justice and helped those in need without ever falling down on the job or resorting to underhanded deeds in order to accomplish the goal. A place that has never once bragged about its record or used the media for self-serving purposes. That place is the Colby Agency."

Time stopped for one second, then two and three. Victoria didn't dare breathe until he finished.

"I can't pay you a dime, and I know my appreciation means nothing to you." He shrugged. "I'm worse than nothing in the eyes of the world. But if you can ignore what you think of me and just do this one thing, I'll know your agency is everything I read it was." Another of those deep, halting breaths rattled his torso. "I beg you, just protect my girls from *her*. That's all I want."

Victoria's heart thudded hard against her chest, then seemed to still with the thickening air in the room. "I'm sorry, Mr. Barker. You're going to have to be more precise as to what your request involves since *you* pled guilty to murdering your daughters twenty-two years ago. Neither your letter nor what you're saying to me now makes sense."

"They're alive." The words reverberated against the cold, white walls. "My girls are alive."

Adrenaline burned through Victoria's veins. Still she resisted any display of her anticipation. "The first officers on the scene the morning you and your wife were arrested," she countered cautiously, "found blood in the girls' bed. Blood in the trunk of your car along with a teddy bear that your middle daughter carried with her everywhere. The blood was tested and determined to be that of your daughters." Victoria hesitated until the horror of her words stopped darkening his features and echoing in her own ears. "You never denied killing your young children, Mr. Barker. To date there is no evidence to the contrary. In light of those facts, how can you expect me to believe you're finally telling the truth now?"

Fury, undeniable and stark, blazed in his eyes before he quickly smothered it and visibly grabbed back control. "That was to prevent *her* from ever knowing the girls were alive and hurting them somehow to get back at me for setting in motion her discovery." Several moments passed as he discernibly composed himself. "They deserved a chance at a decent life untainted by her poison. I had to make sure that happened."

When Victoria would have responded, he said more. "My daughters are alive and well, and if you don't help me, she will find them and kill them. For real this time." He leaned forward, as close as his shackles would allow, and stared deep into Victoria's eyes. "She's pure evil, and you're the only one I can trust to stop her."

Chapter Two

1:00 p.m., Polunsky Prison

"He's lying." Warden Don Prentice made his announcement and pushed out of his chair, indicating his already thin patience had reached an end. "You know what this is, and I'm not taking the bait."

Lyle McCaleb waited for a reaction from his boss, Simon Ruhl, head of the Colby Agency's new Houston office, or from the agency's matriarch, Victoria Colby-Camp. Simon exchanged a look with Victoria then turned to the warden. "Mr. Prentice, we genuinely appreciate your indulgence in this matter. I must admit that I concur with your assessment in light of the facts as we know them."

"That said," Victoria continued as if the rebuttal were a well-rehearsed strategy and she was about to play bad cop, "as warden of this institution, you have an obligation to report this theoretical threat to the proper authorities. Our agency does not have that same legal obligation. However, we have a moral one. We cannot just walk away and pretend this incident never happened."

Prentice shoved back the sides of his jacket, planted

his hands on his hips and gave his head a frustrated shake. "Do you have any idea what stirring up this mess in the media will do to those families?" He paced back and forth behind his desk like an inmate in his compact cell. "There's no way to keep it out of the press." Prentice stopped and stared at Victoria, then Simon. "The folks who thrive on this kind of heartache have been waiting for this moment for twenty-two years!"

"I do understand," Simon agreed once more. "That's exactly why I hope you'll see the logic in our proposition."

Lyle figured things could go either way from here. Prentice had agreed to this conference after Victoria's brief meeting with Barker this morning. Three hours had elapsed since that time with Victoria, her husband, Lucas, and Simon organizing a feasible strategy and the necessary resources. Lyle had jumped at the assignment. As the former head of one of Houston's most prestigious security firms, he knew the business of protection, and his tracking skills were top-notch from his days as a county sheriff's deputy. Add to that the fact that he was a lifelong resident of Texas and the combined bonus of high-level connections with a number of those in law enforcement, and he was the best man for the job. Initially, Simon and Victoria had hesitated. Texas was home and perhaps that made him less than objective. Though he'd only been seven at the time of the Barkers' arrest, his parents had followed news of the high-profile case for years after that.

He might not be the most objective investigator on staff, but in his opinion, that deep-seated understanding of how the entire travesty had affected the community as well as the state could prove useful in solving this puzzle. Fortunately, Simon and Victoria had concluded the same.

Lucas was not happy about his wife's insistence on being so deeply involved in this case. Recently retired from the day-to-day operations of the Colby Agency, the two were in Houston for only a few months. Just long enough to get the new office staffed and running efficiently. Simon was clearly more than capable of getting the job done on his own, but Lyle sensed Victoria and Lucas were dragging their feet with the whole retirement thing. Suited him just fine. Lyle was grateful for the opportunity to work with the esteemed Victoria Colby-Camp. Lucas was more or less an unknown to him, but Lyle was acquainted with the Colby name. The moment he'd heard the agency was opening an office in Houston, he was ready to sign on. This would be his first case, and he was itching to get in the field and start proving his value to the agency.

"You have my personal assurance, Mr. Prentice," Victoria said, drawing Lyle's attention back to her and the challenge she would absolutely win, "that this matter will be handled in the most discreet manner. No one outside this room and a select few at my agency will know the details of this case. The Colby Agency's reputation speaks for itself."

Lyle studied the warden's face, analyzed the way the muscles relaxed as he slowly but surely admitted defeat. He wasn't totally convinced, but he had likely done his homework. A guarantee like that from the head of the Colby Agency was the best offer he was going to get. And, as Victoria said, there was no turning back at this point. The cards had been dealt, the wager on the table. Someone had to make the next move.

"If this gets out—"

"It won't," Simon assured the warden. "Not from the Colby Agency."

"How can you protect these children—" Prentice closed his eyes, shook his head in resignation before opening his eyes once more "—these women when you don't know if they're even alive, much less where they are. My God, this is ludicrous."

Lyle wanted to give the man a good, swift kick in the seat of the pants. They were wasting time with all this beating around the bush.

"We already have someone in place monitoring Clare Barker's movements," Simon enlightened Warden Prentice. "We took that measure immediately."

Surprise and confusion cluttered the warden's face. "How is that possible? They took her out of Mountain View in the middle of the night. Half a dozen decoy vehicles were used to elude the media and the horde picketing her release. No one—not even me—knows where she is!"

Lyle had learned quickly that at the Colby Agency the enigmatic Lucas Camp was an ace in the hole. Former CIA, the man had some serious connections of his own. Clare Barker had requested residence in Copperas Cove, north of her former hometown, Austin. Part of Lyle wanted to be the one keeping an eye of the woman, since the Cove was his hometown. But tracking down the truth was his primary goal.

"Be that as it may, Mr. Prentice," Victoria confirmed, "if we could find her so quickly, others will too in time. If this is a game Barker is playing, perhaps his wife is a target and doesn't even realize it. For all we know, she may be the one in danger. Obviously he has some who support his cause. We can provide protection for her in addition to surveillance if the need arises."

"Mr. McCaleb will be tracking down the daughters through the woman Barker claims helped him get the children into hiding." Simon looked from the warden to Lyle and back. "We hope to locate her before the end of the day. Depending on the situation, if the three are indeed alive, we'll assign a bodyguard to keep an eye on each one until this mystery is solved one way or the other."

Prentice held up his hands. "You've made several valid points." He looked directly at Victoria. "Still, the only way I'm agreeing to this is if you keep me posted on your every step." He scrubbed a hand over his face. "That said, I have no choice but to inform the district attorney. If he has a problem with our decision, he and I will work it out." He exhaled a burdened breath. "There's no denying Barker has something up his sleeve, and I don't want any time wasted on bureaucracy. We'll do what we have to do."

Handshakes and more assurances were exchanged before Victoria led the way from Warden Prentice's office. Conversation was out of the question until they exited the facility. As soon as they were back at the agency's offices, Lyle would prepare to move forward. He was champing at the bit, anxious to get down to business putting together the pieces of this bizarre puzzle of depravity.

"When we have Tolliver's address," Victoria said to Lyle, "I want you to approach her as if she represents a flight risk. Slow and easy. If Barker is telling the truth, she has kept this secret for a very long time. She may not be prepared to let go now. Particularly to a stranger."

For the first time since Lyle had met Victoria Colby-Camp he noted uncertainty in those wise, dark eyes. He smiled. "You have my word. But, I have a feeling you believe I have the skills to handle the situation or I wouldn't be here."

Victoria returned the smile. "I just needed to confirm that *you* are as convinced as we are. This case will be anything but simple, I fear."

Lyle imagined he'd have to wake up pretty early in the morning to get a step ahead of this lady.

In the visitors' parking area, Simon hesitated before settling into his sedan. He pulled his cell phone from the interior pocket of his suit jacket and checked the screen before accepting the call. "Ruhl."

Simon Ruhl had the look and the bearing of a lead agent in a Secret Service team rather than a mere P.I., but then this was the Colby Agency. Made sense that Ruhl set the classic high-end example, since he was former FBI. Lyle had never met a federal agent that he cared for until now. Maybe he'd misjudged the whole barrel based on a couple of bad apples. Whatever the case, Simon knew his stuff and Lyle respected him. So far his experience at the Colby Agency was a good fit. The Houston office was nearly fully staffed, and Lyle was impressed with the lineup.

"We're on our way," Simon assured the caller before putting away his cell. "That was Lucas," he said, shifting his attention to Victoria. To Lyle he added, "Janet Tolliver is dead."

Frustration drilled deep into Lyle's gut. "When?" Not five minutes before the meeting with the warden Lucas had notified Simon that Tolliver's last known address was in the process of being confirmed. Prentice had been kept in the dark about this update until the address and the woman's connection to Barker could be verified. This news was seriously going to set back Lyle's efforts to determine if the Barker girls were alive. Janet Tolliver was the only name Barker had given Victoria. Allegedly, she was his co-conspirator in getting the children to safety before the law descended upon the Barkers' modest home in Granger. Tolliver had moved from Austin immediately after that. She'd jumped around for years. Obviously her final location had been found…along with her body.

"Sometime this morning." Simon hit the remote, unlocking his sedan. "A neighbor found her. The police aren't talking yet." Lyle opened the front passenger door for Victoria as Simon continued, "Turns out she had relatives in Copperas Cove. She had moved there just a few months ago. Coincidentally, only a few miles from Clare Barker's new Five Hills address." Simon held Lyle's gaze a moment before tacking on, "your hometown, McCaleb. That may prove the only good thing about this news, as long as you don't have any conflicts with going back home for at least the first step of your investigation."

Lyle shook his head. "No conflicts." None to speak of anyway. He hadn't been *home* in a while. Looked as if that was about to change. He closed Victoria's door and gave Simon a nod. "As soon as we're back at the office I can move out."

No big deal. Lyle had dug up the deads' secrets

before. He could do it again. As long as no one else died before he got what he needed, he could work with that.

And, for the record, he didn't believe in coincidences.

11:00 p.m., Copperas Cove

LYLE WAITED IN THE darkness. The local detectives had finished their initial investigation of the scene and called it a night. According to his contact, a retired sheriff's detective, the fifty-eight-year-old woman had been bludgeoned to death. In spite of that fact, there was no sign of forced entry, no indication of a true struggle. A broken lamp, an overturned table, both the result of her fall, but nothing else, discounting the blood-stained rug. If not for the blood and the obvious blows her body had absorbed, she might have merely suffered a heart attack and crumpled to the floor.

The violent attack came suddenly, unexpectedly, from a perpetrator Janet Tolliver had known and allowed into her home. The estimated time of death was between 2:00 and 4:00 a.m. Lucas's contact had located Clare Barker's position at ten that morning, moments after Victoria's meeting with Rafe Barker. Sufficient time for her to have committed the crime, except that there was no indication she'd left the apartment rented by her attorney not half an hour's drive from the Tolliver home. Barker had no vehicle as of yet, and no taxis serving the area had a record of a pickup at that address during that critical window of time.

Robbery didn't appear to be the motive, since Tolliver's purse still contained fifty dollars in cash and her one credit card and none of the usual targets in the home appeared to have been disturbed. Tolliver's great-niece would arrive tomorrow to confirm that presumption and to handle the deceased's final arrangements. The police had not questioned Clare Barker, since they were unaware of any connection between her and Tolliver. Clare's whereabouts between her arrival at her new home at 2:00 a.m. and when Lucas ferreted out her location could not be confirmed beyond the apparent lack of transportation. Seemed pretty damning that Tolliver was dead only a few hours after Barker's release. Even more so since Clare had requested Copperas Cove as her landing point. Had she known about Tolliver? Did this brutal murder confirm Rafe Barker's allegations?

Then again, based on what Lyle had read about Clare in the trial transcripts, she was one sharp cookie. Definitely not the type to act rashly. She'd had a long time to lay out a strategy for life after her release and any revenge she hoped to wield. Seemed to him that she would have taken a bit more care. Then again, anyone involved with murdering young girls couldn't be called logical or rational, and *care* wasn't likely a part of the person's psychological makeup.

Lyle emerged from his truck and locked the doors manually to avoid the *click*. He surveyed the quiet neighborhood until he was satisfied the residents were tucked in for the night. Moonlight and streetlamps washed the eight houses lining this end of the street with a grayish glow. There was only one way in or out, since the street dead-ended here, abutting a copse of trees that flanked the rear parking lot and playground of a school. He hoped his investigation wasn't headed

for a dead end, as well. All the homes were owner occupied. The police had questioned the neighbors. No
one had seen or heard anything. Most of the residents
were older folks. Chances were every last one had been
sound asleep between two and four this morning. By
tomorrow the detectives on the case should be able to
determine if Tolliver had received any phone calls that
might have preceded the late-night visitor.

Since Tolliver was the only person who could
have confirmed Rafe Barker's story, her murder had
changed Lyle's strategy completely. There were a
number of alternative steps he could take. Search the
house, and that was called breaking and entering. Not
to mention tampering with a crime scene. He could
check out any items she might have stored in bank
security-deposit boxes or with an attorney in hopes
a journal or notes of some sort related to her dealings
with Rafe Barker existed. If Lyle played his cards right
he might get an interview with the great-niece, who
could facilitate the other steps on his agenda. A list of
Tolliver's friends, the church she attended and any enemies she might have had would be useful. The down-
side to collecting that kind of information was the time
required, and time was the enemy, on several levels.

He strolled along the sidewalk, studying the modest
architecture with the aid of the streetlamps. Felt strange
to be this close to home without having seen his family
already. The ranch where he'd grown up wasn't far
from Copperas Cove proper. His folks would be disappointed if he didn't stop by and at least say hello. But
stopping by the old home place meant risking running
into *her*. And that was a risk he had no intention of

taking. The longer he was in the Cove, the more that risk increased.

This was not the time to get distracted with ancient history.

Lyle slipped into the darkness at the corner of the last house on the right and moved across the well-manicured back lawns until he reached the home belonging to the victim. Both the front and rear entrances were secured with official crime-scene warnings. A cat crouched on the rear stoop yowled for entrance. Lyle supposed the great-niece would see after any pets now orphaned. Or maybe one of the neighbors would step up to the plate. He'd been lucky so far that no dogs had spotted him or sensed a stranger's presence.

The houses were only a few feet apart, boundaries marked with neatly clipped shrubs. Moving silently, Lyle eased toward the front of the Tolliver house once more, scanning the dark windows as he passed and mentally measuring the distance between the crime scene and the neighbor on this side. Most of the houses were one-story bungalow-style homes. Few had garages or fences, just decades-old shrubs setting the perimeters agreed upon nearly a century ago. Other than the different makes and models of the vehicles in the driveways, one house looked much like the other.

The distinct thwack of a shotgun being racked stopped Lyle dead in his tracks. The threat came from behind him, beyond the row of shrubs.

"I've already called the police."

The voice was female. Older. Steady. No fear. Gave new meaning to the concept of neighborhood watch.

"I don't want any trouble, ma'am." He raised his hands. "I'm going to turn around now."

"You do anything I don't like and I'm shooting," she warned.

Lyle didn't doubt it for a second. "I can guarantee I won't do that, ma'am," he offered. "I grew up in the Cove. Worked as a sheriff's deputy for two years right out of high school."

The elderly woman's gray hair hung over her shoulders. A patchwork robe swaddled her slight body. The shotgun was as big as she was. The streetlamp five or so yards away provided sufficient light for him to see that the lady meant business. Folks in Texas didn't play with guns. If they owned one, they were well versed in how to use it.

"My neighbor was murdered this morning." Her gaze narrowed as she blatantly sized him up. "You got no business prowling around out here in the dark unless you're an officer of the law." She looked him up and down, concluding what she would about his well-worn jeans and tee sporting the Texas Longhorns logo. "You don't look like no cop to me."

"You a friend of Ms. Tolliver's?" He decided not to refer to the victim in the past tense.

"Maybe. What's it to you?"

Well, there was a question he hadn't anticipated.

"I came all the way from Houston to talk to her." He jerked his head toward the crime scene. "I wasn't expecting this. You mind telling me what happened?"

She kept a perfect bead on the center of his chest. "You got a name?"

"Lyle McCaleb."

She considered his name a moment, then shook her head. "I know all Janet's friends, and I've met her niece and her husband. And you ain't none of the above." The lady adjusted her steady hold on the small-gauge shotgun. "Now, what're you really doing here, and who sent you?"

There was nothing to be gained by hedging the question. She'd called the police. No point avoiding the inevitable. For now there was no confirmed connection between the Barkers and Tolliver, no reason to provide a cover to protect his agenda for now. "I was sent by the Colby Agency, a private investigations firm in Houston."

Something like recognition kicked aside the suspicion in the neighbor's expression and in her posture. She relaxed just a fraction. "Let's see some ID."

Her reaction was something else he hadn't anticipated. There had been a lot of that on this case, and he'd barely scratched the surface of step one. He reached for his wallet.

"My finger's on the trigger, Mr. McCaleb," she warned, "don't make me shoot you."

"Yes, ma'am." He removed his wallet from his back pocket and held it up for her inspection, then opened it and displayed his Colby Agency identification.

She studied the picture ID a moment then lowered the weapon. "Well, all right then. Come on in. I've been waiting for you."

Lyle mentally wrestled back the astonishment that wanted to make an appearance on his face and gave the lady a nod. "Yes, ma'am. After you."

It looked as if surprises were the theme for the night. He parted the shrubs and followed the lady to her front steps and across the porch. At the front door he hesitated. This was beyond strange. She had been waiting for him?

"Come on," she urged, obviously waiting to close the door behind him.

Lyle played along. Why not? A lit lamp on an end table and the discarded newspaper on the sofa suggested she had been up watching television or watching for someone. Seemed a reasonable conclusion that she would be, since after seeing his ID she announced she had been expecting him. Though he couldn't fathom how that was possible.

"Have a seat, Mr. McCaleb." She gestured to the well-used sofa. "I have something for you." And just like that, she disappeared into the darkness around the corner from the dining room.

Not about to put the lady off by ignoring her hospitality, Lyle settled on the sofa. A couple of retirement magazines lay on the coffee table. He picked up one and read the address label. Rhoda Strong. Since this was her address, he assumed his hostess and the subscription recipient were one and the same. Her demeanor certainly matched the surname. To say it was a little out of the ordinary to invite a complete stranger into one's home in the middle of the night after the murder of a neighbor would be a monumental understatement. But then, Ms. Rhoda Strong appeared fully capable of protecting herself.

Still toting her shotgun, the lady of the house returned with an armload of what looked like photo albums.

"You have me at a disadvantage." Lyle stood as she approached the sofa. "I don't know your name."

"Rhoda." She plopped down on the sofa, leaned the shotgun against her right knee and settled the albums in her lap. "Rhoda Strong. Now, sit back down."

"Yes, ma'am." Lyle couldn't wait. Whatever the lady was about to reveal, he didn't want to miss a word. The possibility that she was a brick or two shy of a load poked into the lump of perplexing conclusions taking shape in his head.

"Okay." She huffed as if the whole effort of reaching this point had proved taxing then rested her attention on him. "Don't bother asking me any questions because I have no answers. All I can tell you is that I've known Janet her whole life. She came here from Austin every summer as a kid to spend time at her aunt's house. Janet never married or had any children of her own. She never got into any trouble I know about, but—" she stared down at the albums "—a week ago she said she needed me to keep these three picture books safe for her. She didn't offer any explanations and I didn't ask any questions. I promised her I would and that was that." Her expression turned troubled and distant. "Until yesterday. She come over here and asked if I'd be home all day. Said she might be coming over to get the albums if the company she was expecting arrived. I told her I reckoned I'd be here. Before she left she got this funny look on her face and made me promise one more thing."

Lyle searched the elderly woman's eyes, saw the understanding there that the items she now held had cost her friend her life.

"She made me swear that if anything happened to her I wouldn't go to the police with these pictures or even to her niece. I was to stay right here and be on the lookout for someone. When that someone arrived I was to give these books to that person and that person only."

Before Lyle could assimilate a reasonable response, Rhoda thrust the stack of photo albums at him. He accepted the load that carried far more weight than could be measured in mere pounds and ounces.

"There. I've done what she asked."

Lyle shook his head. "Ms. Strong, I'm confused. There is no way your friend could have known my name."

The older woman shrugged. "Don't suppose she did. She just said someone from the Colby Agency would be coming." She stared straight into his eyes with a certainty that twisted through his chest. "And here you are."

Not ashamed to admit he was rattled, Lyle opened the first of the three albums. Page one displayed a birth certificate for Elizabeth Barker. Parents: Raymond and Clare Barker. His heart pounding, he turned to the next page. A new birth certificate, this one for an Olivia Westfield. There were newspaper clippings and photos, obviously taken without the subject's knowledge, from around kindergarten age to the present. The woman, Olivia, according to her birth certificate was twenty-seven—the oldest of the three missing Barker girls. The second album was the same, Lisa Barker aka Laney Seagers, age twenty-six.

"These are…" Incredible, shocking. No word that came to mind adequately conveyed what he wanted to say. He had to call Simon and Victoria. They had held out some hope of finding Rafe Barker's daughters alive, but this was…mind-blowing.

"I know who they are, Mr. McCaleb," Rhoda said to him, dragging his attention from the carefully detailed history of the Barker children—women. "My friend is dead because she kept this secret all these years. You do whatever you have to do to make sure she didn't die for nothing, and I'll do the same."

"You have my word, ma'am." Adrenaline searing through his blood vessels, Lyle shuffled to the final album. Selma Barker aka Sadie Gilmore.

His heart stopped. *No.* Not possible.

"Yes," Rhoda countered.

Lyle hadn't realized he'd uttered the word aloud until the woman still sitting next to him spoke.

"That one lives right here in Copperas Cove." She tapped the photo of the young woman touted in the newspaper clipping as an animal rights activist. "Do you know her?"

Lyle stared at the face he hadn't seen in seven years, except in his dreams, his gut twisting into knot after knot. "Yes, ma'am. I know her." If he lived a hundred lifetimes, he couldn't forget *this* woman.

Chapter Three

May 21, Second Chance Ranch, 6:30 a.m.

"Get off my ranch." Sadie Gilmore held her ground, feet spread wide apart, the business end of her shotgun leveled on that no-good Billy Sizemore's black heart. Maybe he thought just because he played straw boss for her equally no-good daddy that he could tell her what to do. Not in this lifetime.

Sizemore laughed. Threw his head back so far if he hadn't been holding his designer cowboy hat it would have hit the dirt for sure, and he hooted. This wasn't the first time Sadie had been blazing mad at her daddy's henchmen, especially this knucklehead. Well, she'd had enough. She poked him in the chest with the muzzle of her twenty-gauge best friend. The echo of his laughter died an instant death. A razor-sharp gaze sliced clean through her. She gritted her teeth to conquer a flinch. "Three seconds," she warned, "or I swear I'll risk prison just to see the look on your sorry face when this ball of lead blasts a great big hole in your chest."

"You stole that horse," he accused. "Don't even try denying it."

Sadie was the one who laughed this time. "Prove it."

The standoff lasted another couple of seconds before he surrendered a step. "You'll regret this," he warned, then turned his back to her. It took every speck of self-control she possessed not to shoot him before he reached his dually. But then that would make her the same kind of cheating sneak Gus Gilmore was.

Sadie lowered the barrel of the shotgun she'd inherited from her Grandma Gilmore and let go the breath that had been trapped in her lungs for the past half a minute or so. Sizemore spun away, the tires of his truck sending gravel and dirt spewing through the air and the horse trailer hitched to it bouncing precariously.

"Lying bastard." Billy Sizemore might be a champion when it came to bronc riding, but as a human he scarcely hung on the first link of the food chain, in her opinion. Cow flies had more compassion. Could damn sure be trusted more.

Sadie swiped the perspiration from her brow with the sleeve of her cotton blouse and worked at slowing her heart rate. Usually she didn't let guys like Sizemore get to her, but this time was different. This time the stakes were extra high. No way was she allowing her father to get his way. She'd bought old Dare Devil fair and square. The gelding was done with his rodeo career. Too old to perform for the bronc riders and too riddled with arthritis for chuck wagon races or anything else. Just because Gus claimed the former competition star had been shipped off to the auction by mistake was no concern of hers. Sadie knew exactly what happened to those horses in far too many cases, and she couldn't bear it. Gus didn't need to know that she still had a friend or two on his side of the five-foot barbed wire fence that divided their properties.

"What you don't know won't hurt you, old man," she proclaimed with a hard look to the west before visually tracking Sizemore's big old truck and trailer roaring down the last leg of her half-mile-long drive.

When the dust had settled and the dually was long gone, Sadie walked back to the house. Three furry heads peeked out from under the front porch, big soulful eyes peering up at her hopefully.

"Worthless." She shook her head at the mutts. "That's what you three are."

Gator, the Lab, Frisco, an Australian shepherd mix, and Abigail, a Chihuahua, scurried from their hiding place and padded into the house behind her. That first cup of coffee was long gone, and the lingering scent of the seasoned scrambled eggs she'd turned off fifteen minutes ago had her stomach rumbling. The enemy's arrival had interrupted her peaceful morning.

With her shotgun propped in the corner near the kitchen table, she adjusted the flame beneath the skillet to warm up the eggs. Another more pungent odor sifted through her preoccupation with the sharp gnawing pains in her belly. Smelled like something scorched...

"My biscuits!" Sadie grabbed a mitt and yanked the oven door open. "Well, hell." Not exactly burned but definitely well done and probably as hard as rocks. She plopped the hot tray on the stove top and tossed the mitt aside. How could a grown woman screw up a can of ready-to-bake biscuits? "One who's spent her whole life in the barn," she muttered.

Her mother had passed away before Sadie was old enough to sit still long enough to learn any culinary skills. The rodeo was all her father had bothered to teach her, and most of the lessons she'd gleaned were ones she wanted to forget. Gus Gilmore was heartless. But then, she'd understood that by the time she was fifteen. He'd tried to keep her away from her grandparents when she was a kid, but she always found a way to sneak in a visit. He had worked overtime to keep her away from everything she loved until she was twenty-one. That date had been more than a significant birthday; it had been her personal independence day. Prevented from taking anything from her childhood home other than the clothes on her back, she'd walked into the lawyer's office and claimed the inheritance her grandparents had left for her—despite Gus's every attempt to overturn their will—and hadn't looked back.

Nineteen months later she had created the life she wanted, just outside her father's reach yet right under his nose. They had been at all-out war since. Fact was, they had been immersed in battle most of her life. The stakes had merely been upped with her inheritance. Gus, being an only child, had assumed he would inherit the small five-hundred-acre ranch that adjoined his massive property. But life had a way of taking a man down a notch or two when he got too big for his breeches.

Sadie poured a second cup of morning-survival liquid and savored the one thing in the kitchen she was pretty good at—rich, strong coffee. She divided up the eggs and biscuits with her worthless guard dogs and collapsed at the table. Mercy, she was running behind this morning. If that low-down Sizemore hadn't shown up, she would be feeding the horses already instead of stuffing her face.

First things first. She had to calm down. The animals sensed when she was anxious. And fueling her body was necessary. Gus's pals had intimidated the last of her ranch hands until they'd all quit, leaving Sadie on her own to take care of the place. She didn't mind doing the work, but there was only so much one woman could do between daylight and dark. She'd narrowed her focus to the animals and the necessary property areas, such as the barn and smaller pasture. Everything else that required attention would just have to wait. Things would turn around eventually. As long as she was careful, her finances would hold out. Between the small trust her grandparents had left and donations for taking care of her rescues from generous folks, she would be okay in spite of her daddy's determined efforts to ensure otherwise.

Gator and Frisco stared up at her from their empty bowls. Abigail stared, too, but she hadn't touched her biscuit. Not that Sadie could blame her. Maybe her ranch hands had fled for parts unknown to escape her cooking. Sadie didn't like to waste anything, unlike Gus, so the dogs were stuck with her cooking until she figured out how to prepare smaller portions.

Before she could shovel in the final bite of breakfast, all three dogs suddenly stilled, ears perked, then the whole pack made a dash for the front door. Sadie pushed back her chair, her head shaking in disgust. If Gus had decided to show up in person and add his two cents' worth, he might just leave with more than he bargained for. Or maybe less, depending upon how well her trigger-finger self-control held out.

Shotgun in hand, she marched to the door and peeked out around the curtains her grandmother had made when Sadie was a little girl. The black truck wasn't one she recognized. Too shiny and new to belong to any of the ranchers around here, at least the ones who actually worked for a living. Ten or so seconds passed and the driver didn't get out. The way the sun hit the windshield, it was impossible to tell if the driver was male or female, friend or foe.

She opened the door and the dogs raced toward the truck, barking and yapping as if they were a force to be reckoned with. If the driver said a harsh word, the three would be under the porch in a heartbeat. Sadie couldn't really hold it against them. All three were rescues. After what they'd gone through, they had a right to be people shy.

With the shotgun hanging at her side, she made it as far as the porch steps when the driver's door opened. Sadie knew the deputies in Coryell County. Her visitor wasn't any of them. A boot hit the ground, stirring the dust. Something deep inside her braced for a new kind of trouble. As the driver emerged her gaze moved upward, over the gleaming black door and the tinted window to a black Stetson and dark sunglasses. She couldn't quite make out the details of the man's face, but some extra sense that had nothing to do with what she could see set her on edge.

Another boot hit the ground and the door closed. Her visual inspection swept over long legs cinched in comfortably worn denim, a lean waist and broad shoulders testing the seams of a shirt that hadn't come off the rack at any store where she shopped, finally zeroing in on the man's face just as he removed the dark glasses.

The weapon almost slipped from her grasp. Her heart bucked hard twice then skidded to a near halt.

Lyle McCaleb.

"What the...devil?" whispered past her lips.

Unable to move a muscle, she watched in morbid fascination as he hooked the sunglasses onto his hip pocket and strode toward the house—toward her. Sadie wouldn't have been able to summon a warning that he was trespassing had her life depended on just a simple two-letter word. The dogs growled while matching his steps, backing up until they were behind their master.

"Sadie." Lyle glanced at the shotgun as he reached up and removed his hat. "Expecting company?"

As if her heart had suddenly started to pump once more, kicking her brain into gear, fury blasted through her frozen muscles. "What do you want, Lyle McCaleb?" Somehow, despite the outrage roaring like a swollen river inside her, the words were frail and small. It still hurt, damn it, after all these years, to say his name out loud.

"Seeing as you didn't know I was coming, that couldn't be for me." He gave a nod toward her shotgun.

This could not be happening. Seven years he'd been gone. This was...this was... "I have nothing to say to you." She turned her back to him and walked away. Who did he think he was, showing up here like this after all this time? It was crazy. He was crazy!

"I know I'm the last person on this earth you want to see."

Her feet stopped when she wanted to keep going. To get inside the house and slam the door and dead-bolt it.

"We need to talk."

Sadie closed her eyes. Why was she standing here listening to anything he had to say? This was crazy all right. Crazy of her to hesitate like this. Hadn't she been a fool for him one time too many already?

"It's about your daddy."

She whipped around and glared at him but still couldn't find her voice. For Pete's sake, she hated the way her eyes drank in every single drop of him. His hair was as dark and silky as before. Those vivid blue eyes still made her want to sink into him, as if wading deep into the ocean with no care for how she'd stay afloat since she'd never learned to swim. He'd changed in other ways though. The cute boyish features had developed into rugged, handsome male assets. And in the face of all she had suffered because of him, he still made her body burn with need. With the primal urge to run into his arms.

Seeing him somehow made her momentarily forget those years of misery she'd endured because of something he had refused to give her seven years ago, and he damned sure wasn't here to give her his heart today.

She kicked the momentary weakness aside and grabbed back her good sense. "What about him?" she demanded. To her immense relief she sounded more like herself now. In charge, independent. Strong, ready to do battle.

"There's an investigation under way that I'm hoping is groundless." He flared those big hands that as a wild teenager she would have given anything to feel roving over her body. "I don't know if I can help him, but he's in way over his head. The only chance I've got of derailing the situation is with your help. I *need* your help."

Narrowing her gaze, she searched his face, tried her level best to look beyond the handsome features and see what he was hiding. He was hiding something. Didn't matter that it had been seven years. She knew Lyle McCaleb. He'd never been able to lie to her, even when she would have preferred his lies to the truth. He couldn't love her.

Whatever he wanted, he could forget it. Her heart had mended in time. She wasn't giving him a second shot at that kind of pain. "I hope you didn't drive all the way here from wherever you came from just for that."

"Houston."

If he'd sucker punched her, her physical reaction couldn't have been more debilitating. He'd been that close all this time? Gus had told her he'd moved to California, had a wife. Someone mature enough and smart enough to hang on to a man like him. A new rush of anger blasted her, obliterating the ache he'd resurrected with that one word. "Whatever. You wasted your time. Go away."

Before she could turn her back a second time and escape this surreal encounter, he opened his mouth again. "I was wrong not to call." He shook his head, stared at the ground a moment. "I was wrong about a lot of things."

Now she was really mad. "Let me tell you something else you're wrong about, McCaleb." She propped the barrel of her shotgun on her shoulder. "You're wrong if you think I give one damn about what kind of trouble my daddy might be in, because I don't." She amped up the go-to-hell glare in her eyes. "And you're dead wrong if you think for one second I care what you need."

LYLE WATCHED, HIS HEART somewhere in the vicinity of his throat, as she stamped up the steps and across the porch. She stormed into the house, slamming the door, without even a glance over her shoulder. The dogs stared after her, then turned to him in expectation.

That didn't exactly go the way he'd planned. Not even close. There was no denying that she did have every reason to hate him. He'd foolishly hoped that wasn't the case.

He blew out a breath and opted for plan B. Sit on the porch and wait. The dogs did the same, keeping their distance and eyeing him curiously but not bothering to bark. She wouldn't call the sheriff's office and have him escorted off her property. Not considering what he'd learned about the war going on between her and the rodeo kings around the county. Sheriff Cox was a good man as far as Lyle knew, but he held an elected position, and in this territory the rodeo kings ruled.

Lyle chuckled. Sadie Adele Gilmore had always been a hellion. In that respect she evidently hadn't changed one bit. She liked bucking the status quo, particularly when it involved the good old boys. She and her father had never really gotten along, not since she was old enough to have a mind of her own anyway. The best he recalled, she'd been damned independent since the age of six. His heart swelled a little more at the idea of what had been hidden from her all these years. He hated like hell to be the one to turn her life upside down like this, but he sure wasn't allowing anyone else to do the job. He owed her that much. He'd hurt her, but he'd made the only choice he could at the time. Nothing he said or did now would change that tragic fact, but he had to protect her.

He couldn't *not* protect her.

Her daddy wasn't going to like it. The last exchange between Gus and Lyle had been several degrees below amicable. The old man would be livid when he learned Lyle was back. The one thing Lyle could absolutely guarantee was that he wasn't walking away this time. For Gus or any other reason.

Wrestling aside his emotions, Lyle focused on what he'd come here to do. Whatever happened from this moment on was his responsibility. Whether she liked it or not. That part he'd just have to figure out. This battle between her and Gus had gone too far, if all he'd discovered was accurate. That was a whole different ball of wax and complicated an already dangerous situation. It pained him that she had been fighting a man like her daddy alone all this time. Lyle had left seven years ago when he should have stayed. He dropped his head. Staying hadn't been possible, no matter how he looked at the past. Things had been far too volatile. He'd had no choice but to leave.

By God, he was here now.

Sadie had a soft spot for animals, all of them. He surveyed the herd of furry critters lounging around his feet. Apparently she'd made it her life's mission to save every one she could, especially those involved with the rodeo that, for one reason or another, were neglected or otherwise abused. That decision had made a lot of folks unhappy around here, particularly Gus Gilmore. She'd gotten more than one, including her daddy, fined by the rodeo association for crossing the line when it came to the treatment of the animals they owned. Many times the incidents were mistakes or oversights, but others were intentional acts intended to ensure a crowd-pleasing performance. The latter could prove hazardous to the person or persons who got in the way.

Lyle stared at his hat, turning it in his hands as if an answer could be pulled from there, but there was no easy answer. Sadie's troubles with the ranchers were the least of her problems right now. Making her understand that reality without revealing too much too soon would be the hardest part. Her cooperation was absolutely essential, but he despised keeping anything from her for any reason.

The fact was he couldn't protect her fully if she didn't cooperate. The situation presented a precarious balancing act. The last thing he wanted to do was hurt her again. Or to let anyone else hurt her. Unfortunately, whatever happened, protecting her from the shocking truth was not possible. She had to know all of it, eventually.

Movement beyond the end of the house caught his eye. He watched her march out to the barn, her shotgun still propped on her shoulder. She'd captured her long, silky blond hair into a haphazard ponytail that hung to the middle of her back. She'd worn it that way for as long as he could remember. The scrap of leather she used to tie it back always ended up barely clasping that gorgeous mane below her shoulders, as if she didn't possess the patience to bother with securing it adequately at the nape of her neck. Her grandmother had scolded her about never staying still long enough to properly brush her hair, much less prepare a suitable ponytail. The memory of running his fingers through her hair warred with the logic required to stay on track. He banished those snippets of lost moments the same way he'd been doing for the past seven years.

The dogs, one by one, got up and moseyed out to the barn to see what their master was up to. Lyle stood, settled his hat into place, and followed. Her soft voice stopped him at the wide-open barn doors. She'd set her shotgun aside and filled a bucket with feed. One by one she served the stabled animals. Chatted softly with each one and gave the old horses a scratch behind the ears. When she'd finished she walked right past Lyle and released all but one horse into the pasture.

The barn and the house were a little run-down. In all likelihood there was fencing that needed mending. Had she been trying to handle this place all alone the better part of the time? The thought made his gut clench. Damn Gus Gilmore. Lyle shook his head. Damn *him*. She hadn't deserved the raw deal she'd gotten from him anymore than from her daddy.

Sadie made eye contact with him as she strode back to the front of the barn. "You haven't left yet?" Her arms went over her chest as her chin lifted in challenge.

"I'm afraid leaving isn't an option."

"You're something." She shook her head, fury blazing in those green eyes her grandmother had sworn came from her Irish roots. Lyle knew different. Sadie was the only one of the Barker girls who had her biological mother's green eyes. "You take off, stay gone for seven years and now you show up needing *my* help. I don't know what you've been smoking, but I think you'd better find some place to clear your head."

"Like I said before—" he folded his arms over his chest, matching her stance and, partly, to keep from grabbing her and shaking her or worse, kissing the hell out of her "—I was wrong."

"Like *you* also said," she echoed, "you were wrong about a lot of things, but that changes nothing."

"I really need your help, Sadie. This isn't just about Gus."

A frown furrowed her soft brow. Damn, she looked good in those work-worn jeans and that pink button-up shirt that hugged her body the way he had dreamed of doing for too many years to count.

"All right, I'll bite. What's this about then?"

At least her question was a step in the right direction. "The trouble involves you, too."

She rolled her eyes and made a sound of disbelief. "I don't believe you. Besides, I'm always in trouble. What's new?"

"This could get ugly fast." Urgency nudged him. "There's no time to say what I need to say the polite way." Might as well spit it out. "I've been sent here to protect you 24/7, until this is over."

He'd expected her to get her shotgun, maybe rant at him a little more, and attempt running him off. He was prepared for that kind of reaction. He wasn't set for her laughter. The sound burst out of her. "You really are out of your mind, Lyle McCaleb. You should go now, before I lose my sense of humor."

He had one last ace up his sleeve. "You think you're unhappy to see me." He chuckled. "Imagine how Gus will feel when he finds out I'm back." Lyle grinned, couldn't help himself. "He's really going to hit the roof. You know how much he hates me. I'll bet word has already climbed its way up to that pedestal he lives on."

That gave her pause and maybe a little anticipatory pleasure. It flashed like a neon sign across her pretty face. "I'm not saying you can stay or even that I believe anything you're saying," she countered, but her resolve had weakened ever so slightly. He heard it in her voice. "But I'll hear you out and then I'll make my decision."

"Rumor has it you're out here all by yourself." That worried him the most.

Anger darkened the features he knew by heart, yanking the step he'd gained right out from under his feet. "I don't appreciate you checking up on me. I'm perfectly capable of taking care of myself."

"I'm just doing my job, Sadie. My orders are to make sure you're protected. To do that I have to know what I'm up against."

Suspicion made an appearance amid the other emotions visibly tugging at her. "Who sent you here? You working for the law again? I thought you went off to be some hotshot security specialist."

The Colby Agency never failed its clients, particularly not where their safety was concerned. Yes, he was here representing those high standards. He supposed one could reason that he was operating under Colby Law. "The answer's complicated, Sadie. There's no simple way to explain it." He didn't dare say more, much less breathe. All he needed was half a chance to protect her with her cooperation…to do right by her this time.

"Well." She dropped her arms to her sides, hooked her right thumb in a belt loop and pursed those perfect bow lips the way she had at fifteen. The image made him ache to trace those sweet lips with his fingers, then with his lips. "You're right about one thing. Gus ran off all my help and there is a lot of work to be done. I can't deny your conclusions there."

"It's been a while." He glanced around, noting the repairs that immediately jumped out at him, such as the barn's old tin roof. It could use a little TLC. He shrugged. "Just like riding a bicycle. Point me in a starting direction and I'll get back in the swing of things faster than old Dare Devil used to toss his riders." He'd noticed the old champion among those under her care. Dare Devil was the only one she hadn't let out to roam in the pasture. Had to be a reason for that. Gus, he suspected. And more trouble.

Something wicked glittered in her eyes as she pointed up to the barn roof. "The extension ladder's in the toolshed. You'll find anything else you need there, too. Long as you stay busy and out of my way. You've got a deal. *For the day.*"

Lyle surveyed the first step toward gaining her co-operation if not her trust, three stories up at the very least. Nothing he hadn't done before.

Sadie headed back into the barn. "Come supper," she called back at him, "I'll expect some answers, and then you'll have my final decision."

Lyle pointed his boots in the direction of the tool-shed. If it kept her alive, he could walk a tightrope all the way across Texas.

If he was lucky, he would live through the experience.

Chapter Four

What now? What now?

It wasn't supposed to happen this way. She had a plan, a carefully laid plan. This could ruin everything! She paced the small studio apartment. Back and forth, back and forth. Perhaps the problem was only temporary.

At the window, Clare Barker peeked through the slats of the yellowed blinds covering her one portal to the outside world. The car was still there. Oh, no, no, no. Who was this man watching her? The warden had relished telling her that as soon as she was delivered to this location she was on her own. She knew what he wanted—he wanted some vigilante to carry out the justice the whole world believed had been denied by an appeals court. Her lips tightened. But this man had not gone away. He was not supposed to be here! He changed everything.

Her fingers knotted together as the worry rose in her throat once more, the taste as bitter as yesterday's coffee dregs. *He* had sent this man to kill her. She knew it! She just knew it. It was the only way to stop her, that was for sure. He would know his options were limited. Had he prepared so well?

Rage boiled in her belly. But he would fail. The fury stretched her lips into a knowing smile. *He would fail.*

More than twenty years she had planned this moment. *He* would pay for what he had done to her. No force on earth could stop her without sending her to hell first.

Time was her most fierce enemy. There was no room for distractions. Clare turned away from the window. Her reflection in the mirror mounted to the bathroom door of her efficiency apartment snared her attention. She was old now. The lines of her frown were deep and ugly. Her hair more gray than the blond it had once been. She touched the shaggy ends she had bobbed off to her ears. No use making it easy for anyone looking for her. She studied the hollows beneath her eyes and the crow's feet nothing short of a face-lift would remedy. All those years within those stark, punishing walls had stolen her youth, her beauty. She had nothing left, save for this long-awaited final act of retribution.

Clare went to the tattered sofa, where her most prized possessions were arranged like a shrine. She lit the small candle on the end table and dropped to her knees. Confident in her ability to overcome all blockades thrown in her path, she studied the photos lined up against the back of the worn cushions. Each one would soon know the truth. Each one would feel her pain and finally understand what only a mother who had sacrificed so much could.

And before they answered to their maker for their sins, each one would realize that it had never been

what if wicked old Clare won one of her many appeals.
It had always been simply a matter of time.

There was no escaping destiny.

Clare bowed her head and began to pray. She prayed
for strength, for courage to stay her course. Once it was
done, she cared little what happened to her.

She lifted her gaze to the photos worn by time and
the caress of her fingers. Mommy was here now. The
waiting and wondering would soon be over.

Chapter Five

Second Chance Ranch, 6:00 p.m.

Sadie washed up and tossed the hand towel aside. What was she doing? Her reflection didn't give her the answer she wanted to see. All she saw in the mirror was a woman who still wanted the only man she'd ever loved. The man who'd left her with painful words that rang in her ears to this day.

I can't do this, Sadie. You're just a kid. I don't have time for games.

Anger and hurt—yes, hurt—twisted her heart. He'd left and she'd cried herself to sleep every night for months. What the hell was she doing allowing him to worm his way back into her life for any reason? The answer resonated in her brain as clearly as the last words he'd uttered to her all those years ago. Despite their miserable history, a tiny piece of her wanted to believe that it could be different now. Yeah, he was still six years older than her, but she was twenty-two—soon to be twenty-three—a lifetime away from fifteen.

Did that really change anything? Of course not. Just because he was here to do a job didn't mean he felt any different today than he had seven years ago. Did she?

She'd thought she was way over Lyle McCaleb ages ago, but apparently she'd been lying to herself.

As angry and disgusted as she was with her own stupidity and his audacity, she might as well get this over with. Her excuses for hanging out in the bathroom had run out. Time to face the reality of this bizarre turn of events and get some answers from the man.

Taking a big breath, she opened the door and stalled. What was that smell? Fried potatoes? She sniffed the air like a beagle on the scent of a rabbit. Corn bread? Her mouth watered as much at the memory of her grandmother's cooking the scents evoked as at the delicious smells themselves wafting from her kitchen right now.

Lyle cooking? No way. Had Walley, the last employee to leave her high and dry and the only one who could cook, come crawling back? Not likely. He was far too afraid of Gus. She wandered to the kitchen, pausing in the doorway to get the lay of the land. No Walley in sight. Hat hanging on a kitchen chair, a red-and-white striped dish towel slung over one broad shoulder, Lyle McCaleb stirred what she presumed to be the potatoes revving her appetite. Sadie leaned against the door frame, too shocked to speak or maybe too curious to risk interrupting. This was a side of Lyle she had never seen. Then again, the fact that their every encounter before had been on the sly might have something to do with that.

He checked the oven, allowing more of that heavenly aroma of fresh-baked corn bread to sift through the air. Still apparently oblivious to her presence, he rummaged through the slim pickings of her supplies, opening one cupboard after the other, and came up with a can she recognized as beans she'd forgotten was there. Probably some of her grandmother's left-over supplies. While the electric can opener whined with the effort of releasing the contents of the can, her attention somehow got trapped on Lyle's backside, specifically the fit of his jeans. He'd been handsome and nicely built before, but now he was…she licked her lips…just plain hot. As if her traitorous body needed to prove the theory, heat simmered through her limbs, settling in that place she had ignored for way too long.

Stop, Sadie. Lyle was here. Out of the blue. She'd tried to reason out his explanation for showing up, but it didn't add up. As far as she knew, Gus wasn't doing anything differently than he'd done for years. Why would the authorities be interested in him now? Just because he was a greedy, ruthless SOB didn't make him a criminal. Just a heartless bastard who happened to be her father, unfortunately. Lyle had suggested her name had been mentioned in whatever trouble was brewing. That was nothing new. She spent most of her time on somebody's horse manure list and ignoring the sheriff's stern warnings.

No. She straightened and steeled herself for a fight. This excuse of his for requesting her cooperation didn't hold water. She wouldn't accuse him of lying, but he was most definitely hedging the truth. As curious as she was about him and what he'd been up to the past seven years, everyone knew that curiosity killed the cat.

"Looks like you've picked up a few new skills while you've been away." She crossed her arms over her chest and strolled over to the stove. Yep, fried potatoes. Browned to a nice crisp. Her stomach rumbled.

She hadn't eaten anything that fit into the home-cooked category in ages. Eggs didn't count unless they were a part of a casserole or other dish. Walley had been the one to dare to stock fresh vegetables. After he'd gone, they'd all ended up horse treats before going bad. Except for the potatoes. She'd been known to pop one in the microwave and wait for the explosion indicating it was done.

"When you live alone—" Lyle wiped his hands on the towel then deposited it on the counter "—you learn to fend for yourself."

Well, well. It appeared things hadn't worked out with the other woman. She had noted there was no ring on the appropriate finger. No rings at all, as a matter of fact. Was that glee flittering around in her tummy or just more hunger pangs? *Get to the point, girl.* If she was nice she would start by telling him how much she appreciated the work he'd accomplished on the barn roof, but she wasn't feeling too nice right now. "We have to talk."

He bent down and pulled the bread from the oven. Her knees practically went weak with desire—only this time it was about the way that fresh, hot corn bread smelled. She was starving! He flipped the iron skillet and a perfect, round cake of bread settled on the plate. Hers never came out looking like that. She generally had to scrape it out of the skillet in a crumbled mess.

"How about we eat first?" He emptied the beans into a pan. "Five minutes and I'll be good to go here." He flaunted one of those sexy smiles that came naturally to him. "Milk sounds good. You could pour us a tall glass and set the table."

Milk? What was she, fifteen again? She squared her

shoulders. "I have beer." She hoped she had beer. And he could set the table himself.

He gave the beans a stir. "None for me. I'll stick with the milk."

For some reason his declining ticked her off. "That's right, you're working."

He gave her another of those cute-as-hell smiles. "What kind of bodyguard would I be if I allowed my senses to be dulled on the job?"

Bodyguard? She started to challenge the idea, but the thought drifted away as she got lost visually measuring those broad shoulders. She really needed to get out more. It took some effort and a mental knock upside the head to redirect her attention to ferreting out the beer she hoped she had. Sadie opened the door of the fridge her grandmother had bought several decades before she was born and studied the meager contents. Milk, eggs, half a stick of butter. One beer lying on its side way in the back. Thank goodness. She wasn't really a beer drinker, but if she'd ever needed one it was now. Three or four might have better served the purpose of escape from this weird situation.

She popped the top while Lyle served up the goods he'd prepared. Her stomach demanded that she follow his suggestion and eat first. Fine. She dragged out a chair and dropped into it. They would talk after dinner. Lyle placed a plate laden with potatoes, beans and corn bread in front of her, along with a fork and a napkin. A cloth napkin. Sadie frowned. "Where—?"

"In the middle drawer of the buffet in the dining room." He placed the same on his side of the table. "You've got napkins and tablecloths in several patterns and colors."

She'd lived in this house going on two years and
didn't have a clue where those napkins were stored.
She fingered the yellow one he'd chosen. Sniffed it,
the aroma of cedar-lined drawers taking her back.
Her grandmother had saved her best cloth napkins for
special occasions, but the solid-colored ones like this
had been on the table every day. How had she forgotten that? Sadie shook off the memories and placed the
napkin in her lap.

Lyle poured himself a glass of milk and downed half
of it before he reached the table. Sadie looked away.
The way his throat moved as he drank or the way he
licked his lips afterward shouldn't bother her. He was
the enemy. Funny, it seemed all the men in her life
were enemies of one sort or the other. Didn't say much
for her relationship skills. Or her choices in associates.

A long swallow of beer didn't make her feel any less
flustered. Maybe another would do the trick. By the
time she settled the can on the table it was more than
half-empty. Reluctantly, she picked up her fork. She
was starving but she detested the idea of him seeing
he'd done good. And man, had he done good. The potatoes were crispy on the outside and soft on the inside.
And the bread was moist with a firm, rich crust. How
the heck did he know how to do this?

Sadie blocked out all else and devoured the meal.
She swallowed the last bite of bread and barely stifled
a satisfied moan. Using the cloth napkin she was glad
he'd found, she dabbed her lips, all the while considering seconds. That feeling of being watched scrambled
across her skin. She looked up to find him staring at
her. She blinked. Her fingers found and curled around
the half empty can of beer. She finished it off to pre-

vent having to speak or maintain eye contact. Maybe she hadn't kept all those appreciative moans to herself.

Lyle ate more slowly than she and he was nowhere near finished. Sadie worked hard at waiting him out but she couldn't do it. Watching his lips wrap around the fork was too much. She pushed back her chair and stood. "I'll clean up." He started to argue but she waved him off and moved on. As badly as she wanted to know the details of his unexpected appearance, she couldn't talk right now.

She'd fed the dogs, stored the leftovers, washed the cookware and her plate and utensils by the time he arrived at her side, his plate and fork in hand. Before he could strike up a conversation—the one she'd come in here to have and then chickened out—she thrust the hand towel at him. "Wipe down the table."

Rushing to finish first, she washed the last plate, rinsed her hands, dried them on her jeans and got out of there. Out of the house—the house that was suddenly filled with him and his hot body and wondrous new talents. Pretending seven years ago hadn't happened was mentally beyond her at the moment, yet somehow her body hadn't gotten the message. Sadie collapsed in the old wicker rocker that badly needed a fresh coat of white paint and pulled her knees up to her chest. Her dogs stretched out around her, full and happy.

For the first time in her life she felt good about herself and what she was accomplishing. Why did he have to show up now and stir around all those old feelings of inadequacy? She'd finally moved on with her life. What did fate have against her? Was it too much to ask for a small reprieve between dramatic episodes?

The screen door grumbled as he pushed it open and

joined her on the porch. He walked over to the chair right next to her and lowered his tall frame there. As much as she recognized that there were many things that needed to be said, she didn't want to talk. Definitely didn't want to hear his voice or smell that earthy male scent of his. His presence was driving her nuts. The longer he was here, the more jittery she got. Why couldn't she shut out all that stimuli and pretend it didn't matter?

Because she was weak when it came to him, and she hated weakness.

"I was wrong not to call."

He didn't look at her as he said the words. Not that she looked at him either, except a sneak peek from the corner of her eyes, but she wasn't the one seemingly trying to make the past right. "You said that already." Twice.

"When it became clear that this case involved you," he went on, still staring off across the land that had been in the Gilmore family for six generations, "I asked myself if coming here was the right thing to do or if it would be best to let another, more objective investigator take over."

The idea shouldn't have unsettled her. But like everything else about him, it did. "Why didn't you?" She resisted looking at him, but failed. His profile was exactly as she remembered. A little more chiseled and defined. The one night they had spent together in each other's arms, she'd lain awake and watched him breathe. He'd refused to make love to her, kept telling her it would be wrong. She was too young. The memory hurt her chest. The next day she had pleaded with him to stay. He'd left anyway, breaking her heart into a thousand pieces.

He'd better have a damned good reason for barging back into her life now. Whatever the reason, she wanted the whole truth. She willed him to meet her gaze so she could confirm the words he intended to say. As difficult as being this close was, she wasn't letting him take the easy way out. Sadie Gilmore used her brain for guidance more often than her heart these days.

Finally, he surrendered his full attention to her. "I couldn't risk that someone else might fail to protect you the way I would."

There it was—that shiver his voice had always set off deep inside her when they were this close. "I can protect myself," she argued for all the good it would do. He was as stubborn as she was. "I've been doing it for quite some time now. Maybe you hadn't noticed." Sadie held up her hands stop-sign fashion. "Wait, that's right. You weren't here." Good grief, could she wave her woman-scorned flag any more vigorously? She should be handling this better. No, she shouldn't be talking to him at all. He was the one with the explaining to do. *Stay calm. Keep your mouth shut.*

He exhaled a frustrated breath. "I don't doubt your ability to take care of yourself, Sadie. Not for a minute." He twisted in the chair, putting himself face-to-face with her. "You've done a damned good job. I admire what you've accomplished. But you have to trust me when I say you can't do this alone. This is different from any of the troubles you've faced head-on in the past. You need my help."

She searched his eyes, fear trickling into her chest.

The reality of the situation abruptly sank past the bitterness and resentment she'd used as a defense against
him and his memory all this time. Whatever he hadn't
told her, she suddenly knew without doubt it was bad.
Really bad. His eyes told the story his words hadn't
quite given her yet. That was why he was here. He
hadn't finally returned to make amends. Gus was in
big trouble. Her, too, apparently.

"That's ridiculous. What could possibly be so terrible?" Her voice trembled with that blasted fear she
couldn't dismiss and a tad of silly disappointment. She
loathed showing him that infernal weakness. She hated
even more that she so desperately wanted to lean on
him. Sadie Gilmore, the girl who thought she could
take on the world. How could he still possess the power
to make her feel needy when there wasn't a man in this
county who could even come close?

LYLE HESITATED. He had to choose his words and his
actions carefully. The photo album was in the truck.
He could show it to her. Get it all out in the open and
shatter her world in one fell swoop. But that would be
taking a major risk. The shock would make her irrational, and cooperation would go out the window. He
needed her complete cooperation in order to protect
her from this threat. There were steps that needed to
be taken. Confirmation that Sadie really was Sarah,
the same for the other women pointed to as allegedly
being the Barkers' missing, presumed-dead children.
Two of the Colby Agency's best were already in place
with the middle and older daughters.

"More than twenty years ago," he began the cover
story he'd decided upon, "a couple in Granger were

arrested for a series of murders. The Barkers, Raymond and Clare." He watched for any recognition in her eyes before continuing. If she remembered the murders he saw no indication in her expression. She'd been just a toddler at the time. "Two days ago Clare Barker was released after winning an appeal that reversed her conviction. There are those who believe she should not have been released and that she poses a threat to anyone she may have had association with before her arrest."

"What does that have to do with me or Gus?"

Now for the sticky part. "That's where things get a little murky. We don't have a definitive link between your father and Clare Barker, but there is some indication that he may be on her list of former associates and, as I said, that makes him and his family a target. Particularly his family. Generally, in these cases, the family is used to ensure the desired outcome."

The beginnings of true fear clouded her face. "If it's Gus's name on her list, then it's my father who needs protection. The idea that she might come after me is just speculation."

"Considering the personal security he surrounds himself with, we felt you were the most accessible target. If Gus has something or knows something that Barker wants, you would be the fastest way to pressure him for cooperation."

"Like he cares what happens to me." Sadie made a sound of disbelief, even though his theory made an undeniable sense that showed in her eyes. "He'd like nothing more than to get me out of the way."

"I think you know that isn't true. The two of you

have your differences, but you're still his only child."
At least legally. Damn, this wasn't going to be easy.

"So this threat is real." She hesitated. "The real
reason you came back."

The disappointment in her voice, in her eyes was
impossible to miss. The last thing he wanted to do
was hurt her again, and apparently he'd already done
that. "The threat is real. I am here to protect you, that's
true. But I should have come back a long time ago.
It shouldn't have taken something like this." He had
to look away. "The way I left things was wrong and
there's no excuse for that."

"Well." She dropped her feet to the floor and stood,
avoiding eye contact. "I have chores."

He got up, blocked her escape. "I need to know I can
count on your cooperation, at least for a little while.
Until we know what Clare's intentions are."

"I have to think about this. You can stay the night
in the barn or in your truck." She met his gaze then,
anger simmering in hers. "I'll give you my decision
tomorrow."

At least he had the night. That was a beginning.

Sadie stopped at the bottom of the steps and turned
back to him. "Does Gus know about this?"

More dicey territory. "The fewer people who know,
the less likely the waters will be muddied. You know
Gus, he'll have his own security folks trying to track
down Barker. That would be a mistake. It's imperative
that we catch her in the act so that she can be properly
prosecuted. Otherwise she may get away with more
heinous crimes." Like Janet Tolliver's murder. He kept
that to himself for now. "There's a lot we haven't nailed
down yet. Revealing our hand too soon could send this

woman into hiding, and then you might never be safe again."

Sadie started for the barn once more. "What can I do to help?" he called after her. When she glanced back at him, he added, "With the rest of the chores."

She shook her head. "I've got this."

One step forward, two steps back. He'd expected shaky ground. He just hoped the ground didn't crack open and swallow him up before this case was solved.

Simon had called with an update on Janet Tolliver's great-niece. Nothing appeared missing from the house as best she could determine. Her aunt had no safe-deposit boxes and no known attorneys. For some reason, Tolliver had decided to move back to the home that had belonged to her own aunt a few months back. She'd told her niece it was the one place she'd always felt at peace. The niece had nothing more to offer. Whatever else Tolliver knew, that information had died with her.

The rumble of engines dragged Lyle from those troubling thoughts. With the dust flying it was difficult to make out how many vehicles were roaring toward Sadie's house, but he estimated three. The first, then the second and third skidded to a halt not twenty feet from the porch. He recognized the driver of the first vehicle before the man launched out the door, rifle in hand.

Gus Gilmore.

The man was obviously losing his edge. Lyle had anticipated an appearance hours ago. Word traveled fast to men like Gilmore. Lyle took his time walking out to meet him. No need to hurry into trouble. From beneath the porch, Sadie's herd of dogs yapped that strange harmony of high-pitched Chihuahua and deep, booming Lab.

"What the hell are you doing here?" Gus stopped in front of his truck, four of his cohorts lined up around him. Lyle recognized only one—celebrity bronc rider Billy Sizemore. He'd been a cocky bastard before. Lyle doubted that caveman flaw had evolved much.

"Hello to you, too, Gus. It's been a while." Lyle braced his hands on his hips. His weapon was secured in his truck. As smart-mouthed and bullish as these men wanted to appear, Lyle wasn't afraid of one or all. It took more than mere guts to shoot an unarmed man. These bozos were lacking in that department, along with a few others, like morals.

"I warned you once before," Gus threatened. "You better stay away from my little girl."

Lyle glanced toward the barn, hoped Sadie stayed put. "Your little girl is a grown woman now. She can make decisions for herself. Word is, she doesn't take orders from you any more than I intend to."

Sizemore started forward. Gus stopped him with an uplifted hand. "I've kept up with you, McCaleb. Just because you work for some fancy P.I. agency doesn't make you any better than the green deputy you were before." His face tightened with his building rage. "I don't know what you're doing back here, but I will find out. Meanwhile, you'd better watch your back."

The unmistakable racking of a shotgun punctuated his warning. "Lyle is my guest."

Lyle's gaze swung to his right. *Sadie.* The woman had a way of sneaking up on a man. Not a one of the bunch had heard her approach. She stood a few feet away, her shotgun readied for use. If she spilled the beans...

"You go on in the house, Sadie," her daddy ordered. "This is between me and him. The fact that he's standing here proves you don't have a lick of sense, much less any pride."

Lyle resisted the urge to grin. Gus should have known better than to take that approach. Lyle braced for the inevitable explosion.

Sadie, shotgun still positioned and ready for firing, walked right up to her daddy. "This is my property, in case you've forgotten, Gus Gilmore. Now take your low-down friends and get off my ranch."

Gus moved closer to her, allowing the muzzle to burrow into his chest. Lyle held his protective instincts in check. Any move he made would escalate this scene and wouldn't have a good ending.

"I ran him out of town once," Gus reminded her. "I'll do it again. And that horse you stole from me, I will get him back, one way or another."

"You'll try," she countered fearlessly. "But I bought him fair and square. The sheriff already told you the papers were good. So don't waste your time, old man. That horse is done, just like you."

Gus glared at her another five seconds before turning back to Lyle. "You heed what I say, boy. Or you'll wish you had. Your connections back in Houston don't carry any weight here. This is my county."

Lyle didn't rise to the bait. He held his temper and let Gus and his minions go on their way. There would be a day when he and that old bastard resolved their differences. Just not today.

When the dust had settled, he considered the woman

caught up in all this turmoil. How did she deal with that man on a regular basis? Living right next door, though hundreds of acres separated Gus's mansion from her modest home, had to be a real pain in the butt.

"You okay?" He noted the slightest tremor in her arms.

"Course." Sadie lowered the business end of her gun. "But he'll be back." She shook her head. "Once he gets his teeth into something he never lets go."

Now Lyle understood why Sadie hadn't permitted Dare Devil to roam the pasture with the other horses. "What's the deal with Dare Devil?"

"His rodeo days are done." She dusted the front of her shirt, removing the hay that had stuck there during her work in the barn. "Gus had him parading around in all kinds of absurd trick shows. Dare Devil couldn't take it. A friend of mine who works for Gus loaded him up with the horses for auction and I bought him. Gus can't prove I tricked him. The only thing he can prove is a series of mistakes that more than one of his employees made. Even the sheriff had to agree with me." She pointed a knowing look in Lyle's direction. "Trust me, that was a first."

Prior to his arrival, Lyle had discovered there was some frivolous trouble between her and her daddy, but this felt more complicated than he'd been led to believe. As much as he disliked Gus, he couldn't see him hurting his daughter physically. But then, she wasn't his daughter. Had his own mother's choosing Sadie as her heir over him been the last straw? If so, why hadn't he shattered Sadie's world by telling her that truth? "Doesn't sound like he's ready to let it go," Lyle suggested.

"That's his problem." Sadie climbed the porch steps. "I'll be sleeping in the barn tonight. Sleep where you want."

Since the house wasn't nearly close enough to the barn to suit him, he'd be sleeping in the barn, too. "I figure there's plenty of room for both of us out there."

Sadie glanced back at him, opened her mouth to say something then snapped it shut. Halfway across the porch, she mumbled, "Suit yourself."

He planned to. The air was too thick with the trouble brewing to let her too far out of his reach. He just had to remember that every square inch of that gorgeous little body of hers was off-limits. There would be no finishing what they'd started that final night seven years ago. She deserved better.

Keeping her safe was the easy part, as long as he maintained his focus. It was the part that came after that tore him up inside. If there was any way in the world he could protect her from what was coming he would…but there wasn't.

The only thing he could do was keep her safe until the imminent physical threat passed. He couldn't shield her from the rest. Not without kidnapping her and disappearing. But then, someone had already done that once, and look how that effort turned out.

Clare Barker wanted her girls back. Whether to finish the job her husband didn't complete or for a happy reunion, Lyle couldn't say just yet. But she wanted something, and the only side of the story they had was her husband's.

Between Lucas Camp watching Clare and two of the agency's researchers digging through the Princess

Killer case files, they had to piece together the truth soon. For Sadie's sake. As well as the others.

For now, anyone who tried to get to Sadie—Clare Barker or Gus Gilmore included—would have to go through Lyle.

Chapter Six

May 22, 2:00 a.m.

Sadie stirred from the dreams plaguing her sleep. She swiped at her nose and frowned. The sweet scent of hay sifted into her groggy senses. Scrubbing her face with the back of her hand, she sat up. It was dark. Darker than when she'd bedded down in the vacant stall closest to Dare Devil.

What happened to the light she'd left on in the tack room? She felt for the shotgun lying next to her, untangled herself from the blanket and stumbled to her feet. A low sound brushed her awareness. She froze.

Listening for the faint rasp to come again, she maneuvered her way out of the stall by touch. The barn doors were closed, blocking out the glow from the moon and stars. She stilled a second time and listened. Scratching? Whimpering?

The dogs.

Bewildered, Sadie moved slowly along the corridor between the stalls. One of the horses shuffled, likely awakened by the same noise that had dragged her back to consciousness. She checked each stall she passed, sliding a calming hand over the animal's forehead. The urge to call out to the dogs burgeoned in her throat, but she preferred not to give her position away if trouble was lurking around outside.

Damn that Billy Sizemore. If he'd come back to try to scare her, she might just shoot his sorry butt this time.

Sadie sensed the stall closest to the big entry doors was empty before she felt around on the fresh haystack and found Lyle's abandoned blanket. Where the hell was he? It wasn't enough that he'd invaded her dreams. He had to be missing in action now that she might actually need him?

That was just like a man. All talk and no action of the right kind. When had honor become obsolete?

At the doors, she crouched down to calm the mutts. She whispered softly to them and gave each a soothing back rub. Allowing them outside would be a bad idea, seeing as the three were all bark and no bite whatsoever. Ushering them into the stall with Lyle's blanket would be futile. They'd only follow her right back to the doors.

What she actually needed was a vantage point with a view to assess the situation before barging out those doors anyway. She glanced around the dark barn then looked up, and a smile slid across her lips. Of course. *The loft.*

Slipping back to the center of the barn as quietly as possible with three dogs on her heels, she listened for any sound coming from beyond the old batten-and-board walls of the barn. Satisfied that all was quiet for the moment, she climbed the ladder to the hayloft. The loft door at the front of the barn that provided access for loading hay was open, allowing enough light for her to make her way there without tripping over any misplaced bales. She surveyed the grounds between the house and the barn. If anyone, including Lyle, was out there, they were well hidden. The only vehicle was her old truck and his shiny new one. No lights in the house.

Where the heck was he?

Sadie heaved a sigh. The man had her on edge. He was probably out there taking care of necessary business and she was in here worried about intruders and *him*.

"Ridiculous, Sadie," she muttered.

Picking her way back to the handmade ladder, she cursed herself for being such an idiot. Why had she let him stay? His explanations for his sudden appearance after all this time were far too vague. If he couldn't tell her exactly why he was here, why was *she* assuming he was on the up-and-up? She stepped off the final rung and walked back to her makeshift bed.

If she were honest with herself about her own motives, she would have to confess that she was curious, hazardous to her health or not, about him. Still had a crazy attraction to him. And she loved that his presence drove Gus nuts. None of those were good reasons for this situation. She lay back on her blanket. Then again, who said she had to have a good reason? The tightening sensation in her chest warned that the wrong reason could set her up for more of the heartache that still twisted her up into knots from time to time.

The distant sound of splintering wood fractured the silence. Gator, Frisco and Abigail burst into unharmonious barking. Sadie shot to her feet, shotgun in hand, and was at the barn doors before her brain had completed an inventory of the possible sources of the racket. Grabbing back control in the nick of time before she burst out of the barn, she eased one door open just far enough to scan the darkness. Still no lights on in the house. The two vehicles hadn't moved. No one swaggering about. Where in blazes was Lyle?

Squeezing out that same narrow crack, she pushed the door back into place before the dogs could hurtle out after her. The big pecan tree was her first destination, the disabled tractor next, then the toolshed and the outhouse as she crept closer to the house. She stilled, listened hard to determine the source of what sounded like distant thudding or pounding. *Thump, thump, thump.* The sound grew faster. Someone was running...in the woods that stretched out from the edge of her side yard all the way to the road.

Sadie summoned her courage and sprinted to the back corner of the house. She flattened against the peeling clapboard siding. The hurried footsteps had stopped...but there was a different activity now. Thrashing, maybe. The distinct splat of flesh slamming against flesh smacked the air. *Fighting.*

Her movements painstakingly slow, she rounded the corner of the house and moved toward the trees beyond the clothesline. The sound of running started again, accompanied by the crash of underbrush being disturbed.

Enough with the tiptoeing around. She couldn't see a damned thing, but this was her ranch and she intended to protect what belonged to her, especially the animals. Heart pumping hard, propelling the adrenaline-infused blood through her veins, Sadie dashed across the backyard and into the acres of woods that separated her house from the road.

Gunfire split the air.

She hit the ground, knocked the breath out of her. A third shot, then a fourth.

Oh, damn.

Staying in a low crouch, she scrambled forward. Fear pressed in on her. Did Lyle even have a gun? She hadn't seen one. Who knew? He could have anything stashed in that truck. Surely Gus and his men had not stooped to this level.

The ensuing hush had her pushing back to her feet and moving forward more quickly. Damn it, if Lyle was lying out here bleeding somewhere…

A trig snapped.

She froze. Leveled her aim in the direction from which the crack had resonated.

Close. That was really close. Her finger readied on the trigger. Her heart quieted, allowing complete focus. Someone was coming straight at her.

"Sadie, it's me."

Her heart dropped all the way to her bare feet. "What in the hell is going on, Lyle?"

"Let's get back to the house."

The fingers of one hand curled around her arm, and for a whole second she felt helpless and her knees went all rubbery. He lugged her back in the direction of the house, mumbling something about hurrying.

Reason abruptly slapped her in the face and she stalled, yanked against his hold. "What the hell is going on?" she repeated. "I am not a child. Stop treating me like one!"

"We're not safe out here like this," he urged in that deep voice that possessed the power to make her tremble. "Let's get inside first."

Furious for the wrong reason and just a little dazed, she trudged and stumbled alongside him, part of her attention on their backs even as they moved forward. Who had he chased off? Had someone broken into the house? Why hadn't he awakened her before he left the barn? It was her house!

Why was it men always thought they could boss her around? She was a grown woman and she was smart. There wasn't a damned thing in this world that she couldn't handle just as well as any man, including the shotgun she carried.

Lyle shoved the back door aside and hauled her into the kitchen. She staggered to a stop. "What…in the world?" The back door was hanging on only one hinge. The knob and locking mechanism as best she could tell hung slightly askew from their standard position. Who kicked her door in? Or out? Even the frame was no longer square and plumb.

He set her aside and proceeded to lift the door back into its damaged frame. Wood scrubbed against wood. "You got a hammer and some nails in the house?"

Her mind reeled with questions and conclusions, and her heart fluttered with the evaporating bewilderment and no shortage of fear. She wrestled it back the best she could and bobbed her head up and down. "I'll round them up."

Sadie flipped on the overhead light and gasped. The kitchen table was overturned, a couple of chairs had gone down with it. Her grandmother's antique stoneware sugar bowl lay in shards on the floor. Oh my God! Someone had been in her house! Her fear and confusion morphed into fury.

"Lock the front door and bring me those tools."

The stern order prompted her from the churning emotions making her feel disoriented. That was the first time she got a look at Lyle in the light. He was bleeding! "You're hurt!"

"It's just a scratch."

Closer inspection confirmed his typical male proclamation. "We need to clean it. At least."

He waved her off. "We'll deal with that when we're secure."

Secure. Did he think trouble was still out there? "Fine." That was just like a man. He could be bleeding out with the enemy bearing down on him and he'd swear he was good to go before he'd permit a glimmer of weakness. And he'd leave her in the dark about the trouble as long as possible. She locked the front door and stalled. Why was her door unlocked? She expressly remembered locking it before going to the barn for the night.

Frustrated and mad as hell, she stamped back to the kitchen in search of the tools. Where had she put them? She'd moved a painting in her room, then…now she remembered. The antique Hoosier cabinet near the sink. Which drawer? *Get a grip, Sadie!* Bottom one on the right.

She picked through the clutter in the drawer. She grabbed the hammer. The nails proved more difficult to get ahold of, especially after she knocked over the little box they were in. Her grandmother had kept them handy for hanging her collections. Framed photos, antique dishpans and most anything else that caught her eye. Sadie hadn't changed a thing except the placement of that one painting. It was her home now but the concept of change still felt wrong, disrespectful somehow.

Appalled all over again at her door now that she could see the full extent of the damage, she thrust the tools at Lyle. The feel of his fingers on her skin as he plucked the nails from her palm made her shiver in spite of the idea that they were in the middle of a crisis. Dummy!

"The way the door is damaged," he said, placing a nail and preparing to drive it into the wood, "this is the only way to secure it for now. It's not going to be pretty when I'm done."

"Do what you have to do." Suddenly deflated, Sadie regarded the chaos that had obviously blown through her kitchen. Someone had been in her house. The actuality sank in all the way for the first time. What could they possibly have wanted? She had no marketable values. No fancy electronics or jewelry. Heck, her television was older than she was. And if they had been looking for cash, this was the last place they should have come.

On the front porch, Gator and his crew were letting her know they didn't appreciate that she'd left them stuck in the barn. Rascals. It hadn't taken them long to figure out there were places in that old barn even Gator could wiggle through. "I have to let the dogs in."

This was crazy. She shook her head as she stamped through the house. If she found out Billy Sizemore or one of his blockheaded friends did this, she was seriously going to shoot at least one of them, maybe both.

The grandfather clock bonged quarter before the hour. Nearly three o'clock in the morning. Anger flamed higher, burning away the last of the fear and anxiety. Damn her daddy and his no-good friends. The notion that this might have something to do with why

Lyle was here elbowed her, since she apparently had tried to ignore that prospect. The jury was still out—way out—on that scenario.

With the dogs trailing her steps, she returned to the kitchen and the sound of her back door being disfigured. With his back to her, she didn't miss the butt of the weapon tucked into the waistband of his jeans. More fuel splashed on the anger already at a steady blaze inside her.

She waited out the final nail required to secure the door into its splintered frame. "So what happened?" Some parts were obvious, but there was plenty she didn't know. Such as what did he hear and see? Why didn't he warn her? And why hadn't he told her he had a gun? "How did my front door get unlocked? Did you see anyone?"

Lyle threaded his fingers through his hair, pushing it from his eyes. "How about I start with your last question first?" She didn't protest, so he went on. "I watched two males enter the house through the front door after some tinkering with the lock. It's an old lock, by the way. You need to take care of that."

Sadie motioned for him to go on and to shut up with the lectures.

"One man came right back out." He gestured ambiguously before walking over and up-righting the table and chairs. "The other was in the house maybe five minutes before I entered and tracked him down. In your room."

"My *bedroom?*" That was…nuts. There was nothing in her room worth the trouble of borrowing, much less stealing.

Lyle nodded. "We should make sure nothing's missing."

There wouldn't be anything missing. She had nothing anyone would want. She started to say as much, but she couldn't get past what she saw in his eyes. Fear. Worry. Uncertainty. Her breath trapped beneath her breastbone. "What is it you're not telling me, Lyle?"

"Sadie." He looked away. "Let's take this one step at a time. Right now—" those blue eyes zeroed in on hers with an urgency that unsettled her further "—we need to know what they were after."

The air jammed in her throat broke past its blockage and rushed into her lungs. "Okay. But then I want the truth."

Lyle checked the weapon at the small of his back as she led the way through the house. The living room had been ransacked. The first of the two bedrooms, as well. The bastard had just gotten to Sadie's room when Lyle interrupted him. She needed to confirm what he already knew. There wouldn't be anything missing in her room or the rest of the house.

The objective, he suspected, was secured in his truck.

Lyle had spooked the guy attempting to noiselessly break into his truck. He hadn't gone into the woods after him, considering the other man was in the house and the possibility of Sadie waking up and coming to the house was too great. The second had gotten a little trigger happy with his escape after bursting through Sadie's back door. Lyle hadn't fired his weapon. Instead, he'd caught up with and tackled the guy. He'd hoped to subdue him and get some answers. Unfortunately it hadn't worked out that way. It had come down to either shooting him or letting him go. The former was out of the question since the intruder was fleeing the scene. Lyle damned sure couldn't protect Sadie from behind bars. Gus would have the sheriff looking for a way to nail him.

Sadie was shaken. He saw her hands tremble more than once as she sorted through her belongings, putting things back in order as she went. Lyle helped as best he could and as much as she would allow. He didn't ask any questions, just let her do what had to be done. The skimpy lingerie she stuffed back into a drawer introduced another reaction into this already explosive mix. He worked at suppressing the response, but it wasn't as easy as he'd hoped.

When her home was set to rights, she shrugged. "Nothing's missing. Not that I can tell, anyway."

That wasn't the answer he'd wanted to hear, but it was the one he'd known was coming. He feared this break-in was about Sadie's past, not about her present.

She looked ready to drop, but she grabbed him by the arm and ushered him toward the bathroom. "Now we take care of your face."

He'd forgotten all about that. "My face will survive," he argued. The dead-last thing he needed was her touching him, particularly right now. As much as he'd like to profess complete objectivity, that would be a flat-out lie.

"You expect me to take orders from you—" she hesitated at the door and gave him a pointed look "—but I'm not allowed to give you any? Reciprocity, McCaleb. Look it up."

"Ha-ha."

"Sit." She pointed to the closed toilet seat.

Arguing would just be a waste of time. Her hard-headed determination had not mellowed with age. He sidled past her and did as she asked. "I could do this myself, you know."

She searched the cabinet under the sink. "No doubt. But then—" she straightened with a bottle of rubbing alcohol in hand "—I wouldn't get to do this." She dampened a washcloth with the alcohol and dabbed his cheek.

Though braced for the sting, he flinched, bit his tongue to hold back a hiss. "I'm glad you're enjoying this." Her hair hung around her shoulders, close enough he could have easily reached up and touched those silky strands. The slightest hint of the rose-scented soap she'd used, combined with the earthy essence of fresh hay, made his throat ache to tell her how good she smelled.

How much that sweet smell made him want to touch her. Another sharp sting from the alcohol caught him off guard, and he swore. Those plump, pink lips stretched into a smile. "Sorry," she said with absolutely no remorse.

"You really are enjoying this." He attempted to stay focused on the alcohol's burn rather than the one between his spread legs.

"More than you know." She made another nongentle swipe. "Just a scrape. You'll live."

"Thanks." He stood, but wished he had stayed put when the size of the room ensured his chest brushed her shoulder. Even that generic contact sent his heart into a frenzied gallop. He pretended to ignore the punch of high-charged electricity that jolted his body by surveying the damage to his face in the mirror.

She stared at him, or rather at his reflection. The hard questions were coming. He could feel her tension. He mentally scrambled for a way to evade the looming storm, but that wasn't happening, barring his suddenly dropping dead. On the other hand, since her shotgun sat in the corner by the door, that was not completely impossible.

"What is it you really want from me?"

If her voice hadn't sounded so small, so scared, so incredibly vulnerable, he might have gotten through this without meeting her eyes. The uncertainty he heard in her voice was confirmed right there in those jewel-green eyes, drawing even more deeply on his protective instincts. His fingers fisted in an effort to resist reaching out to her. He wanted to hold her. To promise her it would all be fine, but he couldn't make that promise. Her whole world was about to change, and there was nothing he could do to stop it.

"I just want to protect you." His throat tightened.

"What were those men after?" she demanded, sounding more like herself.

He wanted to blink. To break the spell, but that wasn't possible. "Like I told you, your father—"

"You're lying." She turned, brushing full against him, breast to chest, and stared up at him with a determination that would not easily be put off. "There's a lot more you're not telling me, and I want to know. Now."

"Sadie." He moistened his lips, to buy time and because he wanted to taste her so badly he could hardly endure the yearning. "You're right, there is a lot you don't know. I explained that I'm not at liberty to give you all the details at this time. I have my—"

"I don't care about your orders." She grabbed him by the shirt front and tried shaking him, maybe to make him see she wasn't taking no for an answer. All she succeeded in doing was sending him teetering closer to the edge. "Tell me the truth, Lyle. Tell me right now."

There was no time to develop an intelligent strategy to outmaneuver this precarious situation. No evasive explanation that would satisfy her. His only alternative was distraction.

His fingers dived into her hair. He pulled her mouth up to his and kissed her, hard at first out of sheer desperation, and then softer…because the taste of her melted him from the inside out. To his surprise, she didn't resist. She relaxed into him, the contours of her body molding to his but not where he needed her to be. His hands glided down her back, formed to her gorgeous bottom and lifted her against him. Right there. God help him, he wanted her. Right now. Right here.

She made a desperate sound that instantly hardened his already taut body. Her fingers threaded into his hair and pulled his mouth more firmly against hers. Desire and need swelled until he thought he might explode. He wanted to say things that hadn't been said seven years ago. Wanted to keep kissing her like this forever. Most of all, he wanted deep inside her…to have his body joined with hers the way he had craved before but couldn't.

She stopped and started to draw her mouth from his. His entire soul protested.

"Wait." Her voice was husky and breathless, her face flushed with the same desire raging out of control in him. "What're we doing?"

His diversionary tactic had worked a little too well.

"I shouldn't have…taken advantage of the situation."
He knew this and yet he hadn't released her. He still
held her tight against him in all the right places.

If she hadn't looked at him that way, he might have
been able to resist kissing her again. He brushed his
lips across hers. Her breath caught but she didn't draw
away. Utilizing a restraint he wouldn't have thought
he possessed at that moment, he kissed her tenderly.
But there was nothing tender about the way his fingers kneaded her bottom. She arched against him and
he almost lost his mind.

Then she froze, the change so abrupt his knees
weakened.

Her gaze locked on his. "They didn't take anything
from the house because that wasn't the reason they
were here."

Her rationale ruptured the haze enveloping his ability to reason. Hellfire. She was right. "Dare Devil."
The thought launched out of him, propelling him into
action. He deposited Sadie on the floor and was out the
narrow bathroom door before his next breath cleared
the emotional bottleneck in his throat.

"I should've thought of that." She sprinted for the
front door, almost getting ahead of him. "They lured
us to the house to gain access to the horses."

He drew his weapon. "Stay behind me." His hand
shook with the receding desire as he fumbled with the
lock. He moved across the porch, then motioned for
her to join him.

The barn doors stood open. Damn it! Sadie was
right. Neighing resonated in the early-morning darkness. The sound of scrambling hooves warned more
than one horse was loose.

Sadie called to the horses, at once calming and luring the animals with soft words. Lyle moved on to the barn and turned on the lights. The stalls stood open, every single one empty, including the last one.

"He's gone," Sadie said from the door, her face drawn with worry. "The others are all here, but Dare Devil is gone."

Fury bolted through Lyle. Damn Gus Gilmore.

Chapter Seven

Bucking Horse Ranch, 5:15 a.m.

Dawn was taking its sweet time arriving. Sadie didn't care if it was still dark. She wasn't waiting another second, much less a minute. She'd wanted to do this over an hour ago but she'd needed to get the other horses settled first and then Lyle had given her a hard time about calming down first. When he wouldn't turn over her truck keys, she started walking.

Before she'd gotten a hundred yards, he'd rolled up next to her in that fancy truck of his and ordered, "Get in."

She'd thought about telling him to go away and never come back, that she didn't need him or anyone else. But the truth was, as mad as she was, she understood she couldn't do this alone—not if she was smart. If she just hadn't allowed that kiss to happen. Maybe she could have fooled herself for a little longer that she didn't want him…but she'd showed her hand. And now he knew what a truly pathetic person she was.

Sadie closed her eyes and cleared her head. It wasn't the end of the world. She had been a fool before. Seven years ago she had pleaded with him to stay, to ignore her daddy's decree and her age. What an idiot she had been. The more important issue just now was getting that horse back. Dare Devil, like all her other rescues, deserved to live out the rest of his days in peace without performance expectations. She'd just gotten started with her rescue work really. The long-term goal was to make her ranch a haven for abused and neglected animals from all over Texas. Eventually she hoped to start a camp for underprivileged children where they could learn about the animals and the animals could enjoy their love and attention, a stark contrast from the strict life they had known in the rodeo. Sadie wasn't trying to be a martyr or to call attention to herself. With this ranch she'd inherited she had an opportunity to do something good. And maybe to make up for her father's lack of compassion.

The idea that part of her motive included doing exactly the opposite of what he wanted her to do, to take over his ranch one day, niggled at her. She dismissed the notion. This wasn't about him or her. It was about the horses.

From the moment Lyle turned onto the road at the end of her driveway, the land that stretched across the landscape on each side of the pavement belonged to the Gilmore family.

To Gus, actually. Since Sadie was the last in that line, so far and Lord knew she wouldn't be in her daddy's will, that left only him. She wasn't sure who that was the saddest for, him or her. At the moment she could not care less. Her mind was on Dare Devil's safety. If that horse had suffered at the hand of any of Gus's men, she would make him pay if it took the rest of her life.

Lyle slowed for the turn into enemy territory. Sadie stared out into the darkness. Her grip tightened on her trusty shotgun. The chances of her getting the horse back were next to none. Gus was too smart for that. But she had to try. Going about this the proper way required focus, despite the ungodly hour and the formidable man—she stole a glance at the driver—who would inevitably get in her way. The heat he'd generated when he'd pulled her against him swirled even now if she allowed the mental images to filter through her head. How could she still want him so very much? Maybe if she'd paid attention to her social life instead of ignoring those basic needs, she would have been better prepared for this. For him.

Focus, Sadie! This was definitely not the time to be distracted by neglected hormones.

Though it was fairly early, Gus would be up. Work started at the Bucking Horse by daybreak, around six-thirty. By that time the crew had better be dressed and fed, because there were no acceptable excuses for being late. *Late* equated to *fired*. That rarely happened, since the whole county knew the way Gus Gilmore operated. He stood by the motto that hard work never hurt anyone, idle hands were the devil's tools and all that holier-than-thou stuff. Sadie had nothing against hard work or anything holy, of course—though the only time she'd gone to church in her life was when her grandmother had taken her. What steamed Sadie the most was men like her father pretending to be something they weren't. He didn't keep a pew warm on Sunday mornings, but that didn't stop him from believing he would be the first through the pearly gates on Judgment Day.

The drive up to the mansion was a full mile. She didn't need the sun to know that every blade of grass in the pastures on each side of the paved minihighway sporting the Gilmore name would be the same height. The lush grazing pastures would be clean of horse droppings. The Gus Gilmore world had to be perfect. There was no room for the slightest flaw. Up ahead the house sprawled across the land a full eight thousand square feet, the exterior a pristine bride-white with massive columns and expansive porches. The barns and other outbuildings were a brilliant red without a single chip of missing color and not a lick of fading evident, since they were repainted every spring. No one, save visitors, was allowed to park a vehicle in front of the house, particularly one that might lessen the impact of elegance and sophistication. A little piece of the Hamptons in central Texas.

All the working pastures and corrals and stables, including the bunkhouse, were well beyond the main house. Like a general in charge of his troops, Gus conducted surprise inspections to ensure all met with his rigid standards. Lack of order and cleanliness were other reasons for a speedy departure from his employment. His expansive, powerful world operated his way and his way only. Failure to agree with him would cost a person his or her position, even the position of daughter.

Sadie fought the sting of tears. She would not cry. The rift between them was his doing, his decision. After her mother's death, he seemed to focus that impossible-to-please self-righteous conviction on her. Nothing she did or said had been right. Whoever said that blood was thicker than water had never met Gus Gilmore.

"Stay put," Lyle said, shutting off the engine, "until I determine how this is going down."

"Whatever you say."

Lyle stared at her for a moment as the interior light faded to black. She held her breath, hoping he would buy her no-questions cooperation. After a moment he reached for the door handle and got out. She restrained the urge to bail out immediately despite the new blast of fury detonating inside her. As soon as Lyle had started up the wide steps leading to the porch, she was out of there. She bounded around the hood just as the massive double doors leading into the house's grand entry hall opened. The ostentatious overhead porch light came on and Gus himself stepped out to stand beneath its spotlight.

Sadie took aim even as Lyle whirled toward her and ordered her to put down the shotgun.

"Where's Dare Devil?" she demanded of the man who cared more about power and position than his own daughter or any animal he'd ever owned.

By the time her furious words had stopped vibrating the air, Lyle was down the steps and at her side. Gus's cohorts had appeared from around both corners of the house, weapons readied for trouble.

"Put it down, Sadie," Lyle urged. "This is not the way to handle this."

"Not until I have an answer." She didn't look at Lyle. Her full attention remained fixed on the man standing on the porch, hands on hips as if surveying a pile of horse dung his help had overlooked.

Unafraid of what he likely perceived as a nuisance,

Gus descended the steps. He glanced to his left then his right, giving those gathered to protect him a slight nod. The men faded back into the darkness on each side of the house. Then he lowered his attention to Sadie. There wasn't a more arrogant man alive.

"What's the problem?" Gus walked right up to where they waited. "It's not even daylight yet. What is it you think I've done now?"

For a second Sadie couldn't speak. Why had everything changed between them all those years ago? When had he stopped loving her? Loving anything or anyone? Just because he'd lost his wife hadn't given him the right to quit loving his daughter. Sadie had lost her mother and she had still loved him…until he stamped the life out of those feelings. No one else around here had the guts to stand up to him. As dysfunctional as it sounded, she had made that another of her quests. She relished every opportunity to undermine his superiority and arrogance. Didn't he get it that she'd been trying to send him a message all these years?

She squashed those weaker emotions. "You stole Dare Devil. Where is he?" This, she had to admit, was low even for him. Wielding her shotgun and making threats appeared to have become the norm for her.

Gus shook his head. "You're the thief, little girl. Not me. You stole him from me."

If she hadn't known what a liar he could be, she would have sworn he was telling the truth. "You're avoiding the question," she charged. "Did two of your men trespass onto my property and steal him?"

"What do you mean trespass onto your property?" He swung his interest toward Lyle. "Is this your doing? You know mine and Sadie's relationship is on rocky ground." He took what he likely hoped to prove an intimidating step toward Lyle. "You'd like nothing better than to finish tearing us apart." He jammed a finger in Lyle's chest. "Is that why you're here? Who are you representing, McCaleb? Maybe your own selfish interests. I know for a fact you have an agenda, so don't deny it."

Lyle laughed, but there was no hint of amusement in the strained sound. "You don't need my help destroying your relationship with Sadie. You're doing an amazing job of that all on your own. And as for my agenda, Sadie knows why I'm here. What you do or don't know is of no interest to me."

"Maybe you've got Sadie fooled, but not me," Gus warned.

"This is not about Lyle or me," Sadie argued, not about to let this turn into a what-did-I-ever-do-to-you session. "Where is Dare Devil? I know you took him, so don't bother lying."

Gus turned back to her. Even in the faint light she could see the fury in his dark eyes. "Whatever our issues in the past, you're wrong about this one."

He was lying. There was no other explanation. "Then you won't have any problem allowing me to check the barns and other outbuildings. Maybe even the house." She added that last bit just to be a smart aleck.

He didn't answer, just glared at her with that same disappointment he'd showered upon her since she was twelve years old. When she was certain he would deny her request, he turned back to the house. "Billy!"

Sizemore swaggered from the shadows. "Yes, sir."

"Escort my daughter around the property. Whatever she wants to see."

With that stunning announcement, Gus walked back into the house and closed the door.

The impact of his decision shook Sadie far harder than it should have. He hadn't denied her request. What the heck? He never gave in that easily.

"Load up and follow me," Billy suggested, "unless you want to walk."

LYLE WASN'T SURE WHAT Sadie's intent was here. If Gus was responsible for the break-in and the horse's disappearance, there was no way he would bring Dare Devil here to his ranch. Lyle settled behind the wheel of his truck as she and her shotgun loaded into the passenger seat. He started the engine and executed a three-point turn so that he could catch up with Sizemore in his dually beyond the back of the house.

"Dare Devil isn't here."

He'd been about to say the same thing, though he hadn't expected it to come from her, considering she insisted on checking the property. "Yeah, I know."

Sadie watched out the window instead of looking at him. "But that doesn't mean he didn't do it."

Well now, he couldn't debate that conclusion. "So we go through the motions?"

"Yep." She twisted around in the seat and stared back at the house. "As convinced as I am, I'm not taking his word for anything." Sadie faced forward. "Gus would take that as a sign of weakness."

Lyle wondered if Gus's relationship with his daughter would have turned out differently if she were his own flesh and blood. Did he know the truth about her former identity? How had he and his wife been chosen to be a part of this? Had someone selected the Gilmores based on their financial status and approached them? What reason would Gus and his wife have had for going along with the offer? Sadie was the only child they'd had. Was there a reason for that? Was that reason the explanation for how they had come to be involved with a backdoor adoption? There were a lot of questions, and so far Lyle had no answers.

The one thing he knew for an absolute certainty was that he was in deep trouble with Sadie. What he'd irrationally intended as a distraction—however selfishly motivated—had proved without question that he couldn't maintain his objectivity, much less his professionalism, when it came to her. That made an already perilous situation *crazy* dangerous. If she decided to confront him about what happened, he would be in even more trouble. He'd already skirted the truth about why he was here. Outright lying about that kiss was out of the question. He suspected she wouldn't like his answer.

AS REQUESTED, SIZEMORE escorted them to every building and corral on the property. Dare Devil was not on the Gilmore ranch, unless he was tucked away on the proverbial rear forty. Lyle wasn't surprised. Gilmore was far too smart to have allowed himself to be caught so easily. Sadie had called off the tour after more than an hour of futility. It would take days to carry out a thorough search of a ranch the size of this one. The horse would be tucked some place out of reach until the dust had settled. Lyle got it that Sadie had needed to see, to show Gus she wasn't going to take this sitting down. The two had this business of one-upping each other down to a science.

"Stop at the house."

He sent her a questioning look and she added, "I have to talk to him."

Lyle parked in front of the house and prepared to get out, particularly if she opted to hang on to that shotgun.

"Alone."

A frustrated breath puffed out of him. "We've been over this already. I don't want you out of my sight."

"This will only take a minute and I'll be inside the house. He's my daddy, he's not going to kill me."

Lyle shook his head to stop the voice suggesting that her real daddy had been accused of exactly that. "Two minutes, and I'm coming in after you."

"Fine."

She climbed out of the truck and hustled up to the entry doors of her father's home. The house where she'd grown up. With parents who had kept a dark secret from her. Lyle scrubbed a hand over his face. How was he ever going to tell her the truth? He thought of the album hidden in the storage compartment behind his seat. Whatever happened, even if he told her right now, the result would be the same as if he'd told her the instant she came to her door yesterday morning.

There would be no forgiveness for the messenger. Particularly one who had shattered her life once already.

GUS SAT BEHIND THE BIG polished desk in his study, as he did every morning at this time, savoring coffee brewed from freshly ground beans imported from some place she couldn't pronounce and scanning the morning paper. Sadie burst in without a knock or announcing herself. "Wherever you took him," she warned, "you bring him back unharmed before dark today and I won't go to the sheriff and press charges."

Carefully placing his fragile and expensive china cup—from France, if she recalled—in its saucer, he let go of the newspaper and settled his attention on her. He studied her a moment over the tops of his reading glasses. "I don't have Dare Devil, Sadie. You should consider the other possibilities before making accusations. He may not be a competitor anymore, but his reputation carries some value." He removed his glasses and neatly folded them before placing them on the desk. "I'll make some inquiries and see what I can find."

The laughter burst out of her. She couldn't help herself. The man wanted to be a comedian now? What else would explain his sudden need to play daddy. "I don't need your help, Gus Gilmore. I need *my* horse back."

Another of those long assessing looks sent her frustration level skyrocketing. "You are in way over your head, little girl. Do you know who Lyle McCaleb is *now?*"

"Don't try to change the subject." He loved to play mind games. Well, she wasn't playing his games. Besides, he'd hated Lyle seven years ago, and she doubted that had changed. This diversionary tactic was nothing she hadn't expected. "This isn't about Lyle."

"Are you certain? What was his excuse for showing up after all this time? Don't you think it's ironic that he suddenly comes back after you've inherited your grandmother's property? That makes you quite a financially secure woman with valuable assets. Not to mention he knows how I would loathe you falling for him again. I don't want to see him hurt you."

This time she laughed for real at his comment. She was basically flat broke. A few folks donated feed and hay to her on a fairly regular basis for the horses. The tiny trust took care of property taxes and insurance along with a few other basic necessities. The only *asset* she owned was that ranch, and she wouldn't sell it for anything. She would always find a way to survive. Oh, and her grandfather's old truck, which was on its last legs, belonged to her. "Where is the horse? I'm not letting this go."

"As I said, I'll look into it." He sipped his coffee. "Meanwhile—" he set his cup aside once more "—why don't you ask your friend what interest the Colby Agency has in you? Or me, for that matter."

A frown furrowed its way across her brow. "What's the Colby Agency?" Lyle hadn't mentioned that name. He was here in an official capacity for some branch of law enforcement, but she wasn't giving Gus a speck of information.

Gus made a disparaging sound. "I knew he'd leave that part out, which, my dear, smacks of deceit." He shook his head. "I expected as much. He'll do nothing more than break your heart again, and, foolishly, you'll allow him to do just that."

Sadie held up both hands. She wasn't listening to this. "By dark today," she reminded him.

"Watch yourself, little girl." Gus stood, pinned her with an intensity that made her uneasy. "The Colby Agency is a private investigations agency. McCaleb's client is anonymous, so far as I can ascertain. I haven't been able to glean any information on that aspect of his assignment just yet. But there is a client and whoever that client is, your friend is being paid to be here and do whatever it is he's doing or planning."

Sadie didn't believe him. Lyle wouldn't have lied to her about that. What would have been the point? She couldn't tell Gus why he was here…she'd promised, sort of.

"I'll be waiting," she reminded him.

Before he could throw out some other bit of purposely twisted information, she left. She'd done what she came here to do. This nonsense about Lyle he'd tried to confuse her with would prove more of his lies. Even knowing how Gus loved proving she had no real friends, the mere idea that there could be some smidgen of truth to what he said made her sick to her stomach. Made her want to cry hard, but, by God, she would not.

She didn't utter a word as Lyle drove back to her house. The sooner she was out of this truck the better. She couldn't breathe. Couldn't think. Gus had planted the seed, and like that damned bean stalk story her mother had read to her as a kid, the seed had sprouted into something overwhelming.

Wrenching the door open before the truck came to a complete stop, she slid out, staggered a little and headed for the barn. Her stomach roiled with the bitter silt of remembered betrayal. Gus was a no-good, lying, mean son of a gun, but he never made that kind of mistake. She didn't want to admit it. With the fading of the initial shock, reality had taken root. If he said Lyle worked for a P.I. agency, it was likely true. It was always the murky details he warped into his own version of the truth. Something as cut and dried as place of employment was too easy to prove. Gus wouldn't waste his time.

Lyle had lied to her.

He'd kissed her as if he meant it—as if he still had feelings for her and wanted her. He'd been back in her life barely twenty-four hours, and he'd already lied to her.

Halfway to the barn, Sadie stalled. Set her hands on her hips and closed her eyes against the swaying landscape. Why had she let him fool her this way? Because she'd wanted to believe he'd finally come back for her. What an idiot she was!

"Sadie." Lyle moved in close. "What happened back there?"

She didn't want to open her eyes and see. His eyes, his face, the mere scent of him made her fuzzy-minded, made her want to fall into his arms and just forget. But that would be an even bigger mistake than the whopper she'd already made.

She forced her eyes open to the truth. The sun was up and showering its bright, unforgiving light over the land…over them. The worry she saw on Lyle's face was real, but that meant nothing. She'd been a fool for him, twice now.

"I want to see your official ID." Her chest ached beneath the ever-tightening band of emotions wrapping around and around her, keeping her unsteady. "Not your driver's license, but whatever proves who your employer is."

His hesitation told the tale before he uttered a single word. "What did Gus tell you?"

She turned away, couldn't bear to look at him.

"I want you off my property." She shot him a look that she hoped cut to the bone. "Now."

"I was sent here by the Colby Agency. A private investigations firm looking into exactly what I told you. I didn't lie to you, Sadie."

Renewed fury ignited. "No, you just left out the parts that didn't fit with what you wanted me to believe. You kept your mouth shut while I assumed precisely what you wanted me to presume. I filled in all the gaps you left." She slammed her hands into his chest, shoving him away from her. "You succeeded. Good for you." Too heavy to hold, she dropped her arms to her sides and dragged in a breath that hurt her heart. "Now get out of here."

"I can't do that."

The blast of outrage that burst inside her then made her tremble. "Don't you dare pretend you want to stay to protect me. I don't believe anything you say."

"It's the truth, Sadie." He reached out, tried to touch her. She backed away. "You're in danger. I can't leave until this is over."

And there it was. The other truth. He would leave when the job he was being paid for was done. The kiss hadn't meant a thing. His decision to take the job, if that part was even true, was about nothing more than the job.

When it was done, he would leave. And just like last time, he would take a part of her with him, leaving her damaged all over again. He'd been gone seven years, and it had taken a measly twenty-four hours for him to take her back to that same place he'd left her in all those years ago.

"I'm calling the sheriff. If I need protecting—" she

glared at him, barely kept her voice shy of a scream
"—that's his job, not yours."

She walked to the house. Her pulse thundering in
her ears, her body trembling with an agony that was
all too familiar. He followed, not ready to give up. She
doubted his employer would be pleased if he failed to
get the job done. Well, that was tough. She wasn't about
to do him any favors. One way or the other, he was out
of here. Now. This morning.

She didn't need Lyle McCaleb.

Seven years ago she had been a wild, starry-eyed
teenager who was so in love she couldn't see the forest
for the trees. He had never loved her the way she loved
him. He'd had other plans that didn't include her. She
had been a distraction. A way to pass the time until
better things came along.

She was a grown woman now. And she had other
plans that didn't include him. If she died single and
alone it would be better than risking his or any other
man's betrayal ever again. To hell with them all!

"Sadie, be reasonable," he urged as she stormed up
the steps to her porch. "This situation is too volatile
and too dangerous to play games. That's Gus's style,
not mine."

She turned on him in the middle of the porch, the
dogs yapping as if there was no tomorrow inside the
house. "Back off," she warned. Damn it, she'd left her
shotgun in his truck. "We are finished. No games. No
talking. No nothing."

That he looked away, beyond her, in the middle of
her tirade only infuriated her all the more.

"What the hell are you staring at?" When he didn't

respond, Sadie turned around to see what was so fascinating behind her.

Mommy's coming for you, baby girl.

The words were scrawled across her front door. The red paint had dripped down the weathered white wood in an eerie manner straight off the screen of a horror flick.

"What the hell?" Sadie moved closer to the door, reached out and touched the paint. Still sticky. She smelled it. The air in her lungs evaporated.

Not paint...*blood*. The message was written in blood.

Chapter Eight

Victoria Colby-Camp reviewed the assessment report compiled by the research department. The investigation conducted by the detectives in charge of the Princess Killer case twenty-two years ago was as close to flawless as any she'd reviewed for that period, considering the science and technology they had to work with at the time. A joint task force from several counties surrounding the small community of Granger had come together to find the killer and eventually the bodies.

Over the course of ten years, more than a dozen young girls had gone missing. The M.O. was always the same—the girl simply vanished with not a single clue left behind. The victims were loosely connected by age, but even the ages weren't consistent. Social status was all over the place, some from very poor families, others from considerably wealthy ones. Race, religion, none of it was truly consistent. The killer's territory extended over several counties. In the end, the single thing all the victims had in common was that each one had a family dog adopted from a small veterinary clinic located outside Granger. But that connection had not been discovered until after the anonymous tip that led the police to the Barkers, the owners of that unpretentious clinic.

Raymond Barker was a beloved member of his community. His wife, Clare, was always at his side. Their small clinic barely stayed afloat, considering the extensive rescue work the couple performed. The family, including their three little girls, never failed to be present on the front pew at church. The children's clothes appeared homemade, their shoes hand-me-downs. Veterinarians from surrounding counties often suggested those looking for pets drop by and have a look at the many available at the Barker Clinic. Rafe and Clare's compassion for animals was known far and wide beyond the boundaries of their small hometown. Since the visits to the Barker Clinic and the disappearances were sometimes months, as much as a year, apart, the remote connection wasn't detected by the authorities.

The case might have gone unsolved if not for that anonymous tip provided early one morning. That tip brought the authorities to the old farmhouse owned by the Barkers. Photos of each "princess" as well as thank-you letters sent by the victims to show their appreciation for their new pets were discovered in the Barker home. The remains recovered from the property were identified as eight of those who had gone missing. The half dozen other missing girls from the surrounding area had not been recovered to this day.

Once the news broke, parents remembered their daughters interacting with Dr. Barker. He'd affectionately referred to their daughters as "princess," prompting investigators to call the case by that moniker. Each victim whose remains had been recovered from the property, as well as several whose remains were still missing, had written to thank Dr. Barker, weeks, sometimes months after the pet adoption. The letters were presumed to be the tipping point—the impetus that solidified the selection process for a heinous serial killer.

Victoria closed the file and her eyes. The images and words were gruesome. How could anyone, much less a mother or father, have committed such horrific acts? The evidence that connected Clare to the murders was far more circumstantial than that connecting her husband. Ultimately that was the reason she eventually won an appeal. There were those who would never believe her innocence, however, simply because of her dark past. Clare Barker's parents, the Sneads, had been murdered when she was barely thirteen. Some who knew the family always suspected that Clare had somehow been involved in their deaths. Given that the latter surfaced only after the arrests, Victoria had to wonder if that were the case at all.

Though a quiet, seemingly work-oriented family, the Barkers had earned the respect of their neighbors. Not social folks by any means, Rafe and Clare had stayed to themselves when not working, ostensibly completely focused on and devoted to their children. But the findings inside the home had told another story. Closets turned into prisons for the girls when they were in the way. Evidence of other, despicable abuse was also discovered. How had this travesty gone on for so many years without anyone noticing?

A rap on her door drew Victoria from the disturbing thoughts. She smiled as best she could as Simon Ruhl entered her temporary office. It would eventually be his conference room. For now he graciously lent it to her and Lucas whenever they were here.

"Is there news?" Victoria had spoken to Lucas earlier that morning. Had something happened since that call? She sincerely hoped not.

Simon settled into a chair across the table from her. "Research just uncovered a small but stunning piece of information. We may have a lead on Janet Tolliver's connection to the Barkers."

Victoria hoped this would prove the break they had been eager for. There had to be more information out there, and they needed to find it. Otherwise, their investigation was going to end similarly to that of the detectives more than two decades ago. "Finally." Tolliver's name was not mentioned in the previous investigation in any capacity. "Does this give us a starting place?"

"Actually," Simon said as he passed a report across the table, "it gives us another ending place. Janet Tolliver was Clare Barker's biological sister, older by two years."

How was that possible? "The police never found that connection? That's quite a strong tie to be overlooked."

"The Sneads were different," Simon explained. "They lived more or less outside society. Religious extremists. The girls were homeschooled. Clare was three and Janet five when they were separated. No one noticed. The Sneads, minus Janet, of course, moved to Austin. Nine-plus years later the parents were murdered. Clare was found covered in their blood and in a semicatatonic state. She spent several months in an institution before being introduced into the foster care system. Meanwhile, the Tolliver family took Janet in as their own. Eventually the adoption was legalized through a private attorney."

"Have you spoken to Lucas?" The need to hear his voice was suddenly a palpable force in Victoria's chest. "Have you briefed him on this new information?" Lucas was doing surveillance on Clare Barker. He needed to know immediately that there was reason to believe she was quite possibly dangerous, no matter that an appeals court had overturned her verdict and the evidence against her alleged past deeds was wholly circumstantial.

"I briefed him first," Simon assured her. "I felt he needed the information, pronto."

Of course he had. Victoria had worked with Simon for many years. He was well versed in the critical steps in a case such as this. She was unsettled this morning. The case file on the Barkers had gotten to her in a very personal way. The evil acts committed against children hit far too close to home, considering her own son had been missing for twenty years before finding his way home. During that time, Jim had suffered every manner of atrocity.

Victoria had to find and hang on to her objectivity. Funny, she and Lucas were supposed to be retired, and here they were embroiled completely in this case. But this one was different. Victoria sensed that there was a profound injustice here, and she needed to set it to rights. To do that, she needed clear, unbiased focus.

"How is Lyle doing with Sadie?" Victoria wanted these women protected above all else. Finding a way into their lives so quickly had not been an easy feat for the Colby Agency. Since Lyle had a history with Sadie, his way in had proven a bit more of a natural entry.

With the other two, the investigators had no choice but to watch from a distance until they were accepted, which made their protective efforts much more difficult.

"Lyle hasn't checked in this morning but all was under control last night."

"How is the confirmation process going?" Research was attempting to verify the thumbprint in each photo album provided by Janet Tolliver to that of the women allegedly the long-missing, presumed-dead children of the Barkers.

"Laney Seager's was easy," Simon explained. "She was arrested on assault charges as a teenager. Olivia Westfield's work mandated a background check, which required fingerprints. Sadie we can't confirm until Lyle gets fingerprints to us. She has seen her share of trouble with the law but her father has kept her from being arrested." Like everyone else working on this case, Simon looked tired. This kind of case was hard on the emotions. "I feel confident with the other two having been confirmed, that it's a safe bet to assume Sadie will be a match, as well."

The story was an incredible one. The sheer number of confusing layers was nearly overwhelming. Victoria could now better understand how so much was overlooked twenty-two years ago. The connections were vague, disjointed and deeply buried.

The reality of the investigation at this point was that investigators were in place with all three women. Clare Barker was under surveillance. And Rafe sat in prison, another day closer to death.

Still, if Clare didn't kill Janet Tolliver and with Rafe in prison, one of the two had contacts who willingly committed murder. Janet Tolliver had been expecting a visit from the Colby Agency, which seemed to indicate Rafe was the one to order her murder. Clare had no way of knowing Victoria had met with Rafe. But why have her murdered and at the same time have her expecting help from the Colby Agency? Not reasonable or logical. But then, what about this case was?

With Clare's chilling past, it was an easy leap to conclude that she was the most likely of the two. But then the justice system had deemed her not guilty, if not entirely innocent. Rafe was the one whose guilt no one questioned. Then there was the letter. Victoria could not get past the letter when considering his guilt or innocence. That gnawing instinct went against how the evidence had stacked up against him. Victoria's instincts were never that far off the mark. Had Clare purposely been setting up her husband to take the fall if she were ever caught? Could either of them been so blind as to not know what the other was up to, considering the evidence of abuse taking place inside the home?

"We still have no connection between any of the adopting parents and Janet Tolliver. All three of the Barker children were legally adopted in private transactions. The paper trail was difficult to follow, but having the birth certificates provided by Tolliver is helping. Olivia, the oldest, is the only one who knows she was adopted. She has never sought her birth parents."

Victoria rubbed the back of her neck. That would change soon enough. Would that be when the next tragedy in this ongoing travesty occurred?

No matter how hard the Colby Agency tried, there

was no protecting these women from the reality of who they were when true justice finally found its place in this complicated and chilling story.

Allison Ingram, Simon's secretary, appeared at the door. "Simon, Lyle McCaleb is holding on line one."

Simon thanked her. He and Victoria exchanged a worried look.

What now?

Chapter Nine

Second Chance Ranch, 8:50 a.m.

Lyle had tried to reason with Sadie for more than an hour. She refused to listen. He sat on the porch now, her final order still resounding in his ears.

Leave! And don't ever come back.

He'd just gotten approval from Simon to do what he'd hoped to put off until the danger had passed.

Lyle pushed to his feet and walked to his truck. His hands shook as he unlocked the storage compartment behind the driver's seat. He removed the leather pouch containing the album. How had he come to be the person who would exert this shocking blow? Chance? Fate? Whatever the reason, he prayed that God would give him the wisdom to do this right and the strength and opportunity to protect Sadie afterward.

He hesitated at the door, took a deep breath, then rapped on the wood still marred by the threat the sheriff had taken one look at and chalked up to one of Sadie's many enemies pulling a prank on her. Sheriff Cox had additionally suggested that the missing horse was the same. He'd show up, Cox had declared.

Clearly the man had concluded exactly what Gus

Gilmore had told him to conclude. Gus had been using his power to manipulate Sadie for years. To his credit, he had protected her once or twice when she'd pursued her goals a little too passionately. But manipulation was manipulation. Neither Gus nor the sheriff understood that some of the events occurring now were about far more than Gus and Sadie's relationship. The danger was real.

Had Gus learned that the Colby Agency was looking into Rafe Barker's request? Discovering that Lyle worked for the Colby Agency had probably been easy. But to learn the case he was on and to use some aspect of it to scare Sadie, that was just plain evil. As stern and hard as Gus Gilmore had always seemed to Lyle, this was a new low even for him—if he was the one responsible.

Sadie opened the door and glared at him, fury emanating from her whole body. At least now she wasn't toting her shotgun. "What is it going to take to get you out of my life, Lyle McCaleb?"

"You wanted the truth." He indicated the package he held, emotion crowding into his chest. "I've been authorized to give you that now, if you're sure that's what you want." Misery dumped another load on his shoulders.

She stared at the leather pouch he held, the color seeping from her face even though she had no idea what was inside. Deep in her heart she suspected something was off with her history. Lyle had sensed that uneasiness since his arrival early yesterday. Her frustration with life in general was about a little more than Gus or him.

"You have five minutes," she said as she stepped

back and pulled the door open wider, "to convince me
to hear you out. Don't test my patience."

"Fair enough."

"If I think for one second that you're giving me the
runaround, I'm done," she added, leading the way to
the living room. "So don't waste my time." She plopped
down on the same old sofa he'd waited on seven years
ago when he'd dared to visit her at her grandmother's
house. Adele Gilmore had liked him, he'd learned. He
wished she were here now to referee. And maybe to
explain some of the missing details. Sadie was going
to need someone to lean on through this. He hoped she
would allow it to be him.

Lyle had considered at length the best way to start
when it came to this part. None of the options were
ideal, but starting at the beginning seemed best. During
his call to Simon earlier this morning, he'd learned yet
another piece of the puzzle. Janet Tolliver and Clare
Barker were related by blood. The layers were slowly
peeling away.

He sat down on the opposite end of the sofa.
"Twenty-two years ago," he began, "a man and his
wife, Raymond and Clare Barker, were arrested for
multiple murders." He removed the copies of the newspaper clippings from the leather pouch but left the
album inside for now. He spread the clippings on the
coffee table. "You might want to look over these."

Sadie picked up the first article. "This is the woman
you mentioned might have some bone to pick with
Gus?"

Lyle steadied his breathing. "Yes."

The black-and-white photos in the articles wouldn't
show Clare Barker's green eyes. Sadie had those green

eyes. And the blond hair. When they got to the photo album, she would see. His fingers clenched on the case. He'd give most anything not to have to show it to her. But there was no way around it. Part of him wanted to be the one to help her through this, but the more selfish part hated to be the one since she would most assuredly despise the bearer of this news long after the dust had settled.

After reading through the articles, Sadie looked up and asked, "They still haven't found the other bodies?"

He shook his head. "A lot of folks had hoped that Rafe would eventually suffer some sense of remorse and give up that information. But he has never acknowledged or denied any of the murders. Clare has claimed innocence the whole time. She stood by her word that she had no knowledge of the murders."

Sadie stared at the decades-old black-and-white photo of the infamous couple. "How could they do this? What kind of monsters are these people?"

The agony churning inside him twisted more deeply. "I can't answer that question, Sadie."

"How could no one have suspected what they were doing?" Her head moved side to side. "Those poor little girls. There's no telling what they endured before they were murdered."

Lyle understood that she was referring to all the victims, and the Barker daughters in particular. He held his breath and waited for her next question.

"I can't see how Gus would be connected to these people." Her gaze leveled on Lyle. "What is it that you're keeping from me?" She searched his eyes. "I knew there was something. You're not a very good liar."

He opted to take that as a compliment. "A few days ago my agency received a letter from Rafe Barker." Lyle closed out his emotions. He couldn't do this otherwise. He explained the contents of the letter, summing it up with, "He swears his daughters are alive and that he fears Clare intends them harm."

Sadie frowned, her confusion visible. "How does that connect her to Gus? He..." The bewilderment cleared and disbelief took its place. "You're looking for the daughters."

Lyle nodded, unable to speak.

"You think..." The article she'd looked at last slipped from her grasp and floated to the floor. "That's impossible. I have baby pictures. They're all over the place at Gus's house. Me and my mother. Me and Gus. The three of us." Anger lit in her eyes. "You've known me my whole life. You know this is not just a mistake. It's crazy."

Lyle braced his hands on his knees and held on. He wanted to hold her and make her understand how sorry he was to have to do this. "Barker gave us a name. Janet Tolliver."

Sadie shook her head adamantly. "I don't know anyone by that name."

"I know," he said gently. "She was murdered the day before I arrived here. But she left something to help us find the truth." He withdrew the album and offered it to her. "This is the connection."

Hands trembling, Sadie took the album and settled it on her lap. She stared at the first page that displayed Sarah Barker's birth certificate. She turned to the next page. She gasped, one hand going to her chest.

Lyle couldn't suppress the crash of emotions. The

best he could hope to do was conceal the outward display of the turmoil whipping inside him. His best effort wouldn't chase away the burn in his eyes.

Sadie's life would never be the same.

THE LITTLE GIRL IN the photos could be her twin. Some part of Sadie knew that wasn't the case. Hot tears spilled down her cheeks and perched on her trembling lips. How could this be? She moved from page to page, photo to photo. Someone had taken pictures of her all through the years. Who had been close enough to take such intimate family shots?

Sadie swiped her face with both hands, then closed the album. She took a breath for courage and turned to the man waiting quietly on the other end of the sofa. "You should have told me this the moment I opened the door and found you on my porch." With each word, the rage built deep in her soul. How could he, of all people, hide this from her for one minute, much less a day?

"The risk to you was too great," he offered softly. "I couldn't take the chance that you would refuse to cooperate given how you might react to this information."

He spoke so damned softly she wanted to slap him. There was nothing soft about any of this! "What risk? I still don't get that part." The whole story was insane. Her mother and father were Gus and Arlene Gilmore. This was a mistake!

"Rafe Barker is convinced his wife intends to do what he allowed the police to believe he had done twenty-two years ago just to have her final revenge against him. He thinks she knew from the beginning that he could not have murdered his daughters. His theory is that she realized he tipped off the authorities all those years ago, and he claims he did, and that she has worked relentlessly to get free just to settle that score."

No way this involved Sadie. None of this sounded or felt familiar. "It's a terrible tragedy, no question. But the names, these photos, they don't stir any memories." She tried to show Lyle with her eyes what he might not get from her words. "Don't you think I would feel something if there was any truth to this cracked story?"

"You were just two years old, Sadie. You might not remember anything even when prompted by evidence like this." He gestured to the album. "I'm not an expert on matters like this. The one thing I know with complete certainty is that you'll need help with this. Counselors." He shrugged. "I don't know. But we have to get through this threat to your safety first, then there are tests you can have that will confirm what I'm saying to you."

Sadie tossed the album aside as if it were poison and might absorb into her skin. "You mean threats like the message some nimrod left in blood on my door?" Cox insisted the words weren't written in blood, but Sadie knew better. He'd promised to have it analyzed, but she didn't need a test to prove what she recognized any more than she needed a test to establish that she was Gus Gilmore's daughter. Whether it came from road-kill or a human, the message was written in blood. Lyle agreed with her, not that she had needed his endorsement, either.

"The message on the door tells me she's found you. And somehow she's keeping an eye on you despite being under surveillance by the best the Colby Agency has to offer. Obviously she has someone working for her, in view of the fact she hasn't left her apartment since we started surveillance."

"I want to talk to her. Right now." Sadie fought back the fear her own words ignited. Her body shook from it. "I want her to say that nonsense to my face."

Lyle held up both hands. "No way. We can only speculate that she left that message. If it's unrelated, we don't want to hand her your identity or your location."

Sadie got up. The talking was over. It was time to take action. "Who else would know to leave a message like that?" That option wasn't even plausible. Other than Lyle and his employer, who would have access to this pack of lies?

Lyle stood, looked her dead in the eye and said, "Gus."

That was the one prospect she hadn't considered, and it took the wind right out of her sails. "That doesn't make sense. Why would he do that? He definitely knows I'm his daughter."

"He's bound to have some idea why I'm here. He tossed out the Colby Agency name as you recall. He's a powerful man. He may have decided to use the situation to his advantage in this war you two have going on."

The idea that her own daddy would have sent one of his hoodlums to do this fired her up all over again for completely different reasons. She had to calm down and think rationally. What if this crazy tale was real? She pushed away the idea. "On the other hand, if he wants to take this place away from me, I guess he could just say that I'm not really his daughter—if any of this is so, which it absolutely is not."

"He legally adopted you. That makes you his daughter in the eyes of the law."

Wait, wait, wait. "How do you know that?" How in the blazes did he know all this stuff about her and she didn't? Because it wasn't real. She refused to believe that her entire life was one huge lie.

"It was done legally, but carefully hidden through private channels."

"And you found it?"

"My agency did." He plowed his fingers through his hair. "As far as the law is concerned, you're as much a Gilmore as Gus. If—" Lyle emphasized the *if* "—he's behind any part of this, it's because he wants to provoke the kind of reaction that would give him what he needs to overturn your grandmother's will."

"What kind of reaction?"

"You threatening to shoot anyone who crosses you. If you were considered unstable, any of the judges he knows would gladly appoint him a conservatorship."

Sadie shook her head. As often as she'd wanted to kill him, she would never really *kill* him. He was her father, for what that was worth. She would never do him physical harm. And she'd never shot anyone else. Half the time that old shotgun of hers wasn't even loaded. That uneasy feeling nudged her a little harder when she considered how many of Gus's friends considered her a little wild and crazy.

"I'm not unstable." She just had a bad temper when it came to protecting the animals.

"You'd end up in the institution of his choosing and he'd take over this place." A frown marred Lyle's face. "Do you have reason to believe he wants your grandmother's will overturned badly enough to go to extreme measures?"

Sadie had to think about that one. That she'd stood on his property with her shotgun aimed at him filled her head. If he was trying to make it look as if she'd gone over the edge, Lyle was right. That incident probably hadn't helped her reputation. "He's made the statement on several occasions that my grandmother had no right to do this. This land was supposed to go to him first."

The whole concept made her furious. As angry as she was, that didn't come close to blotting out the pain of the other. She didn't want to feel it. She didn't want to know it. "I need to talk to him." If there was any truth to this, he would confess if confronted with evidence. Or she'd hold him at gunpoint until he did. No, Lyle was right. That would be a mistake. If Gus wanted her out of the way that badly, she had to watch her step.

Would he really go that far?

She struggled to clear her mind. "Gus can straighten this out." Lifting her chin in defiance of the emotions warring inside her, she decided on a course of action. "I'll bet he can explain all of this. He'll make you see that this is a mistake." Gus would explain everything. Lyle would see.

Lyle moved closer, placed his hand on her arm as if to comfort her. She drew back. Couldn't bear to feel him. She wanted it to be because she was angry and felt betrayed by him all over again. That wasn't exactly what she felt. The truth was she didn't trust herself. If she let him touch her, she might just collapse into his strong arms. It would be so easy, but she couldn't do that. Strength and determination were needed here.

Her whole life was on the line and she had to figure out how to deal with this…this movie-of-the-week drama. Sensory overload was already an issue. Did she scream? Cry? Run away?

Calm down. She had to calm down. And think.

"If Gus doesn't know why I'm here," Lyle explained in that low, quiet tone that made her want to shake him, "he doesn't need to know. There are already too many complications cropping up. Any additional trouble could create a chain reaction. We don't need Gus's money and power delving into this right now. And we damned sure don't want the media getting involved. We have to keep this low profile for you and for the others."

The others. Sadie hadn't considered the others. The Barkers had three children. This had to be a mistake.

Pounding at the front door shattered her efforts to pull it together and concentrate. Before her brain had strung together a reasonable reaction, her feet were taking her toward the sound. Maybe the sheriff had come back with those test results? Not likely. He'd left only about half an hour ago. Damn, she'd lost all perception of time and certainly all grasp on reason.

Before she could open the door Lyle cut in front of her, opened the door with one hand while resting the other on the butt of the weapon tucked into his waistband.

Gus Gilmore loomed in the doorway. "What the hell is going on over here? I got a call from Sheriff Cox. Said I'd better get over here and see this for myself."

Sadie slipped around Lyle before he could step in her path. "Why don't you tell me?" Lyle cut her a look, and his words of warning about the others echoed in her mind. Oh, God. How did she do this?

Gus stared at the door and shook his head. "How on God's green earth would I know?" He nodded toward Lyle. "Why don't you ask him? All the trouble started after he got here."

He had a point with that statement. Confusion zoomed around in her head, making her hesitate. Things around here had been a little weirder than usual since Lyle showed up at her door. But he had nothing to do with Dare Devil or her grandmother's will or this awful story that couldn't possibly be right. What would he have to gain? Had he told her who the agency's client was? Gus had made a big deal out of that. Wait, yes. Rafe Barker. Her stomach roiled at even the thought of the man.

Sadie wanted to cry. To fall to her knees and beg her daddy to fix this nightmare. To make Lyle believe her. But there were other lives at stake. She stiffened her spine and grabbed on to her composure with both hands. "This is between you and me, old man." Her voice still sounded a little shaky. Not nearly as shaky as her emotions just now. She glared beyond Gus to the two henchmen who had accompanied him. "Did you do this, Billy Sizemore?"

He sniggered. "Damn, girl, I spent the best part of the morning escorting you around. How the hell could I have done anything over here?"

Sadie blinked, refused to be flustered by the lug-headed bully, even if he was right. That didn't mean one of his pals hadn't done it for him. "What about you?" she demanded of the man at his side, Chip Radley. "Where were you this morning?"

"Taking care of business for me," Gus answered for him.

Her attention shifted back to her father. He was livid. She knew that face. Her throat felt dry and tight. Gus Gilmore wasn't her father, if Lyle had his story right. The pictures and the newspaper article swam before her eyes. Some awful killer was her daddy. She shuddered, hugged herself to hold her body still. "What kind of business?" She had a right to know, seeing as Gus Gilmore was the prime suspect, in her mind, where this whole mess, Dare Devil and all, was concerned. By God, she had a right to know his business under the circumstances, even if he didn't understand that fact.

"As soon as you told me what happened with Dare Devil, I sent Radley out to check on some folks lowdown enough to do such a thing."

It took every lick of self-control Sadie could rummage up not to demand what he'd learned. But that would be the same as admitting she didn't really believe he was the one responsible. Maybe he wasn't. What did she know? She didn't even know who she was. "You mean, besides you?"

A glimmer of emotion, so faint she wondered if she had imagined it, flickered in his eyes. "I have a few leads to follow up on." He turned away from her and said to his men, "Clean up this mess before anyone else sees it." He muttered something about sacrilege.

"No." Sadie's announcement had him turning back to her. "I'll clean it up myself. I don't need anything from you."

Gus held her gaze for an eternity, something sad and disappointed in his. That was nothing new. He'd been disappointed in her for most of her life. Maybe now she had a clue as to why.

She didn't move until they had driven away. Her knees went weak, making her sway.

"Whoa." Lyle caught her and pulled her against him. "I think maybe you need to take it easy for a bit. I'll clean this up."

Weakness, she hated it! Sadie pulled away from him, squared her shoulders. She was not weak. Whatever happened, she could handle it. "I'm perfectly fine."

"Neither of us has had much sleep," he argued gently. "Let me do this for you, Sadie."

"Just go away, Lyle." She set her hands on her hips and exhaled the breath she hadn't realized she was holding until now. "I need to do this. If I'm still, I'll just obsess on that photo album."

He backed off. "I understand. I'll take care of the horses and feed the mutts."

Damn. She had lost all track of time. Swallowing her pride, she said the right thing for once. "Thank you."

She watched him as he walked to the barn. The way he moved had always made her burn for him. There was a sleek fluidity to the way he walked. His strength had made her feel safe and cared for. Something her father had turned off when she'd needed him most. Mercy, she couldn't hang on to a thread of thought. Her mind was all over the place.

Sadie dragged her weary body back to the living room and collapsed on the sofa. She stared at the photos on the pages of the open album. Her as an infant. The man and woman with her and the other two little girls were strangers to her. Maybe the baby wasn't even her. Sadie closed her eyes. Yes, it was her. There were several photos of her as a baby in the Gilmore family album. Just none with Gus and Arlene until she was two or so. Now she knew the reason why.

She felt like a stranger in the living room—parlor, as her grandmother had called it—that she'd loved as a kid. All the trinkets. Little statues and framed photos, the graceful old oil paintings. It all seemed suddenly foreign to her. Had her grandmother known about this? Of course, she had. You don't come home with a two-year-old and announce you've just had a baby.

The ache swelled so big and so fast inside her that Sadie couldn't breathe. How could this be? All that she had thought she'd known…all that she'd trusted was a lie.

Sadie propped her elbows on her knees, put her face in her hands and did something she hadn't done since Lyle left her all those years ago.

She cried.

THE HORSES WERE HAPPY to see him. Lyle managed a smile. He'd missed being around the animals. He shook his head. Somehow, he had to manage a visit with his folks. He'd let far too much time pass already. Work was always his excuse. But with what was happening to Sadie, he suddenly felt the need to hug his mother and even his father. A handshake just wouldn't be enough.

It took all his willpower not to go back to the house and hug her. She'd fight him like a wildcat, but he knew that was what she needed. The stubborn woman just refused to admit it. He took his time feeding the horses. Gave them all a quick rubdown and their freedom into the pasture. He folded the blankets they'd left in the stalls and hung them over the railing. Sadie kept the place so clean there was little to do in the way of mucking out the stalls, but he did it more or less to put off going back to the house too soon. Maybe she needed some time alone to think. He couldn't blame her. He'd sure needed a minute when he'd first heard this incredible story.

Gus showing up had given Sadie an excuse not to do anything rash. For once, Lyle was thankful for the old bastard. As much as Sadie wanted to believe her daddy didn't love her, Lyle was pretty damned sure he did. He just had a hell of a way of showing it. He was immensely grateful that she hadn't demanded answers about the photo album from Gus. He wasn't sure his warning about the danger had gotten through the emotions bombarding her, but it seemed he had.

Looking at the whole situation between Sadie and Gus from Gus's prospective, Lyle supposed he had withdrawn emotionally after his wife's death to protect himself. It wasn't the right thing to do, but folks didn't always do the right thing. Maybe Gus was only guilty of taking this competition between him and his daughter too far. But then, who had taken Dare Devil? The horse was worth a few bucks, even as old and worn out as he was. Could have been any outlaw out to make a fast dollar.

Lyle would enjoy learning it was Sizemore. Kicking his butt would feel good. But that would be too easy. Nothing about this situation had been easy so far, and he suspected that wasn't going to change.

He'd like nothing better than to wake up in the

morning and find that this was over for Sadie. Every minute that she suffered tore him apart a little more.

The dogs hadn't done any yapping, which he had decided to use as an alarm while he was at the barn and Sadie was in the house, but he didn't like having her out of his sight.

Rain clouds were moving in. This time of year it wasn't unusual for a storm to blow up. Since the barn roof was in good shape now, there were no worries about leaks. Maybe he could talk Sadie into taking a ride to town for lunch. Her cupboards were bare as hell.

Before climbing the porch steps, he checked his boots. His mother had drilled that habit into his head as a kid. *Don't bring anything in this house that belongs in the barn or the pasture, young man.* This was a strange time to think of something so mundane. Maybe mundane was what both he and Sadie needed.

She had scrubbed the blood, and he knew it was blood, from the door, but the fresh coat of paint was still in the can sitting on the porch. Sadie wasn't in the living room or the kitchen. His pulse hitched instantly, but his gut told him she was here. That was something he remembered from before. He could feel her presence. Whenever she was close, his pulse reacted. That the connection was still there after so many years was just further proof of what a fool he had been to walk away. He should never have allowed Gus to exert such influence over his decisions.

On the way to her bedroom he found all three dogs waiting outside the bathroom. Water spraying sounded on the other side of the door. Guess she'd decided she couldn't stand any trace of that mess on her skin. He could use a shower himself.

He tapped the door. "Hey, save me some hot water!"

"Maybe," she shouted back.

Despite having sensed she was okay, relief rushed through his blood at hearing her voice.

"Come on, boys." He glanced at the Chihuahua. "And girl."

Finding the dog food wasn't easy. By the time he did he understood why Sadie kept it hidden above the fridge. Gator, the Lab, was as adept at opening the lower cupboard doors as Lyle.

He poured the kibbles into the different-size dog bowls.

The mutts chowed down. Lyle wasn't a fan of kibbles, but he had to confess to a hunger pain or two. To tide him over he guzzled down a glass of milk. Good thing he was consuming it. The expiration date was only a day away.

Sadie showed up just in time to catch him going for a second glass. She was dressed, hair back in that loose ponytail, jeans snug on her slender body and a plain white tee that looking anything but plain on her. He finished off the milk and put his glass in the sink.

"You hungry?" he asked, knowing she had to be.

For a long time she stood there, watching the dogs, as if she hadn't heard him. Then she lifted her gaze to his. "I want to go to Granger."

"Granger?" That little hitch he'd experienced in his pulse a few minutes ago hit him again, only harder.

"I want to see the house."

That was what he figured. "Sadie."

"Don't try talking me out of it. You're either going with me or I'm going alone."

"There's nothing there to see," he countered. "It's been over twenty years."

"One of the newspaper articles said the house was bought by the parents of some of the victims. They boarded it up, didn't want anyone else to ever live there, but they didn't want to burn it down." She moistened her lips. "They wanted folks to remember what happened in that house."

He moved toward her, had to. He needed to touch her. His fingers curled around her shoulders and squeezed with all the reassurance he could convey in that small gesture. To his surprise she didn't resist. "Sadie, I know this is tearing you apart inside, but you've already had to absorb a lot today. I don't think this is a good idea."

"I'm going."

There was no use fighting it. He couldn't deny her, whatever she asked. "If there's no changing your mind…"

She searched his eyes, hers bright with desperation. "I need to remember something…anything. I have to try."

Chapter Ten

Granger, Texas, 2:00 p.m.

"It's smaller than I expected." Sadie craned her neck to see all she could beyond the truck's broad windows. Lyle had just driven past the welcome sign for Granger proper. *Where history lives.* That cold sensation Sadie had been fighting all day crept through her veins now, making her feel chilled, no matter that the sun shone strong and bright. The town's population hovered just under two thousand. Really small. Too small to have been the home of a monster like Rafe Barker.

"You drive through here before?"

"I don't think so. Maybe." If she'd been here as an adult, it had definitely been a drive through and she hadn't been the one driving. Nothing looked familiar.

The queasiness that had started the instant she read the message painted in blood on her door was still her companion, but Lyle had been right about eating. She'd forced down a burger and it had helped.

She glanced at the album lying on the console between them. A couple of times on the drive here she'd started to pick it up, but each time she'd lost the nerve.

"Drive slower." She didn't want to miss anything.

The town was an old one with a few historic features still intact. She'd noticed the railroad tracks before. Lyle had explained that this had been an important cotton-trade intersection back in the day when the railroad ruled mass transit.

Another of those icy shivers went through her as they passed the police department. She wondered if any of the policemen who'd been involved in the arrest twenty-two years ago were still on the force. Did any of the teachers at the schools remember the older girls? Probably not, she decided, since none had been old enough to go to school.

A church caught her eye and she pondered whether or not it was the one the Barkers had attended. Had she sat on one of those pews as a toddler? She squeezed her eyes shut. No, no, no. She had gone to church with her grandmother.

Eventually the little town gave way to open road. She turned to Lyle. "How much farther now?"

"According to the GPS—" he tapped the dash "—about two miles."

Sadie's heart kicked into a gallop. Oddly, her mind kept tripping over the irony that the Barkers had rescued dogs, cats and other small pets. The concept made her throat hurt. Was that kind of thing in one's DNA? *Breathe, Sadie. Don't think about that part right now.*

Lyle flipped on his right-turn signal and slowed. A big old farmhouse sat off the road, flanked on all sides by ancient trees that shaded the aging tin roof and the overgrown yard. The wood siding might have once been white, but it was more gray now and peeling badly. The windows and front door had been boarded up, just as the article she'd read had said.

Lyle parked in front of the house. The driveway had disappeared in the thick grass. Beyond the house she could see the roof of a barn, not red like hers at home, more a brown. According to the newspapers, the veterinary office had been operated out of a renovated barn. The property was fenced for horses, but there had been no mention of horses in any of the articles.

"You want to get out?"

She'd been certain about the answer to that before they left the Cove. For some reason she wasn't so sure now.

"We don't have to."

"Yes." She gathered her courage. "I need to see."

Lyle opened his door first. He got out and came around to her side. Despite her determination, she hadn't moved. When her door opened, she managed a stiff smile. "Thank you." He didn't say anything, but the worry in his eyes said all she needed to know. He was here for her. Whatever happened, he had her back.

There was still a sparse layer of gravel beneath all that overgrown grass. It crushed under her boots. The sky was clear but the air seemed thick and sticky in her lungs, no matter that the temperature was relatively mild for late May and there was a robust breeze. The front porch leaned to one side, so it wasn't surprising that the floorboards creaked as she walked toward the boarded-up door.

Overhead, remnants of birds' nests and spiderwebs hung on every available ledge and in every nook between old, cupped boards. The front of the house beneath the porch had been whitewashed recently to cover up vandalism, but the ghost of graffiti lingered just below its surface. Sadie thought of the bizarre message left on her door, and that frigid rush ran through her again.

She wandered to the end of the porch and stepped back down to the overgrown grass. The house was deeper than it had looked from the road. Back home her barn stood a good distance from the house. Here the barn-turned-clinic was only fifty or so feet from the house. A screened-in back porch overlooked the yard, where more massive trees offered shade from the Texas sun. Between the house and the barn the hand-stacked rock skirt of a well interrupted the flow of knee-deep grass. A bucket, bent and abused, hung from a frayed rope. The well drew her in that direction. She rested her hands on the cold stones and looked into the seemingly endless black hole.

Had they looked for bodies down there?

A squeak hauled her attention to the far side of the yard. A child's rusty swing set stood beneath a tree, the broken slide squeaking with each puff of the wind. Her boots grew heavier as she walked in that direction.

For a long time she stood there. Just looking. Then she touched one of the swings, set it into motion. Laughter whispered through her mind. Her heart jolted at the imagined sound. Had to be her imagination. Or had she hung on in one of these swings while her older sibling pushed her forward and laughed as she squealed with equal measures of fear and delight?

Dragging a shaky breath into her lungs, she turned to Lyle, who stood by patiently while she explored. "Can we go inside?"

Lyle cocked his head and considered the boarded-up back door beyond the wall of ragged screening. "We can try. It's called breaking and entering if we succeed. Malicious damage of property if we fail."

He smiled at her, and a burst of heat chased away some of the chill. "That's only *if* we get caught."

"I can't argue with that." He hitched a thumb toward the house. "I'll move the truck back here so we don't attract any attention and see what kind of tools I have."

As crazy as the idea was, considering where she was standing, she still enjoyed watching him walk away. The continuity of that feeling was reassuring. The breeze picked up. She hugged herself. The leaves rustled as the tree branches swayed. That whisper of child-like laughter swirled with the swishing of the leaves, making her shiver. A limb scraped the house, attracting her attention there. That window, though she couldn't see it for the rustic boards nailed over it, seemed kind of familiar. The limb scraping against the house felt incredibly familiar. There were no trees that close to her house or Gus's.

"Got a hammer."

Sadie gasped as the sound of his voice snapped her back to the here and now. He'd parked his truck near the swing set, gotten out and closed the door without her being aware he'd moved. She'd been completely immersed in a *memory* that shouldn't be hers. A glance back at the window confirmed that unnerving feeling.

"I want to go up there." She pointed to the window on the second floor that was barely visible between the leaves.

He held her gaze a moment, then offered the flashlight he had in his other hand. "Okay then."

The screen door whined as they entered the screened-in porch. At the door, Lyle dug the claw of the hammer beneath the first board and tugged. The board groaned then popped loose. Sadie flinched. Five more just like that—she jumped each time—and the door was exposed.

Sadie grasped the handle, anticipation detonating in her veins, and gave it a turn.

And it was locked.

"Give me a minute." He hung the hammer in his belt and body-slammed the door, twice.

The door burst inward and the musty smell of disuse wafted out to greet them. Sadie couldn't move for a moment. If she went inside, would she feel any different than she did now? Would she remember something that would confirm she was Sarah Barker and take away her sense of self?

Only one way to find out. Sadie stepped across the threshold. It was dark. She remembered the flashlight and clicked it on. The beam spilled across a cookstove. The kitchen. Made sense. Cobwebs clung to the beadboard ceiling and walls. A thick layer of dust covered everything else, including the floor. She rubbed at the dust with the toe of her boot, revealing the green-and-yellow pattern of worn linoleum beneath. Images flickered, disturbing her vision. She blinked repeatedly, shook her head.

"You okay?"

"Yes." Sadie elbowed aside the heebie-jeebies and focused on the room. Typical farm-style kitchen. Stained and chipped porcelain sink. Old laminate countertop with metal trim. Ancient fridge, reminded her of her grandmother's. Big wooden table with chairs on each end and benches along the two sides.

"Looks like the place was left as it was that morning."

Sadie nodded. "Seems so."

"Why don't I lead?"

"Sure." Sadie thrust the flashlight at him. She didn't need it anyway. None of this was familiar to her. No. She shook her head. She'd probably seen the linoleum somewhere. Maybe at the home of one of her grandmother's friends.

The kitchen led into a long narrow hall that divided the house down the middle and ended at the front door. Or began there, depending upon the way you looked at it. Along one side of the hall a staircase climbed to the second floor. Doorways on each side of the hall near the front door led to twin parlors. One was furnished more formally with what Sadie generally referred to as old-people furniture. Uncomfortable and out of date. The other was obviously the one the family had used most often. Sagging sofa. Box television set. A recliner. Bookshelf lined with the expected, mostly books about dogs and cats.

The house was spooky quiet. She hugged herself and wrestled with the trembling that had started deep in her bones. She started back to the hall before Lyle. He caught up with her in time to prevent her from tripping over a broken floorboard.

"Watch yourself," he warned.

Her attention drifted upward.

"Upstairs?" he asked, directing the flashlight's beam that way.

Sadie nodded then remembered that unless he shined the flashlight at her he wouldn't see the gesture. "Yes." She cleared her throat. "I want to see the other rooms."

Lyle checked each tread before moving upward. Ensuring the steps were still stable enough to support their weight. Sadie couldn't get a deep enough breath. The dust, probably. Couldn't be anything else.

At the top of the stairs was the first bathroom they'd encountered. A rubber duck sat amid the dust and rust in the tub. Three doors lined the corridor. The first appeared to be the parents' room. Plain. Faded wallpaper coming loose in one corner where a water leak had stained the wall.

Sadie backed away from the door. She didn't need to go in there. She followed Lyle to the next door. A bed and chest of drawers were the only furnishings. A guest room, she supposed. There was no window. Lyle checked the closet, closed the door before she had a look.

"What's in there?"

"Junk mostly."

Something she'd read in one of the articles bobbed to the surface of the turmoil in her head. She reached for the door and opened it. With obvious reluctance he pointed the light into the small space.

Ropes and chains lay on the floor. Articles of clothing were twisted into gaglike devices. Her heart bumped hard against her sternum. This was where the children had been imprisoned. Clare Barker had denied the charge, but the evidence had proved otherwise. She wondered why the devices were still here. Hadn't they been used in court as evidence? Or had they used photos instead?

She closed the door and walked out of the room.

"You okay?"

She ignored his question. But no, she wasn't okay. Saying it out loud wouldn't help. "That's the one." Sadie moved toward the final door. The window of this room would look into the massive branches of the tree next to the house.

The room was the same size as the parents' room. There was only one bed, full size. A chest of drawers was the only other piece of furniture, just like in the windowless room. At some point the walls in this one had been painted pink. The toe of her boot bumped something on the floor. She leaned down and picked up the stuffed dog. Her hand shook so hard she held it more tightly than necessary to hide the tremors. More toys were scattered over the floor. She turned to the bed, the covers tousled.

I'm 'fraid. The words whispered through her mind. Images of baby-doll pajamas and long blond braids flashed like images cast on the wall by an antique projector. Screaming. Not children's screams. A woman's. *Let me out! Let me out!*

Sadie reached for Lyle's arm. Her fingers curled into his shirtsleeve. "I'd like to go now."

She couldn't get out of the house fast enough. She needed air and there was none in this place. It was a tomb. Misery and death lingered with the dust and cobwebs.

Sadie rushed out the back door and through the screen door, letting it flap closed. She gasped for air and struggled to restrain the heaving that threatened to humiliate her. She braced against the big tree trunk, the one closest to the house, while Lyle banged on the boards until they covered the door sufficiently.

Beyond the barn, deep in the woods would be the burial ground where the remains of those eight young girls were found.

Sadie stared up at the window of the children's room.

That had been her room. She blinked, understood that cold hard truth with utter certainty. This had been her home.

With at least one murderer.

9:30 p.m.

SHE WAS FINALLY ASLEEP. Lyle covered Sadie with a blanket. The old sofa couldn't be that comfortable, but he didn't want to risk rousing her by carrying her to her bedroom. The day had taken a lot out of her.

Gus had called twice. She had refused to talk to him. Lyle kept expecting him to show up at the door, but that hadn't happened. When they returned from Granger, she had pored over the newspaper articles. She'd asked him dozens of questions he couldn't answer.

Then she'd finally given up the battle with exhaustion and wilted on the sofa. He was damned tired, too, but that demand would have to wait. The dogs had been fed but the horses needed tending and the barn secured for the night.

When he was sure she was down for the count, he grabbed her house key, locked the doors and headed for the barn. What had to be done would take only a few minutes. Make sure the animals had food and water, close the doors and then he might try catching a few minutes of shut-eye in the upholstered rocker that had been Adele's favorite chair. She'd crocheted the doily draped over the back of it. He remembered Sadie complaining that she'd attempted to teach her to no avail.

Sadie wasn't the domestic type. She preferred rubbing down horses and mucking stalls to crocheting and serving tea. All the Gilmore women had been genteel Southern ladies. But not Sadie. She had been too full of life and curiosity to sit still long enough to play refined. She loved getting her hands dirty and her body sweaty.

Lyle had fallen in love with her the first time he laid eyes on her at the Long Branch Saloon. He'd just turned twenty-one and had bought his first legal beer. Sadie and a couple of her friends had gotten in with fake IDs and claimed a table next to the dance floor. One dance was all it had taken, and every cell in his body had burned to tame the girl. But she was having none of that. No one was going to tame Sadie Gilmore.

They had met for several dates before he found out her real name and the truth about her age. Fifteen. Beautiful and dangerous to a guy over the age of legal consent. He'd tried to break it off with her, but she was as stubborn as she was beautiful. She'd teased and taunted him, and he hadn't been able to say no to anything she wanted, much less to their secret rendezvouse. The last night they had been together she had begged him to make love to her.

As much as he had wanted to, he'd refused. She was too young. Her daddy was already on to him. He'd threatened Lyle on more than one occasion. Not that Lyle could blame him. His daughter was barely more than a child. In his brain, Lyle had understood that. But his heart wouldn't deny her. He had known that final night that if he didn't leave he would cross the line. He couldn't do that to her or to himself. She deserved the chance to grow up and become the woman she was destined to be without him charting a different path for her. Gus had warned him that he would disown Sadie if she ran away with Lyle.

So he'd walked away and never looked back. It had been the right thing to do in his mind at the time.

But he'd never stopped wanting her…never stopped loving her. On her eighteenth birthday he had tried to call, but she'd been in Cancún or some party place. He'd left a message, even sent a card, but she never responded.

That was the last time he'd tried. He closed the barn doors and started back to the house. For some reason he hadn't bothered to get involved with anyone else. The occasional date here and there. A few one-night stands. Work kept him busy most days, and dreams of Sadie had filled his nights.

Sadie's old truck snagged his attention. The front fender on the driver's side was dented. He was pretty sure he would have noticed that if the damage had been there before. Running his hand over the bent metal, he leaned down to get a closer look.

The force of the blow to the back of his head rammed his forehead against the fender. He tried to raise up, turn around and defend himself, but the night closed in on him.

He had to get to Sadie. That thought followed him into the blackness.

"STOP." SADIE COULD hear the dogs yapping like mad but she was too tired to wake up. She needed to sleep. If she woke up she would have to remember.

She didn't want to remember.

Her chest burned. She coughed.

Abigail was sitting on her chest licking Sadie's face. "Stop." She turned her face into the pillow but the dogs just wouldn't shut up. Abigail was dancing around on her chest. She wouldn't stop.

As if each one weighed ten pounds, Sadie forced her eyelids to open. She blinked. How long had she been asleep?

Not long enough apparently. She didn't want to wake up. Gator stuck his face in hers. Barked in that deep Lab roar.

"Damn it, Gator." Sadie sat up, ushered Abigail aside. She closed her eyes to stop the spinning in her head. What was wrong with her?

She drew in a deep breath to rouse her brain. She choked, coughed like the old man with COPD who shoed her horses. She swiped the tears from her eyes and blinked.

What the hell? Why was the room foggy?

She tested her next breath. More coughing.

Smoke.

Sadie shot to her feet. Staggered. The dogs went crazy.

She turned around in the room. Smoke came from every direction.

The house was on fire.

She tried to feel her way to the entry hall and kept bumping into furniture. She couldn't breathe. Couldn't see.

What was that adage she learned in school? *Stop, drop and roll.*

The dogs were tangling in her feet. Wait, she couldn't stop! She had to find a way out of here.

The front window. Sadie dropped onto all fours. The smoke was thinner down here. She scrambled to the window overlooking the porch. Keeping her head as low as possible, she reached up and pushed at the lower window sash with all her strength. Slowly, an inch at a time, it raised. She lifted the latch for the old-fashioned screen and pushed it out of the window's frame.

"Abigail, come." Sadie poked her upper body through the window, the little dog in hand, and deposited her onto the porch. Frisco was next. He jumped out of her arms and right through the window opening.

Gator was going to take some doing. "Come on, boy." She grabbed him by the collar and dragged his seventy pounds to the window. She patted the window ledge. "Jump, boy, jump." The smoke burned her throat, her nose and eyes. She couldn't get a breath. She needed this dog to cooperate.

Nothing was ever that easy with Gator. Once she got him to poke his head and front legs out the window, she basically lifted and pushed the rest of him out.

Sadie collapsed on the floor, wheezing and coughing.

She had to get up. Her brain knew this but her body would not respond to the commands.

"Get up, Sadie," she muttered.

Didn't work. Just made her cough some more. She was so tired. Her eyes were burning. Something crashed in the kitchen. There were strange crackling noises. Or maybe scratching…

She was in that yard behind the old Barker house. The wind was blowing and the tree limb was scratching the window. Her sister was pushing her in the swing. Only it wasn't old and rusty. It was shiny and new. Their daddy had bought it for Christmas. Another little blond-haired girl chased a dog around in the grass.

Her sister. Sadie had two sisters. Not Sadie. *Sarah.* Her name was Sarah.

Wait… Now they were in that old bed together. Someone was coming. She could hear the footfalls in the hall outside their room.

I'm 'fraid.

Hands were touching her, pulling and tugging. Sadie fought the hands. She didn't want to go. She was afraid. She told herself to scream, but her lips wouldn't form the sound.

Her head hit something. Her eyes were burning. She couldn't see. She fell. Hit the floor.

This was bad. She was going to die…again.

"Sadie!" The voice shook her mind awake. "Sadie, breathe!"

She gasped. Coughed so hard she vomited.

The hands rolled her onto her side. She wasn't on the floor anymore. She was in the grass. Where was the swing set? Where were her sisters? Why couldn't she open her eyes?

"Come on, Sadie. Talk to me!"

Bright lights blinded her. Colors flashed and the sound piercing the air hurt her ears.

Where was she? Home? Where was home?

The dogs were yapping again.

Something covered her face. The air smelled better now. She blinked at the sting in her eyes.

Why was she on the ground?

Who were all these people?

Fire.

Ice filled her veins. She tried to sit up. Strong hands held her down.

Sadie yanked the mask off her face and screamed, "Lyle!"

Dear God, he was still in the house!

"Calm down, Miss Gilmore," the man urged. "You're going to be all right."

Paramedic. She recognized the uniform now. Why wouldn't her brain work properly? People were everywhere. They were spraying the flames shooting up from the roof of her house with their big hoses. Others were shouting instructions. The dogs cowered close to her, but something was still wrong.

What was she supposed to remember?

Lyle. Where was Lyle?

Sadie scrambled away from the paramedic as he reached to put the mask back on her face.

"Lyle!"

She staggered to her feet, turned around and around, tried to spot his face in the crowd.

Where was he?

"Ma'am, please," the paramedic urged, "you need the oxygen. And you need to sit down."

She smacked at his hands. "I have to find Lyle. He was in the house, too." Why wouldn't anyone listen to her? Tears burned her cheeks. What had happened? She didn't understand this. Where was he? "I can't find him."

"It's all right, ma'am," the paramedic said, "your friend is safe. He's in the ambulance already. Got himself a bleeder, but he's going to be just fine. We had a time talking him into leaving you long enough to get stitched up."

Sadie tore away from the paramedic and ran for the ambulance. She stumbled, picked herself up and started running again. Gator, Frisco and Abigail chased her, yapping wildly. The paramedic shouted at her but she ignored him and everyone else tramping around on her property.

Lyle sat on the gurney inside the ambulance. A paramedic taped a bandage to the back of his head.

"Lyle." She felt weak. She needed to lie down.

He pushed the paramedic's hand away and turned to her. Sadie wasn't sure which one did what, but somehow she was suddenly in his arms and that was all that mattered.

"You scared the hell out of me, kid," he murmured against her hair.

"I'm not a kid anymore, I told you." She buried her face in his chest to hide the sobs she couldn't contain.

"Ain't that the truth," he whispered.

It definitely was, and the first chance she got she intended to show him just how much woman she was.

Chapter Eleven

10:40 p.m.

Lucas Camp leaned forward, pressing his right eye to the telescope zoomed in on Clare Barker's first-floor apartment window across the courtyard. He'd leased the apartment directly across from hers, on the ground floor as well. She'd retired for the evening more than an hour ago. The lights had gone out and he'd watched as she closed the blinds.

He wasn't concerned about her escaping without his knowledge, since there was no back door with any of these apartments. Most were studios, a few one-bedrooms. There was a front entrance and one window. The building was brick. Any escape through the wall would require tools Clare Barker had not carried into the apartment with her and which would generate sound.

On his routine strolls of the grounds, Lucas surveyed the back side of the row of apartments that included hers twice each day. So far she hadn't come outside even once. No cell phone transmissions, no conversation at all. The parabolic ear focused on her apartment had picked up nothing at all. He had, how-

ever, picked up more than a few eyebrow-raising con-
versations from one or more of her nearby neighbors.
Occasionally, he got a glimpse of her at the window.

Her attorney had dropped by once. Otherwise there
had been no visitors. Lucas was not convinced by her
pretense of fading into the background like this. She
was up to something. He just hadn't latched on to a
decent theory yet. She was far too smart not to have a
plan of some sort. Whether it was the one her husband
alleged was yet to be seen.

Clare had graduated from Texas A&M's College of
Veterinary Medicine just like her husband. They'd met
in the program and married right after graduation. It
still rattled him that a man and woman who appeared
to have such compassion for animals could be such
cold-blooded killers. His instincts leaned toward the
idea that one of them wasn't. The only question was
which one.

Lucas settled into the chair he had positioned for the
view of his subject's apartment. He'd called Victoria
to wish her a good-night. She had sounded tired and
frustrated. The case had gotten under her skin far too
deeply.

A few hours' sleep and he would check in with her
again. Perhaps after some sleep Victoria would feel
more like herself. Before giving in to the need for
downtime, Lucas checked his equipment one last time.
If Clare Barker spoke to anyone, he would know it. If
she opened her front door, the motion sensor he had
placed on her door frame would trigger an alarm right
here in his place. She wasn't going anywhere without
his knowledge.

May 23, 12:23 a.m.

THE WAIL OF SIRENS startled Lucas from sleep. He sat up. Lights flashed in the courtyard. The sirens heralded the arrival of fire trucks and emergency responder vehicles. He checked Clare's door via the telescope. Still closed and her lights were out. He shut off the parabolic ear and grabbed his handgun. At the door he shoved the gun into his waistband beneath his jacket before stepping outside.

Shouting from the two-story building at the rear of the complex drew his attention that way. Flames were already leaping from the rooftop. Occupants had spilled into the courtyard. Rescue personnel and some occupants were rushing from door-to-door to ensure no one was left behind in the apartments.

Lucas watched for the lights to come on in Clare's apartment. He strode quickly across the courtyard, tuning out the panicked voices all around him. Being pent up in that apartment for the past sixty or so hours had made his gait stiffer than usual.

A *whoosh* loud enough to drown out all else drew his attention to the end of the one-story row of studio apartments on Clare's side of the courtyard. Most of the occupants on that side had already filtered onto the sidewalk in front of their apartments. Dazed and confused residents wandered all around the courtyard. Lucas hurried to cut through the gathering crowd, his attention focused on one door in particular.

"Sir!"

Lucas turned to the police officer who had shouted at him.

"We've shut down traffic. We need to get everyone

across the street. If you could help rather than moving toward the danger, it would be much appreciated."

Lucas thanked him and then headed toward Clare's apartment in defiance of his request. He would like to help, but right now he had to get to that apartment. Two more officers were already moving door-to-door from the end of the one-story row nearest the eruption of flames, checking the apartments to confirm they were empty.

One of the officers reached Barker's door at the same time as Lucas. "There's a female inside," he explained. "Late fifties. Clare Barker. I didn't see her come out."

"Step aside, sir."

Lucas stood aside while the officer banged on the door and shouted instructions for anyone inside. The two-story building a few yards away was already fully consumed. The fire was burning swiftly through the old one-story portion on this side of the courtyard.

"Let's go in," the second officer to arrive at the door ordered. On closer inspection, Lucas realized this one was a member of the rescue squad.

The handheld battering ram knocked the door off its hinges with one blow. The two official personnel rushed inside, one hitting the lights. Lucas was right behind them.

"The place is clear," the officer in the lead yelled.

The second turned and came face-to-face with Lucas. "Sir, we need you to move across the street. This is a dangerous situation."

"I just need a look," Lucas pressed. "She's a little off in the head," he improvised. "She could be hiding in the closet."

The men exchanged a look. The rescue responder said, "All right, but make it quick." To his colleague he added, "Watch him. Get him out of here as soon as he's had a look."

Lucas rushed to the bedroom area that was divided from the living room area by a built-in bookshelf. The closet was empty. No clothes, nothing.

He moved into the bathroom, ignoring the cop's threats to drag him out if he didn't come with him. The cramped bathroom was empty, the shower door pushed inward, revealing dingy tile and no Clare Barker. Lucas started to turn away, but he decided to pull the shower door outward and check that side of the shower stall first.

The tile had been removed in a small area. He dropped into a crouch and checked the hole. It went all the way through to the next apartment. Just large enough for a small, slim woman to slither through.

Lucas shook his head. He had watched the occupant of this apartment come and go. A much younger woman than Clare Barker, the woman who was identified by the apartment manager as Toni Westen had dark hair and carried at least fifty pounds more than the older woman. Lucas had been had.

The officer grabbed him by the arm and pulled him to his feet. "I will remove you by force, sir."

"Sorry." Lucas adjusted his jacket. "You were right, she's not here."

The cop shook his head and ushered Lucas toward the front door. The lights started to flicker. Three feet from the door Lucas stalled.

"Go," the cop shouted with a nudge at Lucas's back.

Lucas stared at the wall between the window and the door. Clare Barker had left a message.

On the wall four stick figures had been drawn. A woman and three little girls, stair-step in size. A big red X had been drawn across the stick figures.

Clare Barker was gone. Her destination and intent as clear as the drawing on the wall. A mother-and-daughters reunion.

CLARE SCANNED THE MOB gathered in the convenience store parking lot across from the burning apartments. She didn't see the man who had been watching her. He would never find her in this crowd or dressed as she was. She had slipped out twice already, just to test her disguise.

A hand clasped her elbow. She jumped and turned to face what she hoped would not be an officer of the law. It was *him*. Thank God.

He leaned close. "This way. We need to hurry."

With his hand clasped around her arm, he hurried her through the frightened people. They rushed around to the rear of the convenience store.

The lot behind the store connected to another that sprawled out in front of a strip mall. She removed her dark wig and the padding that gave the appearance of bulk and tossed them into one of the trash cans that lined the back of the store. She glanced up, thanked her Maker and hurried after her friend.

At the end farthest away from the fray at the convenience store, a small white car waited in the shadows. He moved quickly to the driver's side while she climbed into the passenger seat.

She couldn't draw in a deep breath until he had

driven around behind the deserted strip mall and eased out onto the street running along the back side.

Clare closed her eyes and started to pray an offering of her gratitude for her successful escape. She had waited so long… These past few days had felt like a lifetime.

"Will the police be looking for you?"

His voice drew her to the present and the steps that needed to be taken as swiftly as possible. "Not right away." She smiled at the driver, who had been immensely kind to her. "With all that's happened, I've failed to thank you properly."

He glanced at her. "We do what we have to."

Yes, that was true. "Do you have all that I require?"

"Everything on the list."

That was very good. "I will repay you one day."

He looked at her again as he braked for a traffic light. "I've already been well compensated."

It wasn't until then that she allowed her gaze to rest on his right shoulder. He was preoccupied with driving so he wouldn't notice. She had no desire to make him feel uncomfortable or to injure his feelings in any way.

Her visual examination slid down his right arm, which ended only six or so inches below the shoulder. He'd lost that arm twenty-three years ago as a young man. No one had ever known the truth about that day. Only Clare and him, and the person responsible, of course.

He and Clare both had suffered greatly. Those responsible would all pay. She would see to it.

Her time was finally here.

She relaxed into the seat as he drove her through the

night. The drive would take a while. Sleep pulled at her but she refused its tug. There was too much to do to waste time sleeping. As much as she fully trusted this man, it was best to remain alert and attentive.

Nothing or no one would be allowed to stop her.

"CLARE."

Her eyes drifted open to complete darkness. She jerked forward, but the seat belt confined her. "Where are we?"

"It's all right. You're safe now." He got out of the car. The interior light blinded her until her eyes adjusted. Her door opened. "Come on, Clare. It's okay. We're here."

She released her seat belt and slowly emerged from the car. He closed the door and took her by the hand with his left. "Hurry."

She followed alongside him, her feet getting tangled in the tall grass. When they had moved beyond the trees, the moonlight spotlighted their destination. Her heart shuddered to a near stop before bursting into a frantic race.

"You're home, Clare. You're really home."

She fell to her knees, tears streaming down her cheeks.

Yes. She was home.

Vengeance is mine, the Lord said.

But He had come to her in a dream and whispered in her ear. Because of the special circumstances, He had decided that vengeance would be hers this time.

And it began now.

Chapter Twelve

"I don't want to argue." Sadie turned away from him, stalled on the walkway that led to what had once been her front porch.

Lyle's head throbbed, and he hadn't managed any sleep for the past two nights. He wasn't at his best by any means. They'd spent eight hours at the hospital. Both had been checked out thoroughly. He had a mild contusion and six stitches where some bastard had whopped him in the head with a blunt instrument that had not as of yet been found.

Sadie suffered from a good dose of smoke inhalation. He closed his eyes and shook his head, winced at the pain the move prompted. If he'd been hit any harder and lost consciousness rather than just being rattled, she would be dead now. She'd gotten the dogs out, but the smoke had gotten to her and she hadn't been able to get herself out.

That was Sadie. Looking out for the animals before taking care of herself.

Her house was a total loss. A cleanup crew would arrive in a couple of days to go through the rubble in an attempt to salvage any personal belongings. Sadie had wanted to do that herself, but Lyle had talked her out of it. That was a job for professionals.

He moved up behind her, wanted to hold her more than he'd ever wanted to do anything in his whole life. "You want answers. I get that. But your sisters don't know what you know."

She whipped around, went nose to nose with him. His body tightened near the point of pain. "They should know. This is not a game. They have the right to know."

He worked at calming the emotions tangling inside him, but every minute with her was a struggle. The ability to maintain even a semblance of objectivity had vanished when he'd pulled her through that window. At this point, talking was not what he wanted to do. The atmosphere between them had changed, and there was no turning back. "Two of my colleagues are working 24/7 right now to get close enough to protect them. We can't screw this up. Their safety is at stake. If we get in the way…the worst could happen."

Those green eyes darkened and widened with her own mounting frustration. "Why aren't the police protecting them? If they knew the truth—" she waved her hand as if the remedy should be crystal clear "—they could agree to protective custody!"

Calm, Lyle. Stay on the point. "What do we tell the police? That a man on death row wants his three daughters—who the world believes were murdered twenty-two years ago—protected from their recently released mother!"

The hurt that shimmered in her eyes instantly doused his flare of irrational anger. She looked away. Lyle dropped his head back and blew out a blast of frustration. He had to get a handle on these damned emotions. In an effort to do just that, he pulled in a deep, hopefully calming breath. The air smelled of smoke and charred wood, and yet the sky was clear and blue, as if nothing bad had happened.

"Are they safe?" Her voice sounded too small, trembled. She lifted her gaze to his. "Can the people from your agency protect them right now? This minute?"

"Yes. These men are the best at what they do. They're prepared to risk their lives without blinking." Before she could launch a counter, he went on. "Clare Barker is at this moment unaccounted for. Whoever is working with her is, as well. If she knows your identity, we could inadvertently lead her to the others by making contact. We can't take that risk, Sadie. It's too great to them and too great to you."

She surrendered. The defeat showed in her slumped shoulders and the weary sigh that hissed past those pink lips. "She's just gone? This woman, Clare?"

Lyle nodded. He had briefed Sadie on the news from Lucas. "Simon, my boss, and Lucas reviewed the video security footage at the convenience store across the street from the apartment complex. She left with a man in a white or gray car. We didn't get a model or license plate number. The only identifying factors we did get were that her accomplice was tall, had light brown hair and that he was missing his right arm. He never looked back, so we didn't get a face or profile shot." Clare, on the other hand, had looked back, almost as if she knew there was a camera and she wanted whoever was watching to know it was her under that disguise.

"You think this one-armed man left that message on my door? Gus said Sheriff Cox got word from the lab that it was deer blood. God knows, there's always one getting hit on the highway. Finding a carcass wouldn't be that difficult."

Lyle turned his palms up. "We don't know who left the message. The one-armed man is certainly a prime suspect." There hadn't been any rain in days. The storm that had threatened earlier had blown around Copperas Cove. The ground was too dry for a vehicle to leave tire impressions. There was no way to say who or how many uninvited had driven up to Sadie's house. The sheriff and the fire marshal couldn't tell them anything conclusive just yet about the fire. One thing was definite, it was one hell of a coincidence that Sadie's house had burned within hours of Clare Barker's apartment complex going up in flames. Fortunately, no lives had been lost in either event. That in itself was an outright miracle.

Sadie gave her head a little shake. "I don't want to believe it was Gus. But the list of those who know about my birth parents is seriously limited. That message was meant to scare me, and whoever left it knew the trick to use."

Lyle recognized she was scared, even if she would admit it only in a roundabout way. He also grasped that even though she and Gus didn't get along, he was her father and she loved him. She just didn't like to say it out loud. "There is also the possibility," Lyle suggested, "that Barker is orchestrating certain things from prison. And don't forget the stick-people drawing Clare left on the wall of her apartment. We can't be sure of anything right now."

"Jesus." She chewed her bottom lip.

He bit back a groan. This wasn't the time to be feeling this way, but there was no stopping the intense response to the way she was torturing that lush lip. He was in no shape to be that strong. They were both exhausted and in need of clean clothes, which only made him think about stripping hers off. They'd had showers at the hospital, but their clothes reeked of smoke. Pretty soon they would need to find clothes and a place to stay.

"Have you seen him?" She searched Lyle's eyes, the question surprising him. "Do you think he killed all those girls?"

Somehow he had to find his focus, for her. "I watched the interview Victoria Colby-Camp, the head of the Colby Agency, conducted with him." Lyle lifted one shoulder in a shrug. "He was thinner than in the photos you saw. Older, of course. Hair was gray." He met that searching gaze. "He looked tired and resigned to his fate. But when he spoke of his desperation to have his daughters protected…there was a glimmer of the kind of compassion that you'd expect from a man who rescued small animals."

Her lips trembled and her face pinched with the misery his words had elicited. God almighty. He didn't know how to choose the right words to give her what she wanted and still protect her feelings. Would it have been better if he'd said Barker looked like the monster the newspapers reported him to be?

"And her?"

"Older, thinner. Gray." The prison photos he had seen of Clare Barker showed a woman who was every bit as determined as her youngest daughter—unfortunately, for the wrong reasons it seemed. He opted to leave that part out of his answer.

"Do you think she did it?" Again, she watched his face and eyes closely, looking for signs that he was keeping anything from her. "Could she have been the one doing the killing instead of him, like he said?"

Lyle implored her with his eyes to see the truth in what he was about to say. "I honestly don't know. But those girls didn't kill themselves. One of them, or both, has to be a killer."

She pressed her fingers to her lips to hide their trembling. Tears, glittering like tiny diamonds, perched on her lashes.

Damn it. He'd said too much again. "Sadie, you know who you are. As difficult as this crazy story is to reconcile, it doesn't change the person you are."

"Maybe."

"That's more like it." He smiled, tried to relax. Him stressing out wasn't helping her calm down. "We're gonna get through this. The house, everything will work out." He glanced over his shoulder at what used to be her home. The move had been an effort to break the tension, but if she didn't stop looking at him that way, he was going to lose his grip on that last shred of control.

"And then you'll leave again."

His heart did one of those dips and slides, all the way down to his boots. She had every right to throw that at him. "I was wrong to leave last time." He'd same as admitted that already, but this time he said the words he should have said before. "That won't happen this time until you're ready for me to go."

"You sure about that?"

"Positive."

Had she lifted her face closer to his, or was he the

one who moved? Didn't matter. All he knew for sure was that he couldn't take it anymore. He was going to kiss her, because he simply couldn't *not* kiss her. She needed it as badly as he did.

The growl of trucks roaring toward them snapped him back, mentally and physically. Her breath caught, as if she too had just been dragged away from the brink of self-indulgence. They couldn't keep dancing all around this thing between them, or they were going to lose it and go too far. Lyle had to do this right this time.

Sadie turned around just as Gus and two of his men, all three driving their big trucks, braked to a stop. Did these guys not understand the concept of conserving? One of the trucks pulled a horse trailer. Gus and the others bailed out and strode toward them.

Sadie put her hand up to shade her eyes. "Is there a horse in that trailer?"

The hope in her voice made his gut clench. "Don't think so." She was still hoping to find Dare Devil.

Lyle took a breath and braced for the battle of wills that Gus's presence unfailingly provoked. He checked the weapon at the small of his back and hoped like hell he wouldn't need to use it. It wasn't enough that Gus had been at the hospital almost as long as they had, hovering and listening. The man was worried about his daughter, for sure. But he was also trying hard to learn exactly what Lyle was up to. If he didn't already know, Lyle felt reasonably certain he had a hunch.

"What do you want?" Sadie crossed her arms over her chest. That appeared to be her standard greeting for dear old dad.

Lyle sensed that to some extent she held Gus responsible for part of this mess that was her history. She understandably felt that he should have told her at some point. In Gus's defense, how did a man tell the woman he'd raised as his own child something like that?

"I found Dare Devil."

"Where? Is he all right?"

"I don't know his status," Gus told her. "But I got word where he was being kept." He shook his head. "The Carroll place. I should've known when that old bastard started drinking again, he couldn't be trusted."

"I'll get my keys." Sadie hesitated, threw her hands up in frustration. "I can't get my keys." She turned back to the house. "They burned along with everything else I own."

"You two can ride with me," Gus offered.

Lyle slid two fingers into his pocket. "I'll drive." Gus shot him a look that declared he wasn't happy about that interception.

"I don't want you digging around in that mess, Sadie." Gus gestured to the heap that had been her house. "My men will be over tomorrow. They'll salvage what they can and bulldoze the rest." The elder Gilmore wasn't giving up on getting his daughter's attention, if not her respect.

"The insurance company is sending someone on Monday," she informed him, visibly bursting his bubble. "Professionals."

"You want strangers going through what's left of your worldly possessions, little girl?" Gus argued.

"I sure as hell don't want your *men* touching my stuff."

Sizemore, Gus's constant shadow, laughed. "You

just don't know how to be a grateful little girl, do you, Sadie Adele?"

"Shut up," Gus growled at him. "Let's go find that damned horse."

SADIE WAITED IN THE truck. Lyle had insisted. She didn't like it one bit, but she wasn't totally stupid. Her house had burned. Someone had whacked him in the head. This was not the time to be foolhardy. Her throat and nostrils were sore as hell. Her chest felt as if she'd sucked in the fire instead of just the smoke.

Gus banged on the door of the shack Jesse Carroll called home, Lyle right next to him. Sizemore and his buddy were walking the property. Sadie didn't see why they didn't go straight to the barn. If Dare Devil was here, he'd be in the barn most likely. Then again, if old man Carroll had hoped to hide him, he might do otherwise. She hugged herself, wished all of this insanity was over.

Another round of knocking on the man's door. Why didn't they just go in? Were all these guys thick-skulled?

Two more minutes passed. Finally, Gus tried the door. Evidently it was unlocked. He and Lyle went inside. Sadie sat up straighter. Lyle had left her his handgun. Her shotgun had gotten charred along with the rest of her personal possessions. She caught a glimpse of Sizemore in the woods next to the barn.

"Idiot."

Seconds ticked off like little bombs in her head. She watched the digital clock shift to the next minute and then the next and still no one came out of the house or went into the barn.

"This is ridiculous." She eyed the barn doors. Not more than fifty feet from the house, about seventy from the truck. It was broad daylight.

She was out the door and headed that way before reason could talk her out of the move. When she reached the barn, Lyle and Gus were still in the house and she had no idea where Sizemore or his pal had gotten off to. Probably relieving themselves. Cocky guys like him loved peeing in the woods.

She lifted the crossbar and the barn doors opened with a reluctant creak. It was pitch dark inside. She let the doors drift all the way open to allow as much light as possible inside. The barn smelled bad. Mr. Carroll clearly hadn't used it for much in a long time and hadn't bothered cleaning it after the last time. She eased along the main aisle, checked the six stalls, her hope withering. No Dare Devil.

There was an odd odor, besides the nasty hay and animal droppings that had petrified. The sunlight that filtered in highlighted the dust and cobwebs that had taken over. Probably spiders, too.

She turned around and retraced her steps. The tack room door stood open. She shifted directions and checked it out. It was even darker in there. She felt on the wall for a light switch. No switch. Smelled a lot worse, too. She moved to the center of the room, her right hand groping the air over her head for a pull string. Maybe there was no electricity to the barn. Had there been any overhead lights in the main area?

Her hand hit something solid. She snatched it back. Not a pull string. She squinted but still couldn't see a damned thing. Gathering her courage, she reached into the darkness again and tried to determine by touch what the object was. Fabric…then something smoother…a boot.

She stumbled back, her heart missing a beat.

A leg. She'd felt a leg.

Holding her breath, she checked to see if there were two legs. Oh, yeah. Two boots. Two legs.

Sadie backed out of the tack room, bumped the door frame on the way.

"I thought you were staying in the truck."

She jumped. Turned to face the voice. Sizemore stood in the doorway, blocking a good deal of the sun.

"There's…" She moistened her lips and reached again for her voice. "There's someone hanging in the tack room. I think it's a man. I'm pretty sure he's dead."

SHERIFF COX SHOWED UP. The coroner arrived a few minutes later. Mr. Carroll was dead. The sheriff concluded that he had hanged himself, since an overturned stepladder lay on the floor of the tack room.

Sadie didn't really know the old man. He had worked for Gus off and on in the past. He had a reputation for heavy drinking and not showing up for days. Gus had fired him a dozen times but he always took him back. Felt sorry for the old guy, she supposed. She didn't like giving him that kind of credit, but when it came to a man down on his luck, Gus wasn't completely heartless. It didn't happen often. In fact, Mr. Carroll was the only example she could think of.

A frown tugged at her brow. He'd sure as hell never offered her any credit for her good deeds.

They hadn't found Dare Devil. Apparently her father's source had been mistaken. Gus didn't like to be wrong. He'd been shouting orders, even to the sheriff for the past half hour. Now that she sat back and watched him in action, she decided that he was upset by the old man's death and this was his way of showing his emotions.

All this time she'd been certain he didn't have any. Maybe the smoke she'd sucked in had damaged her brain.

Twice Gus and Lyle had locked horns, primarily because Gus didn't like that he was here. Lyle didn't abide his intimidation tactics. Not like before.

He'd promised he wouldn't go this time until she was ready for him to leave. Could she trust his word on that?

There was no question that he would finish his job and he would protect her. But could she trust him with her heart? He'd sure stamped all over it the last time.

Her age had been a problem. She couldn't deny that. But why hadn't he written to her or called? He could have come back. But he hadn't. The ache started deep in her chest.

And here she was, risking that same kind of pain all over again.

Shouting yanked her from the troubling thoughts. Sizemore broke the tree line. He held something in his hand. Sadie felt the air rush from her lungs. She pushed off the truck and started forward.

Sizemore was leading Dare Devil.

Sadie rushed to the old horse and gave him a hug. He neighed and snorted as she quickly checked him over. Not a scratch. Her heart felt so big in her chest she couldn't possibly draw in a breath. Apparently, she had wrongly accused Gus and he had been right. That poor old man had taken her horse.

But she had him back now.

Her joy deflated as the coroner took poor old Mr. Carroll away all zipped up in a body bag.

The urge to cry came suddenly. Had that old man killed himself because he'd stolen a Gilmore horse and he didn't know how to make it right?

When had her world turned into this hurtful, scary place?

She felt like Alice after having fallen down the rabbit hole.

How did she climb out?

Her attention settled on Lyle. He was watching her. In that moment, she somehow fully understood that he was her only way out. But the path he offered would change her world again…and nothing would ever be the same.

SADIE HAULED A BUCKET of feed and water to Dare Devil's stall. She rubbed his forehead. "Glad you're home, old boy."

He ate as if he hadn't seen a bucket of feed since he was stolen. She wanted to be angry about that, but it was hard to be mad at a dead man.

Lyle joined her, gave Dare Devil a scratch behind the ears. "Gus wants us to stay at his place until we figure something out."

Sadie shot him an are-you-out-of-your-mind look. Felt bad for being obstinate, considering the small bandage covering the stitches on the back of his head.

"No," he said, reading her look accurately, "I haven't lost my mind."

"Sounds like it." She had no interest in sharing air-space with Gus for an extended period. Besides, Dare Devil deserved a good rubdown. She could use one herself. That Lyle stood so close made her shiver at the idea of him giving her a slow, attentive rubdown.

"Be reasonable, Sadie," he complained. "Sleeping in the barn until your house is rebuilt is not exactly a reasonable expectation."

"The insurance agent said they would bring me a temporary home."

"When? In a few days? Gus has that huge house and there's only him. You can't tolerate being in his presence for a few days? I'm sure you could avoid him somehow in all that space."

Sadie faced him, made sure he was paying atten-tion. "If I take him up on his hospitality, he'll just use it against me later. I know him, Lyle. He doesn't give anything without expecting something back. I don't want to be obligated to him." She was on her own and she wanted it to stay that way.

Didn't she?

The man staring down at her made her second-guess that declaration. She had to stop doing that to herself. This was probably the worst time to even be toying with notions of their nonexistent relationship.

"What do you plan to do for basic facilities?"

She grinned. The problem had crossed her mind. "We'll go to the store and get toilet paper and hand sanitizer. There's water in here and the old outhouse still works."

He laughed. "You've got it all figured out."

"That's right." She planted her hands on her hips. "What? You all out of arguments against staying here?"

His face turned serious. "Someone burned your
house down last night, with you in it. Whoever it was
got the jump on me, which generally isn't an easy feat.
You almost died. I don't want to take any unnecessary
chances with your safety."

"But I have you to protect me," she argued, her in-
sides melting just looking at him and how flustered
he was with the whole situation. She suspected that he
would prefer staying in Gus's house to being here alone
with her. She had every intention of doing something
about that.

"Sadie." His gaze settled on her lips. "I lost a hunk
of my objectivity the moment I laid eyes on you that
first morning. I've been losing ground since. I don't
know if you can count on me the way you should be
able to."

Just like that, she was ready to take the risk to her
heart. Decision made, her arms went around his neck
and she tiptoed to reach his mouth. He let her kiss him
but he didn't kiss her back. So this was how it was
going to be. Fine. She had promised herself that she
would show him just how much of a woman she was
now. She never broke a promise. Leaning into him,
she deepened the kiss. He reacted. His arms wrapped
around her, held her tight against him. She lifted her
legs, closed them around his waist. *That felt good.*

He carried her to the stall where she'd tried to sleep
the night before last and dropped to his knees. Laying
her gently in the fresh hay, he smiled down at her,
slowly settled his weight atop hers. Her breath hitched
as heat filled her in a frantic rush. "I've waited a long
time to be with you like this," he murmured.

The ability to speak eluded her for a moment. She

covered by unbuttoning his shirt. Her fingers felt clumsy. She couldn't wait to touch his bare skin. "I've dreamed of how it would be." She licked her lips. "I wanted you to be my first. Then…" She stared at her shaking fingers, tried to make them work better. "When you left I thought my life was over."

He cupped her cheek, stroked it with his thumb. "Sadie, you're so beautiful, you probably had to keep the guys off with that old shotgun of yours."

She fought the tears. Damn it, she would not cry. Not now. She wanted this moment to be special. "Occasionally."

He swiped a tear with the pad of his thumb. "Please don't cry."

She inhaled a shaky breath. "I'm sorry. It's just…" She blinked to keep more of those stupid tears back. "I don't know how to do this, Lyle. And I want to so badly."

His face darkened with confusion. "Are you saying you've never done this…you…?"

She couldn't meet his eyes. Why did they have to have this conversation? She didn't want to talk. "After you left, there wasn't anyone I wanted."

The tension that stiffened his body wasn't what she'd hoped for. "Sadie, it shouldn't be like this." He shook his head. "Not here. Definitely not a snap decision made under stressful conditions."

Her determination rallied. "Don't tell me what I want or what I should do." She yanked his shirt free of the waist of his jeans. "Stop running your mouth, McCaleb, and show me how you do this."

His mouth closed over hers, and there was no more talk. He kissed her long and deep as her hands moved over his chest, learning every ripple of muscle. The excitement and heat roared inside her. Instinctively, her body started to move against his. He groaned deep in his throat and she smiled against his lips. Oh, how she wanted this man…wanted him to teach her how to make love.

He undressed her so slowly she thought she might die before he finished. She reached for his fly, but he pushed her hands away. "I'll be right back."

Her body quivered when he left her lying there naked on the hay. Where was he going? She heard him murmuring to the dogs. The barn doors opened then closed. Suddenly he was back.

"The dogs are keeping watch outside." Hopping on one leg, he tugged off one boot, then the other. "I wasn't sure they were ready for this."

Sadie laughed. "Good thinking."

She watched, mesmerized, as he stripped off his shirt and then his jeans. Her breath stalled as his boxer briefs slid down those muscled thighs. Her eyes rounded at the sight of his aroused body.

He stretched out next to her and she gasped as that thick muscle brushed her thigh. He leaned over her and kissed her lips before making his way down to her breasts. She cried out at the feel of his mouth on her like that. The sensations were so incredible, she floated away on that delicious cloud of mindless pleasure. He touched her down there…kept teasing her until she couldn't think, then he slid one finger inside. Her body bucked. Her fingers clutched at the familiar hay.

Stretching her until two fingers fit perfectly, he delved deeper, his thumb rubbing that special place fueling all those wild sensations. He kissed and licked his way down her torso, lavished his attention on the part of her that needed more. She had to touch him. Her fingers threaded into his hair, careful of the bandage. Those bad memories tried to intrude. As if he sensed her distraction, he sat back on his knees and lifted her bottom onto his thighs, her legs spread wide and rested on each side of him. One nudge and she moaned with the shock of their most intimate places finally touching.

He gripped her bottom with one hand and guided himself into her with the other, slowly, a fraction at a time.

Sadie wanted to watch but her eyes closed as all those swirling, swelling sensations somehow curled together in one unbelievable rush. He moved in and out, an inch in, an inch out. The stretching sensation made her want to scream for more. She tried to lift into him, to take in more, but he held her back.

"Patience, baby."

The sound of his voice drifted around her, joined all those other beautiful sensations and started to build. He eased in another inch. She cried out his name. His answer was to move a little faster now, in and out.

The swell burst and showered heat over her entire body. She writhed with the pleasure of it...wanted more. Desperate to find that place again, she hurried to get her body into rhythm with his. Moving, moving, as he pushed deeper and deeper. She wasn't sure how much more pleasure she could endure.

He brought his body down on hers, filled her so completely that she couldn't breathe...couldn't speak. She could only feel. That marvelous tide started to rise again. Higher and higher until she drowned in the pull of it. His movements grew more urgent. He groaned with the effort of satisfying his own building need, and she couldn't comprehend how he had held out so long.

She felt the contractions of his orgasm even as her own muscles started that clench-and-relax rhythm all over again, squeezing the last of his climax from him.

He fell onto the hay next to her, pulling her onto her side so that their bodies remained joined.

His fingers sifted through her hair. It had come loose and was all over the place. "You okay?"

She nodded. Not sure of her voice just yet.

"Sadie…"

The worry in his eyes terrified her.

"I…"

She covered his mouth with her own, pushed him onto his back and straddled his waist. She winced as she settled down fully on him, but she knew that small discomfort would quickly pass. "I—" she decided to finish his statement for him "—want to do that again."

Chapter Thirteen

3:00 p.m.

Lyle leaned against the fence and watched the horses graze in the pasture to prevent staring at her. She had finger combed her hair and was in the process of tying it back into that haphazard ponytail that was her trademark. He'd had to bite his tongue to prevent offering to do it for her. But that would only start something he wouldn't have the willpower to stop.

His body hardened at the memory of sinking deep inside her. The ache that accompanied the memories terrified him. All this time she had waited for him, had allowed no one else to touch her the way he had longed to seven years ago. He hadn't expected that. In his mind, she had always been just out of his reach. Now he felt as if she belonged to him.

That was a dangerous position, considering he was supposed to be here to protect her. How could he do that right when she overwhelmed his senses? Blinded him to everything else?

They had talked for hours before making love again. She felt lost. Told him that she trusted nothing and no one but him. Her admission terrified him all the more. Eventually they'd washed each other with the chilly water right from the hose. Those moments had been playful and intimate, strengthening the bond that already ruled him.

Their clothes still smelled of smoke and looked somewhat worse for the wear, but that hadn't dampened their spirits in the least. A drive into town for clothes was next on his agenda. Including a food run. He was starved. She hadn't mentioned food, but she had to be famished.

When all that was done, somehow he intended to persuade her to stay at Gus's tonight. With the security at the Rocking Horse Ranch, she would be much safer. Staying here would be asking for trouble. Especially with him so far off his game.

No time like the present to approach the subject. "I was thinking—"

"I'm not changing my mind about Gus's offer."

She'd cut him off before he'd started. "Sadie, be reasonable. The security is impenetrable. Safety has to be our top priority. Dare Devil is back and that threat isn't likely to be repeated."

Frustration lined her brow as she glared at him with an unrelenting determination. "Not happening, so let it go. I'm not going to put myself at his mercy. Not today. Not tomorrow. Not any day."

Well, damn. "You are one hardheaded woman, Sadie Adele."

"That's what they tell me." She slipped between the fence rails and loped out to frolic with the horses.

What the hell was he going to do with the woman? She refused to listen to reason. He could hog-tie her and take the decision out of her hands. Then Gus would jump him the way he had Sizemore for making a stupid comment.

There was no way to win here.

His cell vibrated. He dragged it from his pocket and checked the screen. Not a number he recognized. That could be good or bad. "McCaleb."

Two seconds into the conversation he understood the news wasn't good. Lyle pocketed his phone and wondered how to break this to Sadie. She didn't need any more pain and stress. He ducked under the top rail and joined her in the pasture. This was something he couldn't protect her from.

She studied his face as he approached and then frowned. "What?"

Apparently he'd completely lost his ability to conceal his feelings. "Gus was in an accident. He's at the hospital. He's pretty banged up, Sadie, but he's stable. They're going to keep him for a while just to make sure." He heaved a burdened breath. "He's asking for you."

The sun-warmed color had faded from her face as he'd spoken. "Take me to him."

HE TRIED TO REASSURE her on the way into town. She said nothing, just stared out at the passing landscape. How much was one woman supposed to take? He hadn't been able to protect her from the pain of any of this. Every aspect of the situation just kept escalating further and further out of control.

She was opening her door before the truck was in Park. He shut off the engine and rushed to catch up with her. The lobby was deserted except for the woman behind the information desk. Sadie stormed her position.

"Gus Gilmore," she announced. "Where is he?"

So much for decorum. "We got a call that he'd been in an accident," Lyle explained.

The woman checked her computer. "Third floor." She looked up and offered a sympathetic smile. "Room 311."

Sadie headed for the elevator.

"Thank you." Lyle gave the woman a nod and rushed to catch up with Sadie. The elevator doors closed as he slid inside. "You need to take a breath before you see him."

"I know what I need to do." Her hands were pushed deep into the pockets of her jeans, as if she were a kid about to enter the principal's office. "I don't know why you insist on telling me what to do." The elevator bumped to a stop and the doors slid open. "You're as bad as Gus."

Lyle let her remark roll off his back. She was protecting herself from yet another harsh reality that had invaded her life. She couldn't be soft and sweet right now. If she allowed that vulnerability, she would be shattered.

SADIE PUSHED THE DOOR inward and walked into the room. What the hell had the old man gotten himself into this time? He lay too still in the bed. His face was battered and swollen, the skin an angry red against the stark white canvas of the bed linens. Her knees betrayed her. Lyle served as her buoy and steadied her.

The heart monitor beeped the same slow, steady tempo as the one she remembered from her mother's hospital room and then her grandmother's. The wavy lines that accompanied the sound didn't seem nearly bright and strong enough, but she had no idea what that meant. An IV line dangled from a bag and attached to his arm. When there was nothing else to distract herself with she looked at him again. He wasn't the strong, mean man she fought with most every day. He was small and weak, and that scared her to death.

"Where'd you get your driver's license?" she asked as she moved to his bedside. "A Cracker Jack box?"

His lids fluttered open and he stared up at her, his eyes bloodshot and puffy. He made a grumbling sound meant to be a laugh. "I know for a fact that's where you got yours."

The air wouldn't fill her lungs and that damned stinging was back in her eyes. "What do you expect? Look who I had for a teacher." At first it had been a tractor, twisting and turning all around the fields. Then that damned old truck of her grandfather's, the same one she still drove. Gus had sworn she'd never make it through the driver's test driving that way.

Gus closed his eyes. "I guess you're right about that."

She braced her hands on the bed rail. "So what happened, old man? Whatever it was you look like you got the short end of the stick."

"I don't know." He blinked a few times then stared at the ceiling instead of meeting her gaze. "Some fool ran me off the road. Probably texting and driving. You young folks don't have a lick of sense."

"You break anything?" She didn't see any sign of a cast or sling.

"Few cracked ribs," he said nonchalantly. "Got

myself a concussion. They're keeping an eye on my spleen." He cleared his throat. "Nothing that won't heal or that I can't live without."

"That's good to hear." He was in a lot of pain, she could tell. That crazy shaking started deep in her bones.

He reached out to the railing, covered her hand with his. It felt cold and rough, but familiar and comforting. Those damned tears wouldn't stay back.

"I told them not to bring me here, that I'd be fine, but you know how they can be." He grunted another pained laugh. "They just want my money. I've got their number."

Sadie produced a smile and nodded. "Most people do."

He chuckled. "Yeah, I guess so."

No crying. She didn't dare say anything else. Her entire powers of concentration were necessary to keep her emotions beat back and to stay vertical.

"Get around here where I can see you, McCaleb."

Lyle did as he asked, standing beside Sadie. She was so damned glad he was here. There were so many questions to which she wanted to demand answers. How could she do that with Gus in this condition?

Gus fixed his attention on Lyle. "I know why you came here."

"We don't have to talk about that now, Mr. Gilmore. You need to save your strength. Focus on recovering."

"To hell you say. I've ignored the situation too long already."

A new wave of anticipation charged through Sadie. She wanted him to make her understand how all this happened—if it was true even though she knew it was. She held her tongue for fear of stopping him. She wanted him to make it all right, as he did when she skinned her knee as a little girl, long before her mother died.

"That woman, Clare Barker, called me the night she was released. Crazy bitch."

The impact of his announcement shook Sadie hard. It was true. Dear God. She had known. She had. But hearing it from her father somehow made it more real. She hadn't wanted it to be true.

"Said she was coming for her baby girl. I told her to go to hell. I had my men watching Sadie before you got here, McCaleb, so don't think you got the jump on me."

"Course not, Mr. Gilmore. I'm very much aware of how much you love your daughter. You made that very clear a long time ago."

"Yeah, well, that's another story for another time."

Sadie's brain couldn't keep up with the dozens of thoughts and memories and theories spiraling there. She didn't want to hear this. She had thought she did, but she had been wrong. Gus Gilmore taught her how to ride a horse and then a bike. How to drive…how to run a ranch. It didn't matter that he wasn't the man who contributed to her DNA, he was her father. Nothing would ever change that. Those hot, salty tears she'd been trying to hold back streamed down her cheeks, and she silently cursed herself for the weakness.

"It was your momma." Gus's full attention settled on Sadie then. "She got cancer a few years after we married and they had to take everything to save her." He made a face that said that loss was irrelevant to him. "I didn't care, as long as she was okay. I just didn't want to lose her. But the idea that she couldn't have children ate at her just like that damned cancer they cut out of her. There was nothing I could do to make her happy. She was just plain miserable. I wasn't always the perfect husband. I made mistakes. But I knew if I could just find a way to fix things for her, she would be happy. Nothing else in this world mattered to me."

"She never told me about the first cancer." Sadie hated the wobble in her voice. She wanted to be strong. This was all so confusing.

"It was a hard time for us both." Gus found that place on the ceiling again, avoiding eye contact. "We kept to ourselves, too broken to be social. The ranch became our refuge. We didn't have to see anybody, didn't have to talk about it. But I knew that wouldn't last forever. Eventually we'd have to deal with the issue."

Sadie tried her best to prepare for what came next. Lyle placed his hand at the small of her back. It was all she could do to keep from throwing herself against his chest and sobbing like a child.

"I talked to a friend of mine up in Austin. He was one of those fancy lawyers you know would do most anything for money." Gus fiddled with the sheet with his free hand and kept the other one clasped tightly over Sadie's. "I didn't care. I just wanted him to fix this for us. I told him what I needed and how much I'd pay. Six months later he called me and said he had a little girl who needed a home. He took care of all the paperwork and I gave him the cash."

"Mr. Gilmore," Lyle said quietly, "do you have any idea who was on the other side of that deal."

"My friend," Gus went on as if Lyle hadn't said a

word, "he'd made a reputation for himself in Austin. Folks knew who to go to without having to worry about it making the news or hitting the police's radar. He said the woman called him with three little girls who needed good homes. He wasn't a fool any more than I was. It was all over the news, the papers. We both knew where they'd come from, but neither one of us cared."

"Did you meet this woman?"

Sadie felt Lyle's tension mounting almost as fast as hers.

"I did not." He looked directly at Lyle then. "But her name was Janet or Janice, that I know for sure." He turned to Sadie, his eyes watery with emotion. "I knew you were sisters. I tried to get all three of you, but the lawyer said that was impossible. He wouldn't accept any offer I made. I figure he was trying to protect you from being discovered. Or maybe himself. The law was looking for three little girls, not one."

"Can you give me the attorney's name?" Lyle asked.

"Wouldn't matter. He died eight or ten years ago. I saw his obit in the newspaper. Fact is, I don't think he knew any more than I did. This Janet or Janice was smart. She wasn't about to get caught."

"You never heard from her or the attorney again?"

"Nope. Not after we picked up Sadie, along with a few baby photos." He chuckled softly. "She was the prettiest little thing in that fancy dress they stuck on her. She kept pulling at it, trying to get it off. I knew she was going to be a handful."

Gus turned to Sadie. She tried to smile but she had gone numb about two questions ago. She couldn't conceive the proper words to say.

"I'm sorry, little girl. I should have told you a long

time ago, but I couldn't bring myself to do it. After your mother died I was scared to death of losing you, too." Tears leaked from the corners of his eyes. In her whole life, she had never seen her father cry. "I guess I managed to do that anyway."

Pride and affection burst inside Sadie. "What're you talking about, old man? I'm here, aren't I? You think I don't have better things to do?" She leaned down and kissed his bruised cheek. "I love you, Daddy," she whispered. "I always have."

They cried together for a while. Sadie knew it was time to go. He needed his rest and this emotional exchange had taken a toll. She promised to be back soon. And Gus made Lyle vow that he would keep her safe or die trying. Lyle gave his word without hesitation. Sadie could have sworn his eyes looked a little watery, too.

Outside the room, Sizemore and Radley waited on opposite sides of her father's door. "Cox is looking for the two of you," Sizemore said with a sneer.

God, Sadie despised the man. "Good for him." Sizemore wasn't worth the energy required to get angry. Cox, either, for that matter.

Lyle kept his arm around her shoulder as they moved through the hospital. Sadie felt some sense of relief. A truckload of sadness. And determination. But relief to understand how this happened. This woman, Clare Barker, was not going to destroy her family. Whatever happened twenty-two years ago was way, way over now. Sadie was a Gilmore, and by God no one was going to change that.

Sadie leaned into Lyle. He and the Colby Agency would find a way to stop this insanity. She was safe with him.

They had reached the parking lot before running into the sheriff. He waited at Lyle's truck.

"Sadie." He nodded at her. To Lyle he said, "We have a little problem."

She rolled her eyes. What now?

"That vehicle that ran your daddy off the road was a truck," the sheriff informed them.

"Is that why you've been inspecting *my* truck?" Lyle asked pointedly.

Sheriff Cox nodded. "I also sent one of my deputies to take a look at your truck, Sadie."

All those painful emotions that had been tearing at her since she'd heard that Gus was in the hospital coalesced into one—outrage. "What the hell are you talking about?"

"Seeing how you and your daddy have been at odds for a good long while now and you've publicly threatened him several times, I would have been remiss not to follow that lead."

"Are you that inept, Cox," Lyle blasted him, "or just desperate for a big payoff from whoever put that crazy notion in your head?"

Cox got in Lyle's face. "I don't care who you work for, McCaleb, I will arrest you and then you can have all the time you want in jail to think of a way to get back in my good graces."

Sadie put her hand on Lyle's arm. "The sheriff's right. He's only doing his job."

Lyle didn't want to let it go so easily, but he backed off when Sadie sent another silent plea his way with her eyes. She had had enough and so had he.

"Your truck," Cox said to her, "has damage on the

driver's side consistent with the kind of ramming strategy that sent your daddy practically to his death."

"I haven't driven my truck in the last twenty-four hours, Sheriff Cox. If someone else did, then you'll just have to haul her in and find their fingerprints. But it wasn't me." She was proud of herself for remaining calm enough to make the statement in a reasonable tone.

"What time did the accident occur?" Lyle asked.

"'Bout two o'clock as best we can assess."

"Today?" Lyle persisted. "As in p.m.?"

Sadie stared at him in confusion. Why would he ask that? They had followed Gus in his truck to the Carroll place this morning before noon. The sheriff had been there, too, as a matter of fact. He knew it had to be p.m., probably while they were making love in the barn.

"You know that's what I mean," Cox fired back.

"That's what I thought." Lyle braced his hands on his hips. "And you're fully aware that Sadie's house burned down last night. You were there."

"That's right," Cox agreed. "If she thinks Gus had anything to do with that, the fire is just additional motive, not an alibi."

Sadie's cool started seeping from her grasp. How dare this knucklehead make such an accusation! Yes, she and Gus didn't get along the better part of the time, but that didn't mean she wanted to hurt him.

"Then why don't you tell me how she drove her truck when the keys went up in flames along with the rest of her stuff?"

Cox was dumbfounded for about three seconds. Long enough for Lyle to toss in, "If you'll read your deputy's report, I stated that when I was ambushed I was inspecting damage to the front driver's side of Sadie's truck. What're you going to call that? Premeditation?"

Cox hitched up his trousers. "I'll be looking into that."

"Good," Lyle groused.

Leaving the sheriff standing there staring after them, Sadie and Lyle loaded into his truck.

"That's what's wrong with this town," he growled as he started the engine, then backed out of the parking slot.

Sadie looked from him to Cox and back. His frustration planted a tiny seed of hope in her heart. "Oh, yeah?"

"Yeah." He drove away from the frustration. "You need a decent sheriff."

Her biological mother was out there somewhere trying to get to her daughters. The man who had been her father her whole life had almost been killed in an accident with which the sheriff thought she was involved. Even with all that going down, she leaned back in the seat and felt a sense of optimism for the first time in days. "I guess we do."

As foolish as hanging on to the idea that he might actually stay was, she needed something to cling to if she was going to get through this.

Chapter Fourteen

Polunsky Prison, 6:00 p.m.

Victoria waited as patiently as possible. Warden Prentice was not happy that she asked for this meeting. He asserted, and rightly so, that each time she was logged in as a visitor he ran the risk of a leak to the media. The press was already sniffing around with regard to the coming execution of the Princess Killer.

But this would not wait. Clare Barker had vanished. There had to be some aspect of her past that would provide a clue to where she would go or to the identity of this one-armed man who had facilitated her vanishing act.

There was no one else to ask. She had no other family and no friends that they were aware of. Whatever Barker could offer might prove useful. He was all they had.

The door opened and Barker was escorted inside by two guards. The usual precautions were taken once he was seated. This time he made eye contact with Victoria the instant he was settled at the interview table.

When the door had closed behind the guards, he asked, "You found my daughters?"

Any sympathy the man had garnered from her on that first visit was gone now. She had concrete reasons not to trust anything he told her. "Janet Tolliver is dead."

He nodded, his expression one of sadness. "I was told."

Anger stirred. Was that all he could say? Victoria restrained the urge to demand answers. "How did she know we were coming?"

The hint of anger that surfaced in her voice had Barker searching her face and eyes. "She would never have entrusted you with the information she had if I hadn't sent word to her."

"So this contact you have developed is so loyal that you don't question how your requests are carried out."

He shook his head, going on the defensive now. "I don't understand what you're getting at. Obviously, you received the evidence, which means Janet must have been alive after my contact passed along the message."

Victoria leaned forward, looked him square in the eyes. "Someone violently murdered her, Mr. Barker. Who else besides you knew she had that evidence?"

"No one."

"Not your connection?"

He shook his head. "Of course not. He only carried the message. *Expect someone from the Colby Agency.*"

Victoria narrowed her gaze and searched his as carefully as he had examined hers. "You don't seem upset that your friend died to protect your secret."

All emotion, even the guarded expression that had gone up as a defense mechanism, disappeared. "I appreciate what you're doing to protect my daughters. There is no way I can hope to repay you. But it feels as if you're accusing me of something, and I don't understand why. I've done nothing but try to ensure my daughters were protected."

The man was good, she would give him that. But not good enough. She had spent some time with the warden before this meeting. He had identified the one-armed man. A nurse in the infirmary, Tony Weeden, had provided medical care for Rafe Barker's allergy-related asthma condition for the past three years. Tony had lost his right arm in an accident as a young boy. His height and hair color matched those of the man who had whisked Clare Barker away. Not to mention the apartment next to hers had been rented under the name Toni Westen. Seemed a little coincidental now that they had the one-armed man's name, though he had not been seen going in or out of the apartment since Clare's arrival next door. He had facilitated her escape. The means had been planned for months.

"Mr. Barker, I warned you from the beginning that unless you were truthful with me, my agency could not help you." He had fallen well short of that single standard.

He shook his head. "I wish you would simply explain what it is you believe I've done."

Victoria tamped back the anger and impatience. "Clare Barker has vanished. Our surveillance ended abruptly after her apartment complex was destroyed by a fire that has been ruled as arson."

"She started this fire? Was anyone killed?"

"No lives were lost, thankfully. We don't believe she started the fire. There is reason to suspect her accomplice used the fire as a distraction to facilitate her getaway."

Barker sighed. Gave a little shrug. "I'm not surprised she has made friends to help her. She is as desperate as I am, only for different reasons."

"There's just one thing." Victoria watched closely in hopes of catching some small reaction besides this annoying nonchalance and indifference. "You seem to have at least one mutual friend."

"That's impossible." A spark of outrage appeared in his eyes.

Victoria nodded resolutely. "Your nurse at the infirmary. Tony Weeden. He was her accomplice. We have the two of them on video leaving the scene together."

"I don't believe you."

There it was. Shock. Disbelief. If Barker had any idea that Weeden and Clare were associates, he did an award-winning job of covering it up.

Victoria reached into the bag the guards had allowed her to bring into the room and removed the photo she'd had printed from a single frame of the video. She placed the glossy enlarged shot on the table. "You're saying that is not Tony Weeden."

Barker stared at the photograph for an extended period. It occurred to Victoria that this might be the first image he had seen of his wife in about twenty years. Would that prompt him to tell the truth, or would seeing her free with his friend fuel a rage that would end his cooperation?

"That is Tony." His tone was blank, low, almost a whisper.

"Then you see how I might suspect you're not being completely honest with me."

"I don't understand why he would do this." Barker

shook his head again. "I thought he was my friend. That he believed in my innocence."

"Does he have information that could prove detrimental to our investigation and how we protect your daughters?" The answer was essential to getting the job done.

"He knows very little. As you are aware, until I sent you that letter I rarely spoke to anyone, verbally or otherwise."

"But he knows something," she pressed.

"He knows I'm innocent and that the girls are alive. He passed the word to Janet that you were coming. That's all."

That was enough. "Is he capable of murder, in your opinion?"

He considered the question for a time. "I would say no, but obviously I am not a good judge of character. I believed he sincerely wanted to help me and was loyal to the cause."

"Is he the one who mailed the letter you sent me?"

"Yes. He read it and insisted on helping me." Rafe looked away as if attempting to regain his composure. "Why would he do this? Surely he understood there would be consequences."

"Only if we can find him."

"He works here every day. He never misses a day."

"He didn't show up for his shift today. He isn't answering his phone and his neighbors haven't seen him in two days. He's not coming back, Mr. Barker. And unless we can find the two of them, my investigators will have no choice but to work in a reactive state under the assumption that both Tony and Clare represent a threat to our clients."

Barker stared at her, blinked.

"Do you understand what that means, Mr. Barker?"

He blinked a second time.

"Shoot to kill, Mr. Barker, that's what it means."

Barker was taken from the interview room five minutes later without having uttered another word.

He knew something or was planning something. Victoria felt it in the most basic minerals of her bones. Either way, the stakes were upped.

These women were in extreme danger. The Colby Agency would do whatever necessary to protect them.

Chapter Fifteen

Second Chance Ranch, 8:30 p.m.

Sheriff Cox ordered two of his deputies and a tow truck to take Sadie's truck away. Not one word Lyle said to the guy had penetrated that thick skull of his. He just kept repeating that same mantra. *I have a job to do.* The strangest part was the idea that Gus would not want him to do this.

Since when did Cox ignore the desires of Gus Gilmore? He'd lived comfortably in the man's hip pocket for decades now. Didn't make a whole lot of sense. It also didn't make him the kind of bad guy who would go to these extremes.

After the deputies had gone, Sadie stood there in the moonlight staring at the charred rubble that had been her home. He wished there was more he could do or say. The promise that this would pass in time just wasn't enough.

Lyle strode over to where she stood. "The horses are tucked in for the night. So are the dogs. Can I convince you to go to a hotel with me?" Sounded like a bad pickup line.

"I don't know about leaving them."

Her hesitation was understandable. "How about a nice, relaxing dinner before we hit the hay then?"

She smiled.

He tucked a strand of hair behind her ear. "That's what I like to see." His chest tightened with the need to hold her and promise her anything she wanted to hear.

"You think he'll be okay?"

Her father's condition was part of the burden weighing down those slender shoulders. Lyle wrapped his arm around her and pulled her close, urged her to lean on him. "The doctor said he's doing fine. He'll be home tomorrow. You'll see."

She shuddered with the release of a heavy breath. "He looked so old and fragile in that bed."

"He's tough," Lyle assured her. "A lot tougher than the truck he was driving." According to the sheriff the truck was totaled. Whoever ran him off the road knew exactly where to strike. Gus never saw the other vehicle. He was making that left turn and suddenly he had overshot the turn and was barreling into the ravine.

It was a flat-out miracle he survived. If Sadie were herself, she'd swear he was too mean to die.

But she wasn't herself by a long shot. If he were in her shoes, Lyle couldn't say he would fare any better.

"Okay." She turned to him, tilted that pretty face up to his. "How about that dinner?"

He pressed a kiss to her forehead and guided her to his truck. The sooner he had her out of here, the happier he would be. After Victoria's report on her last meeting with Rafe Barker, Lyle had a bad feeling that the situation was about to deteriorate fast.

SADIE WASN'T HUNGRY but Lyle had insisted she order. She played with the straw in her water glass, wished it was a beer. Thing was, she rarely drank beer or wine, not since her teenage days anyway. But right now seemed like a good time for one or two. Too much was going on to allow her senses to be dulled. The hospital could call. She'd spoken to Gus a couple of hours ago, but that didn't keep her from worrying. Her father had always been strong, immortal almost.

"Penny for your thoughts."

Somehow she pushed a smile into place for her dinner companion and bodyguard. He deserved all the smiles she could summon. If he hadn't been here…

"I was thinking about Gus. At my mother's funeral he was so solemn and hard looking. He didn't cry. Shook hands and chatted with his friends." Sadie let those memories she usually repressed play out in her mind. "I hated him for that. Then when his own mother died…he was the same way. Like it didn't matter. Just business as usual."

"You were young, Sadie. It's difficult to understand the way some handle emotion."

"I spent most of my life thinking he didn't love me, he loved *controlling* me."

"You're a lot like him."

Sadie didn't know what to make of that. She shook her head. "Seriously, you're kidding, right?"

He laughed that rumbling sound that made her shiver. She'd forgotten how sexy his laugh was. They'd certainly had nothing much to laugh about since he came back.

"Well, let's see." He leaned his elbows on the table and ticked off the similarities on his fingers. "You're both as stubborn as hell. Refuse to give an inch in battle. And you both love your horses."

She waved her hands in his face. "Wait, wait, wait. He doesn't love those animals the way I do." No way. Her father was too driven. He expected the animals to be just as driven, no matter how old and worn out they were.

"Think about it, Sadie. Have you ever actually seen him mistreat an animal?" Before she could argue, he added, "I mean the way some of the other rodeo kings do?"

Well, he had her there. "I guess not."

Lyle raised his hands in the air as if he'd just gone way over the necessary eight seconds. "It's a miracle. You admitted you might be wrong."

She laughed, couldn't help herself.

"Gus just has different expectations and standards. That's all. The same way he had expectations for you."

Sadie flatted her hands on the table and stared at the finger that still had no ring. Yeah, she was young, but she'd been in love with the same guy for her whole adult life. Didn't that count? "He made you leave."

Lyle placed his hands over hers. "He suggested I leave. I left because it was the right thing to do at the time."

She lifted her gaze to his. "You wanted to go?" Of course he had. Just because they'd made love this morning didn't mean he loved her...that he'd ever loved her.

"You were fifteen," he reminded her as if she could have forgotten. "You had a right to be who you were going to be without me taking that away from you before you were old enough to have a clue."

She pulled her hands free of his and leaned as far back in the booth as the padded fake leather uphol-

stery would allow. The disappointment in his blues
eyes almost stopped her from saying what she needed
to say. "I kept thinking you'd call or come back to get
me." The admission hurt even now, seven years later.

"I did call." He held her gaze, didn't cut her any
slack. "On your eighteenth birthday. You were in
Cancún or some place. I left a message. Sent you a
card."

He called. Sent her a card? "I didn't know." She
shook her head. If her daddy wasn't half-dead, she'd
kill him. "Gus told me you'd moved to California and
had a wife."

Lyle scrubbed a hand over his unshaved jaw. At least
something good came of the fire. He hadn't been able
to shave. Inside, she quivered at the remembered feel
of that stubbled jaw caressing her skin.

"Well, I did spend a little time in California, but
there was no woman."

"But you've had girlfriends." Sadie wanted to slither
under the table. How could she have said that?

He shrugged. "No girlfriend really. A few dates." He
hesitated a moment. "If you're asking me if I've been
celibate this whole time, the answer is no."

That hurt. She couldn't pretend otherwise.

"If what you want to know," he offered, "is if I have
ever wanted anyone the way I wanted you, that answer
is no, as well."

Her heart launched into a crazy staccato. "You said
wanted, as in past tense."

The sweetest, sexiest smile she had ever seen broke
across his lips. "You didn't feel my answer to that this
morning?"

Heat rushed across her cheeks. "You made your point."

He leaned close. "If that waitress ever brings our food, I'm thinking we should go to Gus's house and try out that cute canopy bed you told me you had in your room."

Donning a properly affronted face, she declared, "You cad."

Their waitress arrived before he could defend himself. When she arranged their entrées on the table and hurried away, Sadie leaned toward him and whispered, "You take me back to the barn for a few hours and I promise we'll spend the rest of the night at the mansion."

He licked his lips, whether from her offer or from the heavenly aroma of the food steaming between them she couldn't say. As if he'd read her mind, he said, "Deal."

"I THOUGHT YOU SAID you weren't really hungry," Lyle teased as he drove along her driveway, the headlamps highlighting the massive pile of rubble that had been her home.

Sadie flattened her hand on her tummy. "I think I might die. You shouldn't have let me eat so much."

"Hey. I was just glad you left the plate."

"Funny."

She was out of the truck by the time he'd grabbed his weapon and the take-home bag from the restaurant and rounded the hood. She closed the door and leaned against it. "I'm not sure I can move."

Lyle swept her into his arms and started for the barn. "Don't worry, I'll do all the moving."

She banged on his chest. "You are not funny."

He sat her down long enough to open the barn doors and turn on the light. The dogs jumped around in a little dance accompanied by their yapping.

He turned back to Sadie. "One moment."

She made a face. "Hurry up!"

Grabbing a blanket, he hustled to that last stall. After fluffing the hay, he spread the blanket over it and tried to slow the need building to a frenzy inside him. He wanted this time to be slow and awesome. This morning he hadn't been able to hold out as long as he'd hoped to. He tucked his weapon beneath the hay. No need to remind her of the troubles still hanging over their heads.

The horses shuffled around in their stalls as he dashed back to the front of the barn. "Ready."

She strolled past him. Lyle herded the dogs outside and gave them the treat he'd brought from the restaurant. With them occupied, he closed the barn doors and hurried back to where Sadie waited.

He came to an abrupt stop. She had shed her boots and clothes, everything but those cute little pink panties and the matching bra she'd bought while they were in town today.

"Wow." She was way ahead of him...but he was catching up entirely too fast.

She crooked her finger at him. "Come on, cowboy. Let's see what you've got."

The boots came off first. Sadie taunted him into making a show of the rest. He opened his fly and lowered the zipper really slowly. She urged him on, and he refused to disappoint her. By the time he was on the blanket with her, he was more than ready.

Using all the restraint he could muster, he made love to her the way she deserved. He showed her with his every kiss how very much he cared, how much he had missed her and all that he hoped for in the future.

Their future.

She showed him that she was no little girl anymore. She was all woman and she wanted him to acknowledge that. He did his best to do just that. He took great pleasure in acknowledging every womanly part of her over and over again.

Rocking Horse Ranch, May 24, 1:00 a.m.

"THIS IS STRANGE." Sadie leaned forward. "Where is everyone?" The house was darker than the night, not a single light on inside. Even the outside lights were off. Couldn't be a power outage. Gus had a whole-house generator.

"Should we check the bunkhouse? Sizemore and his playmates should be around somewhere."

"Good idea." Sadie didn't like this. With Gus in the hospital, Sizemore was supposed to be in charge. Looked as if he had fallen down on the job.

Lyle drove to the bunkhouse. No lights there, either. He handed her his cell. "Stay here. Lock the doors. Anything happens, get down and call 911."

Sadie hit the lock button as soon as he was out of the vehicle. This was too weird. Something was really wrong. She entered the number on her cell for the hospital and got the nurse's desk on her father's floor. He was sleeping comfortably. Sadie hugged herself, the phone in hand, and tried to see any movement around the bunkhouse. Lyle had gone inside already. The headlights split the night, their beam spreading wide on each side of the truck.

Lyle exited the bunkhouse and started back to the truck. She hit the unlock button so he could open the door. "Did you talk to anyone?"

He slid behind the wheel and shifted into Drive. He met her expectant gaze then. "There's no one in the bunkhouse."

Fear infused her blood. "Maybe...maybe they're in town partying since the boss is out of commission."

"Maybe."

Lyle drove back to the house. Her nerves jangled when he hit the brakes next to the dark house. This was just creepy.

"I need to go in there," he said, "but I don't know about taking you inside, and I can't leave you out here."

Sadie had grown up in this house. She knew the place. There was probably a perfectly reasonable explanation for all of this. Sizemore was likely exercising his newly found power.

"I'm calling Cox." Lyle reached for his phone.

"Let's just go in." They were making too much of this. She reached for her door.

Lyle grabbed her other hand. "Listen to me, Sadie."

The urgency in his voice had that trickle of fear breaking into a raging river.

"You stay behind me. Don't make a sound." He gave the phone back to her. "If we run into trouble, you run, hide, whichever is handiest, and you call for help."

"Okay."

He was out before her. He closed his door silently, so she did the same. Her heart was thumping wildly. Lyle moved up the steps, she followed. She hoped Gus hadn't changed his security code. Otherwise Sheriff Cox would have another reason to suspect Sadie of criminal activity.

Lyle had her stand to one side while he opened the door. It wasn't locked and the security system's warning remained silent. Another wave of intense fear rushed through her veins. She should have let him call the sheriff.

The house was eerily quiet. Lyle closed the door behind her and stopped her when she reached for the light. He clicked on the flashlight she hadn't realized he'd grabbed from the truck. The beam flowed over the shiny marble floor of the massive entry hall. They moved from room to room, Sadie right behind him, clutching the back of his shirt.

When they reached Gus's study, Sadie gasped. The room had been torn apart. "Oh, my God."

"Don't touch anything, Sadie."

She pressed her fist to her lips and bit down to hold back the hysteria. What happened here? A robbery? That didn't explain the absence of all the ranch hands.

Would Clare Barker do this? "Could it be *her?*"

Lyle moved back into the hall. "I don't know, but we're not taking any chances." He reached for the phone. "I'm calling Cox."

"No need to call the sheriff."

Sadie almost jumped out of her skin. She turned toward the voice. Billy Sizemore. She blinked and stared again at his image in the flashlight's beam. He had a gun…*pointed at them.*

"He's on his way," Billy announced. "But he'll be too late to do you two any good."

Lyle moved in front of Sadie. "What's this about, Sizemore?"

"It's about proving to Gus Gilmore that I'm the only heir he needs."

"What?" Sadie tried to move around Lyle, but he held her back. "Have you lost your mind?"

"Oh," Sizemore said with a cruel smirk, "I guess you didn't know he's my daddy. My *real* daddy. Seems like there's a lot he forgot to tell you about."

I wasn't always the perfect husband. Sadie felt light-headed. *No.* She had to keep it together. No way was she going to let this cocky SOB get away with this.

"You've been blackmailing him."

Sadie turned to Lyle. Was he guessing? Did he know something about this?

Sizemore laughed. "I didn't have to blackmail him." His expression darkened. "At least not at first. He said I was the best bronc rider he'd ever seen." Fury tightened his voice. "But that wasn't enough when I told him that little affair he had while his wife was sick was no longer in his past. He didn't like it. Seemed he already had one secret too many."

Sadie tried to push past Lyle, but again he held her back. She shouted over his shoulder, "So you tried to kill him and make it look like I did it? You bastard!"

"The whole town knows you two do nothing but fight. When they find out I caught you breaking into the house, they won't be surprised. It was dark, I didn't know it was you when I fired my weapon. Your boy-friend here fired the first shot, started a domino effect, so to speak."

"You got it all figured out," Lyle said quietly. "Stole Dare Devil to get Sadie fired up."

"Worked, didn't it? She came over here waving that shotgun of hers around."

"Too bad you had to kill old man Carroll to keep him quiet."

Lyle's suggestion sent Sadie's breath rushing from her lungs. "How could you kill a helpless old man like that?"

Sizemore laughed. "He was dead anyway. Cirrhosis."

"Guess your plan worked," Lyle offered.

"Like a charm," Sizemore bragged.

Lyle shoved Sadie to the floor.

Shots fired, the sound echoing off the walls.

The flashlight hit the floor and the beam bounced around the room.

For two seconds Sadie couldn't move. Where was Lyle? Why was it so quiet? She started to get up. A second round of shots shattered the silence. She scooted deeper into the doorway of her father's study.

Someone groaned.

Lyle? She wanted to call out to him...but what if he was down...

The chandelier came on. Light glittered across the shiny marble.

She blinked to force her eyes to focus. Lyle stood over Sizemore, the muzzle of his weapon shoved into the bastard's skull. "Slide your weapon across the floor, Sizemore."

He hesitated but then did as he was told.

That was when Sadie saw the blood splattered on

the marble. Sizemore had caught a bullet in his right leg. Blood soaked into the denim.

Sadie scrambled to her feet, ignoring the ongoing conversation between Lyle and that idiot on the floor. She stared at the splatters. Visually traced the trail. Lyle's free hand was pressed against his side. Blood seeped around and between his fingers.

Oh, God.

She rushed to his side. "You're bleeding."

He flashed a weak smile. "It's not as bad as it looks."

"Where's the phone?" She spotted it near where he'd first shoved her out of danger's path. Almost falling in her haste, she snatched up the phone and entered 911.

Blue lights flashed outside. How? She was confused. Wait, Sizemore had said the sheriff was on his way. The dispatcher came on the line. Sadie pleaded for an ambulance to be sent right away. The dispatcher assured her that one was on the way. Since Sheriff Cox had arrived it wasn't necessary for her to remain on the line.

The sheriff cuffed Sizemore and his deputies took control of all the weapons, including Lyle's. Sadie felt helpless, frantic and exhausted all at the same time. Lyle just kept explaining what happened to the sheriff while his shirt soaked up the blood seeping from his wound.

By the time the ambulance arrived she felt near cardiac arrest. Lyle refused to get in the ambulance unless Sadie could ride in the back with him.

When the doors closed and they were on their way with a paramedic seeing to his wound, she fell apart.

She hated the weakness. But she was entitled. Her world had already fallen apart.

4:00 a.m.

SIMON RUHL HAD ARRIVED to take up Lyle's slack since he was injured and the extent of treatment was not known when Lyle made the call en route to the hospital. At the hospital, Sadie refused to leave his side. The bullet had made a clean exit and surgery wasn't required. Just some cleanup work and closure.

Gus had appeared, much to the dismay of the nurses on the third floor since he had no business being out of bed. Between Gus, the sheriff and what Sizemore had told Lyle and Sadie, they had his story whether he officially confessed or not.

The sheriff had taken Sadie's truck in because both he and Gus suspected Sizemore was behind his accident as well as Dare Devil's abduction.

Sizemore had overheard Gus's conversation with Clare Barker, so he had known what was going down with Sadie. But so far he had not admitted to burning down the house or leaving the message on Sadie's door.

Gus, clad in his boots and a hospital gown, stood at the end of Lyle's bed looking far more like hell than Lyle. Sadie stood at Lyle's bedside, his hand clutched in hers.

Funny, in a million years he would never have imagined this scene. Lyle had to laugh.

Gus glared at him. "Boy, I don't know what you've got to laugh about, so I'm going to assume they're giving you better drugs than they're giving me."

Sadie laughed then, too. Once she started, she didn't seem to be able to stop. The hysteria proved contagious. Gus Gilmore laughed so hard he had to hold his damaged ribs.

When they had caught their collective breath, Gus shuffled over to Sadie and kissed her on the cheek. "I gotta get back to my room."

She smiled and gave him a nod.

Lyle had already seen the turning point. These two were going to be okay.

"Gus," she called out to him before he got out the door. He turned back to her and raised his eyebrows in expectation. "I love you."

"Course you do. And I love you."

The door swished closed behind him and Sadie swiped the tears from her eyes.

Lyle knew it was his turn. He hoped he fared as well as the old man. "I'll be out of here in a few hours."

Sadie nodded. "You were lucky." Her lips trembled. "You protected me and you got shot."

"I had to protect you." He squeezed her hand. "I couldn't let him hurt you."

"I know. It's your job."

"Sadie." He waited until she met his gaze. "Yes, it's my job. Until this Barker situation is resolved, I'll be at your side every moment and I will make protecting you my top priority."

Disappointment flashed in her eyes.

"And when it's over, I'll still be here."

Tears slid down her cheeks, but the disappointment was gone. "You sure about that?"

"I have never been more sure of anything in my life." He pulled her down to him and gave her a kiss. "I love you, Sadie. I have since the first time I laid eyes on you."

She climbed in the bed on his good side and stretched out next to him. "Good," she said finally.

"Because I really didn't want to have to borrow one of Gus's shotguns."

Lyle kissed her forehead. "Does that mean you still love me, or do you just plan to keep me around to help you rebuild your house?"

"I haven't decided yet."

He frowned. Started to ask what that meant, but she turned his face to hers and smiled. "About rebuilding the house," she explained. She caressed his jaw and peered deeply into his eyes. "My life is a real mess right now, Lyle McCaleb, but the one thing that is crystal clear is how much I love you."

That was all he needed to hear. The rest they would figure out as they went.

So far it appeared they were in for a rough ride, but they were both prepared to hang on tight.

Chapter Sixteen

Victoria stared out the conference room window that overlooked Houston's unmistakable skyline. It wasn't Chicago, but it was beautiful nonetheless. She had spoken to Jim earlier today. Things were going well at the Chicago offices. Tasha and the children were anxious to see Victoria and Lucas as soon as they returned.

The transition here in Houston had gone very smoothly. Except for this case.

She turned and walked to the table that served as her desk. Clare Barker remained off their radar. Rafe had not come forward to give any additional information. Victoria couldn't determine whether he was shocked by his friend's betrayal or whether he had received the confirmation he needed and had nothing further to add.

They had found no other connection between Tony Weeden and the Barkers.

Victoria lowered into the chair and opened the file once more. She had pored over the information repeatedly and found nothing useful. And yet she had to be missing something.

Something that made the circle complete.

Rafe Barker had twenty-five days to live. How could they possibly hope to unravel this immensely complicated puzzle in that short time?

Perhaps she wasn't supposed to. The concept had crossed her mind that Rafe had attempted to use her agency to point his wife in the right direction. But that made no sense since Janet Tolliver was the one who knew the whereabouts of the daughters and Rafe had provided that contact.

What were they missing?

"It's time to call it a day, my dear."

The sound of Lucas's voice brought a smile to her lips. He was back! She stood and hugged him. "I'm so glad you're here."

He drew back and smiled for her. Victoria loved his smile. "Ah, but that's only because I lost our mark."

Victoria took his face in her hands and kissed him. "There was no way we could have known she had an accomplice who had set up that arrangement in advance of her release." Much had been revealed since the fire at the apartment complex.

Lucas ushered her into a chair before taking the one next to her. "The complex manager admitted that Weeden had made the arrangements months ago under the name Toni Westen. He leased one apartment with the guarantee that the other would be available for his friend. He gave the manager a hefty bonus."

Victoria doubted the manager would have confessed if not for the fire that had been traced back to Weeden's apartment. He had arrogantly left some of the materials he had used to stage the fire the way he wanted.

The police were searching for him and Clare Barker in connection to the fire.

"The entire sequence of events," Lucas shook his head, "was carefully planned and executed. Clare Barker knew she would be watched after her release."

Victoria didn't understand that part. "It's almost as if she knew exactly what Rafe would do when she was released."

Lucas gave a nod of agreement. "We may be the puppets and he may very well be the puppet master."

That was the part that worried her the most. "Oh, Lyle was released from the hospital. He's fine and insists he can continue providing protection for Sadie until this is resolved."

Lucas lifted a skeptical eyebrow. "From what Simon tells me, we may be losing him."

"I'm certain that's the case." The thought made Victoria smile, no matter that she hated to lose a fine investigator like Lyle.

"What we do for love."

Victoria mentally paused. "Do we have a love triangle here?"

"Are we talking about Lyle and Sadie or someone else?"

Victoria arranged the relevant photos on the conference table. "We have Rafe and Clare Barker. Tony Weeden and Janet Tolliver. Have Rafe and Clare planned this bizarre reunion all along? Or was it Clare and Tony? Tony and Janet? Or Janet and Rafe?"

"We found no evidence that Janet had ever worked for the prison system or had any contact whatsoever with Rafe or Clare since their arrests. Or before actually, other than the fact that Clare and Janet were separated as children."

"Weeden has never worked at Mountain View prison, where Clare was housed."

"Yet," Lucas countered, "there is a connection between Weeden and Clare. Obviously."

"Obviously," Victoria agreed as she surveyed the photos once more. "What does a thirty-three-year-old man have in common with a fifty-six-year-old woman?"

"Well, we can rule out money. The Barkers scraped by before their arrests. There is no hidden savings."

"The house was sold for unpaid taxes."

Lucas gathered up the photos and placed them in the file then closed it. "Our options are limited. We keep an eye out for Clare to surface again and we protect her daughters. That's basically all we can do other than keep digging."

"The other two are much more complicated situations." Victoria worried about Laney Seagers in particular. Life had not been easy on her. She trusted no one and there was a child involved.

"I'm confident the investigators chosen will be able to handle their assigned cases."

Victoria was, as well, for the most part. But the best investigator could not control the actions of an uncooperative principal.

"If Weeden had anything to do with the fire at Sadie's home and the warning message left for her," Lucas reminded her, "then Rafe Barker's assertions may prove true."

Billy Sizemore adamantly denied any involvement with those two malicious acts. But he was about as trustworthy as a snake lying in wait in the grass.

Victoria folded her arms over the case file so she wouldn't be tempted to look at it again.

"You're tired," Lucas suggested.

"I am." She gazed into her husband's wise gray eyes. "I keep asking myself what we're doing here."

He smiled. "We're finishing something we started."

"Perhaps I shouldn't have started this case, Lucas." She was tired. So very tired. They had made the decision to retire. To have a home in Texas as well as Chicago and travel back and forth at their leisure.

Yet, here they were deeply embroiled in perhaps one of the most complicated and heinous cases she had ever taken on.

How long would they be able to keep the media from intruding? The fire had already gotten Clare Barker a mention in the local news.

"My dear." He clasped her hands in his. "Your heart has always been your guide. Retirement will not change that. I don't want anything about you to change."

She lifted his hands and kissed each one. "We'll finish this together and then we'll take a nice long vacation."

"Promises, promises." He brushed a kiss against her lips.

A rap on the door interrupted their little moment. Simon visibly struggled with suppressing a smile. "I hope I'm not interrupting anything that won't wait."

Victoria stood. "Not at all. We were just discussing dinner."

Lucas stood, as well. "Perhaps you and Jolie would like to join us."

"Actually," Simon offered, looking and sounding a bit sheepish, "that's why I'm here. Jolie reminded me that I was supposed to invite you two to our house for dinner as soon as you were both here and available."

Victoria and Lucas exchanged a look. "We're free," Victoria said, "if you're certain this is not too short of a notice for Jolie."

Simon shook his head. "Trust me. She will be prepared. Since our move to Houston she has decided to stay home. She prepares at minimum a three-course meal each evening."

Lucas chuckled. "Sounds like you may need a raise, Ruhl."

Simon smiled. "That's the other thing. She has recently joined the extreme couponing movement. We now have stockpiles." He adjusted his tie. "It's quite unsettling."

They closed up the office and strolled across the parking lot. Victoria was glad to be out for the evening. She had spent far too much time cooped up with the case file of monsters.

She hooked an arm around the arm of each man. But there was no need to worry. The Colby Agency never failed a client. It wasn't going to start now.

At the car she glanced over her shoulder. She frowned. Strange. She had the oddest feeling that she was being watched.

This case was getting to her.
Tomorrow would be a better day.
It always was.

* * * * *

She twisted around to take a look at the person who was going to accompany her on this assignment.

The pressure in the room changed, condensed. The man was six feet of raw energy in a tightly muscled package…clipped to his belt was the gold NCIS badge. The telltale bulge on the other side of him indicated that he was carrying a sidearm. His thick black hair covered his forehead, errant tendrils curling along the nape of his neck.

Sia gasped as she looked into steady, beautiful dark gray eyes, eyes that had gazed into hers full of a smoky passion that only made them darken.

Oh, damn.

Chris Vargas.

Her brother's wingman.

The very pilot who had been directly responsible for her brother's death.

Dear Reader,

Sexy NCIS agents, tough JAG lawyers, rogue navy SEALs, courageous marines—a mix of navy and civilians investigating murder, espionage and crime across a global landscape. These are the characters that will be the fodder for my new series for Intrigue, TO PROTECT AND SERVE!

At His Command throws together former lovers Chris and Sia. He was her brother's wingman and a cocky up-and-coming navy pilot until he made a mistake and crashed into his wingman's fighter jet, killing him. Now, six years later, as a JAG lawyer, Sia is ordered to work with an NCIS agent who turns out to be Chris. They must investigate the death of a high-profile pilot on Chris's former post—the aircraft carrier USS *James McCloud*. He must face not only the memories of that fateful day, but the woman who was as affected by the tragedy as he—one she hasn't recovered from. As they try to track down a killer in uniform, will they be able to overcome their painful past and find a future together?

I look forward to creating more great characters in my upcoming novels for the TO PROTECT AND SERVE miniseries. In the meantime, buckle up and hold on while I kick in the afterburners for a wild ride in *At His Command*.

Best,

Karen

AT HIS COMMAND

BY
KAREN ANDERS

First published in Great Britain 2012
by Mills & Boon, an imprint of Harlequin (UK) Limited,
Eton House, 18-24 Paradise Road, Richmond, Surrey TW9 1SR

© Karen Alarie 2012

ISBN: 978 0 263 89565 0
ebook ISBN: 978 1 408 97251 9

46-1012

Harlequin (UK) policy is to use papers that are natural, renewable and recyclable products and made from wood grown in sustainable forests. The logging and manufacturing processes conform to the legal environmental regulations of the country of origin.

Printed and bound in Spain
by Blackprint CPI, Barcelona

Karen Anders is a three-time National Readers' Choice Award finalist and *RT Book Reviews* Reviewers' Choice finalist, and has won a prestigious Holt Medallion. Two of her novels made the Waldenbooks bestseller list in 2003. Published since 1997, she currently writes Intrigue for Mills & Boon®.

To Kero, for real friendship
and for helping me kill virtual monsters.

Chapter 1

"Aren't you Rafael Soto's sister?"

Sia bristled. She *had* been his sister, but now she was Lieutenant Commander Ambrosia Soto, U.S. Navy JAG. Most of her friends called her Sia, but she didn't think Master Chief Steven Walker was acting at all friendly toward her right now.

He was her number-one suspect in the death of a decorated F/A-18 pilot whose body had been recovered from the bottom of the Pacific, and the man had gone from helpful to belligerent as soon as he discovered who she was. A Navy JAG lawyer often had that effect on guilty people.

The tone of the man's voice said he wasn't a fan of her brother, but highly trained and aggressive fighter pilots were often considered elite jerks by the enlisted.

Ending up on an aircraft carrier in the Pacific was a common occurrence for a JAG officer. She'd been to

many places around the globe, handling all types of
legal issues and investigations. She took this assignment in stride. She had been on temporary assignment
duty, or TAD, investigating another case in San Diego
when she'd been ordered to handle this investigation
aboard the aircraft carrier *U.S.S. James McCloud*—
her brother's last billet. "You can address me as Commander Soto or ma'am."

"But you're his sister, right?"

"Master Chief, are you not getting my drift? I'm here
to ask the questions, not answer them." She flipped open
his file and glanced down. The picture and material
were all neatly maintained. She looked up at him and
narrowed her eyes. "This investigation is about Lieutenant Malcolm Saunders, who lost his life yesterday
when his F/A-18 Super Hornet plunged into the sea. It's
not social hour."

Her sharp words seemed to glance off him. "Yeah,
you'd know about fighter jet accidents, wouldn't you?"

She shot him a cold look and a smoldering fury
burned beneath her skin. She maintained eye contact
with his direct ones with a relentless stare, as if doing
so would give her an insight into his soul. She was re-
warded as he looked away, but before he did, she saw a
challenge and the unmistakable look of a liar. Her scalp
prickled and the hair on the back of her neck stood up.
She always got that feeling when someone was hiding
something. Almost like a sixth sense.

She picked up his folder and studied the man's service record, looking for any inconsistencies. "We both
know you didn't get to your rank by being uncooperative, Master Chief." At her statement, he sat up

straighter. "In fact, you have a spotless service record. The Navy is your life and you've given to it unconditionally."

For a moment, deep regret filled his eyes, but when he blinked they were once again neutral. "I have, sometimes to the detriment of all else."

"And the Navy has given back. You head up Maintenance Material Control."

"Yes."

"Maintenance is the heart of this carrier. Your division is responsible for repairing aircraft and related support equipment."

"Yes."

"One of the branches you oversee is the avionics division?"

"I do."

"Were there any problems with any part of the systems your people maintain?" She set the file down and closed it.

For a moment, the master chief sat in silence, but she could see something she said had caused him concern. But his next words were contrary to the worry he tried to hide. "No. That plane was in tip-top condition."

She lifted her brows and tilted her head. "Yet the pilot and the plane ended up at the bottom of the ocean. How do you explain that?"

"Pilot error."

Sia couldn't help it. She winced and the look on the master chief's face made Sia want to make him pay for his scored hit. "I've been assigned to investigate the reason a forty-million-dollar jet crashed into the ocean and killed the pilot. Lieutenant Saunders was in charge of flying the plane. You were in charge of maintaining the plane. Therefore, I'm asking you questions. I suggest you answer." The authority in her voice was unmistakable. The master chief's lips tightened at her tone.

"I know I'm responsible for the maintenance of the plane. But you have the logs—"

"And I'll inspect them thoroughly. Thank you, Master Chief."

He got to the door, opened it and stopped, his body language aggressive. His aftershave mixed with the unmistakable scent of the ocean and the metallic smell of the ship. A slight breeze ruffled the hair at her nape that had escaped her tight bun.

"Why aren't you looking at pilot error? Are you so sure the pilot didn't make a mistake?"

"I run a thorough investigation. I'll get to the truth of the accident." She rose and set her hands on the small table she'd been sitting behind. "My way."

"Maybe you have a mental block regarding pilot error, Commander Soto?" he said with a soft, accusing tone.

Something snapped in Sia. She was across the small compartment and in the master chief's face before she could stop herself.

"It's no secret what happened with my brother, and it's no secret regarding my insistence for a reopening of the investigation into the incident. I will not have you impugning my integrity. If you do so again, I'll bring you up on charges. Is that clear?"

"Yes, ma'am," he said, his anger barely banked.

"You are dismissed."

Sia had been in the JAG Corps long enough to understand respect was due an officer and some of the good ol' boys left over from the old system didn't take very well to a woman in command. But with the master chief, Sia was sure he had more to hide than his distaste for women in uniform. She had only to prove it.

Maybe you have a mental block...

The master chief's words made her angry all over again. Sia trusted in her brother's abilities as a pilot. When the JAG who'd investigated her brother's F/A-18 accident cited pilot error, Sia had protested loudly. But it did no good. Now six years later, Sia was in another battle. She'd petitioned to have her brother's ashes memorialized at the Naval War Memorial and was promptly told by the official she talked to it wasn't possible. Her brother hadn't died a hero.

That meant she'd have to get her brother's case reopened and that took an appeal to the Secretary of the Navy, or as he was referred to at JAG, SECNAV.

She didn't blame the War Memorial. She blamed the wingman who'd flown with her brother—the man with whom she'd had the most explosive, intimate relationship in her life. Even six years later, the thought of him made her heart beat faster and her palms sweat. She didn't want this reaction, but she couldn't seem to stop it. That promising relationship had ended with her brother's fatal accident.

The loss of her brother had torn her family apart, and she'd simply lost everything except work. The JAG Corps and her job sustained her and honed her into a legal killing machine. Focusing her thoughts back to the investigation, she asked the ship's resident JAG to send in the next person for questioning. In this case, it was the pilot's wingman.

The master chief hesitated when he saw Lieutenant Saunders's wingman standing silently but attentively through their exchange at the door. Then he said something softly under his breath and strode off down the corridor, ducking through the hatch.

Sia focused on the man in front of her in his crisp khaki uniform and aviator's flight jacket. "Lieutenant Russell, thank you for your time."

"I hope it helped in the investigation." His voice was subdued, the grief at the loss of his friend and wingman poignant. Unexpectedly, Sia's throat filled as a result of the memories of the day she'd lost her brother all in one terrible fiery crash. It was the same day she had lost the man she loved, her brother's wingman, who had ejected to safety. "Mal and I were more than wing mates. We were best friends."

"I am very sorry for your loss."

"Thank you, ma'am."

He stepped into the compartment and she shut the door. She indicated the chair in front of the table. "Have a seat." When he was settled and she'd taken her own seat again, she said, "Can you tell me about Lieutenant Saunders's state of mind yesterday when his jet crashed into the ocean?"

He smiled, his eyes brightening. "He was psyched. We always were when we got to fly."

Sia leaned back in her chair. "Anything happen that was out of the ordinary?"

Lieutenant Russell frowned. "The only thing that happened wasn't out of the ordinary."

"What is that?"

He sighed. "Master Chief Walker always seemed to be in Mal's face."

"They didn't get along?"

"No. The master chief was always using what we liked to call good-natured ribbing to put him down, and Mal just ignored his behavior."

"Do you know why the master chief had this perspective?" Sia asked.

"No, ma'am. It seemed to manifest from the first day Mal and I were assigned to this ship."

Sia looked down at the open folder. "I don't see any reprimands in the master chief's file."

Lieutenant Russell shrugged. "Mal wasn't like that. He held his own, he told me. He didn't need to tattle to the Navy command because an enlisted sailor didn't like him. He was as perplexed as I was as to why the master chief immediately singled him out for abuse. We revere master chiefs in the Navy. They know just about every damn thing there is to know. We just didn't get it."

"He should have reported him."

Lieutenant Russell's shoulders drooped and his voice grew strained. "I agree, ma'am. But, Mal is…I mean was Mal."

"Is there any other information you can provide that might help the investigation?" She saw him hesitate and look down as he ran his fingers along the brim of his hat, debating. "Anything," she prompted. "No matter how small and insignificant."

He looked up. The anguish on his face twisted Sia's heart. Her memories were still painful, as if her brother had died yesterday instead of six years ago. Fresh pain flooded through her. "Lieutenant Russell?"

"I hope I'm not talking out of turn, ma'am, but I saw the master chief near Mal's coffee before we took off."

"In the wardroom? Enlisted personnel aren't allowed in there," Sia said.

"No, Mal was just about to step onto the flight deck, and he was finishing it off." He set his hat on the table and leaned forward, his voice dropping. "I don't want to accuse him of tampering with it, but Mal was a top-notch aviator and there's no way in hell he would have downed that plane like that."

"Are you willing to sign an oath to that, Lieutenant?"

"Yes, ma'am. I will." He held her gaze and never wavered, clearly a man who was dedicated to both his friend and the Navy.

Sia dismissed Lieutenant Russell and she moved quickly. She contacted the captain via the ship's phone and requested a search authorization for the master chief's rack, citing the evidence from Lieutenant Russell's oath. With his permission, Sia made her way to the master chief's quarters with a burly master-at-arms in tow. Once inside, she started to methodically search his locker. She found nothing. Sure that she had missed something, she started the search once again. As she went through his underwear and socks, she was about to give up. Her hand brushed against a sock and she felt a hard lump. Fishing out the sock, Sia pulled the garments apart and a bottle fell out onto the deck. Reaching down, she picked it up. When she turned the label toward her, she found she held an over-the-counter product for irregularity.

Her brows furrowed as she looked down at the bright yellow bottle. Why was this in his sock drawer and not in the medicine cabinet? Then it dawned on her. He was trying to hide it.

She would have the contents of the bottle analyzed against anything that was in Lieutenant Saunders's bloodstream. She could be holding the murder weapon in her hand. The hairs on the back of her neck prickled and goose bumps ran along her back and arms.

She needed to detain the master chief and talk to the ME who was doing the autopsy right away.

She motioned for the master-at-arms to follow her as she headed to the legal office to log the evidence and contact the ME. She dismissed the master-at-arms once she reached the office.

When there was a knock at the door, Sia rose to open it. The sea rolled and as the carrier dipped, she lost her balance and got turned around. The door slipped out of her hands. When it popped open, someone shoved her from behind hard enough to send her face-first against the far bulkhead of the office. Her head struck metal with a clanging sound that reverberated against her skull, rattling her brain. Stars exploded behind her eyes. Before she could recover from the suddenness of the push, her assailant hit her with a stunning blow to the back of the head and Sia fell into darkness.

When she woke up, she could taste blood in her mouth and smell the sea air. She opened one eye; the other one, swollen and throbbing, took a bit longer. She focused on a man sitting cross-legged in front of her. Unlike her he was dressed for the weather and the rough seas. Along with his outerwear, he had taken precautions and donned a bright orange life vest. Her hands were tied with a piece of rope in a knot that any sailor would know and that was impossible to untie. Fear sliced through her like the icy wind that battered her hair and exposed skin. She'd never been this open to the elements on the carrier, and it seemed as if they could touch the dark, clouded night sky.

"Master Chief."

"I'm afraid you've stuck your nose where it doesn't belong and your actions have caused me to remember my duty. I'm sorry about this, but you'll have to die."

"Your duty?" Sia spit out. "Murdering an officer is your duty?"

"I can't let you reopen old wounds. Your brother's 'accident' was pilot error just like Saunders's 'accident.'" He raised his hand and shook the bottle.

Sia shifted and studied the determined man before her. He wasn't telling her everything. She got that prickly feeling, only this time more urgently. She wasn't sure if it was because she was in a terrible position.

"Are you saying you had something to do with my brother's death?"

He set the bottle down with secrets in his eyes. "Nope. Not saying it. What I have to say doesn't matter where you're going." He rose and jerked her up by her arm with a painful grip. He pushed her to the edge of the sponson, a platform hanging on the side of the carrier, just below the flight deck. It was a sheer drop to the ocean. The plunge would kill her instantly.

"How did you get me up here with no one seeing?" she asked breathlessly as the ocean churned below her.

He laughed. "I know this ship like no one else. I have my ways. Enough talking. Say hi to Rafael for me."

Sia didn't give the man a chance to push her over. She lashed back with her booted foot and caught Walker right in the kneecap. She heard the bottle roll away against the bulkhead. Walker howled, but the wind whipped the words away. No amount of yelling would bring anyone up here.

He tried to backhand her, but Sia was ready, balancing on the balls of her feet. She ducked, came up with her bound hands and jabbed him in the sternum. He swung widely, sending him off balance. Sia dodged out of the way and Walker's momentum took him over the rail, his scream of rage and fear drowned out by the wind and the ocean.

The soft breeze off the ocean touched her face as she heard the screen door open and close. Remnants of her celebratory graduation party fluttered in the breeze on the table situated on the patio.

As she glanced over, she expected to see her father, but instead a tall, dark-haired man carved out a piece of her cake and sat down.

Sia studied the strong line of his jaw, the width of his broad shoulders encased in Navy khaki. Drawn to him, she sauntered over and he looked up, capturing her with gray eyes as elusive and intriguing as smoke. She said nothing as she straddled his lap, the sun warm on her shoulders, the texture of his uniform stimulating on her fingertips. He smiled, the hint of frosting on his lips tantalizing. Her head dipped down and covered his mouth, the sweet taste of the frosting and him sending her mind into a free fall.

Warmth filtered through her, his groan soft and uncontrollable as he pressed his body against her. His mouth was hot, the press of flesh erotic and needy. If only she could get closer, hang on to the sensation, maybe she could forget what he had done. Forget...

"Miss?"

Sia tried to swim up from the dream, the memory of his mouth on hers.

"Miss? Are you all right?"

The flight attendant's worried face peered down at Sia.

"I'm fine," Sia said, but then she moved and the sore muscles of her arms, face and right shoulder reminded her she wasn't.

"Would you like some water? You were whimpering in your sleep."

Sia closed her eyes to hide her embarrassment. She looked around. Right, she was on the flight back to Norfolk, Virginia. Feeling muddled from the pain medication she'd taken, Sia gingerly touched the huge shiner that ringed her eye, flinching at the pain. She'd looked at it in the washroom mirror before she'd fallen asleep. "Yes, thank you."

The flight attendant left to get the water.

It seemed Sia could not get away from the man who haunted her, even in her sleep. All they had shared, gone in a matter of minutes. She didn't want to think about him. What they had shared was over in the time it took for a fighter jet to break apart and plummet to earth.

The flight attendant returned with the water. Forcing her thoughts back to the *James McCloud* and the now-deceased Master Chief Steven Walker, Sia took a sip of the cool liquid.

Sia's investigation had ended when Walker had gone over the side of the sponson, but she hadn't been able to find the bottle and the ME still hadn't finished the autopsy on Lieutenant Saunders. She was left with unanswered questions in both accidents. Additional statements from the crew confirmed a volatile relationship between the pilot and the master chief. Case closed.

Except Walker's words wouldn't stop eating at her. *Nope. Not saying it.* Did he have something to do with the accident that had taken her brother's life, or was he simply cruel? And what was he talking about when he cited duty as his reason for killing her?

She landed in Virginia at 1700 and intended to go home, take a long soak in the tub and sleep for twelve hours straight. But just as she pulled up to her apartment, her cell chimed and she was ordered to report to the JAG office on Naval Base Norfolk. The crisp March sky, an intense cobalt blue, and the barren trees hinting at a spring that was only weeks away did nothing to invigorate her.

At headquarters, the day was just ending. Sia was greeted by departing coworkers who first were concerned about her injuries, then ribbed her about going the wrong way. As she made her way down the hall, she saw one of her closest friends approaching. Special Agent Hollis McIntyre was one of the Naval Criminal Investigative Service's finest members. She was tough, smart and beautiful. The smile on her face changed to deep concern as they met.

"What the hell happened to you?" Hollis said as she took in Sia's bruises and her arm in the sling.

"It's a long story, one that will take several glasses of wine to tell." Hollis didn't know anything about her family or her brother's death. It was time she confided in her.

"Well, I hope the other guy got what was coming to him." Hollis sent her fist into her palm.

Sia nodded. "He did, but he left more questions than answers."

"Sounds like a thoroughly dangerous and frustrating TAD." Hollis touched Sia's good shoulder, giving her a squeeze.

"It was. Hence the need for wine."

Hollis laughed, but her eyes were still serious. She gave Sia a sympathetic and solemn look and said softly, "I'm so glad you're okay."

Sia nodded and smiled at her friend. "What brings you to JAG?"

Hollis rubbed at her tired-looking face. Her curly blond hair was more messy than usual. "A dead seaman and the guy we caught who did it. Just tying up some loose ends. I'm heading home. Why aren't you?"

Sia smiled wryly. "Boss calls and I answer like a dutiful soldier against injustice."

Hollis laughed. "When can we get those glasses of wine and catch up?"

"I'll give you a call when I'm finished here. Good?"

"Yes. That will give me a chance to go home, shower and change. Been on this case too long and it's starting to…ah…get rank."

Waving goodbye to Hollis, Sia entered the office

space where all the junior grade and clerical staff sat. Around them were the offices of the JAG team. She stopped at the desk of her aide, Legalman First Class Gabriel McBride, a young petty officer from Seattle.

"Commander Soto, welcome back. I've already printed out the report you sent me, and it's ready for the captain's review." He handed her a folder.

"McBride, you are a wonder."

He studied her face and winced. "Ouch on the shiner. Are you all right?"

"You should see the other guy. He took a header off the carrier. So I feel lucky to be alive."

"I'm sure glad you are, ma'am. It would be hard to train up a new boss."

She smiled. "Thanks for your concern." He smiled back and nodded. "McBride, I need for you to do some research for me on Master Chief Steven Walker. I want to know where he was stationed. Cross-reference his stations with any pilot accidents at the time he was serving those stations."

"Yes, ma'am."

After leaving her legalman, she made her way directly to her CO's office, receiving a wave through by his aide.

Entering, she saw Captain Mark Snyder was on the phone behind his desk. The look on his face was less than welcoming, but still he motioned her forward. He finished the conversation with clipped tones and hung up the phone.

Captain Snyder was a tall man, which was evident even when he was seated, as he was now. African-American with close-cropped hair, a wide nose and dark, piercing eyes, he cut an impressive figure in his blue coat and white shirt. As a commanding officer he was fair but tough and often liked to debate with her. "That was the skipper on the *U.S.S. James McCloud*."

Sia came to attention in front of his desk. When he nodded, she stood at ease, reached forward and placed the report on his desk. "Here's the final report on Walker…."

"This particular conversation doesn't have anything to do with the master chief," his voice was low and urgent.

"No?"

"They just had a pilot crash into the deck of the carrier."

"Oh, my God." Sia's heart lurched in her chest and she could see from the captain's grave look there was more. He motioned for her to sit and she sank into the nearest chair.

"Yes, Commander. It's even worse than that. He's Senator Mark Washington's son."

Her commander stared grimly at her, and Sia tried not to flinch. Her boss didn't assign blame. He wasn't petty and he treated her with respect. But at this moment, she saw the unmistakable truth in his eyes. He thought somehow she had let him down. A sick feeling churned in her stomach and squirmed up her spine.

"Send me back to the *McCloud* and I'll make sure I get to the bottom of this."

"It's not that easy, Commander Soto." He leaned back in his chair and sighed. "You are under investigation."

"Yes, it's a matter of routine. I understand, sir. But

I can still perform my duties and cooperate with any type of inquiry."

"I have no doubt of that. You are a meticulous investigator and litigator. But, this time, it's required you have help."

"Help? I don't need…"

Just then the door opened and her boss smiled. "Too late. He's already here."

She twisted around to take a look at the person who was going to accompany her on this assignment.

The pressure in the office changed, condensed. The man was six feet of raw energy in a tightly muscled package. He wore black pants that fit snugly against hard-packed thighs and a trim waist. A gray sweater stretched across his broad chest, with the edge of a plain white T-shirt at his strong throat. Over the sweater, he wore a black leather jacket. Clipped to his belt was the gold NCIS badge. The telltale bulge on the other side indicated he was carrying a sidearm. His thick black hair covered his forehead, errant tendrils curling along the nape of his neck.

Sia gasped as she looked into steady, beautiful dark gray eyes, eyes that had gazed into hers full of a smoky passion that only made them darken.

Oh, damn.

Christophe "Chris" Vargas.

Her brother's wingman.

The very pilot who had been directly responsible for her brother's death.

Chapter 2

Sia looked from her commanding officer to Chris, dumbfounded. It couldn't be. She was suddenly thrust back in time and all the longing, the desire and the need for this man came crashing into her.

It had been the wildest time of her life. He'd been a great fantasy, all hormones and hazard, and she'd been so crazy about him. He had been the only man her father had approved of, saying Chris was a first-rate pilot and the kind of man her father could trust.

Her father's approval had been important. With her father's consent came admiration. A man who could gain the trust and high regard of her father was worth her time.

Captain Snyder cleared his throat.

"Lieutenant Commander Ambrosia Soto, meet Special Agent Chris Vargas."

For a moment Sia's vocal cords wouldn't work, but she was saved from a response by Chris.

"Commander Soto and I are acquainted."

There were layers of meaning in his voice, a tone that touched her deep down and squeezed her heart. So much regret, pain and apology. Her eyes never just met Chris's—they connected like two live wires throwing off sparks. She could see by the look on his face he was studying her bruises and his mouth hardened. Her first thought was it was a good thing Master Chief Walker was dead. Chris's eyes, like polished steel, narrowed.

"Special Agent Vargas comes highly recommended from the director of NCIS," Captain Snyder said. "We're damn lucky to have him."

"Aye, sir," Sia responded. Chris never did anything by half. Sia had had no idea he'd left the Navy and gone into law enforcement. She'd assumed he was still flying.

The way Captain Snyder looked at her, Sia felt adrenaline release into her stomach. The message was loud and clear. Cooperate, don't make waves.

"Special Agent Vargas will take point on this, Commander."

"But it's my case. I'm the one…"

At the look from Captain Snyder, Sia closed her mouth on the words she was going to say. First off, he wouldn't be pleased she would in any way say she'd made a mistake. JAG didn't make mistakes. Second, she'd be usurping his authority. She was often able to get away with it because she was very good at verbal debate. But this time she saw he would yank her off this case in a heartbeat, and she would never get the answers she sought.

She stepped back and came to attention next to Chris. The first scent of him brought back memories of hot skin and heated kisses. She violently pushed those memories away, a resentment building.

Captain Snyder set the folder aside and addressed them both. "You're going back to the *U.S.S. James McCloud*, Commander Soto, and Special Agent Vargas will accompany you. You will look into the death of Senator Washington's son. Special Agent Vargas will be in charge."

"We need to get on a plane as soon as possible, sir," Chris said.

The captain picked up the phone. "That's taken care of. I suggest you get yourselves ready to go. I want daily reports."

"Captain, may I have a word with you? In private?" She glanced over at Chris and he smiled wryly. The protesting tone of her voice made her wince inside. She regretted her blunder immediately.

Captain Snyder sighed. "You're dismissed, Special Agent Vargas."

Chris gave her a sidelong look, but said nothing as he turned and left the office.

When the door was fully closed, Captain Snyder said, "Problem, Commander?"

"I have a history with Special Agent Vargas. It's complicated."

"Uncomplicate it and get the job done. Personal problems don't interest me. Results do. Although you are forcing me to rethink my decision to send you back to the *McCloud*."

"I can handle this assignment," she said quickly, immediately concerned the tenuous connection between Walker and her brother could snap if she wasn't given an opportunity to continue the investigation. "I don't need an NCIS agent breathing down my neck, dredging up old memories." Damn, she hadn't meant to say that. "I'm fully capable."

His eyes cooled. "I know you are capable. But protocol requires it and I'm not going to take a misstep here with the senator's son. You are still under investigation yourself."

"It's a routine investigation." She added "sir" when his eyes went glacial.

"I'm sure you wouldn't want this mishap to mar your record. This is going to be media fodder. I want it put to bed quickly."

Sia clenched her teeth. "Aye, sir."

Exiting the Captain's office, Sia looked for Chris and found him a few feet away. She walked up to him, grabbed him by his jacket and pulled him into an empty conference room. "You could have given me some kind of warning."

"I didn't know you were stationed here. Not until I walked into the Captain's office."

She didn't deserve this twist of fate. Of all the places he could have ended up, it had to be Norfolk. "I don't think it's a good idea we work together."

He shrugged. "It's easy. Work with me or Captain Snyder will assign someone else. Sounds like an easy choice to me."

Sia stared at Chris for several seconds, caught completely off guard again by his presence. After that debacle at her brother's grave site, she hadn't expected to see him ever again. Therefore, she'd had no chance to prepare herself to speak to him after what had happened six years ago. She had strategies filed away in her brain for every kind of courtroom situation, but she had no strategies for dealing with Chris and their short-lived, mind-blowing relationship.

"I don't want to work with you. You know perfectly well why." She wanted—no, needed—him to go away. She desperately needed to sort out her thoughts, and she couldn't do that with him standing less than five feet away, pinning her with that intent gaze of his. Maybe it was better not to confront him so directly. After all, it had been a while since she'd seen him. "Listen," she went on, trying to sound conciliatory, "I don't mean to sound like a bitch, really, I don't. It's just…it's been a very long day, and I'm not really prepared to deal with this *or you* at the moment."

Given her continued, rather visceral reaction to him, even after all these years, perhaps she'd never be ready to deal with him.

"I'm sure it has been a long day. And, yes, I know perfectly well why. Doesn't change a damn thing. Still your choice."

"I can't walk away from this. I want you to."

He shook his head, his gaze resolute. "Not going to happen. I don't answer to you or Captain Snyder, and I sure as hell don't answer to the Navy anymore. This is about Lieutenant Eli Washington."

"Don't lecture me. I know what it's about."

His eyes flared at her terse tone. "Just assign someone else."

"I can't!" She clenched her fists, her outburst startling even her.

"Yes, you can. You just want to strong-arm me. It's always about your precious control. Well, I'm on this case, so get used to it."

It certainly had everything to do with control now. She'd given up her control to him six years ago. Fallen into such passion and heat, she'd barely been able to remember her name. Now standing so close to him, she felt the same damn pull, so overwhelming, so uncontrollable. He looked like the jets he used to fly: sleek, fast and dangerous.

He smelled way too good, musky and male, a combination as potent as a stiff belt of whiskey straight into the bloodstream. But she couldn't back up now and show any weakness. Chris would know he had the upper hand and that wouldn't be a good thing.

She laid it out bluntly, not seeing any reason to sugarcoat anything. "You're being stubborn because of what happened in our past. Is this payback, Chris?"

His face hardened. "Either do your job or pass it on to someone else, Commander Soto."

He hadn't taken the bait, and Sia realized she wasn't going to make him angry enough to walk away from the investigation. "I intend to do my job. Just without you involved."

He laughed then, without mirth. "It would be in your best interest to let someone else handle it."

She stiffened at his chiding tone. "You're alluding to the investigation into Master Chief Steven Walker's death?"

He folded his arms across his chest, the movement

tightening up his chest muscles and arms, pulling the jacket away from the gun clipped to his waist. "The Navy doesn't just casually investigate someone. You're the one who is under scrutiny."

"At the time I handled the investigation, I did it as thoroughly and diligently as I normally do." But in the back of her mind doubts assailed her. What if she had been too distracted by past memories and the fresh mourning of her brother's death? What if she had missed something?

"Is that where you got those bruises? Why your arm is in a sling?"

"Yes. Walker tried to kill me."

He shook his head. "Stupid man. What happened?"

"He took a header over the sponson and died from the fall. They fished his body up just after he went over."

"Really, in that vast of an ocean late at night?"

"He was wearing a life vest. A vest he denied me because I was supposed to be the one dead."

"Let me guess. They didn't find any evidence you helped him over?"

Weary from the day's events, she walked to the conference table and settled into one of the chairs. "No, because I dodged his attempt to throw me over. My hands were tied. It's the biggest indication the events happened exactly as I said they did. I didn't tie my own hands or wrench my own shoulder or give myself this black eye. The investigation is really just routine and to close the loop." She thrust out her good hand and showed him the bruises on her wrist.

He walked over and set his backside on the conference table. Taking her hand gently in his, he studied the black-and-blue marks. "That may be true, but it's the difference between us now. You have to follow the Navy's rules. I don't."

His hand was warm, his palm smooth. Her heart fluttering, she pulled her hand from his hold. "Surely in your job you're required to follow rules."

He smiled. "When it suits me, but as a civilian investigator, I have a lot more leeway than you do."

The smile lighting up his eyes made her remember the potency he wielded with his irresistible charm, all the more reason not to work with him. The other big reason was he'd been directly responsible for her brother's death and the destruction of her family.

It was as if he'd been waiting for her to think that very thought. His eyes changed, got a little harder, a little darker. "I didn't come here to dredge up the past, Sia."

"It doesn't matter whether you talk about it or not. Just seeing you brings it all back."

His mouth tightened and he looked away from her. "I'm sorry for that."

"You said you were sorry six years ago when they handed my mother his flag. It still doesn't help."

He closed his eyes, but not before she saw the flash of pain and, suddenly, she felt sick for the way everything had ended.

"You're not the only one who suffered, Sia. I lost you and your brother. I have to live with what I did to him, to you."

She felt a distinct tug on her heart, but refused to examine it too closely. Yet she did finally give into the urge to reach out and touch his arm, needing that physical contact in a soul-deep way. The leather was warm from his body heat, the muscles beneath taut and corded. "I can't help the way I feel about it, Chris."

"I know you can't, but that doesn't make it any easier to forget what we had. What we shared." He covered her hand with his, the warmth comforting.

"What we have to deal with now is the present. We can't change the past."

"No, we can't," he whispered. "There's no place for us to go at all."

"Don't," she protested.

The warning was diluted to nothing by the sadness in his face. His mouth twisted into a half smile that was cynical and weary. His dark eyes looked a hundred years old.

Even surrounded by family and friends, she'd been so alone when her brother had died. All she'd wanted, longed for, was to have Chris hold her. But the grief of her brother's death tripled when she'd found out Chris had caused the accident. He would never hold her again.

Dangerous, her longing and his proximity.

A quick knock on the door made her sit up straight and release him. She rose, walked to the door and opened it. Her aide was on the other side.

"Excuse me, Commander Soto, Captain Snyder's aide pointed me in this direction. I was able to get you and Agent Vargas on a flight to Hawaii via L.A. The *McCloud* is currently docked at Pearl for repairs to the flight deck. Your flight leaves in three hours. He handed her a folder, giving Chris the once-over. "Your e-tickets are in there."

"Thank you, McBride."

He seemed reluctant to leave her alone. Her legal-man eyed Chris and his gaze returned to Sia. "Can I escort you to your car?"

"No, that won't be necessary. Good night, McBride."

Chris smiled wryly as the petty officer deliberately left the door open. "He's looking at me like I'm a psycho, serial killer."

"You look formidable, that's all. McBride doesn't know you."

"No, he doesn't."

She sighed. "You're not going to change your mind."

"Hell, no." He made his way to the open door and passed her. "Why don't you let this investigation go, Sia?"

"I might have missed something. Something important!" Her voice was loud in the small room. Softer, she said, "I have to fix it or make sure my conclusions were sound. If I neglected to fully handle this investigation and I caused a man's death…"

He stepped up to her until he was close. "I hear you're expected to get over that, too," he said softly.

Her throat ached with the pain in his voice.

"We have to work together. I'll accept that. But don't expect anything else from me," she said, delivering the ultimatum with a tone that accepted her defeat.

Even as the words left her mouth, she knew she was even more than ten times a fool if she believed either of them could forget the fire between them whenever they touched, or looked at each other, or were in the same damn room.

Chris said absolutely nothing. Out of everything that had happened to her in the past twenty-four hours, his silence was more nerve-racking than waiting for a verdict. His silence was downright ominous.

She was in trouble. Oh, man, was she in trouble, but she wasn't going to give in to panic. Later she could panic, but not now while she was standing in front of him. She needed her wits.

Dredging up old memories wasn't conducive to this situation. But it seemed wits and good sense deserted her when he turned those dark eyes on her, when he looked at her as if she were the most desirable, most important woman on earth. She tried to break the spell by thinking Chris probably looked at every woman he wanted that way, but the thought seemed to slip out of her mind like smoke.

Finally he spoke. "I don't have any expectations where you are concerned. I learned that valuable lesson six years ago." His tone was accusing and his eyes brooked no disagreement. It was clear he was disgusted with her lack of support at the grave site. She was smart enough to keep quiet about that.

His face was too close to hers and she couldn't stop herself from thinking about him kissing her. And her mouth ached, waiting a beat, then two, the tension drawing as tight as a wire. Finally he pulled away, turned on his heel and exited the conference room.

It was a while before Sia could make her limbs move.

Oh, yes, she was in deep trouble.

Finally her training slammed into place and she was able to get herself under control.

She needed to get a grip on her emotions—a highly unlikely occurrence when she was still using everything she had not to remember how it was to melt into Chris's arms.

The temptation of him whispered across her exposed skin. These feelings and sensations only made her more resolved not to give in. Her brother was no longer alive because of Chris. She had to remember that information, use it to keep her own emotions from eating her alive.

A little doubt wiggled its way in when she remembered the words of the master chief. Could he have done something to Chris and caused the accident that killed her brother? If he had, then maybe Chris would be exonerated right along with her brother.

And if Chris wasn't guilty of causing the accident that killed her brother, then maybe…

She was jumping the gun here. That was a big if. At this point, she had to keep her distance. She had an investigation to handle. Her baggage with Chris couldn't get in the way of that.

Straightening her uniform jacket, she pushed open the conference-room door and exited, trying to push away the feeling that disaster loomed right around the corner.

Chris stalked out of JAG. Immediately a woman pushed a microphone into his face.

"Agent Vargas. Can you give us any information regarding the death of Senator Washington's son?"

"No comment," he growled and ignored the attempts of the other reporters to get his attention. He pushed the button on his key ring to unlock his car. When he got inside, he slammed the door. Even after all these years, it felt as if they had never been apart.

Shutting out the loud calls of the reporters around the driver's side of his car, his thoughts went back to Sia. He had thought he knew what he would say to Sia when he saw her again. His eyes burned remembering the day of the crash and her face when they'd told her Rafael was dead. He'd never forget the way she'd looked at him. It was shortly afterward that the trembling started every time he sat in a cockpit. It was that look that ultimately forced him to hang up his wings. He'd survived. By sheer luck, he was still standing. But inside he was dying.

After completing his Top Gun training, Chris had been assigned to the *U.S.S. James McCloud* and there met his new wingman, Lieutenant Rafael Soto. Chris was high on his success, his ability to make it to the top of his class. He had his afterburner on and he was flying right into the sun, pulling G's.

He'd shown his father he wasn't good for nothing. Then everything came crashing down.

A sharp rap on the window brought him back to himself. He started his car and drove away without even a glance at the reporters.

Chris had worked with Rafael for two years before he'd met Sia. The *James McCloud* had docked in Norfolk and Rafael had invited Chris to a family gathering. Rafael had been like the brother Chris never had. He was an ace in the air, his knowledge and abilities impressive. He made Chris want to work harder to keep up.

The night he'd met Sia, Chris was cocky and full of himself as only a pilot can be. Feeling he was finally slipping into a family situation he'd always dreamed of, he'd thought Sia would make a fine sister. Then he'd seen her, and any brotherly feelings dissipated in the wake of her sheer effect on him.

Long, coffee-rich hair, dark sensual eyes, and a no-holds-barred attitude only made him want to subdue her in the most carnal way. He took one look at her and knew what would happen between them was inevitable.

She had a knockout, head-turning shape that made the blood in his veins sizzle. But more than her physical appearance attracted him. The minute she opened her mouth and began to spar with him verbally, well, that was the kicker.

Whenever he was stressed, he would revert back to those days when he was on top of the world and seducing Sia had been as natural as breathing. Their first time together still burned in his brain and remained imprinted on his heart.

Chris reached his apartment and was soon out of his car and in his bedroom. Pulling a suitcase from his closet, he started packing.

NCIS had sustained him through the loss of Rafael. But underlying that grief was the agony of losing Sia. Nothing and no one could alleviate that gut-wrenching pain. No one but Sia. He guessed that wasn't the top priority on her list of things to do.

He was on his own, as he'd been most of his life—a reality that had become painfully clear to him after Rafael had died.

Suddenly he stopped packing and straightened, swallowing hard at the memories that flooded over him.

He and Sia had been wrapped up in each other that

summer. With her diploma from Yale, she had easily snagged a prestigious job at a law firm in New York City. Her job was slated to begin in the fall, but they had made plans to be together. Sia was going to break the news to her father that she couldn't go to New York. She loved Chris and wanted to stay in Norfolk.

They had planned a life together and Sia had been so in love with him…until…the accident.

That's when everything had changed. Sia had abandoned him when he'd needed her the most. She'd sided with her family and cut him out of her life as if he meant nothing. For him it had been the ultimate betrayal.

And Chris had lost everything that mattered.

Hollis removed Sia's uniforms from the dryer and walked to her kitchen table, setting them down.

"Here I thought we'd be chugging wine, not doing domestic chores."

"I'm sorry, but I've got to get back on a plane in two hours and then on to Pearl. I appreciate you helping me. This shoulder is still pretty sore and I'm supposed to rest it for another day at least."

"Ah, the glamorous life of a JAG officer."

Sia snorted. "Right."

Hollis gave her a sidelong glance. "What's wrong? You look…unsettled."

"You know what? To hell with it." Sia walked to her kitchen cabinet and pulled out two wineglasses. Hollis smiled, stopped fussing with Sia's uniforms and walked over. "I've neglected to tell you about someone from my past."

"Oh, does this someone have to do with that unsettled look I mentioned?"

Sia pulled a bottle of Riesling out of the fridge and popped the cork, pouring a generous amount into each glass. "He does. I have to work with him and I have to take orders from him. I think it might be someone you know."

"Really? Who?" Hollis took a sip of her wine.

"Special Agent Chris Vargas."

"Chris? You were once up close and personal with Chris Vargas? Oh my, he is a hottie. All the female agents drool over him."

"Including you?"

"Well, come on, he's gorgeous and I'm female."

Sia took a sip of her wine, her emotions ragged. "We have a painful past, Hollis, and I'm not sure how I'm going to work with him."

"Oh, sweetie, I'm sorry to trivialize your feelings." She took Sia's arm and led her over to the table. Settling in her seat, Hollis set her wineglass down and reached for a uniform shirt and a hanger. "Okay, spill."

Sia told Hollis everything. Afterward, Hollis was quiet for a moment, then in one swallow she finished off her wine. "I can only respond in one way. Chris is a decent guy and a top-notch agent. You couldn't have a better partner out there watching your back."

After Hollis left and Sia was driving to the airport, she felt even more uncomfortable with the situation. Sia trusted Hollis, and her observations of people were always accurate. It unsettled Sia to think that all those years ago, she might have been so mired in her grief that she'd unfairly judged Chris.

Chapter 3

It was easy to pick Sia out of a crowd. It was true being in Navy service khaki helped her to stand out, and it was also true she had her arm in a sling and had a very dark black eye compliments of a dead master chief. But it wasn't any of those things that made her easy to find.

Sia commanded attention, she moved and breathed confidence. Her dark hair was ruthlessly pulled back, her Navy cap situated firmly under her arm.

She also had a long line of reporters dogging her steps, but she said nothing to them as she approached.

He had no illusions he would get a welcoming smile. She'd made it quite clear she didn't want him on this case, but that was too bad. He should have turned this assignment over to another agent, but he couldn't. Whether it was to be contrary or something else, he didn't know. From the look on her face, it was clear she was still royally pissed off at him.

He was okay with that. Seeing her had stirred pain and regret, but it had also stirred emotions he had long forgotten. How he had loved this woman. His chest still ached with it; his body still yearned for her.

"All set?" he asked as the same woman from last night tried to once again get his attention. "No comment," he replied.

Her mouth tightened as she asked him another question he blatantly ignored.

Sia gave him a curt nod, and they headed for the security checkpoint. As soon as they reached the staging area, he showed his badge to the official and indicated the sidearm at his waist. The official checked all his papers and then Sia's, as well.

"You're not carrying a firearm, ma'am?" the TSA official asked.

Sia smiled. "No, I'm a lawyer. The only deadly things I carry are my mind for litigation and my very loaded briefcase."

The official laughed, and they were allowed to pass. Thankfully the reporters were left behind, but Chris was sure there would be a fresh batch when they landed. Once in the gate area, it wasn't long before the plane was scheduled to take off. Once on board and securely buckled in, Sia sipped at a cup of coffee she'd purchased and remained silent.

After stowing his own gear, Chris settled himself into his seat. Buckling his seat belt, he glanced over at her. She stared resolutely ahead and it irked him. Surely they couldn't sit in silence for the whole flight. He knew that would suit her, but it didn't suit him. "How did you end up at JAG?"

She turned to look at him, taking another sip of her coffee. He accepted her cool look with one of his own. Although she was as impeccably groomed as ever, there was a hint of strain around her mouth that had only intensified since he'd last seen her. The thought occurred to him she worked too hard, but then he did, too. It was mandatory to keep the ghosts at bay. It was certainly better than drinking himself to death. After Rafael died and Sia withdrew from him, he'd tried that route and discarded it as a coward's way out.

"I applied shortly after Rafael was killed." Her tone was clipped and didn't invite him to ask any more questions, but of course that wasn't going to stop him.

"Why?"

"Why?" she repeated through clenched teeth.

"Yes. Why did you join JAG?"

She huffed out a breath. "It was a way to carry on what he had wanted to do in the Navy—serve his country. I'm not a pilot so I served in the only capacity I knew—the law."

"Did they send you to Newport?"

She turned to look at him with a steady gaze. "Are we playing twenty questions? That could work both ways."

"I'm only trying to find out what happened to you after we parted. I'm curious."

As a cop he was adept at reading body language. He noticed she didn't turn hers toward him as one would do in an intimate conversation. Sia was setting the boundaries, and it seemed they were impenetrable.

"Yes, I went to Newport, Rhode Island, and completed Naval Justice School after I finished Officer Development School."

"You sound like you're reciting your name, rank and serial number. I'm not the enemy."

"We may be on the same side, but that is as far as it goes. You refused to cooperate with me and you are in charge of an investigation that should have been mine. So excuse me for thinking of you as the enemy. Besides, I'm only relating the information you wanted, Special Agent Vargas."

"And you got to pick where you wanted to go?"

She sighed, but when he made it clear by his look he wasn't going to give up, she answered. "Yes, I did."

He smiled now.

Sia frowned. "What's so funny?"

"You're just answering the question."

Her eyes, steamed to a volatile brown, regarded him with pique. "Isn't that what I'm supposed to do?" When she spoke, her tone gave no indication of how she felt about his unwanted questions. Still the cool cucumber. With her dark hair pulled back, not so much as a dab of makeup enhancing her smooth-as-silk skin, and her crisp and unwrinkled uniform ruthlessly fit to her small frame, she was every inch the woman in control.

He ran his fingers through his longish hair. He should have had it cut weeks ago, but his caseload had been brutal. It was a mechanism to keep himself from reaching for her to see if he could muss up that too-perfect control a little. "You're being deliberately obtuse and you know it."

"Oh. You want me to elaborate like we're old friends," she said, but her casual tone was belied by a quick swallow, and the way her hands flexed in her lap. "We're not old friends."

"I know that. But I thought since we're going to be together for a while it might be a good idea to get re-acquainted."

"I think I made myself clear yesterday. We're working together because you forced the issue. Doesn't mean I have to cooperate or make small talk."

"No, it doesn't, but I want you to indulge me."

"If I don't, will you make a report of it to Captain Snyder in the vein of, 'Commander Soto is a competent investigator but she won't indulge me in small talk'? Oh, no. I'll have that on my record. How will I live it down?"

She frustrated him to the extreme—in ways he remembered and, surprisingly, cherished. All she had to do was look at him in a certain way and there it was. It was why he reacted to her in this crazy way when there was even a hint of banter.

He should have given in to her request to let someone else at NCIS accompany her to the carrier. Handling his caseload was enough without this long-term temporary assignment. Chasing Navy and Marine Corps killers, thieves and criminals was a full-time job and then some, but it was preferable to dealing with all this inner turmoil. He'd spent the last six years trying to forget Sia. It should be telling he hadn't been able to do it and he was right back where he started.

She wasn't looking at him, and her tone was flat and hard. But he saw the tremor in her jaw, the vein standing out in stark relief along the side of her creamy neck, and the white knuckles as she gripped the arm-rest of her seat.

"I know how you feel about me being here, but you better suck it up like a good sailor. I'm going to lead this investigation and make sure it's done right. I have the experience and I have the authority. Hell, you should be grateful for my help and a second pair of eyes on this whole mess."

Her cheeks drained of color and she swallowed hard.

"You almost died the last time you were on the *Mc-Cloud,* and I will do everything in my power to see you're never put in that position again. So, stop being so damn stubborn and release your backbone a bit."

Her chest rose and fell more quickly.

"Look at me."

Her throat worked.

"Sia."

She swung her gaze to his, and there was no mistaking the fatigue, the wariness and the healthy dose of anger he saw there. "What?"

"To be perfectly honest, I believe if not for these whacked-out circumstances, we would have never set eyes on each other again. But we have. That may give us a chance to finally put the past behind us and move on. Seeing you again has stirred up a bunch of stuff I thought I was long done with."

She looked away, blinking rapidly.

He dropped his gaze, the emotion building in his chest. Oh, damn, please don't let her cry.

He felt her gaze flicker to his and looked up in time to catch it, hold it. He saw her overcome her emotions and get herself under control. Ah, yes, Sia was certainly made of sterner stuff. If she let herself go, just once, maybe she could learn it was okay to be vulnerable, to lean.

"I think you are mistaken, Agent Vargas. I have put you and what happened in the past. I think you're the one who needs something more. I suggest you get over it because I have no interest in dredging it up. What we had got destroyed."

"Did it?" He held her gaze for a few heartbeats as the color seeped back into her cheeks. "That remains to be seen."

"You didn't let me finish. It got destroyed by you. Now you can suck it up." She rose. "Excuse me. I have to go to the head."

He stood so she could pass, her body contacting with his all the way from his chest to his knees. The plane hit some turbulence and Sia was thrown against him. He held on to her instinctively so she wouldn't fall onto her injured shoulder. The interior of the plane was dark; only the small overhead light on their panel was on. Most of the passengers had decided to sleep since the red-eye flight wouldn't get into L.A. until early morning.

Once the turbulence passed, he didn't let her go. They stared at each other, her face close to his, her mouth soft and damp, glistening in the dimness. Their silence expanded in a way that lent texture to the very air between them. In the close quarters, the air was warm, with little ventilation. Her face was in shadows, but the dim light only outlined her beautiful bone structure, her startled eyes that had green and gold flecks in the deep brown.

"Thank you for not letting me fall," she said softly, her voice cracking, showing how unsettled she was.

He let her go as she pushed at him with her good arm. As she disappeared down the passageway, he had a hard time tamping down his own roiling emotions.

No matter what she said, her feelings weren't in the past. Far from it.

He didn't let himself hope. That would have been foolish, but he did crack the door to perhaps let in hope, if it was so inclined to sneak in when he wasn't looking.

Sia leaned against the head's door. With a soft sound of protest she sank down onto the seat. She turned her head and looked at herself in the mirror. She squeezed her eyes shut, but it only made the images in her head starker, clearer.

Chris was potent at a distance, but close up…he was lethal. She felt the power in his hands as he'd gently supported her through the turbulence. His eyes were a window into his soul, straightforward, sincere and tough. He was all those things and more. How could she have forgotten how much he stirred her blood, how easily she could fall into those fathomless eyes, like descending into a mist that cast a magic spell over her.

She scrubbed at her face with her free hand. Her shoulder throbbed and her eye looked especially ugly with the purple-green-and-black bruise standing out starkly against her white skin.

All of her feelings for him rushed back and she couldn't control them. The pain at her memories of him, of making love to him, of being with him and living with him were more than precious to her, more than sacred. But she had to be smart. The memory of how she'd felt when she'd learned about her brother's death and Chris's pilot error that had allowed him to eject and her brother to die also came rushing back, warring with her need and regard for him.

She couldn't dredge this up, couldn't allow this to color her life or mess with her head. She had to stay focused and do the job she'd been sent to do and do it right.

"This time, I have to make sure it's right," she whispered, her voice breaking. "I have to."

Her shoulders slumped a tiny bit as she tried hard to fight off the inevitable reality check.

It didn't help that she was exhausted. She hadn't slept in twenty-four hours and now she was headed back to the carrier where she'd almost lost her life. Where the master chief had died trying to kill her.

She only wished she had thought to ask him the burning question that was now troubling her. Why? Why had he tried to kill her? What had she gotten close to or stumbled on to or would have stumbled on to if she'd been given the opportunity to question him and bring him up on charges? Had she taken a misstep and been blinded by her own emotions? Was she responsible for Lieutenant Washington's death? Could she even make this right at all?

All the answers were aboard the *U.S.S. James Mc-Cloud,* the ship of memories.

When she got back to her seat, she slipped past Chris as quickly and impersonally as she could. He didn't say anything and that suited her fine. She reached down for her purse and fumbled inside trying to find her pain-killer, but with one hand it was awkward.

Chris took her purse from her and reached inside and found the bottle. He popped open the top and handed her the tablets. Motioning for the flight attendant, he requested water for her.

Sia took the medication and leaned back in her seat.

"Get some rest," Chris whispered, reaching up to turn off the panel light. Sia closed her eyes and sighed as the medication started to do its work.

How was she supposed to shore up her defenses, resume her steely-eyed distance from a guy like Chris? Half of her wanted to fall into his lap right now.

She needed to get back to the no-nonsense woman she'd made herself into or she wouldn't have any hope of surviving the next few weeks with him and keeping her heart intact.

A prayer was on her tongue as she fell asleep, but she wasn't sure exactly what she was praying for.

The sound of the captain's voice and the dim lighting of the plane woke her with a start. She sighed dreamily and snuggled deeper against the firm pillow, her hand reaching around a trim waist to come up against hard metal.

She opened her eyes to find her face pillowed against Chris's hard, muscled chest. His sleepy eyes regarded her with interest and something a drowsy Chris couldn't conceal. She jerked back and groaned softly at the pain in her shoulder and that look disappeared from his eyes. It made her feel almost sad about it, but knew it was better for her own equilibrium.

"Steady," he said softly. "No harm in resting comfortably and God knows that's tough to do on a plane."

Her awareness of him was as finely tuned as her senses were in the courtroom. Except with him, there was all that sexual energy jacking things up. She cleared her throat, maybe squared her shoulders a little, and then made the mistake of looking back at him before reaching for her purse.

Something about the morning beard shadowing his jaw, the way his dark hair was all mussed up, made his smoky eyes darker, and enhanced how impossibly thick his eyelashes were. His mouth looked way too sexy and kissable in the dim light.

She turned away and raised the shade on the window and saw LAX below her as they lined up with the runway to set down. The captain came back on the speaker to let everyone know the temperature and that they would be at the gate shortly.

As soon as the plane stopped, passengers were up reaching for their stowed luggage.

Chris rose, too, and Sia tried not to stare at the way his muscles flexed and elongated beneath his clothes as he reached up for their luggage. How his sweater went tight over his biceps or the way it made his shoulders look wider.

He dipped down and eyed her. "Are you ready? Do you need help?"

"No," she said quickly, not sure how she would handle having those powerful hands on her again. Let him think she was just a bit stiff and sleepy. More the better for her if Chris never knew the level of fascination she'd had for him. Still had, apparently. Dammit.

She reached down and grabbed her purse and briefcase. Rising, she moved out from the seats and slipped into the space in front of him.

She tried her best to appear unaffected and coolly in control as they deplaned. But Chris's long-legged stride kept him right at her back. And she could feel him there, just behind her, in a rather primal way that had the power to skew her internal equilibrium.

Chris took her arm when she headed for the escalator and directed her toward the elevator. He reached past her and pressed the button. When he stepped in after her, she felt a bit claustrophobic, as if he was suddenly taking up too much space, using up way too much of her precious air. And yet he was standing a respectable distance from her, not so much as looking at her. Which did nothing to stop her from thinking how satisfying it would be to push the emergency stop and caress his face, kiss that sexy mouth, watch his eyes heat.

It only made her mood swing to the nasty. "Afraid you wouldn't be able to hold my hand on the escalator like my mommy?"

"Yes," he simply said.

It only made her fume.

Then her stomach growled so loud it was audible above the din outside the slowly descending elevator.

"Sounds like you need something to eat, little girl."

She let his dig go with a perfectly sweet smile.

"Let's get some breakfast, then. We have two hours before our flight leaves."

"I can't hide the fact that I'm starving."

"When was the last time you ate?"

"I don't remember."

After breakfast, it was a short walk to the gate, then on to the flight. It wasn't long before they were touching down at the Honolulu airport, where they were picked up by a Navy car to take them to the *U.S.S. James Mc-Cloud*. A large crowd of reporters were only able to get in a few questions before Sia and Chris were tucked inside the vehicle.

At the sight of the ship and the sponson in particular, a chill ran over Sia's skin. She could see where part of the flight deck had been scorched and that crews were working on the damaged area of the vessel.

The *U.S.S. James McCloud* was only one of a large fleet of carriers in the Navy. The flight deck, angled at nine degrees, which allowed aircraft to be launched and recovered simultaneously, took up the majority of the available space on the ship. The ship carried a full wing of 12/14 F/A-18F Super Hornets as strike fighters, another two squadrons of 10-12 F/A-18C Hornets, as well as early-warning aircraft, a helicopter and anti-submarine squadron. Each carrier-based aircraft used a tailhook bolted to an eight-foot bar that extended from the craft to catch one of four cables on the deck of the carrier. The cables were engineered to stop any aircraft at exactly the same spot on the deck no matter the size or weight of the craft.

The prominent bridge was situated to starboard, which Sia learned early on in her career was the right side of a ship.

Once on board, they were directed to the NCIS agent a-float, Clarissa Weston.

"Ahoy," she called out as they entered her office. "Chris! It's good to see you. I got word you and Commander Soto were coming aboard to investigate this tragedy. My office is at your command."

"Thanks, Clarissa. It's good to see you again. What do you have so far?"

"I'm sure you'll want to do your own investigations, Chris, but so far all I've done is make sure no one has left the ship. That went over big. Most of these people have been cooped up on this vessel for three months, but this port stop isn't for fun. It's to get repairs to the flight deck Lieutenant Washington tore up when he crash-landed." She turned to Sia. "It's good to see you again, ma'am. Wow, that's a nasty shiner. I sure hope you're healing okay."

"I'm doing fine, Clarissa. Thank you for asking."

"The legal office is also at your disposal, Chris, ma'am. Commander Stryker is expecting you."

"Thank you," Chris said.

"The captain asked that you report to him as soon as you were aboard. He's at Pri-Fly, the Primary Flight Control center. I'll take you to him now."

Sia was now familiar with the carrier after spending time on the ship during her investigation. They headed toward what was called the "island"—the command center for flight-deck operation as well as the ship as a whole. The island was about one hundred and fifty feet tall, but only twenty feet wide, so it wouldn't take up too much space on the flight deck.

The top of the island sported an array of radar and communications antennas, which kept tabs on surrounding ships and picked up satellite phone and TV signals. Below that was their destination, Pri-Fly. At the next level was the bridge, where the captain directed the helmsman who actually steered the carrier.

Sia clumsily navigated several ladders due to her injured shoulder as Clarissa ushered them into the Pri-Fly main area, where Captain Thaddeus Maddox was looking through a set of binoculars at the damaged part of the deck.

Without turning around, he said, "Commander Soto. I can't say I'm thrilled to have you back aboard my ship."

"Good morning, sir. Under the circumstances, I can't say I'm thrilled to be back." He was an intimidating man, with a strong, iron-hard jaw and salt-and-pepper hair. His posture was ramrod straight and he commanded the very air around him.

The captain set down the binoculars and turned around. He walked forward and nodded to Clarissa. "Thank you, Agent Weston."

She nodded and took her leave.

Chris reached out his hand. "Special Agent Chris Vargas, sir."

The captain shook his hand, but only briefly met Chris's eyes. He returned his gaze to Sia, and she stood at attention until the captain said, "At ease."

He turned to a stocky blond man standing next to him. "This is my XO, Commander Seth Tate. If I'm not available, you can speak to him."

He then addressed Sia. "Your report put the death of Lieutenant Malcolm Saunders directly on the master chief's shoulders. How do you explain what has happened with Lieutenant Washington?"

"I've only arrived, sir, and haven't had a chance to even review preliminary information."

The captain's eyes narrowed. "Well, I expect you will have answers for me, Commander Soto. I have another dead aviator, lost another expensive aircraft and have a damaged ship. I'm not happy."

"With all due respect, Skipper," Chris said, "I read Commander Soto's report and I would have drawn the same conclusions. She did a thorough investigation and on top of it almost lost her life. It was clear to her at the time she had the right suspect."

"I concede the investigation was thorough, Special Agent Vargas. I will give her that, and she did put her life at risk. But if this investigation into the senator's son's death turns up he was murdered, then it's obvious there was something more to the story than was evident at the time."

She wasn't supposed to go all warm inside when Chris stuck up for her. "Agreed, sir," Sia said. "But Special Agent Vargas is in charge. I answer to him."

"Noted," the captain said. "Stow your gear and get to work. We'll be leaving port in about a day or two. The needed repairs weren't major."

"Aye, sir," Sia said, coming to attention. She executed a perfect turn and left Pri-Fly with Chris following behind.

Back at Agent Weston's office, Clarissa volunteered to show Chris to his stateroom. Sia had been assigned the same stateroom as on her last visit. This time, though, her roommate had been transferred to another billet, which left Sia enjoying the stateroom all to herself. She only meant to lie down for a moment, but fell asleep. When she woke up, she saw she'd been asleep for a couple of hours. After freshening and changing her uniform, she was free to visit the legal office.

Commander William Stryker greeted her as she entered. "Hello, Sia. Sorry you had to come back here so soon."

"Me, too, Billy. What do you have so far?"

"Not much. I've done some preliminary questioning of personnel and I've compiled that into this file." He handed her a folder. "Agent Weston wanted me to pass the autopsy report for Lieutenant Saunders to you."

Sia opened it and quickly skimmed the contents. "Thanks. I'll read this later," she said and tucked it into her briefcase.

"I've also compiled a list of people who were directly responsible for the two jets and any other personnel who may have witnessed the accident." He handed her a sheaf of papers and Sia went to tuck them into the folder.

"Good work. That's what I'm looking for," Sia said.

Chris's deep, resonant voice stopped the action she was about to perform. "Don't you mean that's what *we're* looking for?"

She turned to find Chris standing in the doorway. "Commander William Stryker, this is the lead investigator, Special Agent Chris Vargas."

Billy nodded, eyeing Chris.

Chris came up to her and looked over her shoulder at the list in her hand. "Let's take the first name and make our way down the list."

Sia nodded.

Billy looked at the name at the top of the list. "Airman Trudy Schover. I'll get her in here for you."

It wasn't long before the woman was sitting across the same table where Sia had interrogated the master chief.

"Tell me where you were and what happened when Lieutenant Washington's F/A-18 crashed into the deck," Sia asked the young dark-haired woman. Her hands were clasped together in front of her and she was wringing them.

"I was in Pri-Fly handling the communication between the planes." She looked at Chris. "I'm like an air traffic controller."

"It's okay, Airman, I was a pilot." She acknowledged that with a nod of her head. "Did you know Lieutenant Washington?" Chris continued, leaning back and folding his arms across his chest.

Trudy shook her head, her eyes sincere. "No, sir. I didn't."

"Continue," Chris said.

"Everything went routinely and that night was clear as glass, no clouds in the sky. Lieutenants Washington and Monroe took off. About three minutes into the flight, Lieutenant Monroe yelled for Lieutenant Washington to get his nose up."

"Did Lieutenant Washington respond?" Chris leaned forward, his eyes intent.

"Yes, he said that he was having problems with his radar."

"His radar?" Chris asked, as he set his hands on the table and concentrated on the airman's words.

"Yes, sir. He said it was malfunctioning." Her voice strained, Trudy stopped talking, her eyes going unfocused. She was trying to remember.

"In what way?"

"Total failure. No instruments," she said solemnly.

"But he was trained to land without them, correct?" Sia asked. With each word her throat got tighter. She'd read her brother's report years after his death, and as Trudy related the incident, Sia became more alarmed.

"Yes, ma'am. I tried to initiate communication just before the crash. He had his nose down. Lieutenant Monroe was yelling at him to bring his nose up and the flight crew handling the meatball were waving him off, but it was too late. He hit the deck hard, skidded across the platform and right off the end of the carrier, exploding as he dropped into the sea." Her voice broke and held a note of the shock she still seemed to be experiencing, her eyes moist.

"He didn't even attempt to eject?" Chris asked.

"No, sir."

"Meatball?" Sia said looking at the airman for an explanation.

"It's a series of lights that are calibrated to the horizon. It serves as a safeguard when pilots are landing on the carrier. If a pilot sees green, safe to land, if red, they need to break off and circle around to land again. The circles of light look like meatballs, so that's how it got its name."

"Any other observations, Airman?" Chris asked.

"Only that he was one of the finest pilots I've ever worked with," she said emphatically. "I didn't know him personally, but I knew him as a pilot. I was shocked to see his nose down like that. It was worse than a rookie mistake, malfunction or not."

"Thank you, Airman," Chris said.

Trudy nodded, but before she left, she turned back, tear tracks down her cheeks. "I hope you clear him of any blame. He doesn't deserve to have his record marred this way."

All Sia could offer her was a quick nod, her emotions in turmoil and thoughts of her brother foremost in her thoughts.

When the door closed behind Airman Schover, Chris turned to Sia. "Sounds like he could have made a mistake with the radar off. But he would have noticed if the meatball lights were red."

"Maybe he was impaired. He could have been too short on oxygen, or some other explanation."

Chris took a deep breath and then released it slowly. "That's exactly how it went down when Rafael died, only my plane was still in the air and I ejected."

Silence filled the compartment, the kind that wove around the heart and squeezed tight.

Chapter 4

Just the mention of her brother's name made Sia remember him and the day he'd died. She'd been figuring out the best way to tell her father she wasn't going to New York. She wasn't going to take a job that was too far away from Chris.

She had answered the door when the Navy had come knocking to break the news about her brother. At first, she thought they had come to tell her Chris was dead and her heart had throbbed painfully in her chest. But when they'd told her it was her brother, the guilt only mixed in with the terrible grief and relief it hadn't been Chris.

She could tell by looking at Chris he was remembering that day, too. His beard-shadowed jaw hardened and his eyes went distant.

"Do you think we're dealing with more than pilot error in all these incidents?" she asked him, watching as his eyes focused again, but the pain and the grief lingered in their depths.

"I don't want to jump to conclusions, but my gut is telling me something. I don't usually ignore it."

She turned away from the emotion that darkened his eyes and set his mouth in a grim line. "What is your gut telling you?" The lack of sleep, the quick trip to Pearl and her injuries were beginning to take a toll. She leaned back in her chair and rubbed at her tired face.

Chris didn't miss the movement and his intense eyes studied her. "That somehow, some way, the two incidents might be connected."

For an instant her heart stopped. Now it was racing. "Do you remember Master Chief Walker from the *Mc-Cloud* six years ago?"

Chris shook his head. "The people who serviced the planes were never really on my radar. I lived to fly and my focus was always on that. When Rafael and I hit the cockpits, we flew for the Navy, but it was pure joy. It's tragedy enough to lose one pilot, but two in such a short span of time is…suspect." His voice was reflective and sad. The sound of it squeezed her heart.

She was finding sympathy in all the tragedy. She was feeling some of the guilt that Chris must have felt when her brother's plane had been destroyed. Although she had no emotional ties to Lieutenant Washington, she regretted any action that she hadn't taken to ensure that no more deaths attributed to Master Chief Walker occurred. Then she realized the truth. It couldn't have been Walker. He was dead. What did that mean?

"Oh, damn, there's one flaw in our suspicions." She

folded her arms and tucked herself back into her seat, some of her doubts beginning to surface.

Chris held her gaze. "What is that?"

"Master Chief Walker died before Lieutenant Washington crash-landed his jet. There can be no way he was involved in the death." Dammit, this was so puzzling. Why had the man tried to kill her? What did Washington and Saunders have in common that they were both targeted? Sia was convinced they both had been. The manner of their "accidents" was too similar and the same exact issue with the radar couldn't have been a coincidence. The Navy was meticulous in maintaining their aircraft. Safety was about protecting their investment in the pilots who flew the sleek fighter jets and the amount of money that was tied up in each piece of high-tech machinery.

"There would be if he tampered with the plane before he died."

She hadn't considered that. But what was irking her was the incoherency of the pilot. "That's a possibility, but why didn't Lieutenant Washington correct the position of his plane before he landed? Any seasoned pilot would have. Lieutenant Washington has executed dozens of carrier landings. His behavior doesn't jive with his training and skill. If a drug was administered, then the master chief would have had to be present in the wardroom before Saunders took off."

Chris considered her words, pressing his back to the bulkhead. "There is information we don't have right now, like the autopsy and the condition of his plane. We'll wait for those before we start building conspiracy theories."

"Well, at the very least, the tie I was hoping existed between my brother's death and Lieutenant Saunders's accident could still be viable, but I'm not sure what it means that we have another similar accident within only a day of Lieutenant Saunders's."

Chris straightened. "You suspect Walker had something to do with sabotaging my fighter?"

"I think he had some beef against pilots. Who knows? Maybe he was a wannabe. But I believe he sabotaged your jet."

"Why do you think that?"

"He told me so."

Chris leaned on the small table, his eyes intent and a bit angry. "He told you? He said he sabotaged my plane? He is directly responsible for Rafe's death? Why didn't you tell me this information before?"

She shook her head, holding up her hand. "Wait. No, he didn't exactly tell me that. He just hinted at the information he had no intention of sharing with me that your pilot error was the same as Lieutenant Saunders's. That he somehow had something to do with it. The rest is my conjecture."

"He could have been baiting you. We can't jump to conclusions."

Sia knew he was in charge and the yoke of that rankled. But she wasn't going to shut up just because he thought her ideas were speculation. It was a way for her to work out her cases. Too bad if he didn't like it. "It's possible he could have tampered with your plane," she insisted, getting satisfaction at the way his eyes snapped.

"It is possible. He was on the *McCloud* when Rafe

and I were stationed here. But we have a lot more in-vestigating to do before we come up with an answer."

"I know that. I'm convinced it's worth trying to get them to reopen the case."

"It's a tall order, Sia. The Navy isn't going to be thrilled to rehash an incident that's already been ruled as pilot error. The report states I'm guilty of channelized attention and it substantially contributed to the mishap."

There was a limit to her patience. Sia was well aware of Chris's ruling. His attention had been so consumed with the radar problem it kept him from recognizing and correcting the airspeed and flight path errors and led to his crashing into her brother's plane. Chris was able to eject to safety, but her brother had been unable to do so in time. They had found him in his plane, still strapped in the seat.

"They will if I have new evidence or a confession from the killer," she snapped.

He noted her anger with a mocking glance, skepti-cism in his eyes. "That's true, but you have to be pre-pared to accept the fact they made the correct ruling. I was examined by a doctor and he found nothing wrong with me physically. Both Rafe and I were guilty of pilot error. It cost Rafe his life. It cost me…everything."

A wave of exhaustion hit her. She wanted him to see the possibility, but he was trapped in what the Navy had told him. Sia just wasn't convinced. Her voice rose a fraction. "Nevertheless, even if there is a small possi-bility, I won't rest until justice is served."

Chris scrutinized her pose, her expression, the pas-sion in her voice, and smiled wryly. "You were born to be a prosecutor, Sia." His gaze intensified, sharpened, as if he had sensed something in her. Slowly he closed the gap between them until he was a little too close.

"You'll help me get the evidence I need, won't you, Chris?" Even though it was a question, Sia had no intention of accepting anything but his acquiescence.

Chris shrugged, avoiding the penetrating stare she turned on him. "What does it matter, Sia? I'm no longer part of the Navy and I'll never fly a fighter jet again." His voice was low and smoky like his eyes, laced with old bitterness.

She crossed her arms and scowled at him. "I care. I want my brother's name cleared."

"Your voice is like a loaded gun, Sia." Chris's gaze melted over her, lingering on her mouth. She just realized he had boxed her in.

"Take it any way you want," she said flatly, and pointedly extricated herself from the tight space he'd cornered her into. "But I would think you would jump at the chance." She was all crisp business and haughty demeanor now. It helped to hide the hurt and disappointment that shouldn't be as crushing as they were. "My brother didn't have a chance to defend himself. He didn't have a voice in the matter. I will be that voice for him." She moved back into the main part of the cabin with a deliberate calm that cost her more than he'd ever realize.

"I'll do what I can."

Sia's jaw tightened fractionally. There was still the thread of disappointment he hadn't been more supportive of her plan. He hadn't been there when the master chief had told her he knew something but wasn't telling her anything. That he expected her to go to her grave knowing the two men she loved most in the world hadn't been responsible for the accident. She wanted to grab his shoulders and shake him and make him question every aspect, every memory of that day. But he seemed resigned to his fate and hadn't even considered something else could have been at fault. And, as irrational as it might be, that hurt. "That's all I can ask," she said grudgingly.

"I think we should focus our attention fully on the case we're investigating right now, Sia. Saunders and Washington deserve that."

Sia nodded. "They do."

"Do we have Saunders's autopsy yet?"

Sia shifted her eyes away from his and hedged. She hadn't meant to lie to him, but unless he directly asked Billy about when she received the report, he would never know she had it in her briefcase. She was just being contrary and she knew it. Being under his thumb for her every move on this case rankled. "I'm not sure. Once the case closed and I was sent home, I really didn't have a chance to follow up." All true.

"Well, that needs to be one of our priorities. NCIS agents always follow up."

She nodded. "Agreed. I could look into that right now. I've just got to find Billy."

"Sia, he's probably turned in. It's late."

"It is?"

"Yes, and you're dead on your feet. Let's put this on hold until tomorrow when we'll both be rested. We need to organize how we're going to tackle and untangle this mess. If Walker is responsible for all three deaths, then we need to figure that out. If not, we need to either confirm the pilot-error ruling or negate it. There's more at stake here than proving innocence or guilt."

"What is that?"

"There are families involved. People who want to know what happened to their loved ones. They need to have answers to put them completely to rest," he said gently.

He opened the cabin door and Sia stepped out. He followed and secured the door. He turned and headed down the corridor and she followed.

It must have been the weariness leeching at her body. His words caused a storm of emotions to rise in her, the remembered pain of her brother's death and shame that it had been deemed his fault, never knowing the real answers, not being able to forgive or forget Chris's part in his death. The tantalizing clue from Walker that he had the real answer, but had no intention of giving her that peace. Her eyes filled and she stumbled on the ladder, which was just what the Navy called the metal stairway that led to the various decks of the ship.

With lightning-quick reflexes, Chris caught her and the movement jostled her sore shoulder. She cried out at the painful twinge. Chris responded by steadying her and swinging her up into his arms. Against her protests, he carried her the rest of the way to her quarters.

The memories whirled around her and intertwined, mixing in a braid of pain and longing that had pulled at her for six long years. To feel his touch again was torture. To have his arms around her again confused her, but was still wonderful.

He was sorely testing her sense of balance. Seeing him again was both unexpected and unwanted. At least on her end. She was going to have to endure working with him—she didn't have a real choice, but she could ill afford to let herself rekindle any of the feelings she'd had for him. She couldn't risk it. Besides, their forced contact was temporary, so there was no point. All she had to do was resist the temptation—the very potent temptation.

"Put me down," she demanded for the third time. Defiantly, he held her against his warm, muscular body. "It was unnecessary."

"You're dead on your feet and this was faster."

His voice had gone rough like whiskey and smoke with a touch of black satin sheets. Sia's body responded swiftly and automatically to those softly uttered words, nonsensical as they were. He might have said anything in that voice, and she feared her response would have been the same—an instantaneous quickening, a flash of warmth, reduced lung capacity. His breath was warm against her cheek. "I don't need you to rescue me." She clenched her teeth at the breathless quality to her voice.

"You were always fiercely independent." A wicked gleam sparkled in his eyes, curling the corners of his delectable mouth. He leaned close as he easily held her in his strong arms, his thumb rubbing against the exposed skin between her sleeve and the sling. The feel of his skin against her sent a shower of sparks through her.

"Damn straight," she said as his gaze intensified and there was more fire in his eyes than smoke. With little effort, he caught her gaze, held her prisoner.

"And stubborn," he breathed, leaning closer still, his lips just brushing the shell of her ear.

She gave him a look that made better men back off

and ground her teeth when he only smiled at her. She wiggled against him and he sighed deep in his chest. Finally, he let her go with a slow slide down his body. For far too long, he kept one arm wrapped around her, as if he couldn't quite bear to let her go.

He had often accused her of being obstinate, and those words brought a rush of bittersweet emotion so strong Sia had to take a moment to compose herself. She was finding it almost as difficult to move out of his embrace.

"My independence has served me well," she said.

"I have no doubt."

He fell silent again, and maybe it was her own mounting tension over the swelling emotional war she was playing with herself that made the air between them seem to crackle. But, at least from her perspective, the awareness and anxiety were operating on another level, as well.

He turned as if to go and she risked a quick sideways glance at him then; she couldn't help it. His profile was solemn, his jaw hard and set. His gaze was fixed on a point at the end of the passageway. This emotion she felt could be totally one-sided. Chances were, he didn't want or desire anything from her other than her collaboration on this case.

She was thankful no one had witnessed her momentary breakdown. She leaned against the door frame and tried to tell herself all the reasons why being disappointed with that probable reality was a really dangerous way to feel.

"Sia, there's no shame in accepting help."

It was a struggle to find her composure. He was far

too close, and every facet of her equilibrium was threatened, physically, emotionally, intellectually. "There is
when I'm an officer in the Navy and in an official capacity aboard an aircraft carrier. I didn't need to defend
my professionalism before you showed up at JAG and
hijacked my case."

"I didn't hijack your case."

"Yes, you did. When you hijacked it, you wouldn't
back down or reassign someone else. You refused. Now
we have this…"

She trailed off.

"This?"

"Never mind. I'm going to bed." She turned her back
to him and grabbed the handle to open the stateroom
door. She felt shame at the need to escape.

"No, wait a minute. You can't leave it hanging like
that."

"Chris, I don't want to rehash old news or old feelings. It's been too long and we both know what we
had ended when my brother died. That's the end of
the story."

There was that palpable danger again. His hand
slipped over hers on the doorknob. She could feel how
close he was to her, her back tingling with his nearness,
the heat of him. The situation between them was spiraling out of control. All the more reason to get the investigation back on track. She'd think everything through
later, figure out what to do about it. When he was far,
far away and not looking at her the way he had looked
at her. Like he still wanted to consume her.

And, damn her memories, she knew what it would
be like to let him.

"Is it? I think you still feel something, Sia."

"No." But her protest was low and breathless.

And if Chris himself wasn't dangerous, then what she felt when he was this near surely was. She couldn't fall for him, not for his body or his tarnished soul or his allure of the forbidden. There was no room in her life for this man. She couldn't have her heart broken again; she was still trying to glue the pieces back together from the last time she had come apart.

But she couldn't seem to remove her hand. It seemed a lifeline, an anchor that bolstered her as the memories, good and bad, flashed over her like an uncontrollable fire.

He grasped her hand and turned her toward him and she was powerless to resist.

Holding her breath, she counted the beats of her heart, her eyes on his, wondering why she didn't take her own advice and let go. Walk away.

His hand squeezed hers and his eyes softened. "Sia," he said, his voice low and textured like raw silk—rough and smooth at once, beckoning a woman to reach out and touch him, tempting her, luring her closer.

Her eyes met his and she was lost in the dark gray depths, so lost. It was as if the world and their problems melted in the heat of their eyes. She trembled with the longing she had buried for six years while she immersed herself in her work to forget. She didn't know if it was her near-death experience, the medication, or her deep-seated longing for him. She swayed forward, into him.

His arms slipped around her, taking her mouth without preamble, his lips sizzling against hers. For the first time in Sia's life, she found herself losing control when she very much needed to maintain control, needed to keep her distance. But she lost her train of thought as her good arm slipped up around his neck, her fingers tangling through his hair. He opened his mouth wider, taking more of her. She knew a single kiss wasn't going to be enough.

His mouth was made for love, for kissing and making love, so soft and lush and captivating. She moved against him, her breasts pressing against his chest, her mouth angling over his and creating a brief moment of suction, and as quickly as that, heat shot through every single inch of her body. She felt her control slip, a quick jerk of it out from under her.

Sia was drowning. Drowning in desire and confusion—and desire won, every second, every heartbeat. She wasn't proud of it. She should be made of sterner stuff.

She had to stop. But she couldn't remember why. It was more than a kiss, more than any kiss he'd ever given her. And her mind focused on that one thought—shamelessly. The feel of him in her mouth, the taste of him, was intoxicating, compulsive. He set her on fire with his kiss, made her gasp, and every inch of her wanted more. It was wild. Wild and hot and utterly sexual in a way she'd thought she would never know except in her fantasies—but the reality of it, damn, the reality of it was so much more intense. The silkiness of his hair sliding through her fingers, the rough edge of his jaw beneath her palm, the strength of his arms wrapped around her. Fantasies were perfect because they were so safe. She was in control. Chris epitomized the loss of control. There was no safety in those dark eyes. The pure physical energy of him was a force to be reckoned with. He was powerful, dangerous and unpredictably seductive.

And she'd be a fool if she thought they could ever have what they'd lost. With a soft cry she pulled away.

"I can't!" Her eyes filled. She hadn't meant to cry, but her barriers were frayed and she was so tired.

"Why?"

Tears spilled out and ran down her cheeks. "You know why." She reached for anything that would put distance between them. "Because of your error the Navy memorial has refused to honor my brother. He was a hero and he's never going to get the recognition he deserved."

Chris stood there, taking her words like physical blows. His dark eyes were haunted and filled with the guilt she knew he felt and she regretted her words. Bashing him wouldn't change anything. Rafael was dead. Her parents were dead. Everyone she loved had been taken from her. If she could find any connection, anything at all to the fact it might have been murder, then she could exonerate her brother. And, in turn, Chris.

Standing there stoically and taking what she had to say right on the chin only made her realize how strong and brave he was. He didn't flinch or get angry, he just stood there and let her vent. She didn't know what to say. She could only feel, feel her heart break, feel her mind try to find a way to reconcile her emotions.

But she couldn't move that immovable wall. She couldn't seem to step forward, past it. It remained, lingering, holding her hostage. Nowhere to go.

Nowhere to run.

He reached out gently and wiped at the tears on her cheek with his thumb, then abruptly he pulled her hard against him. His hand disrupted her bun and sent her hair cascading down her back. He buried his face in her shoulder. "Do me a favor, Sia?"

Her voice, clogged with emotion, was muffled against his shoulder. "What?"

"Keep an open mind?"

She took a deep breath. "Keep an open mind?"

"Yes. Can you do that?" he asked, his voice a shade rougher.

"I'll try," she responded, her voice breaking. "I'll try."

He released her and walked away, his broad back disappearing down the passageway. For one moment, she let herself dream they had a chance, but she knew it was a lie. If he hadn't been so stubborn and had just assigned someone else to this case, it would have been so much easier for both of them. Anger mixed in with the desire and longing.

Slipping into her quarters, she burst into tears, her throat tight, her chest heavy. In the darkness, she let herself cry for the loss, for the memories and for the love she once had for a man who could no longer comfort her.

Chapter 5

He hadn't meant to watch her. He'd only come up to the flight deck to run off some of his disappointment and the desire that had caught him off guard last night, and Sia was already there. Of course, that kiss shouldn't have had him tossing and turning, but it had.

He'd been craving the taste of her since last night. He'd convinced himself he must have exaggerated the hell out of what it had been like to kiss her, because a kiss was just a kiss, right? No way could one kiss be so special, so addicting, so enthralling…so intense.

As it turned out, he had forgotten the impact. *In a big way.*

Her lips had been so soft, and the way her breath hitched in the back of her throat, accompanied by that small, rough moan, immediately made him go rock-hard. It was all he could do not to plaster her back against the bulkhead and take and give until they were both sated.

She'd taken off the sling and was easily moving across the flight deck as if she hadn't been almost murdered two days ago. Her dark, curly hair was caught up in a ponytail, streaming out behind her like ebony ribbons as her legs, encased in black Lycra, fueled her quick strides.

The bruise still stood starkly out on her soft, deep-golden skin, but it was beginning to fade somewhat.

"You going to run, sir, or lollygag?" a flight deck sailor said good-naturedly as he walked past. "Although it's a very nice view." He smiled and returned back inside the carrier, no doubt on some task that needed completing. The work on a ship as large as this one never ceased.

Chris stretched and took off. It wasn't long before he caught up with her. "Are you sure you should be running? You almost got up close and personal with the ocean just a few days ago."

"Yeah, swimming with the fishes isn't my idea of fun." She turned to look at him, not at all shy about what had happened last night. He remembered that was something he had always liked about Sia. Her straightforward manner and her lack of game playing had attracted him from the moment he'd met her. Her acerbic wit and quick comebacks made him admire her even more. It was as if six years had melted away.

They were quiet for a few paces and then Sia spoke. "I have a couple of things I need to confess."

She glanced over at him, but there was no apology in her eyes. Instead he saw a flash of anger. He suspected she had no intention of sharing with him what she was up to, but somehow had changed her mind. He wondered why.

"Well, get the torpedoes in the water then."

She laughed without mirth. "Nothing as explosive or dangerous as that. But I want you to know."

"So it doesn't come back to bite you on the butt?"

"Something like that. Even though you hijacked my case, I guess I can be magnanimous in sharing with you some of my suspicions. After all, we're really on the same mission."

"We are. We just have a lot of baggage to jettison."

She chose not to respond to the personal tensions between them. He could feel it even now as they started another lap on the deck. He was sweating freely now, but his body was warming up to the exercise, his muscles loosening.

"After my run-in with Walker and his intriguing statements, I told my legalman to do some research on the deaths aboard the *McCloud* and other ships in the fleet to see if there are any correlations. It might give us a baseline and data to see if we have a consistent MO. It will also tell us if Walker was in the vicinity of any other *accidents*."

"And the second confession?"

"I stalled you on the autopsy for Saunders."

Chris stopped in midstride, floored. After a few steps forward, Sia jogged back. She took his hand and propelled him forward. "Don't stop running. We haven't finished enough to cool down yet."

"I'm not about to cool down anytime soon," he

growled, anger beating in rhythm with his blood. "Why?"

She didn't flinch under his steady, snapping gaze.

"I didn't have a chance to look it over," she said with a bit of miff in her tone. "I wanted to do so without you looking over my shoulder. I have a copy in my briefcase in my quarters. Billy gave it to me as soon as I met up with him yesterday in the legal office. I read through it after you dropped me off at my stateroom last night."

She offered him no apology and he could understand why. Sia considered this her case and he was along for the ride. Regardless of what her commanding officer said, Sia wasn't one to relinquish what she considered her responsibility. He understood this woman all too well. Okay, so she had more at stake than he did. She wanted to clear her brother's name, get him memorialized and bring a killer to justice on a case she thought she may have botched. Chris was sure she thought she could nail all those tasks. When Sia was on a mission, everyone needed to watch out. He just hoped she wasn't setting herself up for disappointment.

There was something else niggling at him and he didn't want to fully acknowledge it lest he also set himself up for disappointment, but he couldn't help it. She had him to gain.

What if she wanted him back? What if she could justify to herself the accident had been foul play? Would she then be able to forgive him? Would that be enough for him? He wasn't sure.

And that eye-opener changed his entire outlook of his world to some new focus, as if he was looking through a kaleidoscope, trying to make sense of the chaotic colors with a view that was no longer his own to interpret—a potentially danger-filled view. It should have scared him more. He was feeling suddenly off-kilter, like the slowly pitching ship.

Sia's speed diminished and finally slowed to a walk. She was giving him sidelong glances as if he would suddenly explode. He was partly angry and partly frustrated she hadn't trusted him with this information. They walked in silence to the exit that would lead them from the flight deck back down into the belly of the ship.

They reached the point where they had to part ways and, without preamble, Chris grabbed Sia's good elbow and steered her into a shadowed alcove. "You have a lot of nerve."

"Me?" Her chin angled with challenge and her voice was brittle. "You wouldn't take the easy way out. You never do, Chris."

"I'm in command here, Sia. You will not withhold information from me again. Is that clear?"

She breathed a heated sigh and faced him defiantly. "Not now, Chris. Not here."

"Yes, now. Yes, here. Not everything is on your terms!"

And just like that she exploded. "I answer to the Navy, not to NCIS, Chris."

He didn't miss the fact he'd said almost those same words to her. Throwing them in his face only made his ire grow. "I was there when your commanding officer gave you a direct order, so for all intents and purposes you do answer to NCIS. You answer to me."

"What?" she scoffed.

"This isn't a joke, Sia." She shoved at him, but he didn't let her push him away.

He knew she was tired, the kind of tired you didn't get from one difficult day. But he had to be tough with Sia or he would lose ground with her. She was much too strong a personality to back down when she thought she was right. But he wasn't perfect. He lost his grip a little, too. "You could severely damage your JAG career by being insubordinate."

"Is that a threat?" she shouted right back at him. "Are you going to write me up, Chris? For doing my job! Right now I care more about the truth then I care about my JAG career."

"That's evident," he shot back. "But you will heed my authority."

"I chafe at your authority. NCIS is a civilian agency. You don't have anything but a fine thread of influence. This should have been my case. It all started with me and me alone. That's where it should end."

"I was there when it started. Don't forget that," he said flatly.

"How can I forget that? How can I? It destroyed my life." Her words were precise, old fury barely reined in. "Not a day goes by I don't think about it and how it eviscerated me."

He flinched and took a step back at the anguish in her voice. The pain was as sharp as ever, as sharp as a razor blade that had ended his dream of a Navy career, lost him the love of his life, deprived him of the best friend who'd been so like a brother to him, destroyed his hope for a family. It sliced at his heart, mocked him with its cruelty, tried to sever his strength.

Regret burned like acid in his throat, behind his eyes. He clenched his jaw against it, whipped himself mentally to get past it. But it all came rushing back, breaking out of its six-year-old prison. And with it came the sound of his father's voice. His father had been a mean, drunken, good-for-nothing bastard who had told him time and again he would never make anything out of himself. Never be anything. But he'd been smart, smarter than he'd let on, because his father would have taken away every opportunity he had to excel. He would make sure his father never saw his grades. Not that his father ever cared. As soon as he could, he applied to and got accepted into the Naval Academy in Annapolis with his eye on Top Gun and becoming a fighter pilot. The tests were a piece of cake, and the training fit him like a well-worn glove. He had owned the skies for a brief time, as fleeting as the burst of fireworks as they lit up the night sky. It wasn't long before he plunged to earth.

"Oh, God, Chris. I'm sorry. I didn't mean to say that." She brought a hand to her mouth to hold back the cry that tore through her, but the tears still flooded and fell. He struggled with the burden of his guilt. He braced his shoulders against it, trembling inside.

"Chris," she said softly. "I lost so much and it's built up for so long. I never got the chance to tell you how angry I was with you. How devastated."

He closed his eyes, the pain and longing had haunted him for so long, closer to the surface than they had ever been. She touched his shoulder, gripping him as if he were her lifeline, but he knew better.

"You have a right to your feelings, Sia." But God, it

hurt, because she might not have meant to say it, but she was most definitely feeling it.

Then she cupped his face. He opened his eyes and the glistening of her tears totally did him in. He wished he could go back to that day and perish with Rafe. It would have been so much easier to have just simply died.

Her eyes softened as she stared up into his face, remorse as clear as the fine brandy color of her eyes. He wanted far, far more than either of them could give at the moment.

He ran his thumb along her lower lip, watching her eyes darken under his touch, wishing like hell her dragons had already been slain.

But he knew he was one of those dragons.

"We have to keep everything in perspective. We just agreed up on the deck we were in this together." His voice sounded raw and misused.

Sia dropped her gaze and took a moment to gather herself. Breathing deeply, she wiped at her eyes. "I'm always so damn angry. It serves me well in court, but it's murder on relationships." She tried to laugh, but it was half-hearted.

"We owe it to those pilots, Sia. If they were victims, we need to bring out the truth and put a stop to the murders."

She nodded. "We're in total agreement about that."

"About our past, we should bury it and try not to let it interfere with our investigation. I understand how you feel, but you have to abide by the orders you were given."

Temper flared in her eyes, but she banked it. "I'll participate in the investigation." She didn't give an inch and he accepted that. They would probably clash again, but for now the storm was over.

Then without warning her arms went around his neck and she hugged him hard. He stroked her hair and kissed her temple and some of the pain she'd inflicted leeched away.

Sia was so torn, so confused. Their private and professional lives were at odds, but her emotions—damn, they were making her crazy.

Dumping on him had been so wrong, but it released a lot of pressure inside her. It was all so much—unburdening herself, trying to reconcile her feelings for him and her anger toward him, then this…overload of sensations with him holding her, caring about her.

He tipped her head back so their gazes could meet. She trembled a little, wanted to be strong enough to scoot away, but had the presence of mind to finally admit to herself this felt good. It was time they hashed out their past. It was time it was dealt with and then she could walk away and have it resolved.

They held each other for several minutes. Like a fog settling over her, the gray of his eyes held her steadfastly and all she could think was she wanted to be able to look into his whenever she wanted to. Like this, intimate and personal, or across a crowded room, when nothing more than a quick smile would say everything that needed to be said between them. She had lost that and that loss left a deeper hole than anything else.

She started to speak, to try to find the words, but he tucked her against his chest then, and she knew there'd come a time when she would say what was on her mind, no matter how painful. Reality had a way of intruding to keep her locked up in a situation that seemed to have no end. But she was on the scent now and she wouldn't let up until the truth was revealed. She had to have that. Lieutenants Washington and Saunders deserved that. And her sweet, strong, funny brother deserved that.

It was a just cause.

When he finally shifted away from her, she only felt it was too soon.

He kissed her temple, then her cheek.

His expression wasn't readable and that gave her pause. "Go and get cleaned up," he said.

"Is that an order?" she asked, a smile playing with the corners of her mouth.

He shook his head and his lips curved a little, too. "Meet me in the officers' mess when you're ready."

"Should I salute you before I go?"

In response, he lifted her hand up to his lips, kissing the back first, then the palm, before curling her fingers in to seal it there. It was a simple gesture, both intimate and heartbreaking, and because she wanted to hold on tightly to both of those things, knowing what lay ahead, she kept her fingers tightly curled as he responded.

"Get going, wiseass."

Back in her stateroom, she took a quick shower and dressed in her uniform, eager to get to the mess and food. She was starving. She was also ready to continue with the investigation. She mentally reminded herself to check her email to see if there had been any news from her legalman.

Stepping outside, she slipped her briefcase strap over her shoulder and turned toward the mess.

Sia was jostled by several crewmembers as she made

her way to the mess. A lot of hungry sailors were crowding the companionway and the ladders. Sia got her bearings and turned toward the ladder. The way cleared a bit and Sia started down. Suddenly, she felt hands on her back and someone gave her a shove.

Losing her balance, Sia began to fall. Only the quick reflexes of the sailor in front of her kept her and him from falling the rest of the way. She apologized and he smiled and told her it was no problem. Once she righted herself, she glanced over her shoulder, but all she saw was the glimpse of dark clothing disappearing down the companionway, getting lost in the sea of sailors.

Had someone just pushed her? It had felt as if the hands had applied force. Maybe it had been an accident and the sailor was afraid Sia would reprimand him or her. She shrugged it off and reached the deck where the mess was located.

She saw Chris near the door to the mess and she stopped on the stairs. She'd forgotten how handsome he was. Age had only tempered those looks, taking him from overtly brash to silently lethal.

He was sorely testing her sense of balance. Their bond, it seemed, was still strong, unexpected as it was unwanted. At least on her end. She found him to be annoyingly irresistible, but she had to be careful not to feel those old feelings and get confused. She could so easily let herself become more attracted to him.

She remembered how he had held her when they'd had that terrible fight after the run on the flight deck. He'd been so solid as he cradled her against his strong chest. It calmed her, soothed her pain in a way that was completely unexpected. He had helped her so much in that moment it caught her off guard and made her realize the strength of their connection.

At that moment, someone he must have known when he'd served aboard the *McCloud* greeted him with a hearty handshake. Chris smiled. It did something magical to his face, disarming her and making her sigh. What would it take for him to smile like that at her? Too many memories flooded her and her regret was never more poignant than it was at this moment. The man moved on but the smile in Chris's eyes lingered.

When he turned and saw her, it diminished some, but didn't completely fade. With a small smile of her own, she made her way over to where he stood.

They went inside, got their food and sat down. She opened up her briefcase and handed him Lieutenant Saunders's autopsy report. "I won't say anything until you finish reading it."

He nodded and as he ate his eggs, his eyes fastened to the pages. Sia still resented her commanding officer's orders. She didn't want her hands tied in handling this investigation. But she had been right when she'd told Chris he didn't have that much of a hold over her.

So what if she was reprimanded. She was going to do what it took to finish this once and for all.

Chris looked up from the pages, his eyes a strong, steady gray, unique and compelling. "They found nothing in his tox screen."

"Right, but look at this." She pulled out the report from the flight boss and handed it to him. Forking up some fluffy eggs, Sia said, "The lieutenant was complaining of dizziness and then he went incoherent." Sliding the fork in her mouth, she chewed and swallowed.

Chris accepted the report and looked at the testimony. "That could have been hypoxemia, caused by a bad oxygen mix."

Sia nodded. "It could have, but then there would have been evidence of that on the report—his lungs or brain or even the oxygenation of his blood would have revealed that." She tapped the autopsy report. "The ME cited nothing in the report that would have indicated he was oxygen-starved." She flipped to the final part of the autopsy. "In fact, Lieutenant Saunders's cause of death is drowning. But if he was impaired during the flight and it didn't have anything to do with hypoxemia, then it had to have been something else."

Hard and sharp, his gaze cut to her. "Like what?"

She met his eyes and shrugged. "Well, an allergy to something he hadn't been exposed to before is possible." She paused for a moment and said, "But it could also be caused by ingesting a drug."

He reached out and snagged his coffee cup and took a sip. "What drug?"

She leaned back in her chair in frustration. "I don't know. I confiscated an over-the-counter irregularity product from the master chief's locker, but the bottle was lost after he took it from me." She could still see his smug smile and she was convinced the man had been harboring more than the secret of what was in the bottle. It was possible he could have been killing pilots. Or know the person responsible, if there was such a person.

"So what makes you suspicious that Saunders was drugged?"

Pushing away the emotion that was distracting her, she reached for logic. "That's the kicker. The master chief himself. When he talked about the accidents, he shook the bottle. I got permission to search his rack after Saunders's wingman swore an oath he saw the master chief touch Saunders's coffee cup. So he had the opportunity to put whatever was in that bottle into Saunders's coffee cup."

Chris closed the autopsy report and handed it back to her for safekeeping. "Still, all the evidence we have is circumstantial at this point, along with some healthy speculation."

Sia nodded. "Playing devil's advocate?"

He shrugged. "You did enough mock trials in law school to know about that. There's always somebody who can trip you up if you're not prepared."

She nodded, remembering those lessons from the simulated jury trials she'd participated in as a law student. "I know it's circumstantial, but my gut tells me there was or is a liar and a killer on this ship. Lieutenants Saunders and Washington were only the latest victims. I think that you or my brother somehow got caught in that same killer's sights."

"A conspiracy? Is that what you're thinking?"

"I don't know." She tucked the report back into her briefcase. "Yet. But I'll find out."

"We will find out, together."

The inflection on the word *together* held a deeper, more intimate meaning. There was a time she welcomed that meaning, but now all she wanted to do was put distance between them. It kept her focused and sane.

She shivered a little, thinking about how he'd tasted, how he'd kissed as if no time had passed whatsoever, as if they knew each other in a more profound way than even on a physical level. No, she firmly decided. No more of those thoughts. A couple of kisses was already two too many. But she found her eyes falling to his mouth. He didn't miss the movement and his gray eyes went steamy.

She decided the best bet was to ignore it completely. "I couldn't go to court with this kind of evidence. But Chris, even if he had a bottle that was run-of-the-mill medication, it doesn't mean that's what was actually in the bottle."

He smiled, but it didn't diminish one whit the heat in his gaze. "That is true. I don't take anything at face value."

She mused for a moment, a thought coalescing in her brain. "All this negative evidence does add up to something."

"You have a theory." He rose and gathered up his dirty dishes and she did the same. "It's not a bad thing to talk out alternatives. You never know what correlation we might draw, or be able to put together some other lead we might have missed. Speculation isn't a bad thing, even if it's wrong. So let's hear it."

Dumping her trash and placing her dishes in the proper place, Sia turned to him. She wanted to be mad at him, even though she realized it was just an excuse to focus her feelings of helplessness on something tangible. Or someone. Instead, she took a deep breath and let it out slowly, forcing herself to relax. Getting worked up wasn't going to help matters any. Besides, she'd already gotten worked up enough for one day. Her gaze slid sideways across the busy mess as Chris's hand cupped her elbow to steer her through the crowd. It was more of a mechanism to keep them together so he could hear what she was saying. The warmth of his hand shouldn't affect her so, but it was like a jolt of electricity. She reined in her thoughts. "In lieu of any evidence the pilot was impaired or his system was faulty, the Navy will rule it pilot error and close the books."

Chris's lips thinned and his voice rasped out. "And a killer goes free."

Her eyes solemn, Sia nodded. "And a killer goes free."

Chapter 6

Chris followed Sia up the ladder, unable to keep his eyes from her shapely backside. He remembered what it was like to cup her there, to hold her hips against his, giving him the leverage he needed to thrust deep inside her. His gaze traveled up the surprisingly unwrinkled and fresh uniform to her shoulders, remembering how creamy they were, how soft her skin was, so smooth and warm. When Sia looked back down pensively, he hesitated and turned around to look behind him. "You all right?" he asked, meeting her eyes.

She dropped her gaze, and said, "Yes, I almost fell here on the way to meet you at the mess."

"Lost your footing?" he said, his gaze steady on her.

"I must have," she said with a shrug.

He stepped closer to her and he noticed how her body tightened. "You don't sound certain."

"I'm not. It seemed as if I'd been pushed. But I didn't

see anyone and there were a number of people coming down the ladder."

After the talk about a possible killer aboard the carrier, Chris wasn't about to take any chances. "How about you stick with me next time we head for food?"

Sia smiled and his heart stumbled a little. Okay, a lot.

"Ready to hold my hand again," she said with a teasing tone.

It was so much like the old Sia, Chris felt a familiar tug of longing that was almost painful. He smiled back at her and said softly, "I'll always be there for you, sweetheart."

Her smile faded. "That sounded a bit sarcastic. Are you implying something?"

"Just letting you know I have your back." Maybe he had said it that way. Maybe his resentment at her ability to turn her back on him was finally starting to show. Maybe it was time for her to know what she had done to him.

⁓ Their gazes met, warred. If the barb stung, she made sure not to show it. He could almost see her defenses surge, click into place. "But I didn't have yours. That's what you're saying, isn't it?"

He brought his mouth within a whisper of her lips, the potent connection between them made volatile by the words he refused to say. Some people had to come to their own conclusions. "Guilt is a strange emotion, Sia. It comes out of nowhere to hammer at you. It sometimes hides in the shadows, but it dictates every single thing you do. It's a relentless master."

"Guilt? What do I have to feel guilty about?"

Pointing anything out to a person who was unaware

of why they felt the way they did was not productive. Sick of that kernel of pain inside his gut that abraded him relentlessly, he said, "You decide what I'm saying, since you seem to like to put words in my mouth."

"Oh, forget it. We don't have time for this."

The sheen of pain in her eyes gave her away, but he let her retreat. He knew what it was like when guilt cut deep. There would be a better time and place. "Right, Sia. It's all dead and buried in the past." He brushed past her. "Let's get back to the legal office and line up our interviews for today."

"Who's on your primary list?" she said, catching up to him.

"Anyone who touched that plane or had any interaction with the pilot."

She stopped and turned to look at him. "That's going to be a long list."

"Then we'd better get started."

Back at the office, she settled into a chair behind the small table she had previously used for interviews.

She pulled her laptop out of her briefcase and set it on the table. "I think it would be best to organize this by area. That way we're not wasting our time by backtracking."

"Agreed."

"We've already interviewed the airman who had direct communication with Lieutenant Washington. So I'd like to talk to everyone who was on duty that day."

"We could systematically move down from Pri-Fly to the Flight Deck Control and Launch Operation Room," Chris said.

Sia responded, "That's where the handling officer and his crew play with their paper planes?"

Chris snorted. "Right, the table is called the *Ouija Board,* a two-level transparent plastic table with etched outlines of the flight deck and hangar deck. Each aircraft is represented by a scale aircraft cutout on the table. The handlers use those cutouts to represent real planes as they move on and off the carrier. When one is in maintenance, they turn it over."

"So anyone who works in that room knows when a specific plane is down for maintenance?" Sia asked.

"That's correct. Handy for a killer to keep track of both Saunders's and Washington's planes."

"Yes, handy indeed," Sia said.

Sia pulled up the list and jotted down a few names according to priority. "What's next?" she asked. "The control centers, including the Carrier Air Traffic Control Center and the Combat Direction Center?"

Chris nodded. "We will want to speak to the landing signal officer and crew that were present when the jet crashed, along with getting the footage of the crash, as well. The captain can get us that information."

"I think we have enough for now. Let's get started." They made their way out of the legal office and were soon ascending the ladder to Pri-Fly. The skipper wasn't present at this time. Instead, the OOD, or officer of the deck, took his place to stand a four-hour watch. Chris and Sia split up the list and took statements from each of the crew members who had been present during the crash of Lieutenant Washington's fighter.

When they met at the end of the interviews, Chris asked, "Anything pop?"

"No, nothing of significance that I could detect."

"Okay, let's move down to the next deck and then question the handling officer, Lieutenant Susan Cotes."

The Flight Deck Control and Launch Operation Room was small—smaller than Chris remembered. He wedged himself inside the windowless room, followed closely by Sia. The close confines intensified the smell of her fresh hair and the subtle smell he would always define as Sia. Trying to minimize his distraction, he turned slightly away from her. Lieutenant Cotes was a tall, quite beautiful woman with dark brown hair and sharp green eyes. She was wearing the yellow tunic that identified her as an air handler.

After introducing themselves, Chris said, "Lieutenant Cotes, we'd like to ask you a few questions regarding the day Lieutenant Washington crash-landed his fighter jet on the *McCloud*."

"Yes, sir. Anything I can do to help."

"All the information you received from the flight deck LSO was accurate that day?"

"Yes, Lieutenant Jackson is always on her game. She tried to wave off Lieutenant Washington, but it was too late. He hit the edge of the carrier and crashed."

"When was the last time Lieutenant Washington's plane was in maintenance?"

Chris noticed how her hand shook as she smoothed it through her hair. He wondered whether it was nerves or something else. "I can't exactly recall, but I can look it up for you and get you the information as soon as possible."

"Did you know Lieutenant Washington?" Sia asked.

"Yes, I did, but only as an acquaintance."

"We'll look forward to receiving that report. Thank you for your time," Chris said.

"She was a little jumpy," Sia said as they made their way to the Combat Direction Center. "Could be the general unrest after a crash or something more."

"Could be."

In the Carrier Air Traffic Control Center, they talked to several radar technicians, including a young man named Ensign Brant, who was new to the position. Once they were done with that, it was long past the lunch hour. They went to get something to eat and then were back in the legal office. When Sia opened her laptop, she let Chris know Lieutenant Cotes had sent her an email giving her a report as to when Lieutenant Washington's plane had last been serviced. "Looks like it was just a week ago, and it looks like the master chief oversaw the repairs. He's the one who signed off on the log."

"That would be significant if the master chief wasn't responsible for just about every plane that went through maintenance."

"True, but it does tie him to Lieutenant Washington. Let's find out who did the actual maintenance."

In the maintenance hangar below the flight deck, Sia and Chris tracked down someone who could give them answers regarding who had actually worked on the plane.

They were directed to a seaman mechanic who was on record as performing the necessary maintenance. "Seaman Yost?"

A young man with dark brown hair and wire-rimmed glasses turned and came immediately to attention. "Officer on the deck," he said.

"At ease, sailor. Are you Yost?"

"That's me. What can I do for you?" Yost relaxed into an at-ease position.

"I'm Special Agent Chris Vargas from NCIS and this is Lieutenant Commander Soto, JAG. We have a few questions for you regarding Lieutenant Eli Washington's jet. We understand you were the one who did the maintenance."

The man straightened when he saw Chris's badge. He looked at Sia and paled a little. "Yes, I did."

"You can continue with your duties," Sia said.

Cleaning a dirty wrench with a red cloth, he set the tool aside and chose another wrench. "Are you saying there was something wrong with the plane and that is why he crashed?" Turning away, he slipped the wrench inside an open panel.

"No. The report hasn't come back yet. Were you the only person who worked on the plane when it was in the bay?" Chris asked.

He stopped what he was doing and faced them. "You're asking me this question because of the master chief." He looked between the two of them.

"Just answer the question, Seaman," Sia said. Her voice brooked no disagreement.

"The master chief was one of the most knowledge-able people I've ever worked for in the Navy. I still have a hard time believing he had anything to do with that other F/18 crash, but the shiner on your face says otherwise."

Sia said nothing.

Seaman Yost sighed. "The master chief went over my work on Lieutenant Washington's fighter."

"Was that unusual?"

"Very. He oversaw all the departments in Maintenance. I was surprised he would take the time to go over my work here in Avionics."

"Were you present at the time?" Sia asked, stepping closer, her voice steely.

"No. I wasn't," Yost said with a tinge of anger in his voice. Chris suspected he didn't like ratting out the master chief, even if he was dead and all evidence pointed to the fact he was guilty. "Ma'am," he added when Sia's eyes narrowed. "He sent me to start work on another jet."

"So it's possible he could have tampered with the plane?" Sia stepped back and eyed the plane Yost was working on.

"Well, that calls for conjecture, ma'am."

Sia stiffened and her head whipped around. "Are you trying to get into trouble, Yost?"

"No, ma'am."

"Then answer the question," she snapped.

"Yes," he ground out. "In my opinion, I'd say he had plenty of time to tamper with the jet."

"What repairs did you perform on the plane?"

For a moment he didn't answer. Then he sighed. "Routine stuff, but I did notice his radar unit was unseated in the brackets and I fixed that."

"As if it was jarred loose?" Chris asked.

"No, as if it was a hurry-up kinda job. I just figured the last mechanic was in a rush to finish the job."

"You didn't report this?"

"Nah, it was something that was minor and I didn't want to bust the guy's chops."

"That's all for now, Seaman Yost."

He nodded and went back to work.

After they were a safe distance away, Chris said, "We've established the master chief had access to Lieutenant Washington's plane. Could it be he killed Washington from beyond the grave?"

"I guess it may have been possible, if he tampered with the plane. We need to light a fire under them to get that plane checked over ASAP."

"I could get my forensics specialist over to where they've taken the plane and we would have a report in twenty-four hours," Chris said.

"He's that good?"

Chris nodded.

"The salvaged plane was taken to a hangar at Hickam Air Force Base. Saunders's jet is there, as well."

Back in the legal office, Chris connected to his forensic specialist.

"Who's the lovely lady?"

"Keep it focused, Math." Math was the resident nerd at NCIS, but he would be what women called cute. Intensely dedicated to his job, Math did notice a nice turn of ankle and a pretty pair of eyes. He had dark hair that was styled in a bowl cut, with bangs on his forehead. He wore a pair of wire-rimmed glasses and had that perpetual look of an eighteen-year-old. He sometimes acted like one. But Chris often let it slide. The kid was brilliant.

"Hi, lovely lady. Swear to God, Vargas, you get all the good assignments."

Sia smiled at the young man on the computer screen.

"Sia, this is Justin Mathis. Don't encourage him." Chris turned back to the screen. "I have a job for you."

"I'm up to my eyeballs, in eyes, so make it fast."

"I'm not going to ask."

"It's best you don't."

"I need you to fly out here and look over a fighter jet for me. I need a report fast."

Math sighed. "Let me guess, twenty-four hours."

"You got it in one."

"Vargas, I can't promise anything until I see the wreck."

"I don't care what anyone else says, Math, you're the best."

"Ha ha. Bye, lovely lady."

"He's very good at his job, so if anyone can get us some answers, Math can."

"I pulled Lieutenant Washington's record and I found something interesting."

"What?"

"Looks like there was a reason Lieutenant Cotes was a bit jumpy."

"Why?"

"She filed a sexual harassment complaint against Lieutenant Washington."

"When?"

"Two weeks ago."

"Nothing against Saunders?"

Sia pulled up the pilot's file. "No, nothing here I see."

"That doesn't mean he wasn't harassing her. Maybe she didn't get a chance to file a complaint."

"It's possible, but from what I heard from his wing-

man, he didn't seem the type and I didn't find any notes
in his rack when I searched."

"We'll search again."

Sia bristled. "Do you think I'm inept? That I can't
do a competent search?"

"No, that's not what I was implying. It's possible
something got missed. Especially when you're not sure
what you're looking for. Now we know what we're looking for."

"In the meantime, let's get Susan Cotes in here for
some more questioning."

Chris and Sia were seated when Susan Cotes entered
Legal. She was still in her bright yellow tunic as she
took a seat at the table across from them.

"I don't know what I can add to what I've already
told you," she said, to break the thick tension in the air.

"Oh, I think you do," Sia said. "You neglected to
mention you had filed a sexual harassment charge
against Lieutenant Washington."

She closed her eyes and took a deep breath. "I wasn't
trying to hide it from you," she said quickly. "I didn't
want to blurt it out in front of my coworkers."

"Well, we're alone here. Tell us the details now. Did
he assault you?"

"No, nothing like that. He was sending me notes.
They would be tucked into my uniform or slipped under
my door. Once he cornered me in the wardroom and
said we should explore the relationship I'd described in
a note to him. I had no idea what he was talking about. I
wasn't participating in this fantasy note-writing that he
was sure was me. I suggested he had me mixed up with
someone else. He insisted it was me, and he seemed

quite confused by my response. That's when I lodged the complaint. I barely knew him."

"So he'd never initiated direct contact with you before the incident in the wardroom?"

"No. I thought maybe he was shy or something—not that he seemed that way. I'm not about to get involved with a pilot. I'm interested in making the Navy a career. I didn't want to derail it. Lieutenant Washington was a very handsome man, but I just wasn't interested. When I told him so, he seemed completely baffled and said I was a crazy bitch sending him mixed messages."

"Do you have any of these notes?"

"I gave them to the captain when I filed the grievance."

"You submitted your complaint only two days before Washington crashed his plane."

"Yes, it started up about four days before the crash. I didn't want it to get out of hand, so I made the complaint and hoped the captain would reprimand him and it would stop."

"But Washington crashed before the captain had a chance to speak to him?"

"Yes. I'm sorry he's dead. I just wanted him to leave me alone."

"That's all for now, Cotes. We might have more questions for you later."

"Yes, ma'am." She stood and left the cabin.

"How about we split up," Chris suggested. "You go and talk to the captain and I'll question Washington's wingman. He might have some information about Susan Cotes."

Chris shook his head. "I thought we were going to stick together."

"Don't be silly. I just fell. It's nothing to be concerned about. Besides, we need to split up the workload. It's more efficient."

Chris looked skeptical, but nodded. "All right. If you're sure."

Chris headed toward the wardroom and found Lieutenant Monroe drinking coffee at a table. "Hello, Monroe," Chris said, showing the lieutenant his badge. "I wanted to talk to you about Lieutenant Washington's crash."

"Have a seat."

Chris sat down and leaned back in his chair. "What were the conditions like when you both went to land?"

"It was windy, and that's always a tricky landing."

"Thank God for the meatball."

"Amen to that. It got me in safely with no wave-off my first pass, but when Eli went to land, it was a different story. His flying had been somewhat erratic about a half an hour out, but that's understandable as he reported a problem with his radar. So he reported it and we were recalled. Most of the chatter on the radio was about Eli's condition."

"Did he answer?"

"He did, but as the approach got closer, he got more incoherent. Once I landed and taxied off, I no longer was on the radio. I watched as the LSO waved him off, but Eli came in too low and hit the ship. He skidded right past me. I could see him in the cockpit, but he made no attempt to eject. I didn't even realize I was screaming for him to eject. Of course, he couldn't hear me."

"Did he appear to be unconscious to you?"

"He appeared aware, but I only saw him for a split second. If he had ejected, he would have made it."

"Do you know anything about Washington harassing Lieutenant Susan Cotes?"

Monroe sighed. "Eli was shocked when he discovered the woman wasn't interested and it wasn't because of his good looks. Eli never had a problem with the ladies. He said she was into him, but he didn't say why."

"And that's why he was shocked when she filed the sexual harassment charge?"

"Yes, when she told him, he was floored. He called her crazy and accused her of giving him mixed signals."

"He didn't elaborate on what the mixed signals were, though?"

"No. He didn't say. He might have been a ladies man, but he was closemouthed about his exploits."

"A true gentleman, huh?"

"Yeah." Monroe paused. "The scuttlebutt floating around is pilot error. I hope that's not the case. With Saunders's crash and now Eli, there's going to be some serious consequences for us if this is pilot error. A lot of scrutiny."

"Our investigation isn't complete. Let me know if you can think of anything else that might be important."

"Will do."

Sia navigated her way to the captain's quarters and knocked on the door. He answered and she stepped inside. "I have a few questions regarding a sexual harassment charge Lieutenant Susan Cotes filed against Washington."

"You think this is relevant in Washington's death?"

"We still don't have enough evidence he was murdered and we're following the leads we find. Cotes had a beef with Washington."

"She did. She was pretty upset when she came to me about it. It seems she was confused with the way he was harassing her."

"The notes?"

"Yes."

"Could I see them?"

The captain went to his desk and pulled a file.

Sia opened the file and found the notes were typewritten, with lascivious messages printed on them. They were signed simply "Eli."

"These are not handwritten. If you're wooing a woman, seems like you'd pull out all the stops."

"I'm not sure. I didn't get an opportunity to talk to him before he died."

"Could I have permission to search his rack?"

"Yes, go ahead."

When she turned to leave, the captain's voice stopped her.

"Before you go, Commander, footage of both crashes your partner wanted to review are on this flash drive. I've had some pushback from Senator Washington. He wants answers about his son's death. Unless you want the senator touching down on this carrier, you'd better wrap this up." She reached for the flash drive, but he didn't immediately let go of it. She looked into his piercing blue eyes and realized why he was in command of an aircraft carrier. "He's not alone, Commander. I want them, too."

He let go of the flash drive and Sia tucked it into her briefcase.

"With all due respect, sir, rushing an investigation is counterproductive."

"Noted. Do it right, Commander, and do it fast."

"Yes, sir."

Sia left and headed right to Washington's rack. Donning gloves, she began to search. It wasn't long before she came across folded papers tucked under his mattress. After she opened them and read them, Sia realized they shed a whole new light on Susan Cotes and her sexual harassment story.

In lieu of the evidence she had in her hand, she had a couple more questions for the captain. But once she got to his quarters, she found he wasn't there. When she bumped into the XO on the way to the bridge, he told her the captain had been called to the bridge.

She headed there, and as she was going to ascend the ladder she heard the sound of a helo. It was a large one and it hovered over the deck for only a few seconds before touching down.

She saw that the captain was on the flight deck waiting for the helo to land and she changed directions, making her way down to the flight deck. Her stomach dropped when she saw the official government emblem on the side of the helo.

When she reached the small knot of men hovering around a tall, distinguished man, Sia felt a jolt.

Senator Washington had landed on the deck of the

U.S.S. James McCloud, and from the determined look on his face, she could tell he wanted answers.

And he wanted them now.

Chapter 7

She approached the captain, and the steely brown eyes of the senator turned her way. "Is this the JAG handling the case?" he demanded.

"Sir," Sia said, reaching out a hand to him, but he just eyed her, the grief of his son's death plain in his eyes.

"I'm not here for a social visit, Commander. I'm here for who is responsible for my son's death. I've heard that it may not have been an accident."

"We do have some leads, sir. But our investigation is still ongoing and I don't—"

"You will brief me in fifteen minutes, Commander, in the captain's conference room."

"Sir."

"Is that a problem?"

"No, sir."

He indicated for the captain to show him the way,

and with a knowing look, he left with his entourage and the captain.

Scowling, Sia turned back to the interior of the ship. She needed to get back to Legal and talk to Chris before he was blindsided by the senator. He wouldn't be pleased to find out that she'd already had a run-in with him without Chris present. As the lead investigator, it was a responsibility he would consider his. If there was one thing she knew about Chris, it was that he wouldn't shirk this responsibility. She'd better get a move on and find him right away.

Sia headed back to the legal office. As she got to the top of the ladder, she felt two hands in the middle of her back. Before she could react, she was shoved violently. Losing her footing, she tumbled down the first three ladder steps before grabbing on to the handrail to stop herself from falling farther. Looking up, she caught a glimpse of something yellow ducking around the corner of the bulkhead.

"Ma'am. Are you all right?"

A seaman helped her to stand. Feeling shaky, Sia held on to the handrail until she felt more solid. "Can I escort you to sick bay, ma'am?"

"No, that won't be necessary, but thank you for your help." When she faced the young man, she recognized him from yesterday. "Oh, Ensign Brant. We talked yesterday in the Carrier Air Traffic Control Center."

"Yes, ma'am, I remember. I know how easy it is to fall. Takes some time to get used to the movement of a ship. When Lieutenant Cotes was training me…"

She grabbed his arm. The information he'd so innocently given her made her forget about her pain from the fall. "You replaced Lieutenant Cotes?"

Her reaction made his voice hesitate. "Yes, she went on to handling and I filled her vacancy."

Sia's hand tightened on his arm. "She's knowledgeable in radar systems?"

He looked down at her hand and up to her face. He nodded. "I'd say. She's a whiz."

"Thank you, Ensign. I appreciate your help."

This time she was sure she had been pushed and she was now sure she had herself a prime suspect, but that would have to wait until after she spoke to the senator. At least they had something solid to move the investigation forward. She was sure they would soon have a person in custody. Back at the legal office, she initiated contact with her legalman.

"McBride, how are you coming with that search for me on Master Chief Walker?"

His look was apologetic. "I got pulled off it, ma'am, by the captain, but I can get back to it tomorrow," he promised.

"Tomorrow?"

"It's almost closing time here. Remember, a six-hour difference."

"Of course. It's only morning here. If the captain tries to commandeer you again, tell him this is for the Washington case. He'll understand."

"Yes, ma'am."

Sia couldn't keep the excitement out of her voice. "I want you to extend that search for me. In fact, make it a priority over the master chief. Search previous billets for Lieutenant Susan Cotes, and I want to know about any pilot deaths, no matter what they are."

"Yes, ma'am. First thing tomorrow morning."

"You found something on Cotes?"

She turned to find Chris standing behind her and he sounded peeved. "Yes, when I searched Washington's rack, I discovered these."

Chris rifled through the pages and his head popped up, his eyes gleaming. "Typewritten notes from Cotes?"

"Yes, which means she was participating in this game they were playing and if the captain had talked to Washington, then he would have discovered her sexual harassment charge was bogus." The more evidence she gathered on this woman, the clearer it looked that she was the one they were looking for.

"She lied to us," Chris said, his voice a growl. "We'll need her back in here."

"The captain gave me the footage you requested." She pulled the flash drive out of her pocket. He took it out of her resisting fingers. "It would have been nice to know you requested access so I don't look like an idiot."

"Just like you withheld the autopsy from me?" He shot the words back at her like a bullet from a smoking gun.

She shrugged. "It's not the same thing."

He snorted. "Yes, it is. You admitted you still blame me. That's the real reason you're chafing at my control of this case. Admit it."

Sia brought up her arm to press her fingers against her suddenly throbbing temples. The man had a way of giving her a headache.

He grabbed her wrist. His eyes were stormy. "You're bleeding."

"What?" She looked at him as if she'd gone dumb.

"Your arm. You're bleeding. What happened?"

The concern in his eyes was genuine. After all they had been through and were still going through, Chris never changed. She felt the warmth of his body, the strength that poured effortlessly out of him, while he did nothing more than stand there. And she wanted to wrap herself in it, just for a moment or two, just long enough to draw strength from him and get her bearings back. But genuine or not, there was too much between them for a simple tug and hug. "I got pushed—again."

He scowled. "Then the first time was no accident."

She tried to get her wrist back, but he wouldn't let go. "No, it wasn't, and when I looked up I caught a glimpse of yellow."

His eyes flashed. "Like Cotes's yellow tunic?"

"Yes."

"Be careful, you're going to smear it all over your uniform." He pulled her over to a first-aid kit.

"You know, I can handle this myself," she said wryly.

He shrugged off her words and opened the kit, selecting a small, square package. Ripping it open, he unfolded the small pad inside. "It's in a hard-to-reach place on your forearm. I'll get it."

He wiped away the blood with the alcohol pad and it stung a bit. Sia went to pull away, but his grip was too strong. "What were you talking to McBride about?"

"I asked him to compile a list of all pilots who have died aboard the *McCloud*. Everything, including deaths ruled as accidents." He placed a bandage over the cut, his touch branding her with little licks of fire. "She lied about sending Washington notes and I discovered from Ensign Brant in air traffic control she was previously in that position and had been his training officer."

He raised his head from his work and looked at her, understanding dawning. "So she's familiar with radar."

The pain diminished to a dull throb now that the cut had been treated. Sia was happy to put some distance between them. "Yes, that's as far as I've gotten. I was going to look at her file more closely."

"We can do that now."

"No. That's going to have to wait," Sia said.

"Why?"

"Senator Washington is here and he wants to meet with us in the captain's conference room, now."

Chris sighed. "It's counterproductive for him to come here and demand answers when we haven't finished the investigation."

"We both know that. But he's grieving, Chris. We... we both know what that feels like. I can't say that I don't sympathize with him. In his shoes, I'd want answers, too."

"All right, but I want to come back here afterward and look up her file."

"We need to look at that footage, too, before we bring her back in here."

"Agreed. Can we agree on something else?"

"What's that?"

"You stick close to me or, at the very least, call for a master-at-arms if I'm not available or we have to split up?"

"All right. That's something I can agree to." When

they reached the conference room, Chris knocked on the door. The captain said, "Enter."

Sia and Chris walked through the door. The senator was sitting at the head of the table, his two aides on either side of him. One was working on a laptop and the other one was speaking to the senator in low tones.

Sia stood at attention until the captain asked her and Chris to sit down.

"I want to know what progress you've made on the investigation into my son's death. I can't sit in Washington anymore and get no report."

"Sir, as Commander Soto has told you, we are working on some solid leads."

"What are these leads? Did someone murder my boy?" His voice was authoritative, but underlined in raw sorrow.

Sia shifted uncomfortably. She remembered what had happened at the graveside when her father had verbally and physically attacked Chris. She knew he was remembering that day. He had to be.

She just hoped he didn't lose his cool, as he had back then.

She expected Chris to close down, to get tough, but instead his eyes went soft, filled with a knowing sympathy. "Sir, I know how you feel. I've been there. But at this time, we can't really reveal what we know because we haven't fully investigated what we have."

"You damn well will tell me what you know! You'll tell me now!" the senator bellowed.

When Chris didn't answer immediately, the senator rose. "Are you refusing to tell me what you know?"

"It's more complicated than that, sir."

"Complicated? Either someone killed my boy or not! There's nothing complicated about it and I want to know who it is."

Sia understood why Chris was being closemouthed about their leads. It wouldn't be conducive to the investigation if the obviously agitated senator went after Susan Cotes before they could question her.

"We have a suspect that we have identified."

Snarling, the senator rounded the table. Chris rose to face him. The senator jabbed at Chris's sternum hard with his forefinger. "I'm going to ask politely once more."

"Senator…"

"You stay out of this, Captain."

Sia rose, too, and stood shoulder to shoulder with Chris.

Chris's voice sliced the thick air like a lethal knife. "With all due respect, Senator Washington, that information will remain confidential until we have gathered all our evidence."

The senator, fueled by grief and anger, shoved Chris hard against the bulkhead. Both aides and the captain went to intervene, but Chris held up his hand to them. Softly he said, "I know what you're going through. But if you push this, you could ruin the investigation, taint our suspect and derail our interrogation. The suspect could walk. I know you want justice for Eli. That's what we want, too, and we'll do everything in our power to make it happen. We think Eli is worth that consideration and time. Do you?"

Everything inside the senator crumbled. The anger

that had cloaked him vanished, leaving him naked and vulnerable.

"I just want my boy back," he whispered. The captain ushered the shocked aides out of the conference room and shut the door behind him.

Sia put a hand on the senator's arm. His face crumpled and tears ran down his face. Sia's heart squeezed tight and she wrapped her arms around the inconsolable man.

Her eyes met Chris's over the senator's shoulder. He was the one she wanted to hold. The bleak look in his eyes told her that keeping information from the senator about his son's possible killer had taken a toll. But the courage and the skillful way he'd defused the situation made her heart catch in her chest. Hollis surely had been right.

It only made Sia more ashamed of how she'd treated him six years ago.

After seeing the senator to the helo and assuring him that he would have answers soon, Chris and Sia watched him take off. They headed back to the legal office, but found Billy had a few people inside that made it a bit crowded. Since Chris was bunking with a roommate, Sia suggested they go to her stateroom.

Once inside, Sia booted up her computer to check for emails. "Nothing from him yet." She looked at her watch. "Oh, damn. He's probably gone home. I'll check with him tomorrow. Let's review the footage."

Sia plugged the flash drive into her computer and started the file. They watched as the jets approached. It was easy to see which plane was Monroe's and which one was Washington's. It was clear the second plane's pilot was in distress. Monroe landed his craft without incident, just as he'd said.

"Washington is flying too low," Chris said. He watched closely as the jet clipped the edge of the ship and skidded.

As she watched Sia couldn't help thinking about her brother. How it must have been for him at the end. Seeing the crash also made her think of Chris. How it had been for him when his jet had collided with her brother's. Tears gathered in her eyes and she quickly brushed them away. She minimized the footage.

She looked at Chris, but instead of the emotion she expected to see, he looked puzzled and unsettled. She replayed the footage and paused it just as the jets came alongside each other, their wings almost touching.

She could almost imagine the plane on the right was her brother's and the one on the left Chris's. She could also imagine how they must have collided.

Back then it had seemed cut-and-dried. Pilot error. But now in light of the two pilot deaths, Sia wasn't so sure anymore.

Chris snapped out of his reverie and stared at her. His eyes sharpened. He reached out and touched her cheek with the back of his hand, wiping away the telltale tears.

He looked at the computer and gently closed it. The image of the jets winked out.

He wondered if his heart could take any more. If he could, as he had said so many times, move past this source of pain and guilt in his past, in her past. He wanted to let loose the feelings that were still locked up in his heart, but he was afraid of the consequences of her rejection.

And the sight of those two jets so close in the air. Milliseconds away from disaster. Facing death each time he jumped into his cockpit had been easier.

Easier than looking into Sia's eyes and seeing her pain, her loss, seeing that she was holding on to something so desperately her knuckles were turning white. And deep down it hurt that she needed his exoneration, needed to have a reason to believe he wasn't to blame for Rafael's death.

And sometimes, he wondered if it really mattered. Rafael was dead. Dead and gone. But they were here, warm, living flesh. He wanted her. As unreasonable as it might seem, he wanted her. Still.

He went to pull his hand away, not sure if he could offer her any comfort she would accept. When her hand quickly rose to curl around his, his heart twisted with a painful longing that had multiplied for six long years.

"Don't," she said softly.

He could feel the tremors in her as the tears fell freely from her eyes and he wasn't sure if they were now for Rafael or for all they had lost.

Her hand rose along his arm, to his shoulder as she leaned in closer to him. With a soft, low cry, her trembling lips met his, and then covered them, moving gently, sweetly.

Chris was drowning in hunger, fighting a need that rose swiftly, was banked ruthlessly. He didn't want her to just react to him. A ragged sense of honor kept him motionless when instinct dictated he haul her into his arms. It was the memory of the pain in her eyes only a moment ago that kept him from giving in to those urges, that had shouted clearer than words that she was still conflicted about him.

Her mouth moved to his jaw, and he clenched it, hard, when her lips dragged over the stubble. His lungs dragged in the scent of her in a guilty, greedy swallow, and his muscles quivered with the force of his control.

She didn't need this. The thought hammered in his head, keeping rhythm with the pulse in his veins. He didn't know what drove her, but he knew she was vulnerable in a way she hadn't allowed herself in a long time. Knew that even her well-worn defenses must have limits.

And, he had to admit, so did his.

And he was equally certain given time they'd be firmly back in place. She was still reeling from all the memories this case had brought back and adding him to the mix only made it more complicated. He tried to remember that as she caught his bottom lip between her teeth, bit down gently. He had to admit this would be folly for both of them. Keeping their relationship professional was the wiser choice, but where Sia was concerned he seemed to lose his focus, set aside his own pain. But there'd been emotion in her answer, in just that single word. And it was apparent in her kiss. Each touch crumbled his control a bit further.

Her fingers skimmed over his chest. His muscles jumped beneath her touch, quivering. His hands went to her hips, intending to put her away from him. In a moment. This must be a special kind of hell reserved just for him, for offenses committed.

When her mouth touched his again, his arms slipped

around her waist, and he kissed her back with a crushing desire that should have worried her. Should have had her pulling away. Instead it served to scorch them both.

His fingers tunneled in her hair and he held her head still, consumed her mouth. And he imagined just for a moment what it would be like to make love to her without fearing the inevitable moment when her defenses would snap back into place. Keeping him out and the memories locked away.

No barriers existed between them now. The certainty shimmered between them, tempted with a heated promise. And the knowledge was sweet, perhaps made more because he knew how rare the moment was.

He could feel her heart race, keeping pace with his. His tongue pressed at her lips for entrance, and they parted in a provocative way that made him groan. He dragged her closer, one hand sliding beneath her serviceable khaki shirt, skimming over her smooth back. She arched against him, and the last remnant of his control gave way under the weight of his need for her.

After so many years apart, he took his time, reveled in the freedom to touch and savor her. He snagged the hem of her shirt, drew it over her head. Skin against skin, warm and vibrant, made him unravel a bit more. The silk of her bra against his chest was sensual, charging his blood to a torrent. The smooth skin of her shoulder beckoned his mouth, his muscles tense. Breathing hard, he paused to get the surging passion under control.

The bunk was close enough that he could add just the right amount of pressure. They would end up where he wanted her, where he could explore her to his satisfaction, every inch of their bodies touching. They could give their passion free rein, forget all thoughts, all doubts.

He bent, scooped her up in his arms and laid her on the bunk. When he followed her down, it was with passion held in check, and something far more dangerous rising to the surface. He loomed half over her, tangled his hands in her long, curly tresses, rubbing the strands against the sensitive pads of his fingers, moving the mass away from her striking face. An aching path of tenderness carved through him. Her bruises were like a badge of courage against her golden skin, a reminder that life was so fleeting. His lips brushed over the marred skin, one warrior paying homage to another.

Sia froze under his soft mouth, aware that something had shifted in his rhythm. Uncertain of her response, she felt his mouth move to the places on her body where she'd been hurt, sensually identifying each of her injuries, soothing each. His tenderness made the myriad of emotions locked inside her clamor for release. Again he was offering her something she didn't know how to accept, or return. She only knew he tangled her emotions into unidentifiable knots. Wreaked havoc on her system. The minutes stretched, encased in silver.

Chris took his time relearning the contours of Sia's body, saw her eyes, glazed but wary. And understanding rocked him, so sudden and hard he shivered with the knowledge. Walls worked both ways. Barriers were erected and served to protect what was inside, but also worked to keep everything out. He wondered if she knew his defenses seemed to be made of sand.

Their mouths collided, tongues tangled. Passion still sluiced through his veins, but tempered for the moment.

He teased her with supple, lingering kisses as his hands played on her flesh, languid and dreamy. And when he felt her body soften against his, heard her breath hitch slightly, he knew this was what he craved. What he'd always craved. To feel her melt with bliss. To feel her hands frantic on his flesh. To know with every gasp and moan he drew from her she thought of him. Only him.

His hands drifted over her breasts, impatient with the silk barrier. Deftly he reached behind her and released the clasp. Freed, the soft globes gleamed in the light, tipped with tight pink nipples.

His fingers circled one nipple, flicking it with his thumb. Her breath hissed in and she reached for him, her fingers clutching his shoulders, skating over his chest. A thousand points of flame burst beneath his skin, and she pulled his head down to her. With a soft moan of pleasure, he drew her proffered nipple into his mouth, savagely satisfied to hear his name tumble from her lips. Cupping her other breast in his hand, he fondled it until the dual assault had her body twisting against him.

A haze seemed to have formed over all thought, all reason. There was only Sia, her flavor tracing through his system, her scent embedded in his senses. Light from the single lamp in the stateroom slanted across them, illuminating their skin and making it glow. Her fingers were fumbling with his pants, and each slight brush of her knuckles against his abdomen was the most exquisite form of torture.

Desire rushed through him, made a mockery of his control. Stepping away, only a fraction, he stripped the cloth barrier away from his body and kicked it away. He donned protection and pulled her to face him until they lay together, side to side, so that every inch of their bodies touched. Finding the pulse at the base of her throat, he stroked it with his tongue. Restlessly, she drew her leg sensuously up the length of his leg and across his hip.

His breath heaved out of his lungs. The time had passed for slow and easy. His hand kneaded the satin of her thigh, felt the whisper of muscle beneath the silky skin. It was always an erotic delight to rediscover Sia's softness. His fingers trailed closer to her core of heat, and he thrilled as her body twisted with need.

She forgot to breathe. He gave her no choice but to feel. Sia gloried in the choice, even realizing it came with risk. But right now there was only his body close to hers, smooth flesh stretched over padded muscle. Her fingers traced over him, where sinew and bone joined to leave intriguing hollows. Each begged to be explored with soft lips and swift hands.

Longing battled with doubt. He traced the crease where her leg met her hip and she stiffened, her lungs clogged. He was moving down her body, painting flesh with his tongue. Her blood turned hot, molten, and chugged through her veins like lava. Her world, her focus, narrowed to include only the two of them.

Need, Chris was finding, was a double-edged sword, one as painful as it was pleasurable. And, poised on that razor-edged peak, he was as primed as she for a fall. He couldn't find it in himself to care. His mouth found her moist warmth and her back arched. He slipped his hands beneath her hips, lifted her to devour. The soft, strangled sounds tumbling from her lips urged him on,

to take more. To give more. And when she shot to release in a wild shuddering mass, she cried his name.

Sia fought to haul breath into her lungs. Her limbs
were like liquid. And for the moment at least, she felt
utterly tranquil. She felt the bunk move, and her eyelids
fluttered open. Tranquility abruptly fled. Here was the
danger she'd forgotten, in the primal masculine man
bending over her. Her hand rose of its own volition,
curved around his neck and brought his mouth to hers.

His breath heaved out of his chest as her teeth scored
his skin lightly, nipping a path from his shoulder to
his belly. His restraint unraveled a bit more with each
soft touch.

The light illuminated their thrashing bodies, spilling on the bunk. Chris's gentleness had vanished, hunger raging. His vision misted, but his other senses were
alert. Achingly so. The sweet, dark flavor of her tongue
battling with his. The silkiness of her hair brushing
against his skin and the sexy, tight grasp of her hands
as she explored him where he was hot, hard and pulsing.

The teasing was gone. Gentleness was beyond him.
His arousal was primal, basic and immediate. His hands
battled hers, and he rolled her to his side, drew her leg
over his hips. Testing her readiness with one finger, he
watched her eyes, shadows of emotion and desire moving through the soft, dewy brown like comets.

He moved into position, his shaft barely parting her
warm cleft, and stilled. He eased into her, her eyes directly on his, now bare and vulnerable, opening more
than just her body to him. She twisted and moaned
against him as he moved in tiny increments, not satisfied until he was seated deep inside her. Then he took

her mouth with his own, savagely aware every inch of their bodies was touching. Inside and out. And still it wasn't enough.

He withdrew from her only to lunge again, each time deeper, harder, faster. They were caught in a vortex, spinning wilder and wilder. Out of control. He saw her face spasm, felt the clench of her inner muscles, swallowed her cry with his mouth. And then, only then did he let the tide sweep him under and dash him up and over the edge.

Minutes, or hours, later he stroked a hand along the curve of her waist before settling it possessively on her hip. Each beat of her heart echoed with his. Their breathing slowed, and eventually reason intruded. He started to move away and her fingers tightened in an automatic reflexive response. Reluctantly he ignored it. The protection he'd used was fast losing its effectiveness. He took care of it and rolled back to her. To please himself, he pushed the heavy tangle of her hair away from her face and skimmed his fingertips over her shoulder and down her arm.

It would be easy to stay like this, to cuddle and make love, but they were much more than simply lovers. He knew from personal experience it would be wonderful to fall asleep cradled in her arms.

Once before he'd thought they'd forged a bond, until Sia had ruthlessly cut him out of her life and the distance had yawned between them like a deep chasm. He wasn't going to make that mistake again. She would have to come to terms with him, and that was something he couldn't help her with.

Sia could see the change in his eyes and she hated

the emotions and the feelings locked up inside her. The sheer satisfaction of being this intimate with Chris was something she cherished, but the past hung between them like a specter. "We both know this doesn't settle anything, it only makes it more convoluted and complicated. Until we work through our past, it'll be the white elephant in the room. Is that something you want, Sia?"

He picked up her hand and measured it against his. She could see the emotions dance like flame in his eyes. Without conscious volition, her fingers locked with his. He couldn't know what he was asking. She wanted to get past it all, but she couldn't. She didn't have answers yet. Even as she mourned their relationship and all they had lost, she felt locked in her decision.

She hated this. Trying to quench the lick of panic in her veins, she moved closer to him. She didn't want to deal with the jumble of emotions, the mingled doubts and fears. Far better to end this now. Again. Before there was a sticky tangle of recriminations and disappointments to assuage.

But as he drew her chin up to meet his eyes, she couldn't, so she changed the subject. "What was it about Washington's accident that bothered you?"

It took him a moment to change gears and she could see the disappointment in his eyes, but he let it go for now. It was just a reprieve. She knew that. Maybe when she had to make a final decision about Chris, she would have more answers.

"I don't know. I can't put my finger on it. But something about his landing is bothering me. It's been a while since I landed on a carrier at night."

"It'll come to you. Try not to think about it too hard."

He nodded.

Sia slipped out of the bunk, unabashed about her nakedness. It fueled her to know Chris was looking and admiring. She pulled a T-shirt and shorts out of her locker and put them on. Her dark hair obscured her vision of Chris lying on his side in the bunk watching her. With a small smile, she scooped up her laptop and opened it. When it woke, the screen was still on the jets. With a pang, Sia minimized it. "As soon as McBride finishes with that research, I'm sure we'll find Cotes was aboard the *McCloud* when Rafael died."

"Sia, it's best to draw conclusions only when we have evidence that is the case."

"That's true, but I have a feeling about this. It's going to clear his name. I just know it."

Chris hadn't moved from the bunk, nor had he donned any clothes. The sheet was draped over his groin, but his well-muscled chest and every other part of his fine body was displayed. It was hard for her to concentrate.

"Investigations aren't about feelings. Don't let your emotions override your logic," he said as he shifted with a ripple of muscle to his side to pillow his head on his arm.

"I'm not. I'm just stating what I think is the truth. Why are you being so negative? Don't you want to be exonerated?"

He sat up, his face pulling into a frown. "I lost everything that was important to me six years ago, Sia. I've made a new life and moved on. But I can see that you haven't. We can't live in the past."

Sia stood and came over to the bunk. "I know that.

But this isn't about moving on. This is about justice for my brother. Justice for you. If someone tampered with your radar or drugged you, then it's our duty to bring that person to justice. There is no statute of limitations on murder!"

"Sia," he said, grabbing her hand when she went to turn away, "I know you want this more than anything, but you have to be prepared for whatever the truth is going to reveal. I don't want you to set yourself up for disappointment."

She extricated her hand from his. Her overloaded senses only distracted her from her anger. "Maybe this doesn't mean as much to you as it does to me. I'll never stop trying to prove my brother wasn't at fault that day. I just don't believe it."

"But it's easy for you to believe I was. To blame me. You and your family ostracized me. I was already handling a load of guilt, yet I couldn't even get any peace at Rafael's funeral. Your father attacked me."

"He was hurting. He wanted someone to blame."

"And you sided with them," he said, his voice harsh and raw.

"They were my family."

"You said you loved me, Sia. Doesn't that mean anything to you?"

"Yes, it does. But I couldn't go against my family."

"No, because you wanted someone to blame, too."

The air crackled between them and Sia's eyes flared with emotion and anger. "I wanted to support my family, Chris. That is the bottom line. My parents were devastated. My father turned to the bottle and my mother lost her will. I saw her lose the battle with living every day."

"How are they now? Have they moved past—?"

"You don't know? They didn't move past it, Chris. They died five years ago in a car crash because my father was drunk."

Chapter 8

Chris lay quietly, listening to his roommate complete his morning ritual. It was dark in the stateroom except for the dim lights over his bunk. Chris guessed it was only about four o'clock or four-thirty.

He turned over until he faced the wall. Sleep had been elusive and fitful since he left Sia's cabin. His shock at the news of her parents' deaths had hit him very hard, right in his heart.

His loss was now totally complete. Unequivocally permanent.

And he had to wonder. He didn't want to complete the thought, but he wasn't easy, even on himself. Did she blame him for her parents' deaths as well as her brother's? The thought gnawed at him in a place that, even after six years, was still raw. And he had to assume some of the blame. He was indirectly responsible for their deaths. It was his error that killed Rafe.

Being with her again had brought it all back. He didn't have to hear her tell him she couldn't forgive him when forgiveness was what he wanted and needed. He knew she couldn't and that reality shattered his foundations even more.

Like a thirsty man so close to water he could smell it, but wasn't allowed to drink.

He would have been kidding himself if he'd thought there had been any way back into their good graces. The Sotos had cut him out of their lives as ruthlessly as his own father had, but for a short time, he'd had it all. The love of his life, a family who loved him like he was their own and a best friend who had brought all his dreams and hopes together in one neat package.

It had been fleeting, but it had been real, for as long as it had lasted.

Unable to fall asleep, he donned his running gear and slipped out of the ship to the flight deck. It was quiet this morning and almost completely devoid of people.

There was a lone runner and he swore softly. He'd told her it wasn't safe for her to be on her own, but independent Sia didn't think anything of running early in the morning without an escort and he was the last person she wanted to see.

It took him a few lengthy strides to catch up with her. They ran side by side in silence until the sun came up over the horizon.

"I'm sorry about your parents," he said softly, not looking at her. He kept his gaze straight ahead on the pink horizon.

Sia slowed to a walk, not looking at him at first, as if

she was processing all that had happened. He reached out and touched her arm, so she looked over at him.

She held his gaze for a fraction of a second longer, and then dipped her chin, before coming to a complete stop. "I'm sorry, too. I miss them."

"I miss them, too," he said simply and it seemed to be enough. She nodded and squeezed his arm.

"Since I couldn't sleep, I've been thinking about Lieutenant Cotes. She had motivation and means, but did she have the opportunity?" Sia lunged into a calf stretch on first one leg, then the other.

Before Chris could respond, a female voice interrupted.

"Excuse me, sir."

Chris turned to find a tall blond woman approaching them. She was dressed in red, marking her as one of the flight crew. As she got closer, he realized she wasn't as young as he'd first thought. She had a long scar from her temple down to her chin. It was an old scar that had faded with age. Something about the scar stirred a memory, but one that eluded him.

"Special Agent Vargas," she shielded her eyes from the rising sun.

"Yes, and this is Lieutenant Commander Soto."

"Ma'am." The woman nodded her hello. "I was directed to you by the XO. I was meeting with him on the bridge when we saw you running on the flight deck."

"You are?" Sia asked.

"Lieutenant Maria Jackson. I'm one of the landing signal officers and I was on the flight deck when Lieutenant Washington lost control of his jet and skidded.

In fact, I was the one handling the meatball and directing him in."

"We talked with several crew members and watched footage of the crash. If we come up with more questions, we'll be sure to talk to you." Chris didn't see any need to rehash what had happened on deck. They had the footage and had interviewed both Washington's wingman and the air boss.

The woman's gaze narrowed. When he tried to go around her, she moved to block his path. Something flashed in her eyes, something menacing and chilling, but it was quickly gone and Chris had to question whether he'd seen anything at all or if it was a trick of the light.

"Actually," she said impatiently, "I'm not here about what happened on deck that night. I'm here about what happened before Lieutenant Washington crashed."

"What is that?" Sia asked. Standing beside the tall woman, Sia seemed even more fragile.

Maria looked pensive for a moment. "I didn't really think anything about it until today when the XO mentioned you were investigating Susan and if I had any information regarding her and Lieutenant Washington, I should report to you."

"And what do you have to say about Lieutenant Cotes?" Chris prompted.

"She likes to play games with men," she said derisively, not looking away. "I've seen it in the past. With Lieutenant Washington, it was just more of the same. The argument started in the wardroom. When he walked away, she followed him. She continued the dispute with him right near his fighter. She had a piece of paper in her hand and she was waving it around. He was shaking his head and I could tell he was angry."

"Do you know what they were arguing about?" Sia asked.

"Not completely." The woman lowered her voice. "But she made a threat."

Chris regarded her for a moment, and then said, "What kind of threat?"

Her tone ominous, she replied, "That he would regret it if he didn't stop harassing her. She would put a stop to it. I just assumed she would go to the captain, but I'm not sure now what she really meant."

"Now?" Sia asked.

Maria shrugged. "Well, now that he's dead."

"She was near his plane, you said." Looked like they had more to interrogate Susan Cotes about than just the notes and her knowledge of radar. The evidence was mounting.

"That's right. And he stalked away when she made her threat."

"What did she do?"

Maria looked uncomfortable, but resigned to the onerous task of informing on a friend. "She ducked under the plane and I lost track of her. I had to prepare the deck for a landing, so I got busy. It was only after the crash and the XO's information that I thought of it."

"Would she have had access to his radar equipment from underneath the plane?" Sia asked.

"Sure, she could have. I didn't see her, but it's possible."

"Thank you for your time, Lieutenant Jackson," Sia said.

She nodded and walked away.

"Looks like she had opportunity, too," Chris said.

"Looks like it. Let's get her back into interrogation."

Chris nodded. "Let's get cleaned—"

The sound of a shot echoed across the deck. Chris pushed Sia toward the cover of two jets and several more shots rang out. One plinked into the nearest jet, much too close to Sia's head. Chris pushed her down and covered her. She started to protest, but he shushed her. He heard the sound of running feet and the clank of a metal door somewhere above them. Then silence.

He lifted himself off her and looked down into her face. She was flushed with fear, her pupils dilated. He cursed that he hadn't been carrying his sidearm on the deck. He'd left it in his locker. From now on he was going to carry it. He saw the captain approaching with angry strides.

"Are you all right?" he said, checking her over himself.

"Yes. I'm fine. Who is shooting at us on an aircraft carrier?"

"That's what I would like to know." The captain's voice was filled with anger.

A half an hour later in the captain's conference room, Sia and Chris sat at a long brown table.

"All the sidearms that were signed out of the armory are accounted for. None of them have been fired."

"Someone could have smuggled one aboard. I sent the bullets we pried out of the fuselage of the two jets to my forensics specialist at Hickam. Once we find the weapon, he can match the ballistics."

"The only other sidearm that is aboard this ship," Sia said, "is yours."

"Mine is locked up in my stateroom inside my locker."

"It wouldn't hurt to check it, Vargas," the captain said. "We will be getting underway today. Heading back to San Diego for a few more extensive repairs to the carrier. I want whoever is responsible for what's going on caught before we dock. Is that clear?"

The captain pulled open the door and signaled a master-at-arms, the Navy's version of the MP. "I want you to secure Lieutenant Cotes in Legal until Special Agent Vargas and Commander Soto arrive. Then I want you to wait outside for further instructions."

The steely-eyed man nodded and left.

"Why don't you two get cleaned up and conduct a thorough interrogation of Lieutenant Cotes and check your weapon, Vargas. Report back to me with your findings. You're both dismissed. I have a call to make to Senator Washington. Get me some answers and the perpetrator."

When Sia started to walk back to her cabin, Chris followed.

"Where are you going?"

"With you."

"Why?"

"Someone shot at us. You were pushed down the ladder. Not leaving you alone."

"Suit yourself."

She walked down the gangway and navigated the ladders, favoring her recently injured arm, but Chris could see the way her hand trembled on the rail. When they got to her cabin, she reached for the handle and turned it. He touched her arm and she stilled.

Some color was returning to her cheeks. But he remembered how she had looked after the gunshots. She'd been pasty-white and, despite her surprising mettle during the incident, looked like a feather could knock her over.

"I'm fine," she said, her voice catching as he caressed her arm.

"That's good bravado, Commander, but I'm not buying it." He turned her around and cupped her face. Her skin was smooth, soft and warm against his palms. The feel of her calmed something a bit wild inside him.

"Buying what?"

He tilted his head and stared at her. "I've been shot at before. I can lay a bet you never have."

"No. I won't take that wager and it doesn't mean I'm going to back down, either."

"I wouldn't bet against that."

"Good, because you'd lose."

"I won't let anything happen to you," he said, his voice a shade rougher now. He leaned in and pressed his forehead to hers. With his face close to hers, their gazes locked.

"I'm a JAG officer. I'm expected to take care of myself, but this time, I'll take you up on that. You're the one with the gun."

He pulled her into his arms, tucked her against his chest. "And I know how to use it."

"That doesn't surprise me. You have many skills."

He leaned back enough so he could look into her face. "Oh, do I?"

She smiled. The beauty of it caught him off guard. It was the first genuine smile he'd seen on her since he met her at JAG. He liked the softness of it, the vulnerability. It made his heart ache. It gave him hope where there was none, a hope he wasn't sure he could handle.

It was natural for his head to drop, his mouth to home in on hers. It felt right and good when his lips covered her soft smiling ones. And when she softened rather than stiffened beneath his hands and mouth, he gave up any pretense of trying to control himself where she was concerned.

The past and the present were so tangled up in his head and in his heart, he didn't even try to convince himself he knew the difference anymore. He wanted to think he was well past that part of his life. Clearly, he was not, when it came to the one woman he'd never been able to forget.

"If we didn't have work to do…"

She sighed. "Duty calls. It always does and in this case, we have to answer. It's too important not to."

He nodded. When she opened the door, he crowded in after her.

"What are you doing?" She put her hand on his chest to stop him.

"I said I wasn't leaving you." He pushed forward, liking the way her hand felt against him.

"Chris, I'll lock the door," she said, and couldn't help the small smile that lessened her outraged tone.

He smiled back. "That's a good idea, but I'm going to be on this side of it."

"Oh, for the…all right," she said, giving in after taking a look at his face. "But you stay on the other side of the head door."

"I will."

Inside, Sia grabbed her uniform and disappeared into the head. He heard the shower come on as he imagined her getting in under the spray. All that glorious skin wet and gleaming. When the water went off, he shifted and sighed in relief.

"Oh, shoot," he heard her say in distress.

"You okay?"

"I…ah…forgot my underwear. Could you…" She trailed off.

Chris chuckled.

"It's not funny!"

"Oh, it's providing me with great amusement."

"I was in too much of a hurry to get away from you."

"Right." He went to her locker and opened it. "Does it matter…"

"No! Just grab a pair, for God's sake."

He picked out one from all the lacy numbers in her locker and hooked it to his forefinger. He knocked on the door.

She opened it, a towel wrapped around her, her shoulders looking damp and inviting. Her face was mortified when she saw the panties dangling from his finger. She snatched them away and slammed the door.

He chuckled again.

"You'd think an NCIS agent would have better manners," she shouted through the door.

He laughed. "We're a coarse bunch of SOBs. Most of us come from a law enforcement background, the rest from the military."

"I have to say I was surprised you went into the agency. I thought you'd still be flying." Her voice was subdued now, but filled with curiosity.

"I resigned my commission shortly after you left for New York. I tried to kill myself with alcohol for the first month. I'd probably still be there or in the ground."

"What happened?" He didn't miss the anguish in her voice and it made his gut clench at the memories of the worst time in his life.

"A buddy called and he hauled me out of my apartment and read me the riot act."

"Sounds like a good friend."

"He is. He worked for NCIS and encouraged me to apply. I thought it sounded like I could make a difference."

She opened the door. "And have you?"

She looked scrubbed and fresh, her hair pulled back and securely fastened.

"I think so. The work is rewarding, but tough. I used the long hours like I did alcohol. It dulled the pain and after a while it got better."

She put her hand on his chest, her eyes clear and looking deep into his. "That's good, Chris."

Her sympathy made him want to draw her close, but he was aware of the time and their responsibilities. It was the only thing that stopped him.

"Time for my shower," he said, meeting her gaze head-on.

She grabbed her hat and nodded she was ready to go.

Back in his own stateroom, he opened his locker and pulled out his weapon. Sia looked over his shoulder.

"Your gun is here."

It looked the same as when he'd left it. He nodded. He caught a whiff of cleaning oil and noticed his kit was just below the weapon. Reaching down, he opened it. Nothing inside was disturbed. He called the captain and gave him that information while Sia took a seat on his bunk.

While he was in the shower, he mentally went over what they knew. Two aviators were dead. It seemed both of them had had radar issues and both of them had been incoherent at the end. They had a dead master chief who'd tried to murder Sia. Two planes were being thoroughly investigated. Last but not least, an LSO who had seen the suspect under one of the jets.

They needed more answers. When he emerged from the head, they headed to the legal office.

"Your weapon is still in your locker?" Sia asked, her gaze flowing over him like a warm caress.

He was sure it was involuntary, but that thought did nothing to lessen the impact of her eyes on him. "Right now, I have it against the small of my back. I'm not taking any more chances."

She looked pensive. "So someone must have smuggled the weapon aboard."

He reached up and rubbed her shoulder to tell her he would stick by her. "Looks like it."

Two masters-at-arms were standing on either side of the door as Sia and Chris approached. The guards nodded as Chris opened the door and indicated for Sia to enter.

Lieutenant Cotes was sitting at the small interrogation table. Her hands were nervously intertwining, but ceased when they entered.

Sia sat and Chris nestled in next to her. Sia pulled Lieutenant Cotes's file out of her briefcase.

"We have received information you and Lieutenant Washington had an argument on the flight deck the night before he flew his mission," Sia said.

Chris was beginning to think Sia would make an excellent cop. Her interrogation skills were very good. She didn't elaborate or expound on what she was saying. She just gave her suspect a little rope.

Susan shifted and looked away, her lips tightening. "It's true. We had an argument, but I only wanted to talk to him and tell him I was going to the captain because his notes hadn't stopped."

"What was his response?" Sia said, her eyes sharp.

"He got really angry and accused *me* of playing games and said I didn't need to bother because he was going to talk to the captain." She dropped her head in her hands. "This is a nightmare. Nothing good comes from even speaking to a pilot."

"Were you?"

"Was I what?" Susan asked, her head coming up, her eyes moist.

"Were you playing games?" Sia elaborated, her voice even.

"No!" Susan snapped.

Sia arched a brow and studied her so hard that Susan dropped her hands to her lap and glanced away. Without a word, she pulled out the notes she had found in Washington's bunk and laid them out on the table one by one.

Susan's eyes swung suspiciously toward the pieces of paper, and then her face went white as she studied the notes. Color flushed back into her cheeks as her shocked and angry eyes met Sia's. "I didn't write these. I don't know what kind of game Lieutenant Washington was playing, but I wasn't a part of it."

Chris said softly, "Did you tamper with Lieutenant Washington's jet?"

"No! I told you. We fought on the deck, but I left when he did. I didn't touch the plane. I had nothing to do with his death!" She smacked the table with the flat of her hand.

Sia ignored the outburst and fired off another question. "Where were you at zero one hundred hours yesterday?"

"In my bunk sleeping after my shift," Susan said, clearly wondering where this was heading. "Why?"

"Someone with a yellow tunic pushed me down the ladder."

"It wasn't me," she said, even more agitated.

"Can anyone confirm you were there…sleeping?"

Susan's eyes narrowed and her mouth tightened. "No. I don't know. As I said, I was sleeping."

"What about your roommate?"

"She was on duty."

"I have one more question for you. Do you own a gun?"

Susan made a soft sound and looked away. "No, I don't own a gun."

"Have you fired one recently?"

"What? At you and Agent Vargas? Is that what you're asking?"

"Have you?"

"No! All the answers to your questions are no!"

Chris's phone buzzed and when he looked down, he

saw he had a text from Math. He checked the message. *Need to talk to you now.*

"Looks like Math has something for us." Chris got up and opened the door. "Lieutenant Cotes, you may go back to your duty station."

Susan angrily pushed her chair back and with a sullen look on her face brushed past them. Chris shut the door.

"I'll commission us a vehicle and we'll head over to Hickam to talk to Math."

An hour later they were in the procured vehicle and heading over to the base. Chris navigated the streets easily.

"Your old stomping grounds?" Sia asked.

"Yes, we docked here often. I will say that Rafe and I took advantage of the beaches and the pretty women in bikinis."

Sia smiled. "Rafe was my brother, but he was purely male."

After getting through security, they were directed to a hangar on the north side of the base. Chris pulled up to the large gray structure and he and Sia left the car.

Once inside, they found Math examining a large piece of what looked like the fuselage of a fighter.

"Math?"

Math turned around and smiled. "Hey, that was fast."

"The ship is docked less than a mile from here. It took longer to get a car. The Navy and their red tape."

"Hello, pretty Sia."

Sia smiled at him and shook his hand.

"What do you have for us?" Chris said.

Math rubbed at his tired eyes, went over to a desk

and sat down. He indicated two chairs. Sia and Chris settled in.

"What is it?"

"I went over the planes and can tell you there were no structural issues. Both of them were sound, solid pieces of machinery. However, I can't say the same thing about each radar. Both of them were damaged."

"From the impact or from something else?" Chris asked, leaning forward.

"It would be hard to determine. Saunders's jet took less damage when it crashed into the ocean. According to the data recovered from the flight recorder, it was clear he was at the controls most of the way down, so he tried to minimize the damage when he realized he was about to crash."

"Realized? What do you mean?" Sia asked.

"I can only guess that he was in and out of consciousness most of the descent. I think he was unaware his jet was so close to the water. He made no move to adjust his controls between the time of the collision and just before he hit the water."

"He was mentally incapacitated?" she said, giving Chris a knowing look.

"He was most likely mentally and physically incapacitated. Whether it was from something inherent or introduced into his system, the ME has to make that determination."

"There was no conclusive evidence from his autopsy that indicates he was drugged," Sia said, and she looked triumphant that her insistence that a drug had been involved in the pilot deaths had turned out to be true.

"Well, I suggest the ME take another look. That pilot

was not acting normal when handling that jet. It took a long time for him to crash. Several minutes."

"It's true," Sia said. "His wingman confirmed that."

"And the flight recorder corroborates the wingman's testimony."

"Did he have water in his lungs?" Math asked, his brow furrowing in thought.

"According to the report, yes. He drowned," Chris replied, thinking Sia was right and they did have a drugging of a military pilot on a U.S. carrier.

Math nodded in confirmation. "Then he was alive for some time after he hit the water."

"So he had ample time to eject?" Sia said, her eyes shining a bit.

"More than ample time," Math said.

"And Washington's jet?" Chris needed to know if the same things added up there.

Math reached up and scratched his stubbled jaw. "There it is cut-and-dried. The radar was damaged when the jet hit the ship and exploded. It had more extensive damage."

"So then you can't tell if it was tampered with?" Sia said, disappointment evident in her tone. They were both hoping for some kind of evidence they could use.

Math grinned and cocked his head. "On the contrary, I can."

"What did you find?" Chris knew that look. Math had it whenever he'd found something substantial. Chris always liked that look.

"Two fingerprints. I ran them through AFIS and I got a hit."

"Who do they belong to?" Chris said, anticipation curling in his gut.

"Lieutenant Susan Cotes."

Chapter 9

"Chris, I do want to point out to you the fingerprints I lifted off the casing were almost perfect."

"No smudges? No smears?"

"None. But the evidence speaks for itself. Your case is solved thanks to me and I did it in just under twenty-four hours." Math smirked.

"It would seem so."

Sia and Chris made their way back to the ship. Chris reported to the captain and got permission to bring Susan Cotes back to the interrogation. She paced restlessly in her stateroom as Chris entered. "Are you all right?"

"Yes," she said. "I want the truth from that woman."

"Let's go get it."

Sia nodded, her face solemn. Chris headed toward the door, and just as she was going to shut down her laptop, her email notification dinged. She clicked on the icon and her email message popped up. The email was from her aide. He'd gotten the list she wanted of all pilot deaths aboard Navy ships from the time her brother had been killed. She clicked on the list and found eight names, including Rafael's. She also noticed her aide had included pictures. In the email, he said it was important she open the file. She clicked on the attachment. The file loaded and she gasped softly.

"Chris," Sia said, her eyes on her computer screen.

Chris paused with his hand on the door handle. "What is it?"

"Look at this."

When he walked closer to the screen, he swore softly under his breath.

"They look like you. Well, except for Rafael. All of them, including Saunders and Washington. They look enough like you to be brothers.

"Susan Cotes is a serial killer. It's clear from these photos." She was reeling from this information, not quite sure how she should feel. Not quite sure how she should act. If Chris had been targeted by a serial killer all those years ago, then her brother had been nothing more than collateral damage.

And, Chris…Chris had been the intended victim.

Her stomach churned at this news, and in the bright light of day she had to realize she had been so off-base. It was true the *accident* that had taken her brother's life was no accident at all. It was supposed to have been Chris who died that day. He had been the target.

All these years she'd blamed Chris, so sure her brother couldn't have made a mistake. She had been right. He hadn't made a mistake, but then, neither had Chris.

Both of them were blameless. She had wronged Chris. And her mother and father had also wronged him. But they couldn't make amends. That burden fell completely on Sia's shoulders.

Anger she'd never felt before infused her with a searing heat. Without a word, she left the stateroom. She could hear Chris calling her name, but she was too caught up in the emotion to stop, to reason, to give a damn about anything. When she reached the legal office, she burst into the cabin.

Susan Cotes jumped in her seat as the door slammed against the wall. She reacted visibly to the look in Sia's eyes. She rose and started to back up. Without preamble, Sia lunged at the woman, grabbed her by the shirtfront and pushed her into the bulkhead. "You ruined my life. You killed my brother."

Susan Cotes's eyes filled with confusion and fear. She shook her head. "I don't know what you're talking about."

Strong hands grabbed at Sia and pulled her off and away from Susan. Chris stepped forward and said softly, "Get ahold of yourself."

Sia shouted, "You're a monster."

Susan looked at Chris and said, "What is she saying? Why is she so upset? I don't even know her brother."

Chris pulled out his handcuffs and Susan's eyes widened, tears gathered. "No," she said her voice breaking. "I didn't do anything. I didn't kill anyone."

"Susan Cotes, you're under arrest for the murder of Lieutenant Eli Washington."

He turned her around and snapped the cuffs on her wrists. Susan shouted, "This is crazy. I didn't kill him!"

Chris ignored her words and said, "You have the right to remain silent…"

His words faded as she stared at the woman responsible for so many deaths. What sick, twisted mind could have planned eight murders? But she had killed nine men! And only Chris had survived. Guilt rolled and tumbled around in her gut as she looked at him staying calm and doing his duty. She watched mutely as he turned the woman over to the masters-at-arms with instructions to put her in the brig.

Sia turned away from the door, crossing her arms over her chest and trying to tamp down her anger.

When the door closed behind them, Chris turned to her. "Sia, what were you thinking! You have no proof she's done anything but kill Washington."

She turned to meet his eyes, but dropped her gaze down at the way he looked at her, disappointment clear in them. She unwrapped her arms. He continued.

His voice was closer, which meant so was he. She had to look up, but she really needed more space, and more time, before having to handle him, or handle anything. Dealing with Chris up close in her personal space was more than she could take on at the moment. "You're a seasoned prosecutor, and you had better start thinking like one."

"It has to be her," Sia said stubbornly. "Did you see the photos? Did you? They all look like you! Oh, God, you were a victim. She was trying to kill you and yet she stands there looking so innocent."

"You need to step away from Rafael's death. You're

letting your grief and anger get in the way of rational thought. You need to get back on track right now or I'm taking you off this case!"

"You will not!"

His eyes went hard and flinty, and she had to resist the urge to shiver. "I will and I have the authority." Gone were the smooth-as-velvet, dulcet tones. In their place was a flat, steely voice that brooked no argument.

He took a step closer, and she tensed. She tried not to show it, but that much was really beyond her at the moment. The stabilized world she'd thought she'd constructed for herself had just been proven to have very shaky foundations. And she didn't know what to do about that. All these years, she'd gone on the assumption that Chris was at fault, not forgiving him, not allowing herself to pine for him. She had wanted him so badly, for the comfort, for the peace, but she couldn't find it with him. And now she realized, she hadn't found it without him either. She felt adrift and lost.

"We have a lot of work to do. Foremost being looking into those other deaths and getting the details. We will need to be calm and prepared when we talk to her again. You can't come barreling in here and accuse her of a murder where we have no proof. Get ahold of yourself, now!"

The conflagration of her anger dissipated, leaving a small, burning ember inside her. He was right. She had lost it. After so many years of grief and loss filling her up, she'd snapped. Her bottled-up feelings had broken free and if not for Chris, she could have jeopardized this solid case against Susan Cotes. It was a good thing he was here.

She took a cleansing breath and headed for the door. When Chris didn't move, she tossed him a chiding look. "Aren't you coming?"

"Where?" he said, eyeing her warily.

"To the captain. We have to search her bunk."

He nodded and opened the door, "Now you're talking. After you."

Sia donned gloves after they entered Susan's berth, the one she shared with Lieutenant Maria Jackson. Sia started with her locker and Chris worked on searching the bunk.

Without thinking about it, she went straight for the socks and began pulling them apart. After the forth pair a familiar bottle dropped out. Sia looked down, her stomach twisting. Bending down, she picked up the bottle and gasped.

"What is it?" Chris asked.

"This is the exact same bottle I found in the master chief's berth. What appears to be a simple over-the-counter irregularity aid."

"How do you know that?"

"The label was torn in the exact same spot. You find anything?"

"Yes and no. I found her yellow tunic stuffed under her mattress. I bagged it to test for gun residue. But no gun."

"One more question to ask her."

"Let's get this cataloged as evidence and get it to Math. He's still at Hickam. In the meantime, we need to slog through the information your aide sent us regarding those deaths. Let's get to it."

"Yes, sir," Sia said.

After getting the sample off to Math, they returned to her cabin for her laptop, went to the legal office and printed out all the information her aide had sent her. They decided that it would be more comfortable working out of her own stateroom and returned there.

If they were going to tie these murders to Susan Cotes, there was a lot to go over. She was also still waiting on the information regarding the master chief.

"What was her connection to the master chief?"

"He was sleeping with her?"

"He was old enough to be her father."

"Maybe she's looking for a father figure. All we know at this point is he tried to protect her. I think that's why he tried to kill you."

"It's possible. I told him I was going to dig into my brother's death. That could have been the trigger."

"You couldn't have known he was connected at the time, Sia."

"Yes, well, I almost signed my own death warrant." She looked down at his notebook. "You've got a lot of notes there. Care to share?"

"All nine pilot murders involve pilots stationed aboard the *McCloud,*" Chris said.

Sia was surprised no one had put the pattern together, but more than one agent had handled the deaths.

"The first death resulted from a fall from an upper deck of the carrier. It had been windy and storming and the death was ruled accidental. One was during shore leave. The man had been stabbed and left for dead outside a bar in Hawaii. NCIS investigated and classified it as a robbery/homicide. No suspect had ever been found in that crime and it's now considered a cold case." He flipped over a page and continued. "The next was a chopper pilot who had crashed into the ocean and drowned. The ruling had been accidental."

Sia wondered if the pilot had been drugged.

"Then your brother was killed, ruled pilot error. Two more pilots had gone down on a routine mission, but their jets and bodies hadn't ever been recovered."

"Then that left Saunders and Washington," she said, looking over his shoulder.

"Your aide is very thorough."

"That he is. He'll make a very good lawyer one day."

Chris's phone trilled, he flipped it open and said, "It's a text from Math. Get him up on the two-way."

When Math popped up on the screen, he said, "You two look as tired as I feel."

"What do you have for us?" Sia asked.

"For you, sweetheart, anything you want." He wagged his eyebrows.

"Math," Chris growled.

"Oh, right, you have a claim on her."

"Shut up and give us the information."

"Which is it, man? Shut up or talk?"

"Math," Chris said, lower and more menacing.

"All right. The drug in the bottle is Gamma-Hydroxybutyric acid, commonly known as GHB."

"The date-rape drug?" Sia asked.

"Yes. GHB is also used in a medical setting as a general anesthetic, to treat conditions such as insomnia, clinical depression, narcolepsy and alcoholism, as well as to improve athletic performance."

"But it wasn't prescribed for her. It was in an over-the-counter medication bottle."

"That's correct. We can surmise from that behavior she meant to conceal the drug. So if we can infer that, then we can conclude she used it to drug Washington. It would explain his behavior the night he crashed and his inability to eject."

"But there was no evidence Washington had been drugged."

"GHB is colorless and odorless and is easily added to drinks that mask the flavor. A urine test is the best way to detect the drug in the system, and that is problematic, if you're not specifically looking for it. The drug leaves the body about eight to twelve hours after ingestion. Quite frankly, the ME could have missed it, since it is sodium-based and occurs naturally in the central nervous system."

"Is there a way to detect it after death if you're specifically looking for it?"

Math smiled. "You would have made a good forensic scientist, Vargas. As a matter of fact, there is. GHB can be detected in hair for months after ingesting the drug."

"And you already tested Lieutenant Washington's hair?" Chris's smile was easy and made her shiver inside as she became mesmerized by the way his mouth curved.

"I did. He had enough in his system to cause dizziness and drowsiness. I would say if Lieutenant Washington and your suspect were in the wardroom, she could have easily slipped it into his drink. Since he had coffee in his stomach contents, the strong flavor would have easily masked the taste."

"And the tunic?"

"Well, you've really hit the jackpot with this woman. The tunic tested positive for gunpowder residue. She had fired a weapon, but I can't say for certain if it was at you and the lovely Sia or at the pistol range. If you want me to do any tests on the other pilots who were killed, you'll have to exhume the bodies. That's always hell on the families," Math said, shaking his head.

"It may be necessary. Their loved ones have a right to know what really happened to them," Chris said firmly.

"You let me know, cowboy."

"Roger that. Math, thanks as always. I appreciate the effort you made coming all the way from Norfolk."

"Can I go home now?"

"Yes…after I get your reports."

"Aw, damn, that'll take me hours. Looks like I'll have to sleep on the plane."

"Well, you better get started."

"Screw you, Vargas," Math said with a chuckle. "Goodbye, pretty Sia." He blew her a kiss and ended the conversation as the screen winked out.

"He's a character," she said.

"You have no idea. He's brilliant, but eccentric. He loves the ladies."

She smiled. "I can tell." Her eyes locked with his. In this quiet moment, a moment of shared amusement, it was hard to think that six years had passed since she'd seen Chris. It was as if time hadn't passed at all. As if they were in some kind of time warp transporting them back to when her life was full of this man, his kisses, his body, his love.

She couldn't forget the past, but right now it seemed to recede some, to give her some solace in this moment.

Strands of hair slipped from her bun and swung softly against her cheek.

Chris reached out and brushed at it, letting the long strands filter through his fingers. Her hair was free from the bun by some stealth move he made and as it cascaded over her shoulders, Chris sighed. "My beautiful Sia."

Nerve endings on red alert, Sia held his heavy-lidded gaze, his eyes as gray as smoke. It seemed amazing to her, the way her body came alive and aware of him. Her heart picked up a beat; her breasts grew heavy and tingled, her nipples drawing into hard, beaded knots.

Chris was tall and rangy, with strong broad shoulders and slim hips. Sleek skin over heavy muscle. The expression on his lean, tanned face was languid and powerful. He moved closer to her as his hand cupped her face. As he looked deep into her eyes, she remembered easily why she had fallen for Chris so quickly.

He'd been cocky and brash when she'd first met him. Imbued with that fighter pilot aura only a man with deep confidence and amazing skill could have and, damn, but he looked good in the uniform. He was first in his class at Top Gun and she hadn't at first wanted to get involved with him. She had plans and he didn't fit into them. But then she'd seen his sensitive side, when he would coax her mother out of her depressions and make her father laugh with his big whopping fighter pilot stories.

His moniker had been Streak, like lightning, like pure unadulterated speed. And he liked to move fast.

Like a flash, he had taken her breath away.

Moving fast had been in his blood, but it looked like he'd tempered that speed until only the promise of it lay in his dark, soot-smudged eyes.

He caught her first with the magnetic quality of those eyes, glittering with devilish lights, and then zapped her with that grin. She had never experienced anything like Chris Vargas's grin. She felt as if he had turned a thousand watts of pure electricity on her.

His mouth was wide, his lips were sculpted, the sexy dip in his upper lip drew her eye and all she could think about was how he would taste.

He went to his knees on the bunk and cupped her face in both of his hands. His palms were warm against her skin and she closed her eyes as he ran his thumbs along her cheekbones. With a quick intake of air, he whispered close to her ear, "You trying to seduce me, sugar?"

She shivered at his warm breath across the sensitive shell of her ear. His fingers delved into her hair, caressing the nape of her neck.

"Why don't you take your shirt off for me?"

She complied, but not before she slid her hands up his sides, up to the heavy muscles of his shoulders. Her buttons felt small compared to all that strength.

Her shirt off and discarded, Sia opened her eyes. The scent of him filled her nostrils with warm, aroused male, musky and virile.

That mobile mouth skimmed along her face with teasing kisses; the whisper of his heated lips almost made her beg for more contact. "Now the pants," he ordered. And Sia knew, in this case, she was at his command.

She shifted and he shifted with her as if he couldn't bear to let her go. She slipped out of her pants and knelt on the bunk in nothing but her bra and panties.

"Soldier on the outside…" he said as he deftly removed her bra and released her breasts; they ached for his touch. He hooked his fingers around the stretch of lace at her hip, his flesh hot against her skin. "All woman on the inside."

He tugged. Slowly. Excruciatingly slowly. She wanted to tip her head back, close her eyes, and just focus on feeling every sensation, every ripple of pleasure. But she couldn't take her eyes off him. She tried not to tremble so hard, but she couldn't seem to stop. As he removed her panties, the warm cotton of his pullover barely brushing over her nipples, she cried out.

"Sia," he said, his voice strangled. "You're so beautiful."

She watched as he stood and quickly undressed and donned protection. "Lean back and open your knees slightly," he said, crawling back on the bunk. Sia complied, meeting his eyes in a head-on collision of passion.

He knelt before her again. This time his hands circled her waist and slid to her lower back. He put slight pressure there and she helplessly arched. He supported her back as his head descended to lick like flame against her collarbone. A puff of air blown across her nipple was a tease, sending red-hot ripples straight to her groin.

He licked one nipple, then the other and Sia groaned softly in her throat, aching for more contact with his hot, wet mouth.

She reached for him, sliding her hands over his taut, smooth skin, into the silk of his hair. With pressure on the back of his head, she brought his mouth hard against her breast. His mouth closed over it, working the beaded point with his tongue, his five-o'clock shadow pleasantly abrading her skin.

With urging, he clamped his lips over her other breast, suckling her until she thought the pleasure might kill her.

He slipped a hand between her thighs to find the tight, throbbing knot of nerves. Gently he pushed her back, his mouth still on her breast. When she was flat on her back, he slipped away from her, trailing kisses down her abdomen. As he slowly drew his tongue along her most sensitive flesh, Sia restlessly moved against him. Chris moaned as he continued his dedicated assault on her senses, tying her into sensuous knots. He slipped his fingers inside of her, his tongue never stopping its delicious swirling patterns that stole her breath. She buried her hands in his hair, gripping it gently as long moans, one after the other, poured out of her as he lifted her and settled his mouth fully against her.

Crying out, her mind reeling at the pleasure, at the pure carnal joy. Her hips arched and bucked, twisted for the best angle and optimum contact with his mouth.

Hot, wild bliss. Mindless ecstasy. Terrifying freedom from the bounds she had to live within. Her pleasure crested abruptly, strongly, wringing unrestrained cries from her.

Pleasure spiraled through her and she was in his arms, immersed in his embrace, lost in his kiss as that beautiful mouth covered hers. His touch unleashed a host of needs that had lain dormant inside of her for six long, lonely years. Now they leaped and twisted, wild with the prospect of freedom.

As their eyes met, she saw his glittering on the edge of control. He entered her in one powerful stroke, filling her, touching off another explosive climax that only fueled him. He wrapped his arms around her and crushed her to him.

He moved slowly and she could tell by his taut muscles it cost him. He kissed her softly, tenderly.

She slid her hands down his back, over the hot, flexing, sweat-slick muscles. Then her fingers stretched over the tight, rounded mounds of his buttocks. She caressed and squeezed, urging him to increase his tempo until he was pumping his hips into her, frantic with the need for release they achieved, one on the heels of the other.

Afterward they dozed, exhausted, replete. Chris settled on his side with one leg thrown across Sia. She turned toward him and curled up against him as his arms came around her and pulled her closer. She caressed his face, the sharp cheekbones, ran her thumb across his mouth, loving the texture of his skin.

Inside she felt a heaviness settle on her as she met his eyes. There was no satisfaction in them, no triumph, just a deep sadness that connected with her own heavy heart.

Her brain scrambled to make sense out of the constant flux with the reaction of her body and her heart. It was all such a huge jumble. There was no way she could make a rational judgment. Not with him looking at her like that, and her wanting all sorts of things that were on the verge of impossible.

Their past still loomed, and with this new information that still had her reeling, she lost her anchor. Then he cupped her cheek and turned her gaze to his when she looked away in a vain effort to regroup.

"Does it help to know?" he whispered in the dark stateroom.

"Know what?"

"Who might have been responsible for the death of your brother. She used me like a weapon and killed the wrong man. Does it help?" he asked, never more sincere, real concern outlined in every inch of his handsome face.

This time her heart didn't skip; it stopped altogether, then thundered on with such ferocity she felt it might explode from the sudden intensity of it.

"Don't," she said softly, her voice catching. She buried her face in his neck. "Just hold me, Chris. Tighter," she said. "As if you'll never let me go."

"I remember, Sia. All the time. I remember what it was like to be with you, hold you. I thought I had gotten over you, but it seems that I was wrong. I don't know what we're accomplishing with this trip down memory lane, but I can't say that I wouldn't do it again. I've missed you, sweetheart."

Guilt and shame welled up in her that he could be so generous and she was unable to get past what had happened. There were going to be more questions for Susan Cotes. But would there be any answers for Sia?

"Talk to me. Tell me what is in your heart. It's just a matter of saying the words. I won't pressure you after this. Just tell me. Does it make a difference?"

This was killing her, twisting her heart and emotions into painful, complicated knots. Did she still love Chris? Did finding out Rafael's death had been a result of an attempt on Chris's life help? Could she turn away from a once-in-a-lifetime relationship again?

"I don't know, Chris." Her voice broke and she buried her face in his neck, her hot tears spilling out against his smooth skin. He tightened his hold, which only made her cry harder. She didn't deserve his comfort, trapped in her own bitterness and pain.

In that moment, she realized with such clarity how she had betrayed him, abandoned him. Even now, she couldn't come to terms with her own actions. It was easier to continue to blame him, take what little time they had together, then part when it was over.

"I simply just don't know."

Chapter 10

Dawn was breaking across a tumble of heavy gray clouds. Sia tucked her hands in her coat pockets and made her way toward the bridge followed closely by the master-at-arms she'd requested to accompany her. The wind picked up and snatched at her tightly pinned hair beneath her hat.

She was still trying to make sense of everything that had happened in the last day. But she still had a job to do. When she reached the bridge, she removed her cover and found the captain drinking a cup of coffee as he surveyed information on a clipboard.

"Good morning, Lieutenant. I'm afraid we have some rough seas ahead of us. There's a storm between us and the coast. No way to go around it. We're going to push to land. I'm going to clear the flight deck and restrict all crew to their quarters. Are you aware of safety procedures in the case of an emergency?"

"Yes, Billy—Commander Stryker went over them with me after I boarded. I'm up to speed."

He nodded. "Good work on getting Washington's killer."

"About that, sir." She pulled out the sheaf of papers she'd brought with her. "We suspect there are more." She handed him the pages and he shuffled through them, staring at the pictures of all the dead pilots and their resemblance to each other.

"Son of a bitch," he said softly.

"We, Special Agent Vargas and I, believe all these men were her victims. But at this point we don't have any proof."

"What do you plan to do?"

"Get a confession. We think the killer has some deep-seated issues regarding pilots. The first guy was probably pushed to his death. He was either lured to the deck or was a case of opportunity."

"You have my permission to do whatever it takes to get the confession. You're a lawyer. I don't have to remind you of the law."

"Sir, there's something else. Something I didn't mention when I boarded because I didn't know it was part of this investigation."

"Go on."

"Special Agent Vargas and I know each other. We had a relationship six years ago when he was stationed aboard the *McCloud*. He was involved in a midair crash that killed my brother, Rafael Soto. We believe he was the intended target of the killer and my brother died as a result of the attempt on his life."

"I was briefed on the incident when I took control of

this vessel five years ago. I sense you have an agenda here, Commander. Perhaps you should tell me what it is."

"Sir, I never meant to harbor any secrets. Until this evidence came to light, I always believed it had been an accident. I also believed my brother was blameless in the matter. But now, with this new evidence, I was hoping you would recommend to SECNAV that my brother's case get a review so he has a chance to be cleared of the pilot-error ruling. I want to petition to have him memorialzed at the Navy Memorial."

"You get me a confession and I'll petition to clear both their names."

"I don't know how Chris feels about it, sir."

"You didn't consult him?"

"No, our relationship has been strained. I didn't want to presume too much on his behalf, but I will relay your promise to him."

Sia turned to leave. When she reached the door, the captain said, "I'm sorry for your loss, Commander. You're a fine credit to this Navy. Your brother would have been proud."

"Thank you, sir."

When she got to the base of the ladder, she could see the bustle of the crew working to get the deck cleared and the jets stowed below in the hangar. As she turned to go inside and head back to her quarters, she spied Chris standing on the deck. He looked forlorn and alone as the wind caught in his dark hair. His face was impassive as he confronted his ghosts and she had no doubt that's exactly what he was doing. She watched as he clenched trembling hands.

Her heart ached for him. He was part of the past she wanted to forget, part of the bitterness and the grief and the pain.

Chris stood on the windblown deck trying to rein in his emotions. Trying to come to grips with his own loss. *It had been more, Rafe,* he said. *I lost more than you that day. I lost Sia. I lost a family and I lost my nerve. But I've got to finally, finally come to terms with it.*

Once he had known dreams of love and family and the kind of ordinary success that most men strove for, but he'd been shown in no uncertain terms that life had a way of taking you and tossing you around like a rag doll to lie broken where you fell. That life had blown up in his face, and he had had to live with the fact he'd been the one to lay the powder and light the fuse, or so he had thought.

What he had rebuilt for himself in the aftermath was simple and basic, he reminded himself as he watched the last jet sink onto the deck of the carrier; the sound of the hydraulic platforms descending into the belly of the deck was snatched away by the wind.

As it disappeared, he let his pain go with it, let his guilt and his shame disappear. He clenched his hands into fists as he struggled with the hope that one day Sia could do the same. He didn't want simple and basic anymore. He wanted the *more* he had lost.

With the thought of her, he felt her small hand curl around his fist. He opened his hand and grasped hers. The warmth was welcome as it radiated from his hand to his empty heart.

"There's a storm brewing. The captain is restricting crew to quarters for the duration."

"That include us?"

"Yes, but in light of this new information regarding the GHB, I want to reinterview Lieutenant Russell and Monroe. If we can place Susan in the wardroom at the same time as both pilots, that gives us stronger evidence that she had the opportunity to spike both of their drinks. I also have the captain's permission to work on Susan Cotes and get her to confess. We have the information to present to her. I also asked for my brother's case to be reopened and considered."

He turned to her. "Don't you think that was premature? We don't have a confession yet. We don't have anything that links her to that accident."

"We will. We have to. The captain said he would also petition to clear your name."

"I don't need my name cleared. It doesn't matter anymore. The past is over and done with. I'm moving on."

"Surely you can't mean that. What you did with the Navy means something. It has to. If it doesn't, then my brother's death means nothing. I can't bear that."

He turned to her and pulled her close. "I didn't say that what I did here didn't mean anything, Sia."

She wrapped her arms around his neck. "I wish it was as easy for me to let go," she said.

"But you can't."

"Not yet. Maybe never. I don't know."

She grasped his hand and pulled him toward the decks below. They went to her quarters and when the door shut behind them, they didn't pretend.

His mouth found hers with evidence of a keen-edged

need that was reciprocated. This time would be different from last night. He wanted to unleash the need he had for her that lurked just beneath the surface.

The air crackled with the electricity they created. His mouth went in search of hers, and their tongues tangled. He pushed at her clothing until he got it all off her, and she did the same.

He bent his head to catch her nipple in his lips and sucked strongly from her. Her knees buckled in sudden violent response. Her fingers went to his hair, unconsciously drawing him closer as the sensations crashed over him, one wave after another.

She cupped his heavy shaft and he surged into her soft hand. It was shockingly arousing to be touched by her and he knew he would never get enough. He slipped his hand between their bodies, found her warm, wet heat and stroked a finger inside her. She cried out, her fingers tightening around him. His mouth went to her other breast in a dual assault that was engineered to make her unravel fast.

His voice was ragged, muffled against her skin. "The bunk."

Her touch grew more deliberate. "I want you inside me. Now."

His breathing ragged, he gave her a long, deep kiss, and began to move her toward the bunk. She apparently had no intention of cooperating. "The bunk," he panted, his mouth moving to her jaw, her ear, her throat. "Now, Sia."

Instead she went to her knees before him, pressed her lips against his hardness. He shuddered and groaned, throwing his head back at the feel of her soft mouth taking him. She traced her tongue down the length of him, exploring him with lips and tongue, until he hauled her to her feet and into his arms.

Her mouth met his fiercely. Her kiss evoked a violent response in him. He responded to her violence with more of the same, demanding an answer. He backed her against the bulkhead, then reached down and lifted her leg over his hip.

The need in her clear brown eyes aroused him beyond his limits. "Chris." He pressed his mouth to hers and swallowed the sound while cupping her bottom and lifting her to impale her with one long stroke.

The sweet velvet slide of his shaft inside her, the delicate pulsations as her body adjusted to his invasion, was almost more than he could bear.

Surging forward, he heard her moan and went in search of her mouth. Sealing it with his, he positioned his hips, thrusting hard and deep, wringing wild cries from her. Her legs were wrapped around him, her arms clinging to his shoulders. Each savage thrust flattened her breasts against him and the exquisite sensations threatened to send him over the edge.

Fingers digging into her bottom, he held her steady as he pounded into her, his vision graying, beginning to blur. He dimly felt her heels pressing into his back, her body tensing, then clenching around him. He was blind, deaf to all but this woman.

When he felt her release, he lunged harder, buried himself inside her to the hilt and followed her into oblivion.

They made it, eventually, to the bunk. For a few minutes they lay there. Once their breathing softened and slowed, Sia turned to him. "You look like you came to some kind of closure up there on the flight deck."

"Almost. I only need one more thing."

"What is that?"

"You to say that you forgive me, Sia. Say the words."

"Give me some more time, Chris. Just a little bit more."

He sighed in disappointment, but Sia couldn't seem to utter the words. She didn't know why. She should. Chris really didn't deserve this.

She had no idea what time it was when her eyes flew open. Nor could she say what had woken her from such a deep sleep. She went to move, then felt the weight of Chris's arm folded across her back, holding her against him. She didn't want to disturb him, but she was struggling to orient herself and her still-fuzzy brain took a moment or two to remember where she was and what she was doing there.

With the sudden dipping and rolling of the carrier, Sia felt a dull throb of a headache beginning as she lifted her head, willing her eyes to adjust to the dark so she could find her bedside clock. It was just past 0930, which was a relief. She had only been asleep for about an hour. It seemed neither one of them had gotten a decent night's sleep.

Of course, Navy bunks weren't exactly meant to be shared by two, yet she felt completely and blissfully sated. She thought about that for a moment, partly because it pushed the return of fear and panic to the edges of her mind for a few more precious seconds, and partly because she couldn't help but wonder what, in fact, did come next for them. She realized the events currently unfolding could end up robbing her of finding out, but that didn't stop her from thinking about what she'd want if it was up to her.

Slowly, cautiously, she slipped out from beneath his arm and gently shifted her weight off the bunk, her eyes adjusting just enough to keep her from stumbling on her way to her toiletry items.

She hit the shower and the heated water felt good even with the unsteady deck rolling beneath her feet. She was supremely proud her stomach didn't protest. Seasickness would be absolutely no fun.

Her father would have been proud of her, she thought as she exited the head and slipped back inside the stateroom. The thought made her smile and for the first time since he'd died, she was thankful she was able to think of him without the immediate pain that would inevitably follow.

She snapped on a light near the locker. It was enough to illuminate her clothing and she dressed quickly in her service khaki. After she was dressed, she walked over to Chris, who was still sleeping. She noted the smudges under his eyes. They deserved this small bit of rest. He had kept long hours on this case, not to mention the extra pain and baggage each of them carried.

Now was the time to get the confession from the woman who was directly responsible for her brother's death. It was what she hoped for so that she could finally lay him to rest.

Proof, evidence. Her brain hammered on the words, and she paced away from the bunk. Even with Susan Cotes's confession, was there a chance for them?

She suspected that it was up to her.

"You're going to wear a hole in the deck."

Her head whipped to the bunk. Chris was awake, his sleepy half-lidded eyes watching her. His head was propped on his arm, his biceps a thick bulge of muscle. His shoulders gleamed in the dim light and cast shadows on his broad chest and tapered waist.

"I was just thinking about our upcoming session with Susan Cotes."

"Working out a strategy?" he asked, stretching his tall, muscular body like a big jungle cat.

"Something like that," she replied, her brain short-circuiting at the sight of him.

He smiled. "You must be a hellcat in court."

She shook off her fascination and turned away to look for her hat. "If you mean that I get my convictions or garner a good defense, then yes, I'm a hellcat in court."

"Come here."

His voice was thick and velvety and she'd be a fool to even get near him in this mood.

"Chris," she said, her eyes going over his face again, homing in on his mouth. "That's not a good idea. I just got dressed and pinned up my hair. I'm not going to get close enough for that stealth move you do to bring it all back down again."

He laughed. "Stealth move?"

"That's what I call it."

"I can't entice you even a little?" He wagged his eyebrows.

She laughed, but kept herself at a safe distance from him. "It's tempting."

"I guess I'll have to come to you." He slipped out of the bunk, all heavy muscle and testosterone, his maleness emphasized by his wide chest and thick thighs.

She couldn't take her eyes off him. Rooted to the spot, she was helpless when he reached her and cupped her cheek. His mouth covered hers, the kiss full of banked passion and subtle need.

When he raised his head, he smiled. "I'll use your shower, then make a quick trip to my stateroom for clothes."

It wasn't until a full minute after he stepped into her bathroom that she realized her hair was down around her shoulders. With an exasperated, but amused sigh, she went to pin it up again.

Looking at herself in the mirror, she couldn't quite meet her own eyes. Maybe she couldn't say it to him now, but she could—had to—admit it to herself. She was still in love with him, and it solved absolutely nothing.

Fifteen minutes later she was sitting next to Chris, trying not to get distracted by the fresh way he smelled and the heat that radiated off his body, a body she had just done such intimate things with less than an hour ago.

Lieutenant Russell, Saunders's wingman, sat in front of her. She smiled at him and said, "Can you remember who was in the wardroom the day of Saunders's crash?"

Lieutenant Russell looked down as he fidgeted with his hat. "There were a couple of other pilots there, Green and Wilson. Also, I remember the LSO, Maria

Jackson, was getting coffee and Lieutenant Cotes was there talking to Lieutenant Jackson."

Sia nodded her head. "Thank you, Lieutenant. You've been a great help."

After he left, Lieutenant Monroe was ushered in and he recalled that both Lieutenant Jackson and Cotes were in the wardroom. Lieutenant Cotes and Washington were sniping at each other and giving each other dirty looks. This evidence was the last nail in Susan's coffin.

Focus, she told herself as the master-at-arms opened the door and ushered Susan Cotes in. Chris indicated for her to sit at the small table and, with an irritated sigh, she sat down.

"Do you understand the charges against you?"

"I understand them, but you're both off base. I didn't kill Lieutenant Washington. I don't know how many times I have to say it."

"The evidence makes you a liar, Lieutenant."

Susan's face blanched and she brought her hands up, the metal cuffs rattling against the table. "What evidence?" she demanded, fear and defiance in her tone.

"We found your fingerprints on the radar casing from his jet. The one you tampered with, along with the GHB you used to drug him."

Susan stood in outrage, her face a mask of shock and disbelief. "I did not! I had nothing to do with it."

"The evidence is iron-clad, Lieutenant. We didn't bring you here so you could deny your guilt. That's unproductive in the face of the evidence. Both lieutenant Russell and Monroe place you in the wardroom before each pilot took off."

It surprised Sia that Susan was fighting tears and

she suddenly became uncomfortable. Susan's behavior seemed wrong, somehow. She showed no signs of the sadistic behavior of a serial killer. But the evidence was irrefutable and Sia put away her doubts.

"Why did you bring me here?"

"We want to give you a chance to come clean about the other murders."

"Other murders? Oh, my God. You two are insane. I haven't committed *any* murders."

Without speaking, Sia laid out the pictures of the dead pilots. Susan looked down at them with a dull and glassy-eyed stare. "I don't know any of these men."

"We think you do." Sia pointed out her brother. "This is the only man in this array who doesn't resemble the others. Do you know why?"

"No," Susan mumbled and Sia could tell when someone was shutting down.

"It's because he was an unintended victim. Chris was your intended target."

Susan looked at Chris, then back at Sia, then down to the picture. "This is your brother, isn't it?"

"That's right."

She looked at Chris. "He was killed when your plane crashed into his. I remember that report."

Chris nodded.

"Wait a second," Sia said as she digested Susan's words. "Report?"

"That's right, Commander," she said smugly. "I wasn't on the *McCloud* when Lieutenant Soto died. I was thousands of miles away in Virginia, at Norfolk Naval Airbase at a training center."

* * *

Sia looked at the computer screen in her quarters, dejected by the news her legalman gave her. "It's true, Commander. She had orders and it's documented on her record. She wasn't on the *McCloud* the day your brother was killed. I'm sorry." The picture was fuzzy and jumped often as the storm battered the ship.

She tried hard to hide her disappointment. "And the other pilots?"

"Those dates match up to her tour of duty. Her shore leave matches up to the time our dead pilot ended up in that alley."

"Thank you, McBride."

"You're welcome, Commander. When are you headed home?"

"As soon as we dock. We'll process Cotes and Chris and I will hop a plane back to Norfolk. She's going to be handled by the folks in Miramar."

"It's getting hard to hear you. How is it there?"

"The storm is pretty intense, but the captain is competent."

"Good. Oh, I almost forgot. I finished compiling the list of all the personnel aboard the *McCloud* the day your brother died. I can send that to you."

"Please do."

There was a knock at the door and Sia signed off on the two-way.

When she opened it, Chris stood on the other side. "How are you doing?"

"I'm angry and disappointed. How do you think I feel?" She moved away from him, afraid he would try to soothe her. She didn't want that.

"That would be my guess. I warned you not to get your hopes up too high," Chris said.

"Yes, you did, and now that you've delivered your message, you can go," Sia snapped.

"Sia, what is it you're looking for?" Chris began on a long, bone-weary sigh. "What do you need?"

"I want my brother's life to have had meaning. The Navy Memorial is something tangible. Something that people will remember. Oh, never mind. You don't understand."

His big shoulders rose, absorbing the weight of the accusation. "Yes, I do. I understand too well. Do you think that blaming someone, anyone, will somehow give your brother's death meaning?"

"Yes!" she said, slamming the heel of her hand against the bulkhead. "It wasn't his fault he died. He's not to blame."

"No, he's not. I am. There's no hiding it now. There's nobody out there left to blame but me. You can't give me the forgiveness I need because you need to hold on to that blame. It's ruled your life for so long you can't seem to let it go."

"Leave me alone." He was right and she didn't want to hear it. She couldn't let go until she'd attained her goal. She couldn't let her brother down as she had somehow let her parents down.

"Maybe you don't want to let go," Chris said relentlessly, grabbing her shoulders so she would look into his face, into his eyes.

"Leave," she shouted, her lips trembling, her anger getting the best of her. "Now!" She struggled out of his grasp, her eyes on fire and her throat full.

He turned toward the door. "Maybe it would have been easier for you if I had died that day, too. Maybe then you could have moved on."

She didn't answer him. She couldn't. In her disappointment and grief, she was unable to make any sense out of what had happened. And she could get no justice for her brother or for Chris. But she did know one single truth about this whole business. Her world would have been so bleak if Chris had died. The thought of being in a world without him caused her more pain than she could bear.

The door closed behind him and she knew if there had ever been a chance, there no longer was. She'd ruined it by being unable to make that simple concession.

She heard her email ding. It looked as if Gabriel had stayed overtime to get her what she needed. She was sorry she wasted his time. They had their killer and Susan couldn't have been the person who had tried to kill Chris. It was baffling. Sia had been so sure. *All* the other men looked like him, to the point of eeriness.

Unless Susan was telling the truth and she hadn't killed Lieutenant Washington. Did they have the wrong woman? The thought left her feeling dizzy and weak. She stood there for a moment pushing all her pain and disappointment away.

The fingerprints were damning evidence, though. *The fingerprints were perfect.* Perfect...maybe. Sia sat down at her computer and pulled up the internet browser. She typed in "faking fingerprints." Numerous hits came up and she chose a website. It was possible and, furthermore, the fingerprints that were faked were usually flawless.

She quickly pulled up the file of personnel and started to go through the list. She found the master chief's name, and Susan Cotes's. She scanned the list until her breath caught and her senses heightened. The only other familiar name on the list was still aboard the ship. With trembling hands she pulled up the person's file. Not only had the person been on the ship at the time of all the deaths, but that person had also been on the ship at the time of Rafael's death.

A knock sounded on the door and Sia rose to answer, still intent on her discovery. Chris had come back. She should have known he couldn't leave her alone in her state, and she was grateful to him. The ship pitched violently, and Sia held on to the doorjamb before she reached for the knob.

An apology was on her lips when she pulled the door open. But the eyes she met weren't Chris's.

Lieutenant Maria Jackson. She was the only other person who had been on the ship when the murders occurred. In her eyes was the coldness Sia had expected from Susan Cotes.

The eyes of a serial killer.

Chapter 11

"Hello, Sia. Surprised to see me?"

"Lieutenant Jackson." It was all she could get out, because she'd looked past her face now and discovered the gun in her hand.

She gestured with it now. "The Navy JAG got caught off guard. That's so delicious."

Sia couldn't move, couldn't think clearly, couldn't decide on any course of action, because too many things were racing through her brain all at once. Susan Cotes was telling the truth. She was innocent. Would she ever get the chance to tell Chris she was sorry, that she still loved him?

"Move back inside."

She hesitated, not wanting to comply, debating for a split second whether to step back, slam the door shut.

"The bullet is faster than your reflexes, Commander," she said calmly, as if reading her mind. "It's not the way I want it to happen, but…" She shrugged. Once again she gestured for Sia to back up. "You have questions and I have answers. Do you want to go to your death not knowing what those answers are?"

Sia stepped back as Maria shoved her hard into the stateroom and closed the door.

She pointed at the locker. "Change."

Sia's gaze flew to the locker. "Into what?"

"Your dress blues."

"Why?"

"Indulge me and I'll allow you one question."

Sia walked over to the locker and pulled out her uniform. As she took off her shirt she asked, "Did you try to kill Chris six years ago by spiking his coffee with GHB and tampering with his radar?"

"Yes."

"Why?"

"That's two questions."

Sia seethed as she ripped off her shirt and donned the white one, then stopped.

"Aw, the JAG officer wants to play games."

"Answer the question."

"I did you a favor. Men are nothing but abusers and leavers. You can't trust them. I will admit there was a lot of satisfaction killing them inside their fighters. Cocky bastards. But it was even more satisfying up close when they knew they were going to die. You should have seen the look on the face of the one I pushed off the deck. And the one I stabbed to death. So surprised a woman would ever want to do anything more than fawn over him. They made me sick."

Sia listened, shocked and repulsed at the lack of feel-

ing in her voice. She was completely devoid of conscience. Emotionless, soulless. There would be no
appealing to her sense of mercy or humanity, because
she didn't have any. Escape was her only hope, and that
hope was slim with the gun pointed at her back.

"Chris isn't like that."

Her expression changed. "No, he isn't. He was loyal
to you and kind. I will give you that. But he looked like
him and that made it okay to kill him."

Sia put on the jacket. "Who couldn't you trust? Who
hurt you this badly that you kept seeking revenge?"

"The man who asked me to marry him, then left me
at the altar while he ran off with another woman. He
humiliated me."

She donned the pants and fastened them.

"Looks like you're out of clothes, but I'll give you
one for free, since I like a person who has spunk."

"Was your fiancé a pilot?"

"There's no flies on you, counselor...yet. Let's go."

"Where?"

Jackson responded by suddenly grabbing Sia's hair
and yanking her close. Her scalp was on fire; an instant
later she also felt the cold muzzle of the gun against her
temple. The voice next to her ear made her shudder.
"Do not test me more than you already have." Her fist
was still in Sia's hair, and tears sprang to the corners
of her eyes as Jackson gave it a vicious twist. "Now, I
will release you, and you will do as I say, when I say.
Are we on the same page?" To underscore the question,
she tugged harder on Sia's hair.

"Yes," she choked out.

"Good," she said quite pleasantly, and released her as suddenly as she'd grabbed her.

Sia staggered forward and landed hard on her hands and knees on the steel deck.

"Get up. Time is precious. We must go."

Sia obeyed for now. She opened her cabin door, but to her dismay there was no one in the gangway. "Which way do—" She had to break off, clear the sudden lump in her throat. "Which way?"

"Up to the deck."

"Outside? But the storm is in full force." She'd said it perhaps a bit too stridently, but her heart was pounding so hard she could hardly hear over it, and hysteria was edging up her throat, squeezing it tight.

"It's perfect for where we're going. I'm sure you'll remember it." She stepped closer and smiled, aiming the gun at her chest, and then lifting it to her head. "So let's stop wasting time, shall we?"

Sia swallowed hard, trying to remain calm. Panicking wouldn't save her.

She wasn't given time to comply before Maria grabbed her elbow and shoved her roughly ahead of her. "No more questions. No more answers. Not until we reach our destination. Then I'll grant you a few more."

Sia climbed the ladder to the upper deck. As she approached the hatch, she could hear the rain beating on the bulkhead, metallic echoes adding an eerie quality to an already surreal experience.

But she couldn't fool herself. She was in terrible danger. If she didn't do something, she was going to die. There was no doubt where Maria was taking her. Sia didn't know why, but she was sure of it.

"Open the hatch."

She gripped the wheel and applied pressure, the metal cold beneath her hands. It made barely a noise as it turned. Nothing but a whisper of a sound.

Pulling the door was another matter. "It's heavy," Sia said. "I need a hand."

"Don't get smart now, counselor."

"Do you want to be here all night while I struggle to get the door open?"

Maria sighed and jabbed the gun into Sia's back. Pain exploded, radiating down the back of her legs.

"That was just a reminder not to try anything."

As they pulled, the door swung inward and the sound of the rain and wind intensified until it was a pounding rhythm. Gusts of moisture coated Sia as she finally got the door open enough for them to see outside. Her breath caught in her throat at the violence of the sea, roiling with white-capped waves, the dark sky showing only flashes of lightning.

Thunder boomed and Sia jumped. Maria laughed at her discomfort.

"This is nothing compared to some storms I've seen," she said and she jabbed Sia with the muzzle of the gun again. Sia never wanted to hit someone as badly as she did now. "Pull the door closed and secure it."

Stepping out into the tempest drenched Sia straight through her heavy uniform coat. Icy rain poured down, pounding like nails on a roof, taking her breath away. The water was so heavy and came down so fast it almost made it difficult to breathe.

Sia knew she was not in sight of anyone on the bridge. It was a long shot, but if she could run far enough out onto the flight deck, maybe someone would see her from the bridge and send help.

She pulled at the door, her shoulder and arm muscles protesting as it swung slowly closed. She spun the wheel to lock the door in place. She tensed and like a runner off the mark she sprinted away from Maria. She was banking on the lack of visibility and the unsteady rolling of the deck to protect her from any gunshots. Sure enough none came, but Maria was obviously in just as good shape as Sia.

Fighting Maria was her only chance. She had no intention of dying without at least trying to save her own skin. It was about honor and principle. It was about survival.

Maria lunged at her, catching hold of her ponytail and jerking her back hard enough to make her teeth snap together. Sia shrieked in anger and pain and twisted toward Maria, lashing out with her feet, kicking at her knees, her shins, any part of her she could hit.

Maria's lips pulled back against her teeth in a feral snarl, and the back of her hand exploded against the side of Sia's face, snapping her head to the side, bringing a burst of stars behind her eyes and the taste of blood to her mouth. The sky and deck seemed to swirl, her arms flailing to futilely try to maintain her balance. She staggered sideways and fell. On her knees, she tried to scramble farther out onto the flight deck, well aware the lighted bridge was just above her. Adrenaline pumped through her like a drug, driving her forward even when Maria caught hold of her wrist and hauled her up and back, wrenching her sore shoulder.

But her struggles stilled automatically as the blade of a knife glinted off the flight deck lights.

Sia's heart drummed, impossibly hard, impossibly loud as the blade came nearer and nearer her face. It was a military knife, built for one thing and one thing only—killing. The blade was polished steel, the tip tapered and the edge serrated. Sia knew Maria had used this knife to kill once, and she had no doubt she would use it again.

"I would prefer if you would cooperate, Commander," she said, her face close to Sia's as she shouted over the sound of the rain. Maria's left hand slid along her jaw, fingers pressing into her flesh. The knife inched nearer.

The pitch of her voice was the same even tone that struck a nerve in Sia, but it was no longer devoid of emotion. Anger strummed through every carefully enunciated word as she brought the knife closer and closer. Sia's breath caught hard in her lungs as Maria touched the point of the knife to her cheek.

"Be a good, brave officer," she said, sliding the tip of the blade lightly downward. Over the corner of her mouth. "The Navy taught you how to do that, didn't they, Commander?"

Sia said nothing, afraid to speak, afraid to breathe as the blade traced down her chin, down the center of her throat to the vulnerable hollow at its base. If she struggled now, would Maria lose her patience and slice her throat and be done with her? That seemed preferable, but there were no guarantees. If she waited, bought time—even a minute or two—might she find another chance to break away?

She blinked the rainwater out of her eyes and wanted to groan. The bridge was directly above her. She could see movement, but no one glanced down, no one saw them.

The storm intensified, the rain falling harder, pelting the deck like bony fingers.

The knife rested in the V of her collarbone, the point tickling the delicate flesh above. The sensation made her want to gag. She swallowed back the need, felt the tip bite into her skin. The pain came seconds later, throbbing with her heartbeat. Blood slid down her neck to mix with the rain. Every cell of her body was quivering. Sia held back her fear and panic, grabbed her sanity with both mental hands and defied Maria with her eyes.

Maria laughed. "You have more courage than any man I've killed."

"Go to hell," Sia ground out between clenched teeth. She didn't even dare move her jaw with the knife so close to her throat.

"I've already been there. Now it's your turn." In one split second the knife was gone, but the gun was back in Maria's hand and she got quickly to her feet, hauling Sia with her. She pushed her hard in the back to get her to move forward. Sia almost lost her footing on the slick, heaving deck, but regained it at the last minute.

They skirted bridge and moved to the edge of the ship. When they reached a ladder that went down into the darkness, Maria said, "Go." But before Sia could comply, Maria grabbed her by the hair again, twisting brutally until Sia cried out. "If you try anything, I will shoot you in the back and throw your body overboard."

Sia looked up as Maria released her hair. She knew where Maria intended to take her.

The sponson.

Chris stalked away from Sia's cabin, his anger palpable. She was simply the most stubborn woman on the planet. She was hell-bent on saving her brother's memory and destroying any happiness she could have had.

She certainly wasn't doing it for Rafael. He was dead. Long dead. Sia was doing it to assuage her own sense of justice. She couldn't accept the fact that mistakes had been made and as a result he died.

The fact that she couldn't forgive him really had nothing to do with him at all. It was all about her own mission. The trouble was Chris needed it. He needed her to say the words. Needed it down to his battered soul, his broken heart.

He stopped and swung at the bulkhead, bruising his knuckles and sending pain down to his elbow in waves. But it felt good to have some outlet to release the tension roiling in him.

He was done with this. He had to be done with berating himself. He'd let Rafael go earlier, while he was on deck.

Why couldn't he let go of the need for Sia's forgiveness?

He didn't have to soul-search too long to realize why he needed Sia's forgiveness.

He knew why.

He was still in love with her, probably always would be. The pain of that admission made him want to run out on deck and howl at the storm.

He loved Sia just as much as he had six years ago. He'd never gotten over her.

Regardless of his anger and his sense of betrayal, he was in love with her. And he understood her better than he had six years ago when the feelings were raw and burned his gut like acid. It had never been about him. It had always been about her sense of loyalty to her family and to her brother.

Didn't mean her rejection didn't hurt. It did. Immensely. But the knowledge lessened it somewhat.

He headed to his stateroom and lay down on his bunk. Closing his eyes, the pitching and the rolling of the ship lulled him into sleep.

The buzzing of his phone roused him. Blearily he looked at the display, but didn't recognize the number. It had a Virginia area code.

He answered.

"Special Agent Vargas. This is Commander Soto's aide, Gabriel McBride, sir. I'm sorry to bother you, but I'm trying to track down the commander." The concern in the man's voice brought Chris up to a sitting position.

"She's in her stateroom. I left her less than a half hour ago."

"She's not responding to my calls or emails. I really need to speak to her. It's important."

His phone beeped impatiently to tell him he had an incoming call. When he saw it was Math, he said, "McBride. Hold on one second."

"Chris, check for your weapon."

"What?"

"Now, man. Check it now!"

At Math's urgent tone, Chris lurched out of bed to

tear open his locker. His sidearm was gone and his gut clenched hard.

"It's gone."

"The person who shot at you has it."

"How do you know that?"

"The bullets and the casings you sent me! The ballistics match your gun!"

"Son of a bitch. I've got to go."

Chris pinched the phone between his shoulder and ear as he frantically got dressed. He pressed the key to disconnect Math. "McBride. You have information regarding the case?" he asked urgently.

As soon as he was dressed, he bolted out the door, his lungs pumping with adrenaline and fear for Sia.

"Yes, I've got some information that ties the master chief to one of the crew members aboard. I think that's relevant to the case."

When he reached Sia's stateroom, he knocked, but there was no answer. His stomach sank when he tried the handle and discovered the door was open. The stateroom was empty.

"Agent Vargas, are you all right, sir?"

Chris realized McBride had spoken to him, but Chris had been distracted by the empty stateroom. Sia had to have been taken. There was nowhere for her to go. The ship was in lockdown.

"Yes, McBride, give me a minute."

His gaze snagged on Sia's computer. The laptop was open as if she'd been working on it, but the screen was dark. He went to it and pushed a button. The screen flashed on. He saw the website she'd visited. Then he noticed another file was open. He clicked it to open it.

When he saw the personnel list and the name the blinking cursor was on, he swore.

"Sir, what is it?"

"Tell me what tie you have to the master chief?"

"Well, when I was investigating him like the commander asked me to, I stumbled over some records...."

"McBride! The information!"

"The master chief was Lieutenant Maria Jackson's stepfather."

In a flash, memory came rushing back at him. She had been the LSO when he was aboard the *McCloud* and she'd been in the wardroom before he and Rafael had taken off. Both wingmen of the dead pilots remembered that she'd been in the wardroom before they had taken off. She was the one who had spiked their drinks, not Susan Cotes. The woman had been framed as she'd claimed. The scar, he remembered her scar. He remembered he'd gotten dizzy shortly after takeoff. His radar was messing up and he'd focused on it. Tried to see clearly, but his dizziness had gotten worse. Then he'd jerked at Rafael's voice in his ear and the plane had swerved, collided against his wingman's. Rafael had shouted an order, told him to eject as the jet spun out of control, whirling in midair. And it had been Chris's sense of survival that had saved him, that and his training as he lurched for the eject button and jettisoned from his impaired jet.

Jackson was the killer. She'd orchestrated the evidence against Susan Cotes. She framed her to distract and mislead them. She was the one who had taken his gun right before she'd come to them on the flight deck.

She must have shot at them when she'd left, then cleaned and replaced his gun in his locker. He was sure of it.

He was sure of one other thing. She was the one who had Sia and if he didn't find her, Jackson would kill her.

He closed his eyes and swore softly.

Sia shivered as her sodden dress uniform coat did nothing to keep her warm. Her back was pressed to the rail and the ocean churned below her, the waves breaking against the hull in white froth fury. There was no way to survive a plunge from this height. Even if she did, she wouldn't last a minute in the heaving waves below.

Suddenly the rain diminished and Sia faced fury of another kind.

"Do you know why I brought you up here?"

"No, but I'm guessing it has to do with the master chief."

"It does."

"Were you lovers?"

Maria tossed her head back and laughed. "God, no. He was too close to me for that. Or should I say too close to my mother."

"He was your father?"

"My stepfather."

"We were estranged for quite some time. Even when I was assigned to this ship, he didn't recognize me until I told him who I was. He was speechless and told me he wanted to make amends. As if he could. He left us, just like all men do. But—" her voice softened "—he did try to protect me. He took my GHB bottle and tried to kill you. He got scared when you said you were going to get the Navy to reopen your brother's case."

"So it wasn't his duty in the Navy that he tried to kill me. It was his duty to you as a father."

She shrugged. "It came to him later in life, when I was grown up, but I guess it counts for something."

"You're not going to get away with this."

"Yes, I will." With that she pulled aside a black tarp and Sia could see Lieutenant Cotes's dead eyes staring up at a night sky she would never see again. "It was supremely easy to spring her from jail. The master-at-arms was stupid enough to allow me a few moments with my friend. As soon as he turned his back, I grabbed his gun, forced him to unlock the door. I made him go inside and take off his pants. Then I shot him at point-blank range with his own gun. The look on his face was priceless. I wish I could have captured it on film."

"You made it look like he was going to…"

"That's right. No one would be surprised. Men are pigs." Maria pulled the tarp all the way off Susan's body. "She was a fighter, too. I had to be careful not to mark her."

Sia saw the blood on Susan's temple and the hole the bullet had left. "She didn't know she was rooming with a serial killer."

"It's not that black and white, but people like you need a classification. So you'll think what you want. She trusted me. Her mistake. She didn't know I was methodically framing her for Washington's murder. I even typed her suicide note on her computer and printed it out on her printer. It's beneath her body right now.

It is bad luck Chris had his accident when she wasn't on board. Then everything would have gone to plan."

"You're a monster!"

Maria laughed. "No, I'm not. I just need closure. You know all about that. That's what you've been searching for. That's what all the arguments were about with your boyfriend."

"I was searching for justice for my brother."

"Whatever your motives were, maybe now you can forgive your boyfriend. Oh, wait, no, that won't be possible. You'll be dead and he'll never know how you felt."

Her eyes hardened and Sia knew she was at the end of the line.

"Jump. There's no escape. At least it's more of a choice than you gave my stepfather."

Sia had only one chance and it was a very slim one. Her head jerked toward Susan's corpse. "Is she still breathing?"

Maria swung around to look at the body. Head down, Sia lunged for Maria, planting a shoulder hard in the woman's chest. The two of them landed on the hard steel, inches from Susan's dead face, and began wrestling for control of the gun. Sia grabbed hold of Maria's arm and slammed it hard against the landing, but before she could shake the pistol loose, a white-hot pain sliced into her right side, momentarily shorting out all thought and strength.

Howling with pain and rage, she twisted around to find the source. The knife had penetrated the thick jacket and opened up a gash just below her rib cage.

Before Sia could react, Maria swung the gun up and slammed it into her temple.

* * *

Chris swore again and dropped his phone.

He knew where Sia had been taken at gunpoint—with his gun.

He raced out of the stateroom and swore under his breath as he wasted precious time opening the hatch and closing it behind him. He took a risk as he ran across the slippery, pitching deck only to lose his balance and slide to the edge, catching a spinning, stomach-dropping view of the ocean. He was able to stop his momentum by catching the rail. Breathing hard, rain sluicing down his face and soaked to the skin by the icy rain, he pulled himself up and made a beeline for the ladder. Reaching it, he descended frantically, his heart pounding with dread and fear for Sia. If he lost her… he couldn't complete the thought. Wouldn't accept she was already dead.

He reached the sponson and was just in time to see Maria push Sia's limp body over the edge.

Chapter 12

"Sia!" Chris screamed her name, and it snapped her out of the fog the blow to her head had caused. With her last ounce of strength, Sia snagged the rail with the crook of her elbow and struggled to hold on. The arm on her injured side was also weak from the shoulder injury, but she ignored the dull ache. Her feet dangled in empty air.

She panicked for a moment, and then realized she had to keep calm. She could hear Chris's roar of anger and the sound of battle above her. And she understood the cunning of the woman who had wanted him dead six years ago. It was ironic Jackson was now wrestling with the man who resembled the very fiancé who had walked away from her, just as Sia wrestled with her past. Her former fiancé was one smart, lucky guy, it seemed.

Her head cleared some more. Chris didn't know Maria had a knife.

Through sheer brute force and determination, Sia was able to get her body partially on the lip of the sponson. She could see a tangle of bodies as they struggled. Chris was intent on getting her to release the gun; he still didn't see the knife.

"Chris, she has a knife!" Sia screamed as loud as she could above the roar of the ocean and the storm.

He jerked away from her as she struck, the knife hitting empty air. Maria cursed as she looked at Sia and brought the gun up. Chris grabbed her gun hand and then also had to stop the momentum of her knife hand. He rose and pinned her, his knee on her chest.

Sia heard bones break and Maria cried out as she dropped the knife. It clattered to the deck and Chris dropped her hand to knock it away.

With an inhuman howl, Maria hit Chris in the face with a vicious blow. He was knocked to the side but his momentum stripped the gun out of her hand and it slid to the solid wall of the carrier with a ringing metallic sound.

Sia's arms were going numb and she was beginning to lose her grip. She couldn't hold on much longer. A huge, violent wave struck the ship and rolled over the flight deck, stinging her eyes. She lost her grip and slipped, crying out. Chris, distracted by the sound of her distress, looked her way, giving Maria the time she needed to go after the gun.

Chris yelled, "Hold on!" and scrambled after Maria a split second later. If he didn't end the fight soon, Sia was going to fall. Panic made her try to get better purchase on the rail, but the rain-slicked metal made it almost impossible.

Her head spun from the blow, her stomach lurched with nausea and her heart beat in time to her frantic breathing.

She looked up in time to see Chris catch Maria and deliver a powerful punch to her jaw. The woman flew back and landed heavily on Susan's body. Maria remained motionless, finally, thankfully, unconscious.

But it was too late for Sia. Her grip loosened and Chris was too far away. And her regrets piled up one on top of the other. She would never get the chance to tell him what was in her heart.

Her sight dimmed to gray and she started to fall away from the ship. Suddenly, without warning, her wrist was snagged with a warm hand and Chris's face was just above her. "Hang on, sweetheart, I got you."

Bracing his feet against the rail, he strained against her dead weight. With her head injury, she could barely help him at all. With a mighty heave of his powerful shoulders, he pulled her up and over the rail. She heard voices as men swarmed down the ladder and onto the sponson. Chris cradled her in his arms. She looked up at him wordlessly, her eyes shining with gratitude. But she couldn't maintain eye contact, couldn't utter a sound as her world turned to black.

Standing in sick bay, dripping water all over the immaculate deck, he watched as Sia was set on a gurney and wheeled away from him into a separate room. A crewman handed him a towel and gave a pointed look at it and the deck. Chris wiped his face and neck.

"Go get into some dry clothes," the captain said.

Chris didn't move.

"Go, Vargas. She'll be in there for a while. We have a very competent doctor."

Chris went back to his stateroom and showered off the rainwater and Sia's blood. He placed his clothes in evidence bags and zipped them shut. After dressing, he automatically reached for his firearm, but then remembered he'd had to turn it over to the Navy as evidence.

He went down to the brig and found Maria had regained consciousness. She didn't hold back and her sullen face only emphasized her cold and emotionless eyes as she confessed to everything. She'd be transferred from the ship and sent to Miramar, California, where she'd be then incarcerated at the Navy Consolidated Brig, or NAVCONBRIG.

His phone rang just as he was done and he headed back to sick bay. His boss asked him for an update, and Chris filled him in on all the details, leaving nothing out. He listened while his boss told him about a mission that required his expertise. He needed to leave the carrier right away. There would be a flight waiting for him in San Diego headed for Afghanistan.

He tried to protest, but his boss was firm. The *McCloud* case was wrapped up, he insisted. All that needed to be done was the paperwork.

Chris went back to his stateroom and packed. In one of the pockets of his suitcase, he pulled out his wings. He carried them wherever he went. Making his way back to sick bay, he found Sia in one of the bay's beds, still unconscious. She looked pale and so frail lying there. She had fought like a lion and he was so proud of her.

His throat was full as he stood there hoping for some

sign she would wake up. After several minutes, he could wait no longer. He didn't want to leave her like this, but he had no choice.

"Are you ready, Vargas?" the captain asked.

Sia came awake slowly. She could feel warm fingers stroking her face. Then at the material at her neckline, a rustling and then when the cloth was smoothed back a heaviness that hadn't been there before along with metal against her skin.

She struggled to come fully awake as she heard Chris's voice as he spoke in low tones to someone.

"No, I'll just be a few more minutes."

Sia wanted to open her eyes, wanted to make her mouth move, but she couldn't seem to throw off the lethargy. "That's for you, Sia. I've put the past behind me and no longer need them. Maybe my wings will let you soar and you will remember me from time to time."

He was leaving? No, she had something important to tell him. He couldn't go.

"How is she?"

That was the captain's voice.

"She's stable. I stitched up her side and she has a severe concussion. With rest, she should be fine." That unfamiliar voice must be the ship's doctor.

"And you, Vargas?"

"No worse for wear, sir. I appreciate the quick transportation. I have a case in Afghanistan that needs my attention. I just got the call from my superior. They have a transport waiting for me in San Diego."

"We'll be docking in about two hours, but the chopper is waiting for you."

She felt the stare of two men. "It's a good thing you arrived in time to save her. And her legalman should be commended for having the presence of mind to call the ship and alert me to the danger."

"Yes, sir. I've got to be going."

"Take care of yourself, Vargas."

"Thank you, sir."

Sia stirred and opened her eyes. No one was with her as she sat up, her side protesting. She was in a gown, lying in sick bay, an IV in her arm. Her head spun and she wondered how long it had been since Chris had left.

Without thinking, she pulled the IV out and swung her legs to the floor. Her knees buckled, but she pulled herself upright. Pain sliced into her side and her world spun, a terrible throbbing exploding in her head. She felt a heaviness at her neck and looked down. Chris had pinned his wings to her hospital gown and tears gathered in her eyes. She had to catch Chris. She had to talk to him. Now, in person.

She held on to the bulkhead as she made her way to the door and out into the gangway. She picked up speed as she headed for the flight deck. Sailors gaped at her as she passed in her hospital gown and bare feet, but she didn't care if her backside was hanging out.

She had to talk to Chris.

She reached the deck as her strength was waning. And saw him. She screamed his name, but all that she could get out was a croak. She ran a short distance to the deck, but Chris opened the helicopter door and set his bag inside. He followed it without looking back.

Sorrow filled her along with a healthy dose of shame and regret. "Chris," she said softly on a sob, clutching the wings in her hand, the edges biting into her palm. "Don't go." But as the doctor reached her, berating her for getting out of bed, Sia watched the chopper take off. She resisted as the doctor tried to get her back to sick bay. Watched until the chopper disappeared from her sight and Chris from her life.

She resisted the doctor's attempts to move her while time slipped away as she sat there questioning, remembering, hurting, mourning. She released all the tears she had held for Rafael, all the pain she had been so afraid to feel at his loss. It all came pouring out in a deluge, in a storm that shook her and drained her. She grieved alone. Just the way her brother had died. And on the deck of the carrier where he'd lived his last moments, she let go.

Chris faced forward, going on sheer determination. He was exhausted in the aftermath of apprehending Maria Jackson. She had confessed everything in a monotone voice, looking at him with accusing eyes as if she knew him.

In the end, just like her former fiancé, Chris had ruined everything.

He delivered the confession to the captain, who promised he would contact SECNAV and take care of expunging Chris's record of the pilot-error ruling.

Chris had told him not to bother, but he could see the captain wasn't going to heed his request. Chris agreed with the captain that it was important to clear Rafael's record.

It was the last thing he could do for Sia.

He turned his face away from the pilot as his eyes

filled. Blinking away the tears was much easier than trying to clear the pain from his heart. He knew where Sia stood and it was clear from their last conversation she could never forgive him. Regardless of who was responsible for Rafael's death, his jet had caused the accident. He felt raw at the thought that it was easier to forgive him when she thought he wasn't responsible for his actions that day. For him, it was too little, too late. He couldn't be with a woman who didn't fully believe in him and support him no matter what.

He loved her, but it was too late for them.

As the chopper zoomed through the now bright blue sky, Chris closed his eyes and let sleep take him. When he got to Afghanistan he would have to hit the ground running. Best to get the rest he needed now.

As he drifted into sleep, he couldn't help the memory of Sia's beautiful face from being the last thing he thought about before he succumbed to his fatigue.

Washington, D.C., in the spring was beautiful. A late spring had pushed the peak of the cherry blossoms to mid-May. Sia decided to walk from her hotel to Pennsylvania Avenue where the ceremony for her brother would be held. The sidewalk was packed with people celebrating Memorial Day.

Two months had passed since Sia had left the *U.S.S. James McCloud* and she was due back in San Diego in two months to testify at Lieutenant Maria Jackson's court-martial. There was really no need for a trial, since the woman had confessed. But testimony would be taken to strip the woman of her rank and insignia for the acts she'd committed against Navy personnel, along with the destruction of millions of dollars' worth of Navy property.

Sia felt that was wholly justified, as her side twinged from the knife cut that had almost fully healed.

She had made several inquiries into finding Chris, but NCIS was tight-lipped about where he was and had been uncooperative in granting her access to either his contact number or email. She had to wonder if that was because he had explicitly told them to keep his number private from her. She was shut out and would just have to wait until he returned from his mission.

The need to talk to him burned in her gut as she rounded a corner and saw the Navy Memorial across the street.

Stepping off the curb, she checked for traffic and crossed. She approached the rotunda that featured a granite sea map of the world, tall masts displaying signal flags, surrounded by fountain pools and waterfalls.

She approached the statue of The Lone Sailor and stood in front of it for a moment, remembering her brother, remembering his courage and his dedication to defending his country. She remembered his bright blue eyes and dark hair, his handsome, smiling face.

She remembered how she had striven to get him what he was due. A place where she could remember him for all times. A tangible place.

But the satisfaction of reaching her goal dimmed in the wake of what had happened between her and Chris aboard the *McCloud*.

She left the memorial and entered the exhibit area; another statue greeted her—a family embracing their loved one, home from the sea. Tears welled in Sia's eyes as she realized she would only be welcoming her brother home in spirit. For the first time, it was enough.

She located the room where the ceremony would take place and slipped in to take a seat in the second row. There was quite a crowd, all chattering as they settled in.

The ceremony started and a number of Navy personnel were honored. Then, when her brother's memorial was next on her program, she looked up to see the former and current captains of the *U.S.S. James McCloud* walk out onto the stage.

Her breath caught when Chris stepped out after them and seated himself. He looked impossibly handsome, even with beard stubble, his clothes wrinkled and his hair a tousled mess. His gray eyes were filled with pride and sadness.

The former captain of the *McCloud* got up and took the podium. "Today we are here to honor the fine men and women of the Navy. But there is one Naval officer who has been wronged by us. This we need to make amends for. Lieutenant Rafael Soto died when his fighter jet collided with Lieutenant Christophe Vargas's jet on a routine training mission over the Pacific. Unbeknownst to the Navy investigators at the time, the accident was really an attempted murder. Both pilots were sanctioned and had their records marred by a pilot-error ruling. Their records have now been cleared and we are here today to correct our error and honor Lieutenant Rafael Soto."

The captain finished his speech and left the podium. Chris rose, shook his hand and gave him a sharp salute. When he reached the podium, he looked out over the audience. "I am Christophe Vargas. I'm here today to tell you about my friend and wingman, Rafael Soto. He liked jelly beans and thought that Christmas was the best time of the year, more because of the giving than the receiving. He liked to garden and grow vegetables, saying a little dirt never hurt anyone. I don't have to tell any of you what it's like to lose someone who is as close to you as a brother. Some of you have lost a brother, sister, best friend. I carried around a lot of guilt for living when he died. For moving forward with my life. But after I was part of the investigative team to apprehend the person responsible for his death, it's been alleviated. I can't go back and change what happened. But I can honor the memory of my friend until the day I die. He was out there defending his country and I was proud to be at his side. Rafael," Chris said quietly, "I'll always have your six."

As Chris spoke, the lump in Sia's throat got tighter and tighter. Tears gathered in her eyes and she knew at that moment that she had been so wrong, even more than she had on the carrier when she'd tried to catch Chris. She had to talk to him.

He left the podium and sat down. The ceremony came to a close. In the crush of bodies, she was blocked from the stage. She frantically tried to find him, but lost him in the crowd.

Dejected and annoyed, she decided she would go to see Rafael's plaque. Chris would return to NCIS eventually and she'd go over to his office if she had to.

When she approached, she saw a man in rumpled clothing run his hand over the plaque, his head bowed. Her heart tripped and tears filled her eyes. Chris.

She took a few steps forward, suddenly tongue-tied. It took her a moment to find her voice. "Chris."

His head jerked up and he spun around. "Sia," he said, his eyes lighting up at the sight of her.

She smiled and came to him, afraid that if she touched him, he would disappear. They stood there for a few moments in awkward silence.

She looked up at him, her face carefully blank as she tried to assess the shift of feelings between them. "I've been looking for you."

"You found me."

"I wanted to thank you for saving my life. If you hadn't caught me—well, it seems to me that you were there when I needed you. Why is that, Chris? Even after I treated you so badly."

"You were grieving, Sia."

"I was, but what I forgot was that you were, too. At the time, when it was ruled an accident, I should have stood by you. I made a terrible mistake pushing you away, blaming you. I just needed my brother's life to have meant something, and you were part of what destroyed him. What I didn't realize at the time was that his life did have meaning."

Chris slipped an arm around her shoulders and eased her against him, pressing a kiss to the top of her head. It was all he needed to do and she marveled at his capacity to care. She splayed her hand against his warm chest, right over his heart, hoping against hope that she still held a place there.

"I know you didn't kill my brother and that you had no control over what happened."

"No, we know that Maria…"

She covered his mouth with her fingers. "No, Chris, it really doesn't have anything to do with her. This is between you and me. I have to ask you for your forgiveness for not believing in you, for not trusting you, for pushing you away when you needed me the most."

For a moment he looked stunned. He just stood there, waiting, staring past her. His chin trembled as he pressed his lips into a thin line. "My forgiveness?" he choked out.

"Yes. And if you can't, I'll wait," she promised. "I'll wait as long as you need me to wait. I want a future," she said simply, the wish so precious. "I want to go beyond the past. I want you to go with me."

"I forgive you."

"Just like that?" she said, her throat aching with unshed tears.

"Yes, because I already let go," he said, his voice deep and raw, his eyes trained on Rafael's plaque. "I refuse to let the past dictate how I will live my future. Not anymore. I forgave myself. So my forgiveness is easy. I never stopped loving you."

"What?"

"I love you, Sia."

Sia cupped his face and looked into his eyes. Seeing the truth there made her realize she had been wrong. There was more than hope that they could move on. She gave a shaky sigh of deep relief. "I love you, too. I never stopped, either. You are right. We need to put the past behind us. Move forward into the future. Our future."

Her arms went around his neck, her heart overflowing. She pressed her cheek against his chest and let go of everything, the past, the pain, the heartache and the terrible loss. She would always miss her brother and her family, but now, *now,* she finally let him go, let them go. Her gaze landed on his plaque and the tears were finally released. As they flowed, he lowered his mouth to hers for a kiss that was both bonding and beginning, promise and fulfillment…and love.

Hand in hand, they walked out of the building. When they hit the street, Chris smiled. "I sure hope you have a hotel room. I just got in from Afghanistan and didn't have time to check in."

It was Sia's turn to smile. She took his hand and this time she hailed a cab.

In her hotel room, she pushed the worn leather jacket off his shoulders, tugged his shirt loose and lifted it over his head. He raised his arms, accommodating her, and soon she had his bare chest at her disposal. To do with what she wanted.

And the hunger to do that was stirring in her blood.

She took it slowly. Sweetly, deliciously slowly.

He'd tasted her, taunted her, teased her, on several occasions. Now he would be at her command.

Her entire world narrowed down to the smooth expanse of honeyed skin wrapped oh-so-tautly across his chest. She dipped her head and drew her tongue slowly from his collarbone down the valley between his pecs, and then teased her way over to his nipple.

He drew in a sharp breath when she flicked her tongue across the sensitive tip. His hands came up to her hair, and she smiled as it came cascading down around her shoulders.

"If you like that move," he said, his mouth close to her ear, "you'll love what else I can do."

She laughed and looked deep into his eyes.

"Ambrosia," he said, "my Sia," his voice barely more than a rough whisper.

"Chris," she said, making his name a vow.

He cupped her head and slowly drew her mouth up to his, his eyes on hers as their lips met.

She took his kiss, letting her eyes drift shut as sensation after sensation poured through her. He slowly lowered them both to the bed, where he rolled her beneath him and continued his sweet seduction. Their clothes didn't come off in a frenzied rush, but with slow deliberation. As if they both needed to offset the harsh reality of what they'd been through with something pure and honest.

They took turns slowly exploring each other, delighting in discovering again what made them gasp, what made them moan. It was slow but complete capitulation where nothing was held back, nothing was hidden.

When she finally rolled to her back, taking his weight fully on top of her, it was as if she'd reached a golden point, a place she'd been trying to get to for a long, long time but could never quite find. That place where life suddenly became more complete and took on even greater meaning.

Without a word, they locked gazes and he slowly pushed into her, not stopping until she'd taken him fully inside of her. She wrapped her legs around him, holding him there, taking a moment to wallow, to revel a bit, in the supreme pleasure and contentment of being joined to that person who was to be hers.

And in that moment, despite all the fears, all the work yet to be done, and the promise of the future that lay before them, one thing was certain: her time spent with this man was going to mean something to her for the rest of her life.

The rest she let go, and willed herself just to feel, to truly live purely in that moment and that moment only. She moved first, pressing her hips up into his. He began to move inside of her, so deep, filling her so perfectly. It wasn't wild, it wasn't frenzied; it was powerful and necessary. He slid one arm beneath the small of her back and lifted her hips even higher so he could sink into her even more deeply. Their gazes caught, held, and their thrusts came faster, deeper. She watched him climb, watched as his need for her strengthened, felt his muscles gather and bunch as he drew ever closer. She tightened around him, needing to know she could take him to that place, give him that sweet bliss that he so effortlessly gave her, and found herself shudder-ing, too, in intense satisfaction as he growled through a pulsing release.

He kissed her, pressed another kiss to her temple, and then dropped another one just below her ear before rolling to his back, pulling her with him, and settling her body alongside his.

She fell against him with her body as she'd fallen for him with her heart. She didn't question it. Her eyes were already drifting shut as she shifted enough to press a soft kiss over his heart before tucking her arm across his body. Then she draped her leg across his, needing him as close to her as he could get.

It was okay to let go completely; he was there to catch her.

"Chris," she said as the light faded from outside and the city quieted.

"Yes," he murmured.

"In case I forgot to say it. I for—"

He covered her mouth with a kiss, his lips soft and warm. "I know."

Epilogue

"Chris," she puffed, "wait for me." He turned and smiled at her.

"Well, come on, slowpoke." He waited while she slipped her arm through his.

She huffed in mock anger. "You're not carrying around a bowling ball in your stomach, mister, so just be patient with your pregnant wife," she said, laughing as she made the last few steps to the rotunda of the Navy Memorial.

"I said to wait until after the baby was born to do this. You, on the other hand, acted quite unreasonable. 'No, Chris,'" he mimicked in a high falsetto voice, "'I have to be there on the anniversary of my brother's memorial.'"

She laughed until she was breathless. "You know this is important to me, so you even drove me all the way from Norfolk. It was just a few hours' drive, anyway, and I'm not due for another two weeks."

He looked down at her enormous stomach and sent his hand lovingly over the huge mound. "It feels risky to me."

He held her hand as they made their way to the plaque. She stood in front of it and smiled at the handsome picture of her brother. Gently, she ran her hands over the words: *In honored memory of Lieutenant Rafael Soto, loving brother and son, keeper of freedom and liberty, and lover of jelly beans.*

He would have been happy for his sister and his best friend. Sia and Chris had been married now for two years. Two wonderful years. It hadn't been smooth sailing that whole time, mostly because she was stubborn, but Chris had always been there for her and she for him.

Suddenly the dull ache she'd had in her back all the way from Norfolk intensified. There was a popping sound and a rush of water that left a puddle beneath her.

Several people were milling around the other memorials and they turned to look at her. One woman covered her mouth as her husband whipped out his cell phone and dialed.

"Oh, damn," Chris said, looking down, then looking at her. "Is that what I think it is?"

She smiled, not at all panicked as she took Chris's hand. "Yes. We're going to have a baby." Chris didn't move, just stared at her, dumbfounded. "Now, Chris."

"Right, hospital."

He took her hand and started to pull her when a strong contraction took hold of her, sending pain across her abdomen and stabbing into her lower back. She doubled over and several people asked Chris if he needed help. He just shook his head and waited out her contraction.

When it was over, Sia knew. "Ah, Chris, we're not going to make it to the hospital."

"Oh, damn," he said again as he looked frantically for a place to set her down. "That bench." He dragged her over and helped her lie down. He settled her jacket over her hips and legs as he removed clothing to make way for the baby.

"I think I've been in labor all day," she said, breaking off as another searing contraction tightened her stomach into a hard knot of pain. She cried out and Chris went white.

"Hang on, honey."

"I didn't know it was labor pains," she panted. "They were so mild."

"You're just one of the lucky ones."

She cried out as another strong band of pain contracted and she felt a pressure in her groin. "I feel the need to push," she said, the unmistakable feeling of bearing down overwhelming her.

"Then push, honey. I'm here."

Sia let her body take over, since it seemed to know what it wanted to do.

After several minutes, Chris cried out, "I can see the head. Keep going." He ripped off his jacket and his T-shirt.

Sia continued to push and Chris asked her to stop momentarily as he navigated the shoulders. She could hear the sound of an ambulance in the distance. She remembered someone had called for one when they saw her water break. But they were going to be too late as she felt her child slide from her body. Chris caught the small bundle in his hands and wrapped the baby in the soft cotton of his shirt as Sia heard the first cries.

"It's a boy," Chris said, looking up at her with a joyous expression on his face, wonderment in his eyes. And Sia reached down and touched her son. The little boy turned his head, and, like lightning, Sia was struck with instantaneous love, a bond that filled her with the same wonder she'd just seen on her husband's face.

She stroked his head and said softly as the paramedics rushed up to them, "Hello, Rafael."

* * * * *